Flight of the Armada

Book One

by

Jay Michael Jones

Vabella Publishing
P.O. Box 1052
Carrollton, Georgia 30112
www.vabella.com

Cover design by Wille Thompson
Back cover art by Jesse Duke

13-digit ISBN 978-1-938230-16-5

Library of Congress Control Number 2012947164

10 9 8 7 6 5 4 3 2 1

Dedicated to Katie, Drew and Will
Heart, Soul and Spirit

Contents

Other Books in the *Flight of the Armada* Series

Author contact info:
j.michael.jones57@gmail.com
770-834-4132

Chapter 1: What a Bounty

"I am getting some sort of signal on the com," Glendon Garin reported with excitement after months of flight through space. The other five Thuringi scouts took note and checked the communicators in their ships. "There is a good deal of music, but the language is strange."

"Of course, it is strange," Darien Phillipi snorted. "It is only to be expected." He shifted uncomfortably in his seat. The single-pilot triangular ships flew in a tight wedge formation, too close together for him to risk a nice full-sized stretch in the cockpit. It would not do to travel so far only to accidentally run into each other now with their destination within com range.

"No, no; it is more than simply an unknown language. It is either several differing languages or a very clever way of getting around the universal translator."

"I have it, too," Gareth Duncan said as he experimented with the controls in his ship. "I shall try to concentrate on one of the languages and see what I can find. Word! I have never heard such confusion!"

"Look at that world; it is ringed with orbiting rock," Glendon noted. "That is one of the prettiest planets we have come across in a long time."

"Oh, I do not know," Darien mused. "I have seen better." He impatiently tugged his long blonde braid of hair over so it would not rest between his back and the seat. It was times like these when he wondered why he bothered with the Thuringi Air Command tradition of long single braids. They all wore braids but if the others did not complain, Darien would not either.

"Brent? Are you still with us?" Carrol Shanaugh asked as she watched one of the ships stray a little out of formation. Space flight was hard enough on the airbreathing Thuringi, but on an Aquatic like Brent Ardenne it was sure to be even more challenging.

"Mmm, yes," Brent replied, his voice raspy and weary.

"It will not be long," Stuart Phillipi told him hopefully.

"I have a lock on one of their frequencies," Gareth announced. "It may take some time for the com system to digest and translate this language."

"Well, anything is an improvement," Stuart pointed out. "Brent, you are listing."

"I… oh. Sorry."

"Brent," Carrol said, "Would you like a catchline?"

"Yes, I would at that, little sis."

She sent out a towline that fastened onto his ship. She did not like the sound of strain in his voice, and the relief in his reply confirmed her suspicion he might not be able to pilot his ship well enough to make an unassisted landing. "Darien, catch Brent's other side," she directed. "Stuart can go ahead of us and establish contact."

"All right."

"Word, that is a massive world there," Darien muttered as a colorfully streaked planet with shaded bands of red and white clouds came into view. "Is that the source of the communication?"

"No, it is further in toward the sun."

"Well, if they can talk then I presume they can eat," Darien said. "I never thought I would say it, but I could use a nice fat friak right now, roasted and juicy to perfection."

"Stop talking about food," Stuart groaned to his twin. "I am down to my last few ration packets now."

"Look at this; it is a dead red," Stuart commented as they passed by another planet.

"We have seen many of those," Gareth said idly. "I think I have a lock on something! Slow down; the com source is coming up fast."

"Oh, look at it, just look at it!" Glendon gasped as they approached the planet issuing the communications. "Brent, look! All that blue – it must be water!"

"And so much land, and the greenery! What a bounty!" Gareth said with a whistle of surprise.

"There is so much white on it; I wonder what that means," Brent mumbled. He felt a trickle on his lower lip and reached up to touch it. He drew his hand back and stared at the blood. So: his lips were parched. He hoped Glendon was right. It had to be water; it must be water down there. The suit specially designed to keep his Aquatic body hydrated held no liquid now and what little moisture remained was not enough to meet his needs.

"I will lead; follow me, scouts!" Stuart said with a boisterous chuckle and headed down through some clouds near a place where the water met the land. The others followed him. He broke through the clouds and was surprised to find the land closer than he realized and a ground-based vehicle headed right for him. He made an evasive maneuver and watched helplessly as the vehicle swerved off the road. "Oh, damn! I have it, I have it!" he said as he went after the ground craft.

"We just arrived and already he is breaking toys," Darien noted with devilish glee. Brent chuckled but did not reply.

Along a lonely stretch of road in rural Massachusetts, America in the summer of 1961, Michael Sheldon rolled down his car window to enjoy the breeze now that the rain stopped falling. He needed some time off from work to finish his doctoral thesis, and a few days decompressing in the country sounded good.

Out of the corner of his eye, he noted a shiny spot in the cloud ahead that was not the sun peeking through. Suddenly a brilliant blue-white light was in his eyes headed directly for him. He slammed on the brakes and felt the terrifying helpless sensation of hydroplaning as his car skimmed the road surface, left the pavement, and careened down the embankment. His hands clutched the steering wheel, and his legs slammed against the underside of the dash. Over and over from side to side the car tumbled until it came to rest upside down in a creek bed.

Water poured in through the open window and the cracked windshield. Michael struggled but could not twist around to keep his head above the rising water. I'm going to die, he thought in despair. I wanted to live longer than this!

The car shuddered and moved upward. The water drained out as Michael wheezed for air, relieved at first. He lay against the interior roof of his car and wondered what happened. The roadway had been empty moments before. How was it possible that his car was lifted out of the water? How did a crane or a tow truck get down the ravine and hook up to him so quickly, where was it before the accident? Was that what made the brilliant light? What was going on?

The battered vehicle settled on the shore of the creek, and the door came off with a metallic screech. A figure peered into the interior. He grabbed Michael's arms and tried to pull him out, but Michael gave an unexpected shriek of pain. The rescuer saw the young man's legs pinned in place by the dashboard. The stranger reached in and ripped the dashboard apart with one hand and pulled the injured driver out into the rain. He carried Michael to a sheltered area under some overhanging trees and gently sat him down. The stranger made a clucking sound with his tongue as he looked at the injured leg.

"Am I that bad?" Michael croaked.

The man jerked back, startled. He was taller than anyone Michael knew, well over six and a half feet tall. He wore his long blonde hair in a braid that reached well past his waistline, and his eerie bright yellow eyes appeared iridescent in the half-light of the rainy afternoon. The man wore a close-fitting black tunic with a stiff upright collar and flowing sleeves with cuffs snug at the wrists. His fitted white breeches tucked into high black boots that extended in front to shield the kneecap. A small cape draped around his shoulders and a gleaming pistol of unfamiliar design dangled from a holster over one hip. At the other hip, a glittering scabbard and a sword with an intricately carved silver handle hung from the belt at his waist.

Michael looked beyond the figure and saw a triangular aircraft the length of a school bus and nearly as wide in the tail section, hovering silently overhead. It was the color of the rain clouds. Despite the pain in his legs, Michael straightened and looked again at the figure before him. This man did not look like a Soviet, and the aircraft was like nothing close to a Sputnik.

"Holy cow! Are you an alien? From another planet?" He started to get up but fell back with a groan of pain. The man patted his arm and spoke in a comforting tone in an unfamiliar but musical language. Michael remained conscious as he watched a second aircraft arrive. Another alien with humanoid feminine curves to her uniform got out and approached him unsteadily. She cut away Michael's trouser material to reveal a two-inch deep gash that ran down his left leg. Bright red blood gushed rhythmically from the wound, and Michael wildly realized he had severed an artery in the crash. The second stranger pressed a small bulb with a needle against the leg.

Now feeling no pain, Michael watched in drowsy curiosity as she guided a wallet-sized instrument slowly along his leg and placed the tip of a small clear tube into the gash. She carefully maneuvered the tube inside the gash several times, and the bleeding stopped. She stroked the gash carefully from the interior outward, and the gash closed before his eyes. She then took the instrument and bulb and left

Michael's line of sight.

"How did you do that?" Michael asked. The stranger motioned him not to speak and put him into the aircraft. As they flew away from the accident site Michael wondered in silence. He felt no fear but was not passive about his predicament. He glanced around the cockpit and realized his new friend evidently traveled a long time judging from the worn upholstery and the general lived-in look of the cockpit.

There were instruments on the panel Michael could not even guess as to purpose, and the inscriptions on them were not in a recognizable language. In the center of the front console was a screen displaying the area in front of the ship, like a closed-circuit television. Other screens showed the surrounding terrain from different locations around the outside of the ship, even though Michael had not noticed any sort of cameras mounted anywhere.

A series of levers and switches were on the left side of the front panel, with corresponding indicator lights. The ship was bigger than it appeared from the outside, with room enough for the pilot to take a comfortable stretch. Behind the pilot's seat was the seat Michael occupied, and behind him a small door, presumably to the rest of the ship.

They landed on an empty beach. Michael crawled out after the stranger emerged from the cockpit. The ship was no longer cloud gray, but Michael could not pinpoint its exact hue. The metal took on a different appearance in the bright sunlight, mirroring the sky above and the sand, below.

The sandy patch where they stood was only a few yards long. From there down the coastline as far as they could see the shore was rocky. The stranger turned slowly around, taking deep breaths of the sea air. He inspected the pebbles on the beach and observed the waddling sand crabs, the tide and the gently weaving tall pines that crowded the landscape up to the rocks on the beach. He let out a satisfied sigh and turned back to Michael as he adjusted something near his ear.

Michael Sheldon was twenty-nine years of age with wavy brown hair and wide gray eyes. He had a crooked nose, an inherited trait made worse by an unfortunate tackle in high school football, and a solid build that saw many a winning football game at college. At his temples were wisps of premature gray. For a while, the men simply studied each other. Finally, Michael cleared his throat and spoke.

"Thanks for helping me, I owe you my life." He gave a sudden laugh. "You have no idea what I'm saying! I wonder if this is real. I expected a man from Mars to be, I don't know; little and green or something."

"(I am not from Mars)." The stranger's voice had a peculiarly clipped accent, the accent of one speaking a foreign tongue fluidly if not altogether certainly. He was still fooling with his ear, and his voice faded in and out. The surprise of hearing an unexpected British accent from the yellow-eyed stranger caught Michael off guard, but the stranger took no notice.

"Where are you from? You're sure not from around these parts," Michael said.

"(My name is Stuart Phillipi de Saulin, Crown Prince of Thuringa and emissary for my father, King Lycasis Phillipi de Trennon of the Twenty-Fifth Rule. Whom do I address)?" The sound was solid now, and even though the words seemed to come out of his mouth, upon close observation his mouth did not accurately form the words.

"I'm...uh..." Michael felt woefully inadequate. "I am Michael Marley Sheldon, um...from Tulsa, Oklahoma, and... a graduate of Harvard." This information made no impression on the crown prince of Thuringa, so Michael plunged on. "How...I mean, you speak English pretty good for a... a prince. Do all of your people—?"

"(Speak this English? No. I wear a universal translator)." He pushed back his long hair to display an apparatus that circled the outer back of his ear and extended an inch or two toward his jawline. Its circumference was no bigger than a power cord to Michael and was the same color as the man's skin. It was barely noticeable to the younger man who had been occupied with more pressing matters. "(Oh; you have none. I beg your pardon. How are you feeling, Michael Marley Sheldon of Taulsa? Are your limbs adequately repaired)?"

"Are my limbs...I... oh, boy." Michael sat down suddenly on the beach. The prince watched him closely but saw that Michael's abrupt sitting was not from inability to stand, but from the inability to comprehend just how he was able to stand once more. "Yeah, they're just great. You said you're an emissary for your father. Where exactly is this Thuringa, and how did you get here from there?"

"(Thuringa is far away from this sparkling planet, yet it was once quite like this. Are you familiar with the stars)?"

"I got a merit badge in Scouts for it. Yes, a little."

Prince Stuart gave him a perplexed look but continued. "(Our world was dying. We gathered together what was left of our civilization and left in search of a new home. I am a scout for our people)."

"A royal scout from another world," Michael clarified for himself.

The crown prince of Thuringa suddenly broke into a smile, delighted at his new acquaintance's grasp of the situation, and at his own ability to communicate that message. He looked like a teenage boy to the American, but he carried himself like an adult. "(You are quite correct, Michael Marley Sheldon of Taulsa)."

"It's actually pronounced Tulsa, and I'm just Michael, to my friends. And," Michael rose and held out his hand, "here on planet Earth, friends shake hands."

Prince Stuart clasped Michael's hand and tilted his head slightly to one side. "(As do we, friend Michael of Tulsa. You call your world Earth. Interesting; a very solid name)."

"You said you are looking for a new home. Are you all planning to live here?" Michael asked. He felt somehow oddly disjointed from the whole scene, as if maybe it was a dream or hallucination of some sort. If it was a dream, he ought to wake up before any of his questions were answered, if this dream ran true to form.

"(No, we only need a place to rest before moving on. We intend to settle on another world beyond here, an uninhabited one. That is our goal)."

"How long will that take?"

The tall prince sighed and knelt down to feel the water as it rushed over his hand coming ashore. For a moment he gazed at the waves, and at last he replied. "(Not for many years yet. You see, we have an armada coming; our people and our race's culture, history, zoological specimens, botanical specimens, and we cannot rush them through space. My kinsmen and I were able to travel at a higher speed by virtue of our lesser payload and stronger ships. There are far too many of the rest to ask for permanent residency here. It is not our desire to rule another's world. We need an empty but habitable world upon which to begin again)." He squinted up at the sun. "(Ah, the thrill of travel,

7

and the greater thrill of staying still)."

"This is amazing," Michael marveled. He had not expected an answer like that. Maybe this was a really, really good dream. "When did you get here?"

"(Moments ago. I entered the atmosphere and went below the surface cover and found myself head-to-head with a vehicle that ran off its pathway. I am so sorry, Michael. I did not expect to contact an inhabitant so soon)."

"That was you? You just now got here?"

Stuart considered his words. "(I should look for a place to settle, diplomats to contact. Have you any suggestions)?"

"You mean, like, take me to your leader?"

"(Yes. I need to meet and speak with the principal ruler of your world)."

"Well...look, your Highness –"

"(Where)?"

"No, no, that's just an expression. Your Highness, this planet just came out of a worldwide war not so long ago between powerful countries. My country—this one, America – is terrified of the Communist threat from Russia. Things are in such a state that if you just sashay up and say, 'Hi, I'm a royal prince from outer space', well, the world is spooked enough to blow you away just as a precaution. Or even worse, they'll think you're a regular human who's lost his mind. Even if someone were to believe you..."

Michael stopped before he could tell this strange visitor further information. Suppose like the science fiction movies he saw, they were there to take over the Earth. Michael did not want to reveal anything that might compromise his own world. If this were a dream that would be one thing, but it was starting to feel real.

Prince Stuart's face was a study in uncomprehending concentration. "(I will need to learn more about your world, Michael of Tulsa. I have understood few of your words just now)."

"I know, I'm sorry. Just understand that this world is not a bad place, but there are a lot of very trigger-happy people who could give you the wrong impression of it. They might be afraid of you, not understand what you want and try to fight before you say anything."

The air around them took on a glow as other triangular-shaped crafts appeared from the clouds above. Michael counted five more in addition to his new friend's. They landed in a semi-circle around the two standing on the beach. From the crafts emerged more tall people with yellow eyes and long blonde hair, and they took time to get acclimated. After stretching and taking surreptitious glances at the native of Earth, the other Thuringi walked stiffly around on the beach. One talked to Stuart in that strange lyrical language. His hair was a darker blonde than Stuart's and his face was animated as he repeatedly gestured toward Michael with a frown. Unlike the calm prince, this one had sharply angled eyebrows that knotted at his brow and underscored his displeasure. Over his uniform he wore a long black waistcoat with long tails that swirled with every movement he made.

Two Thuringi were in a long-awaited conference. One was a little stockier of build, and he had a hand on the other's shoulder. Michael saw that the other one was the female who repaired his leg. She apparently did not quite have the hang of gravity yet since she clung unsteadily to him. Another man, taller and slenderer than the others, took samples of the beach sand. The fifth one simply stood and stared at the ocean.

"I thought we were going to come quietly, unnoticed! And yet here you are, Stuart, collecting some stray istay, some Outlander, to your bosom! Who is that pathetic looking creature? Is that the best this world has to offer?"

"Stuart, this is beyond our wildest dreams! Why could we not settle here, instead of going to Farcourt? It is just as promising – oh hush now, Darien, who you to complain after a journey like that one!" the tall one exclaimed. "These deposits are much like our own vaguno. Theirs must be a farming race to grow such a rich field of vaguno as this."

"(Be still a moment, both of you)," Stuart said. "(This world, this Earth, will be a good resting place for our people. No, we must continue to Farcourt in time, Glendon. My friend over there is Michael of Taulsa. He offered us a haven from the world's woes. They have apparently been at war recently and there are Communiss? - someone - his people have been fighting. It is apparently complicated. He suggested we take shelter at a location he knows. He seems quite kind; not an istay at all, Darien. Why are you in such a foul mood)?"

"Inspired by Brent, no doubt," Glendon said as he picked up a seashell and shook it curiously. "He has been quite irritable this past week. His skin is terribly parched."

They turned to look at the figure that stared out to sea. Michael was unable to understand anyone except Stuart, but he followed their line of sight to the still figure. He cautiously approached the mesmerized man, who appeared injured by the looks of the four white slightly diagonal slits under each ear on his neck. The man wheezed with every breath, and his face was strained and in pain as he stared at the water before him.

"Um...we call it an ocean. A very...very large body of water. This is water, see." Michael scooped up a double palm's worth of water and held it up to the man. The water trickled out from between his fingers.

The man's eyes widened as he emerged from his trancelike state. "Illick chara-a-a-nay!" he shouted, flinging his arms out in ecstasy. He dove into the water and splashed about like a crazed seal, whooping and laughing. Michael jumped back and wondered if the poor man suffered from some sort of space fatigue. Stuart joined Michael.

"Uh...what does illick chara-a-a-nay mean?" Michael asked as he kept a wary eye on the still splashing celebrator.

"(It means, 'He is a fool who hesitates at such bounty)."

"Sort of, 'the last one in is a rotten egg'?"

Stuart looked at Michael for a moment and laughed. "(I suppose...whatever that means)." He gestured to his kinsmen to join them and introduced them in order of lineup to Michael. "(This is Lieutenant Colonel Glendon Garin)," he said in reference to the slender one taking samples.

Glendon smiled as he reached to finger Michael's wavy brown hair. He had a very elegant way about him, as if dignity and professionalism were his second nature. He was an extremely attractive man by Earthian standards, and his angular features, large expressive eyes and thick long eyelashes were Hollywood quality. "Ver hitum caute?" Glendon asked. Stuart pointed at Glendon's ear, and Glendon smiled apologetically at Michael. He adjusted his own translator and spoke again.

"(Interesting. Are you all colored thus)?"

"No, we're all pretty different," Michael said. Glendon slowly circled Michael and inspected him by observation. There was nothing alarming in the way this was done; Glendon was simply curious about his new acquaintance.

"(This is my brother Prince Darien Phillipi)," Stuart said as he indicated the one who gestured and grimaced earlier.

A long dark gray coat shaped like a wasp's wings in back draped over Darien's black tunic. His clothing was edged with silver piping and small colorful rectangles occupied the left breast of his tunic. They reminded Michael of military medals. A quick glance at the other Thuringi revealed they all had medal-rectangles. Like his companions, Darien wore weapons at his waist: a pistol nestled in its well-worn holder and a beautiful silver sword with an ornately carved handle, a close match to Prince Stuart's. The gleaming blade bore some sort of writing along its surface, and it was hard for Michael to keep from staring at it.

Darien had a rugged face with deep-set yellow eyes and shaggy dark blonde bangs along with a thick ropelike braid of hair that reached to the small of his back. He cleared his throat and spoke with a patronizing tone. "(And is this your kingdom)?" he asked politely.

"No, my property is miles from here," Michael answered with the feeling that should this prince discover Michael was a common nobody, the thin veneer of friendliness might be gone again.

"(This is Major Gareth Duncan)," Stuart said, referring to the stocky one who stepped forward, his translator already adjusted. Gareth had keen eyes that missed nothing, a steady gaze that met Michael's gaze measure for measure. He wore a mud brown tunic with a myriad of pockets full of items he obviously needed or used often. His breeches showed evidence of stains, like oil or lubricant. His voice was unemotional, but his eyes were full of anticipation. "(I would like to see examples of your technology)," Gareth said without preamble.

Michael replied, "I doubt that we could come close to anything like you've already got."

If Gareth looked disappointed, he quickly shrugged it off. "(There is always an opportunity for technological exchange)," he said, and opened a tunic pocket and removed a small palm-sized box. He touched its surface, pointed one end at Michael and studied the box. Gareth looked a little surprised and wore a small, pleased smile. He did not explain what the box was for, and Michael had no chance to ask.

"(That one out there)," Stuart said, gesturing out to sea, "(is Sea

Commander Brent Ardenne)." Brent emerged from the water, his dark blue suit soaked and he, happy. Multiple thin tube-like lines ran across his uniform in a weblike pattern, and they pulsated with a rhythmic beat. His wetsuit was once again full of the liquid he so desperately needed, and he was energized again. "(Brent, this is Michael of Tulsa)."

"(Hail, Michael of Taulsa)!" Brent greeted after arranging his translator properly. He had a roguish smile, not as wicked as Darien but every bit as speculative. He turned again to the sea. "(And a glorious Taulsa it is, too)."

"No, that's the Atlantic Ocean," Michael corrected. "Tulsa's in Oklahoma."

"(I am indeed sorry)," Brent's attention returned to his host. "(Do you wish to retrieve it from their clutches)?"

"No, no," Michael declined. "It's fine where it is, it's all right."

"(Ah)," Brent said, astonished at Michael's words and trying not to be obvious about it. He glanced over at Stuart and made a face that asked, did he say what I think he said?

"Who's that?" Michael asked as he gestured to the loner with the balance problem. Hesitancy swept through the group of Thuringi, and Michael wondered at their reaction to what he thought was a reasonable question. The figure moved to stand next to Gareth Duncan.

"(This is Princess Carrol Shanaugh de Phillipi)," Stuart said. "Darien's and my sister."

She removed her helmet, and Michael could not hold back a welcoming smile. No wonder they hesitated to mention her. A pearl like this should be hidden from potential thieves. She extended her hand gracefully, royally. Taking a tip from Errol Flynn's Robin Hood movies, Michael kissed the back of her hand.

Darien suddenly jerked Carrol away and shoved his face in front of Michael and bared his teeth.

"Dakarte Istay!" snapped Darien.

"(He is not one of us. He does not understand)," Glendon protested in Michael's defense, gently pulling Darien back.

"(Have you ever seen the like)?" Gareth mused and looked at Carrol for her reaction.

She smiled. "(Well, these people are certainly a friendly sort)."

She looked at Darien and smiled at his anger. "(Do not take it so personally! We are here to meet people, not fight them)."

"What...what'd I do?" Michael asked, his eyes wide with apprehension.

"(Nothing. In our society, a man usually is better acquainted with a woman before he displays such an affectionate move. In some families, they even wait until they plan to be devoted to each other)," Stuart explained soothingly.

"Devoted?"

"(With the intention to marry)."

"Oh, heck," Michael moaned. "I'm sorry," he said, and addressed the woman. "Here on Earth, sometimes kissing a girl's hand is like a show of respect and admiration. I didn't mean to insult you or insinuate anything. I sure don't want to start a feud."

"(What)?" they chorused.

"I don't want to start a fight."

"(You did not)," Carrol assured him. "(I find it rather refreshing)." She looked at Gareth pointedly. "(Thank you ever so much for the reading material)." It was obviously a statement only he understood, and he grinned at her.

"(Please accept my apology on behalf of my brother's harsh reaction)," Stuart told Michael. "(He is on edge from the strain of our journey and has always been quite protective of her)." To Darien he muttered, "(We might as well have brought Erich, after all)." Darien curled his lip but said nothing.

Stuart continued. "(Perhaps I should introduce our people as a whole. The royal Phillipi family ruled Thuringa for centuries. Ours was a self-supporting world and we shared our bounty equally. No one was lesser in comforts and goods than another as long as they worked within the community; the nobility and the ordinary people were of equal worth in the eyes of the king. The average lifespan is six hundred years, and six hundred years is a long time to live down a dishonorable deed)."

Brent snickered and pointed to himself to indicate he was living proof of something dishonorable. He did it in a good-natured way, as if his naughty deeds were inconsequential enough not to bother him or his royal companions.

"Six hundred years! How do you measure years, and how long

are the days where you lived?"

"(Our home world was roughly the same distance from our sun, as yours," Stuart explained. "We probably have similar measurements of time)."

"So, what is your society like; what do you do? Do you marry and have families...?"

"(Thuringi usually wait until after the one-hundredth birthday to marry, or once we are comfortable enough with the everyday execution of daily gifted tasks to settle down and have a family. Among the scouts, three of us are married: I have a wife named Aura -)"

"(My sister)," Brent interjected.

"(And we have a son named Erich. Brent and his wife Isador have a son named Triton and Glendon and wife Janis have a daughter named Echo. The children are all the same age and are good friends. They are adolescents now.)" Glendon and Brent exchanged wry glances which told Michael that raising teenagers was no easier on Thuringa than it was on Earth.

"Is everyone in the military, like you?" Michael asked as he noted all the uniforms.

"(No, we have civilians as well. Every citizen performs a task of trade or skill they are judged gifted to perform. The time spent in these tasks is touted as 'hours earned.' Some are gifted in military matters, but others prefer the civilian life. We are all required to perform common duties - gathering garbage for recycling or destruction, or cleaning public buildings or streets, that sort of thing. These tasks are routinely rotated every nine days so no one would be stuck doing the same thing)."

"(No one enjoys gathering friak peels)," Darien said in his low growl, "(but at least everyone has a turn at not enjoying it. That is why they are called common tasks)."

"(Gifted tasks are what a person's natural ability is included to do, such as medical practice, architecture, teaching, animal husbandry, engineering, and military service)," Stuart added. "(Our world had been a happy world where good times abounded, and the Thuringi warriors were sent on missions to other less fortunate worlds. The majority of Thuringa were warriors, but the war with the Shargassi wiped out most of the Sea Command and much of the Ground

Command.)"

"The... the Shar-ga- what?" Michael asked about the unfamiliar term.

"Shar-ga-SAY," Stuart repeated pleasantly. "Even with only fourteen thousand warriors left, the Royal Thuringi Air Command could still outfight any warrior forces of the Stellar Council worlds!"

"Word!" Brent exclaimed proudly.

Stellar Council worlds! The thought of multiple alien races made Michael's head spin. A part of him wanted to announce to the people of Earth this marvelous revelation that was history making, world-shattering news. It was the world-shattering part that held him back. There was no way Earth would be able to digest this information. There would either be wholesale panic, or he would be branded as a nut who watched one too many grade B science fiction movies. There was a lot more to learn about the Thuringi before the revelation of their existence was made, especially if only six were present on Earth.

"I'd like to know more about you, myself. Maybe this isn't the best place to talk right now," Michael said with a glance at the open beach all around them. "I come from a place about a thousand miles from here. There's a house on some property my family owns that's pretty secluded. Why don't we go there, and you can tell me more about yourselves? You could even stay there for a while."

Prince Stuart studied his newfound friend. "(You would do this for us and our people)?"

"Well, how often does a fellow have a chance to help someone from another world? Someone who's helped me?" He patted his legs in emphasis. "If you'll give me a lift – a ride in your ship, that is – I'll take you out to the house."

"(Yes, that would be wonderful)." Prince Stuart and his companions exchanged relieved looks.

Michael worried over what he did. Bam! Just like that, he offered a safe haven for people he literally knew nothing about. Suppose they were here to take over the Earth? Suppose that weapon at the prince's side was meant to kill any resistance to their arrival?

But then, the prince and his sister saved Michael's life. They repaired his wounded leg. The prince asked what diplomatic sources he should contact; it was Michael who suggested secrecy. If there was one thing the movies taught him, it was that the government always had secret weird experiments going on, and this prince seemed too nice for some G-man scientist.

Off in the distance they heard a bell clanging from a beach house down the shore. "Well, maybe we'd better get going," Michael suggested.

They all got back into their respective ships and followed Stuart and Michael's lead. Michel advised them to stay low to avoid radar.

"(This radar of which you speak)," Glendon asked Michael, "(What kind of probe is it)?"

"It can locate a plane in the air," Michael said. "It uses sonar waves."

"(It sounds primitive)," Gareth mused.

"(This Taulsa)," Brent wanted to know because all he saw beneath his ship was land, "(Is it near great waters)?"

"No, but there's a creek that runs through our property and a fair-sized stock pond."

"(This language is like so much Thelan to me)," Brent growled. "(What is a 'creek' and a 'stockpond')?"

"They're water sources. We're almost there," Michael said as he looked out of the cockpit. He felt giddy inside. He was flying inside a spaceship! What an adventure! No one would believe him, of course; no doubt his family and friends would figure he spent too much time at the B movies.

The ship was remarkably roomy inside, even given the fact that the Thuringi were large people. The instrument panel bore identifying face plates in a language which looked like idle scratch marks. There was a definite pattern to those marks, however. He noted some gauges bore scratches alongside small hash marks and Michael presumed these were numerals.

Michael glanced out the cockpit to the land below with ease. He recognized the landscape when he saw the Mississippi river below, and he realized how fast they were going. Oklahoma would be underneath them quickly, at this rate of speed. He tapped Stuart on the shoulder and guided them down to the farmhouse.

The Sheldon ranch house was in sad shape. When Derrick Sheldon struck oil, he promptly moved his family into Tulsa, leaving the ranch to serve simply as a point of reference for his drilling crews.

But it was a large two-story house, spacious and comfortable with a wide front porch that stretched across the width of the house, sheltered by a sloping roof connected to the clapboard siding. The house was surrounded by a three-strand barbed wire fence that enveloped a large overgrown yard Michael always dreaded mowing as a boy. The house sat fifty yards back from the hard-packed dirt road and the weather-beaten barn was forty yards further behind the house. A worn gravel driveway led from the road up to the right side of the house and around to the barn. The side yards measured thirty yards from the house to the fencing. A few free-ranging cows sidled up to the fence.

They landed their ships in the back yard out of sight of the road. Stretching as they got out of their crafts, the Thuringi were cautious about their surroundings but at the same time quivered with curiosity. Glendon went at once toward the cows until caution overtook him, and he stood back from the fence about ten feet. He spoke to them in his musical Thuringi language in an attempt to coax them closer. The cows moved about restlessly but did not leave until they realized there was no food offered.

Michael explained the different features of the farm. Gareth was especially interested in the tractor, the combine, and the hand implements. He also eyed the old truck Derrick Sheldon drove home one day and was never able to start again. Michael told him he could tinker with it all he wanted. "I know it won't fly you around the moon or anything, but it's the kind of transportation most people use here."

"(Hmm)," Gareth said, studying it. "(It is positively elementary. How challenging)!" Once he had the hood opened, he crawled into the engine compartment, a "Hmm!" of discovery issuing from his lips now and then. They pulled him away to continue the tour.

Darien inspected the farmhouse with a critical eye. "(This will take much work to make livable)."

"(But we are grateful for it)," Stuart said to Michael, irritated at his brother's ill manners. Darien belatedly grunted and nodded.

"I'm afraid we didn't do a lot of updating before we moved," Michael said, "but the roustabouts haven't done too much damage."

It had three bedrooms and a bathroom upstairs with a kitchen, dining room, living room and a master bedroom downstairs. Off the kitchen in back was a screened-in porch. The plaster on the ceiling was cracked but still intact and the wallpaper was dingy and peeling in places. To show people he knew around the house would have been embarrassing enough, but to put his old house on display for people from a whole other world, possibly another galaxy, made Michael temporarily wish he could have fixed the place up before they came out. But then, who knew he would have visitors - extremely foreign visitors?

"The thing you'll need to concentrate on is getting some identification for yourselves, something that won't raise suspicions about your origins," Michael continued. "I'll tell my folks that you're friends of mine I'm loaning use of the house. I'm sure they won't mind."

Carrol noticed Brent was missing. They searched and finally found him blissfully floating in the metal water reservoir beside the barn. He repeatedly dunked his head under water, and the weblike pattern on his wetsuit pulsed with each heartbeat. "There's a stock pond down yonder," Michael said at first chance.

"(There is liquid right here)," Brent sighed, sloshing around in the reservoir languidly. "(I shall observe your stockpond of which you are so eager to introduce, eventually. And just what is this stockpond down yonder)?"

"A stockpond is a pool of freshwater, about...oh, about as big as this fenced in yard."

Brent abruptly stood up. "(Stockpond, you say)?"

"(No, no stock pond now)," Stuart told him. "(Are you more comfortable)?"

"(Yes, I am refreshed for the now)," Brent said, emerging from the tank.

"Are you... do you need water to live, or something?" Michael asked.

"(We all do)," Glendon explained, "(but our kinsman Brent is of a liquid heritage that begs a kinder climate for his skin)."

"He's amphibious?"

The Thuringi looked at each other. The translators strained to decipher Michael's unfamiliar language.

"(I adore females)," Brent stated almost indignantly.

Glendon explained, "(He will dry out and weaken without the touch of water on his being)."

"Yes, that's what I meant," Michael said. Brent nodded,

apparently satisfied that his virility was no longer impugned.

"(Does this world have anything edible? We are no longer parched but we do hunger)," Darien said as he rubbed his abdomen in emphasis.

"Oh, I guess you do, at that! There's a store about ten miles from here," Michael volunteered. He checked his wallet. He planned to buy groceries for himself that weekend and so had a good amount of cash on hand.

"(What is a store)?" Darien asked suspiciously.

"(A store is a trader's center)," Glendon said brightly, and Michael nodded in confirmation. "(It is a marketplace, correct)?"

"Right," Michael agreed, and showed them his greenbacks. "This is our monetary system. I exchange these... tokens for whatever price they put on what I need."

"(Oh, I see)," Gareth remarked, "(it is the way of the D'tai and the Gharadee, vaguely similar to our hours)."

"(And of our way, in the older days)," Stuart agreed. "(Before the Reform of the Phillipi)."

"(So, we have returned to the barbaric past)," Darien snorted. "(Stepping backward in time. I had hoped it would be as Thuringi as possible, this world)."

"(It is closer than I ever dared dream. Darien, we are no longer on Thuringa)," Stuart reminded him sternly. "(We are guests, guests of a market-based society. You sound more and more like an Elder and that is unnerving)." He turned to Michael. "(I do apologize for my brother, friend Michael. Our people do not use coin to measure the worth of our toil, but we do – or rather did – trade with others and we understand the use and utility of monetary systems)."

Stuart took Michael to the outskirts of the nearby town in his aircraft, as the others remained behind in the farmhouse.

"This will take some doing. What a disgusting way to live!" Darien exclaimed as he kicked at some crumpled paper in the floor.

"He said no one lives here, Darien; what is the matter with you?" Carrol reproved. "It is not that bad, and I am glad we are in a secluded area. He does not quite look like us and none of them probably will. We will not fit immediately into this society. We do not know their strengths and they have been at war. Does your hunger allow for the six of us to fight for landing rights here against an entire planet? How do you know this Earthian is not somehow connected to a powerful lord and your insults will bring us trouble?"

"No, you are right," Darien said crossly, annoyed at his own behavior. "I cannot seem to help it. I am too hungry to do much else than listen to my stomach object to its hollow state. I could not understand some of his words. What is 'Aye-m'? And 'Yer'?"

"And a 'yonder'?" Brent added.

"What is this, Gareth?" Glendon asked about an object in the house's front room.

"How should I know, this world is alien to me too," Gareth replied, but he checked it out just the same.

"You are the mechanical answer man," Glendon told him. "Surely you can hazard a guess."

Gareth looked the object over from every vantage point, muttering as he tried to figure out its purpose. "It is made of a heavy metal. Large, square and... dark dirt, or ashes! Hmm! There are holes with coverings on top. This hollow tube runs out of it and into the wall, but there is no engine attached... no power source... hmm." Gareth poked around in the hollow metal object, unfamiliar with a wood-burning stove. "I do not know."

"Do not know?" Darien laughed. "Gareth Duncan, the man who can make lifesaving repairs to a gigantic oceanic ship, does not know what a little metal box does?"

"I said I do not know. Did you hear that? I shall say it again then. I – do – not – know." He grinned. "Are you glad that the processes for waste removal on the ships all worked? I can make basic bodily functions on a fighter craft an afterthought even after many ginta of flight, yet you take me to task over an iron box on a strange world. Yes, I am at a complete loss as to its purpose. However, there is an engine of sorts out to the side of this building; Michael said something about a generator. If it has an engine I can be of service. But this," he said, kicking the stove, "This is a waste of time."

"I will go with you," Carrol said. As they walked through the door, she patted his head. "If you are a good lad, I will give you a music box."

"Dig yourself into trouble a little deeper, Your Nibs," he grunted, and elbowed her. They shoved each other playfully back and forth all the way down the steps.

"Some things never change," Brent observed.

Stuart waited hidden in a stand of trees while the young man he befriended walked into the grocery store. As he waited, he rubbed the rough bark of a tree with his hands. These were not the firm proud Dorea trees of Thuringa, and they were not like the gracefully arching Sarden trees that lined the grand streets of Thelan, either. These were scrawny, tough, squatty trees that appeared to fight gravity to meet the sky. Dull green leaves clung tenaciously to the branches, unwilling to give up their places. Only a few feet away grew another kind of tree. It was larger, with a domed canopy of leaves and long armlike branches. The lower limbs nearly touched the ground. It was vaguely similar to a Thuringi Sarden that centuries of children assumed grew specifically for them to climb.

What a world, Stuart marveled. The variety was astounding. Different types of colorful flowers grew in riotous display all around him, and tiny buzzing creatures flew from flower to flower, touching them briefly. He heard the steady rasping of a fat green bulb with wings before it also flew away. In some ways Earth was similar to Thuringa and Thelan and Borelliat, and other Stellar Council worlds: flowers and grasses and tended landscape around buildings. In the details flying buzzing creatures were things even Stuart in all his travels never saw before.

Perhaps in the depths of the oceans, a power source similar to what Thuringa's oceans once held could be found. Only the Phillipi family could control the fabled Arda liquid of Thuringa, and Stuart wondered how he might discover who wielded this world's power. Did this world even have the equivalent of Arda power? The Phillipi did not speak of their unique talents to the general populace, so it would hardly be likely that this world's power structure would announce the same. He wondered how much damage had been done during this large war Michael mentioned. So many questions! He peeked around the tree again and waited for Michael's return.

Meanwhile in the store, his Earthian friend carefully considered his options. What does one feed a hungry group of aliens? Michael wondered. Do they cook? Will they be allergic to Earth food? How much are six people going to need after such a journey as they must have had? He decided to get as much variety as he could and then arrange to get more of what they liked later.

On the way home, he answered Stuart's questions. The trees he saw were blackjack and chestnut trees. Some of the flowers were day lilies and irises and sunflowers, and the buzzing creatures were "insects" called "bees". The raspy green bulb with wings was a "cicada".

"(Beez)," Stuart repeated, and laughed. "(The names for your creatures are amusing)."

"I guess they are, at that," Michael replied. He never really thought about it before, but he was eager to discover the differences between cultures.

Michael was astonished to see the lights on at the farmhouse. He thought there was not enough time to work on the generator, but then that Gareth fellow seemed to thrive on things mechanical. And sure enough, Gareth stood next to it as he wiped his hands on a cloth, pleased. The beautiful girl Carrol pulled his arm to remind him to join the others in the kitchen.

Michael emptied out the grocery sacks on the kitchen table. They looked on with great curiosity at the collection of foodstuffs. Darien opened a can of peaches with his very lethal-looking sword before Michael showed him how much easier and less messy it was with a can opener. Darien sheathed his weapon and inspected the can opener seriously.

The slender Glendon was quick to smile and quicker to pick up on Earth ways. He was especially interested in plants and animals and did not hesitate in the least to pick up an item to inspect it. He was strikingly handsome and nearly seven feet tall. Michael had the impression that Glendon always managed to maneuver himself to stand between a Phillipi sibling and anything new or unexpected until they could determine its threat level.

Darien tried to improve his attitude, but his eyes still held a wary disdain for his surroundings. His hands were never far from the grips of his weapons. Each new, unfamiliar sound caused him to snap his head around in alert. Flies especially annoyed him until Michael found an old flyswatter and showed him how to use it. Darien hunted down flies with an unnerving vengeance.

Gareth was told he checked out a wood stove in the front room. He was at a loss to explain to the others what it was, and Michael's explanation sounded so logical that Gareth felt stupid. This was a source of great amusement to the others, who teased him about not figuring out the fundamental workings of an inanimate object.

"(Thank me for the lights some other time)," he advised them. "(Burning wood for heat inside a house without a hearth; who knew)?" He poked around in the stove's empty interior as Michael continued to unload the groceries.

"What was that thing you were looking at, that little box when we were on the beach? Just before Brent yelled 'Illick charr-aa-nay'?" Michael asked him.

Gareth replied, "(It is a medical device called a burillier. It told me you were much like us physiologically. The inhabitants of the worlds of the universe are richly varied, friend Michael, but you and I are quite close in composition)."

"Kind of, galactic cousins?"

Gareth's smile widened. "(Quite kind of)."

"(And the phrase you quoted is not usually drawn out the way Brent shouted it)," Glendon explained. He manipulated his universal translator so he could pronounce it correctly. "Illick charanay. (But it is perfectly understandable for such enthusiasm in the face of such a welcome body of water!)"

Carrol wanted to apply a cream to Brent's skin, but he waved her away with a reminder of the stock pond and water tank by the barn. Carrol went on to check the rest, and it was clear to Michael that she was the doctor of the group. She checked the groceries and decided nothing appeared harmful for them to at least try. The Thuringi all loved the fruit; the apples were wiped out in minutes. The bread was nibbled on but apparently too dry after weeks of travel rations to enjoy yet. They all looked in morbid fascination as Michael formed the ground beef into patties and explained the relationship between the cattle in the pasture and the patties.

"(You eat gakkis)?" Glendon asked sadly.

"(Yes, most of us do. What do you do with your cows)?"

"(We would use them for transportation)."

"(Oh! Then gakkis must be like horses)." He nodded toward a crooked faded picture still hanging on the wall. Glendon examined it.

"(Oh yes, quite. Ours have a horn)."

"(The cows have horns. The cows, you eat)," Carrol mused. She stood next to Michael and watched him in a friendly manner, but it made him uneasy. They took offense to his hand kissing, but just where was the line drawn? Suppose her kinsmen thought he was trying to seduce her by a simple flirtation and decided to make rubble out of him?

"Now, we'll fix up a fire and grill 'em," he said when he finished enough for one burger apiece. He led the way to the old grill outside. He found a batch of wood chips on the back porch but had no matches. "I need some flames going, here," he muttered as he put the wood on the grill grate.

"(Very well)," Gareth said, removing a weapon from his side holster and tinkering with it. He fired at the wood, and it flamed up with a roar. Michael jumped back.

"You're pretty handy to have around," Michael said shakily, as he put the patties on the grill.

"(What does this 'yer' mean, friend Michael?" Glendon asked.

"You're? It's a – it is a contraction for the words 'you are'."

"I see. Um, why?"

Michael thought for a moment. "Well, there are a lot of words we contract. It's – it is – just a quicker way to respond, that's all. That is all," he corrected himself. "You mean you never, er, put words together that way?"

"No. We simply speak faster."

Michael chuckled. "Ah, I see."

Gareth asked, "(Why do you not use the stove in the house)?"

"It'd – it would make the house too hot this time of year. Anyway, that's – that is what this grill is for. They'll taste really good this way. They will taste good."

"It was not my intention to make you self-conscious about your manner of speech," Glendon said reluctantly.

"No, that's – that is all right," Michael assured him. "It probably does not help your translator any, trying to interpret my contractions and my Okie accent at the same time."

"Luket," Brent said, as he saluted them with a bottle of milk.

"Look at what?" Michael asked.

"Luket," Brent repeated, showing Michael the bottle.

"Oh, that is milk. We get it from the cows, too."

"(How? The cows become red)," Brent said, indicating the meat.

"No, we milk them. See, we take their...boy, howdy, this is tougher than I thought. We don't – do not – kill all our cows for meat. We drain certain ones of their extra milk. It doesn't – does not! – hurt them. Sometimes it makes them feel better, especially dairy cows."

The Thuringi all eyed him with mixed expressions. Stuart and Glendon were puzzled and re-checked their translators. Gareth was interested in knowing more but seemed unsure how to ask. Carrol seemed disappointed and almost ill, and Brent was amused.

Darien smiled wickedly. "(On D'tai, the men have spouses for that, when they become dahree)."

"Oh no, NO!" Michael sputtered. He quickly flipped the burgers onto the grill as his face flushed red with embarrassment. "The gakkis, I mean the cows, give us food, nourishment! No, we have spouses, wives and girlfriends and stuff, for...for..."

"(For)?" Gareth asked apprehensively.

"Sex." Michael blurted out.

"(Oh. Yjass)," Stuart clarified. "(The act of union between genders. Darien, if you are trying to be difficult, you have succeeded; now stop)."

"Yes, Yjass," Michael emphasized, hoping he meant to say what he just said.

"(There are females here like you, then)," Carrol said, not without relief.

"Well, of course," Michael said, flustered. "Where do you think our babies come from?"

They looked at one another, not realizing the question was rhetorical. Finally, Carrol ventured, "From... cows?"

"(From our females! Where do your babies come from)?" Michael snorted, and she slapped his hand. The blow made him jump back, rubbing his hand gingerly.

"(I do not think he meant, specifically, to see from whence they come)," Gareth said dryly.

Stuart was extremely annoyed with his siblings, and it showed in his curt tone of voice. "(Do not strike him! This culture is a different one from ours, but we must assimilate. We must keep away from these people until we learn more about them. It will not do to antagonize them simply because we do not understand their culture)." Stuart patted Michael gently on the back. "(I am sorry, friend Michael of

Tulsa. We are bad guests, but we deeply appreciate your help)."

"Well, you're hungry, you're tired, and you're new. Maybe it's better if you don't get out much at first. Have a pattie," Michael replied. Why were pretty women always the touchiest? He showed them how to eat burgers between two slices of bread. All but Brent enjoyed them; Brent tried to be polite and appreciative but could not stomach the strange food.

"(I prefer Luket)," he admitted.

"Yeah," Michael muttered as he sank down onto a stump, "and I prefer red-hot Yjass in the back of a Ford with a redhead from Sallisaw."

They all burst into laughter.

"(I am sorry, Michael of Taulsa)," Carrol said, "(I did not realize I struck you so hard. It has made you take leave of your senses)."

"I'm not saying anything more to you, lady," Michael said warily as he rose to head for the back door, "God knows what you'll do to me if I try to describe petting."

"(God)?" Glendon's attentive voice stopped Michael in mid-stride. "(What do you know of...what God do you worship)?"

"God. God is God."

"(What kind of God, what do you call it)?" Glendon pressed the issue as they returned indoors. Although the Thuringi still inspected the other items from the grocery bags, they all tuned in to the conversation.

"Well...my God doesn't have a name. He is just God. See, in this world there are a lot of different Gods worshiped ever since...well, ever since time began. But for me, there's just one God," Michael said.

"(The God with no name)?"

"Yes."

"(Yjass? You worship Yjass)?" Darien howled with amusement.

"Not Yjass, Y-E-S. Affirmative? Agreed? Okay?" Michael sighed. "I worship the God with no name: that is correct."

"(You have a bent mind)," Stuart said disapprovingly to Darien. To Michael, "(We, too, worship one God, and we have no name for him. He is simply the God of All)."

"Are you Christian?" Michael asked.

"(No, we are Thuringi. What is Christian)?" Stuart asked.

Michael smiled weakly. "This is gonna be a long one, Your

Highness. Let's go sit down on the front porch and talk."

They sat on the porch and leaned against the wall of the house or against the support posts for the porch roof as Michael Sheldon attempted to encapsulate his world and religion for alien visitors. "Most scientists believe the Earth was formed millions of years ago and that all life evolved from lower life forms. Our religious leaders say that God created the universe and the Earth and created man. What does your religion claim?" Michael asked.

"(The God of All created each world in accordance to His ultimate plan. All lives are guided by the alignment of the stars God placed in motion)," Stuart explained. "(We usually do not know the reason or plan but place our trust in the God of All to guide us accordingly)."

Michael nodded. "That sounds like what most of our Judeo-Christian beliefs follow. There are a number of religions on our world. Not all of them believe in a singular God or that God is a male figure or even believe in God at all."

"Yeep!" Glendon uttered, a startled response to something that rattled him. "(Why not)?"

"Some people just don't believe; they are jaded or stubborn and want concrete proof. It has been agreed by many scientists that mankind evolved from primitive creatures. This sort of belief has only been widely accepted in the last few decades." The Thuringi did not know how to reply to this statement, so they did not. Michael continued.

"History was passed down word of mouth from generation to generation until writing was developed. Early man was pretty ignorant. God was seen in different ways by different groups of people. Many things in nature were explained through superstition and signs. Believers in God hold that God created mankind in His image to populate our world, but a fallen angel named Lucifer corrupted man. He told man he could be like God, too.

"This was a sin in God's eyes, so man and woman were driven from the Garden of Eden, the perfect place God created on Earth for them. Mankind became mortal and could sicken and die then. Many beliefs and practices sprang up over time. Prophecies claimed a savior would be born that would save man. Eventually the Jews, a sect of believers in monotheism, were at odds with a powerful pagan group called Romans. Now, Christian beliefs state that God loved this world so much, that he gave his only begotten son to bear the sins of world after he was born to a Jewish woman. His son Jesus died so we could live with God in heaven forever when we die here."

"(Gave his what? God has a son)?" Stuart asked.

"Yes. Jesus was the Son of God. He suffered at the hands of Romans when He was a man of Earth, and because of His suffering we believe He didn't die forever. We believe He conquered death and still lives in spiritual form." The words that Michael knew since childhood now took on a different texture now that his view of the universe changed.

Gareth shivered and shook his head in confusion. "(But how could he die? Gods cannot die)."

"He was born on this world through a human mother. He was therefore human while he was here, and when He died, he took on the sins of the whole world. If you believe in Him and in God, then your spirit also will never die when your human body dies. You will live in heaven forever in spirit."

For a long moment, the otherworld guests stared at their host. Then they began to chuckle until it grew into uproarious guffaws.

"(What a tale)!" Glendon whooped. "(You are an imaginative people)!"

"There are millions of people who believe it."

This simple statement stopped their laughter. "(How many worlds believe in this)?" Stuart asked.

"Just this one," Michael replied.

"(How many people are on your world)?" Darien asked.

"Roughly three billion."

A unified gasp issued from the crowd. "(That is more than on all the worlds of the Stellar Council)," Stuart mused. "(Please forgive us our mirth, Michael, but your tale is so impudent! Aside from sheer number, what is it about your people that make them so grand as to host a son of God among them)?"

"Well, up until this afternoon nearly everyone on this planet including me thought we were the only people in the universe."

"(You are not as imaginative as Glendon claimed)," Darien commented wryly.

"Well, what are your beliefs, what is your culture like?" Michael asked defensively.

Stuart jumped in to answer before his caustic twin could. "(We believe in the God of All, who made all the worlds. Each planet has variations, I suppose, but most worlds embrace the concept of some sort of God, all-powerful and compassionate in equal measure. We read from the Thuringi Book of Prayer and attend services every ginta. We uphold our honor and duty with equal devotion in the name of the God of All. We have never heard of this perfect place, this Eden of which you speak. We accept sinful behavior as a challenge over which we must exercise control in order to live the proper life of a devout Thuringi. Our prayers are no different for our Aquatics as they are for Airmen)."

"Each planet, you say. What planets; what are they like?" Michael asked eagerly.

"(Our closest neighboring planet was D'tai)," Darien told him. "(Their prosperity and industry were thanks largely to the peace we held in place for them)."

"(Our defenses did not have that much to do with their economic success; only their safety)," Stuart objected, and explained for their Earthian host. "(Several worlds were made to pretend that they were forced to give us supplies after we fled our dying planet and approached them for help. The D'tai are a generous people normally but were desperate to remain in our enemies' good graces. After what happened to our world, they were uncertain they could escape the same fate if they defied the Shargassi)."

"What happened to make war between you and these Shargassi?"

"(It started long, long ago. The Shargassi have a history of aggression and brutality and pillaged outposts and murdered innocent folks since before any of us were born. We are known as a warrior race under monarchical rule, but we urge peace and use our military to enforce the peace. The Shargassi are a military empire and believe in taking what they need rather than trade peacefully)."

Glendon seconded Stuart's words. "(The Shargassi wanted Thuringi power and might without developing their own. They killed two hundred thousand of our people but still they failed their main objective. They did not annihilate their rival. We survived)."

Darien grumbled, "(Other worlds caved in to the Shargassi's

demands to not aid us, despite knowing we were desperate for supplies. After all the times we literally saved those worlds from everything from aggression to natural disasters, some did not have the sand to take care of their own! At least the D'tai created a plausible excuse in order to help us)."

Stuart did not want Michael to get the wrong impression. "(There are societies with powerful defenses who are not afraid of the threat and others who have only trade goods for appeasement. And then, there are the Chassiren)."

"(Ahh)." Brent, Darien, and Gareth all smiled at the mention of this name. Glendon did not comment and looked uncomfortable instead. Carrol looked at Gareth and raised an eyebrow, along with a smile.

"(The Chassiren are a race of beautiful women who help visitors put aside the cares of the day for more, shall we say, welcome distractions)." Michael smiled and nodded in understanding at Stuart's words. "(They are gracious and well versed in the customs and courtesies of all the known worlds)."

Glendon shrugged and muttered, "(I would not know; I have never met one)."

"(Our Glendon is a proper Thuringi; his family does not dally with Chassiren. Garins are far too couth to stoop to a little what-what with desirable women)," Brent chuckled.

"(Those that we do, we prefer to call our wives)," Glendon replied with dignity.

Michael traced Earth history as briefly but as detailed as he could. The Thuringi were impressed with the tales of kingdoms and exploration, and even more impressed with peace treaties and scientific advancement. They were disturbed by the notion of plagues and untreatable illnesses. These were things they had just left behind on Thuringa. Michael could not help but notice how appalled they were at Earth's comparatively primitive technological status. The stories of war interested the Thuringi, and their history likewise interested Michael.

One Thuringi name in their history kept cropping up, and the name Maranta Shanaugh made the beautiful Carrol Shanaugh nearly swoon. His story was told by Darien; Carrol could not bear to speak of it. Maranta had also helped explore their future home Farcourt, 'a

fair, promising world uninhabited by creatures of intelligent thought.'
According to Glendon who quoted the report from memory, it was 'a
gakki's paradise.' As far as they knew, Earth was the only habitable
world in this far-flung area they called the Unknown Territory.

"(Maranta and his crew visited Farcourt on a scouting
expedition)," Stuart explained, "(They were able to travel to it along
the wormholes. But to travel the wormholes, ships must be hardy, and
we cannot transport the entire Armada's contents through a man-made
physical transporter. There is no transporter available large enough to
hold anything bigger than our cargo shuttles. We need every battleship
we have to protect the fleet. Some of our ships could not withstand the
kind of buffeting a wormhole trace produces, and for an exceptionally
long stretch there are no wormholes to venture through as even a
shortened passage. We have powerful engines but without use of the
traces it will take a long time.)."

"Uh... wormholes. Gotcha," Michael replied, not getting him at
all. "You must have trusted this Maranta fellow's judgment a lot if
you're banking your future on his exploration."

"(He was our Warrior General as well as our brother-in-law),"
Stuart said with a nod of his head at Carrol. She sat with her head
bowed, gazing at the floor in thought. Gareth stroked her shoulders in
comfort.

Darien stretched his arms upward and his rowdy voice cut
through the somber mood like a sword. "(Ordinarily I would wonder
at the judgment of any man daft enough to marry a troublesome
package like Carrol, but he was as trustworthy a man as ever there
was! I trusted him with my dear only sister so yes, we are going to
Farcourt on his word)." Carrol glanced at him, and Darien gave her a
saucy wink. She smiled and playfully wrinkled her nose at him.

The first rays of dawn peeked through the darkness from the
horizon when Michael awoke. What am I doing back home at the old
house? he wondered. He looked around and remembered. It was not a
dream, then.

Aliens from space really were here on Earth, on his porch. They
were awake until the wee hours of the morning on the front porch of
the farmhouse in a cultural history exchange, until one by one they all
fell asleep where they sat. He was glad he did not report them to the

authorities. Now that he had a chance to know them, he warmed to the Thuringi more than he ever warmed to anyone or anything in his life. They were people with feelings and hopes and fears just like anyone on Earth and as far as Michael Sheldon was concerned, they were to be protected.

Glendon stood nearby as he watched the sun rise. He took deep breaths as if he could not get enough clean cool morning air, or at least not in a very long time. Michael watched in fascination as tears ran down the tall man's cheeks.

"Are you alright?" Michael asked gently.

"(I have not seen such a beautiful sight in many years)," Glendon said equally as quiet. "(It is a wonderful world here, friend Michael)." He adjusted a blanket at the shoulder of the slumbering Prince Stuart.

"You take very good care of them," Michael observed.

"I am a Naradi Famede, a member of the Royal Family Guard. It is my duty to look after my Phillipi charges, but it is also an honor and a joy. I would look after them even if it were not my task to do so."

"That's very admirable," Michael noted. He suddenly sat up with a start, awakening the slumbering Thuringi with his exclamation. "Oh my gosh! My car is still upside down in a creek in Massachusetts! If I'm considered missing or someone calls in the wreck, they won't know where I am. They'll be worried. They'll call my parents, and they'll be worried and pissed."

"(What is that)?" Gareth asked as he yawned and stretched.

"Pissed. Uh..." Michael answered, "Not happy at all."

"(I will take you back)," Stuart offered. Michael got up to go, and Stuart put his hands on Michael's shoulders. The top of Michael's head was equal to Stuart's nose, so he tilted his head back and looked up at the tall alien. "(You are the best friend we could have possibly made, Michael of Tulsa. I am certain that the God of All has guided us to you for safety and aid. We will always be in your debt)."

"I appreciate that," Michael said, trying not to wince. He had been through quite a bit in the past eighteen hours, and he was sore all over. "I'm not sure how much food you have left over for a breakfast meal."

"(We still have travel rations)," Gareth pointed out, and this made the others groan. "(We have no way to barter for food)," he pointed out, "(and we cannot expect our generous host to continue to feed us. He already houses us)."

"(Gareth is absolutely right)," Stuart said. "(We will live on our travel rations until we can come up with a way to assimilate into this society)."

"(...and get more peaches)," Glendon added. He liked the tasty treat from the can Darien slashed open. It was devastatingly sweet, but one can divided among six Thuringi did no harm.

Stuart took Michael back to the store, where Michael spoke to the owner, Ed Gentry. He explained that some foreign friends were staying at the ranch for a time, and would Ed help them when they came to shop? The owner remembered Michael from the old days and was happy to help. Michael bought sunglasses for his guests to hide their yellow eyes. He went outside and gave Stuart a pair so Michael could introduce him to Ed. Michael bought some more fruit and other supplies. The ship was hidden out of sight of the store, and they pretended they had walked into town.

They returned to New England where Michael went to a theatrical supply company and ordered blue contact lens, the kind film actors used. They then returned to the creekside wreck site and set the plane down among thick foliage for camouflage. Michael's car was still there. He shook Stuart's hand.

"I'm so sorry I can't drop everything right now and help you, but it would raise a lot of questions if I just quit what I'm doing without a logical explanation. I'll try to get the phone hooked up out there. In the meantime, I'll have those lens shipped out to you to the ranch as soon as they come in. The local postman will bring the package to you. Let him know you were expecting it and act casually. You can get away with a lot if you behave as if whatever you do is an everyday affair."

"(I cannot possibly tell you how grateful I am, Friend Michael. We are in desperate straits. We will do our best to be good guests, but we are bound to make mistakes)."

Michael smiled. "I understand. Just try not to draw attention to yourselves, okay? You guys are kind of hard to miss, you know." They heard a screech of tires from the roadway above. "Somebody must have seen the car, so I'll go be found. Take care, Your Highness."

"(And yourself, Michael of Taulsa)." Michael went out from behind the rocks and trees shielding them from view.

"Geez Louise, have you been here all night?" Tom Scott hollered in relief as he gave his old college friend a big hug. "You had us all worried! Are you okay, Michael? How did you manage to get out of a crash like that?"

"It was a miracle," Michael said truthfully. "Take me back to town, will you? I need to call my family and let them know I'm okay."

"Clarence Burton's already got every policeman and state trooper on the lookout," Tom laughed. "The guy is a rich drip sometimes, but boy, he's a loyal rich drip. Say, did you know there were all sorts of reports about mysterious lights and ships and stuff? My ham radio was smoking with reports. Did you see anything out here? What happened, anyway?"

"I swerved to avoid an animal, and I lost control. Lights and ships, huh? What kind of ships?"

"Oh, man! Rocket ships, alien ships, you know. They were sighted up the coast too."

"You don't really believe in little green men, do you?" Michael laughed. Tom shrugged sheepishly. Michael continued easily, "Come on, then. Give me a lift back to the house. The only aliens I know work in the kitchen at Clarence Burton's home." Tom burst into laughter. With a backward glance toward the rocks, Michael got into the car and the friends headed for Boston.

Stuart Phillipi peered out from behind the rocks. Never in all his wildest worried imaginings did he dare hope for fortune as good as this! The God of All was surely watching over the scouting party. A bountiful planet with edible food and for the aquatic Brent's sake especially, water; being befriended by a kind, patient young man who remained kind and patient even after Stuart's people were so rough on him. Michael was a teacher, working on his doctorate at the Earthian Academy with the curious name of "Harvard". With so much on his agenda already, it was kind of the Earthian to offer to help at all and his Thuringi guest was incredibly grateful.

That they had a safe haven in a strange, violent world was not what Stuart expected to have on their first day. At the very least, the Thuringi scouts were prepared to negotiate a treaty for squatter's rights and eventually hoped to soften the populace up to allow the Thuringi Armada to rest in a peaceful truce. At the worst, they were prepared to battle for a resting place. It would have been difficult as they were all tired from travel and dangers, but possible in this relatively elementary civilization. Stuart returned to the Sheldon ranch, thanking the God of All that Michael Marley Sheldon of Tulsa, Earth piloted a ground vehicle at just the right place at just the right time in the Thuringi's lives.

Chapter 2: Beginnings

Michael Sheldon called his father and told him some friends needed to stay at the old ranch. "They lost everything in a storm, Dad," Michael lied. "They really need help. They'll keep the place up and probably even make some improvements."

Darryl Sheldon agreed to the arrangement. Michael was a practical man, a son in whom anyone would take pride, and Darryl was pleased Mike was so considerate of those less fortunate than he. The matter was a simple one, and Darryl had more on his mind than Mike's luckless friends. Michael's brother Derrick never did like the ranch and said he felt sorry for anyone so bad off that they would want to live there.

Michael had no idea how to go about contacting anyone who could help the new arrivals. Ordinarily he would have gone to some authority or the military, but a strange chill seized him the moment he reached for the phone to call the number in the phone book. Every time he reached for it, a peculiar buzzing sound filled his ears, and he was suddenly consumed with doubt.

The military was jealous of anyone who had better weaponry and even though the Thuringi were strong, there were only six of them. Sheer numbers would overcome them. There was no telling what kind of experiments would be done on them and like so many other unsolved mysteries, such experiments could be done in secret. Michael might never see his new friends again.

"I'll just have to think about this for a while," he decided aloud to himself. "I don't want to call just anyone, for sure not the military. I'll give them some time to rest up and then I'll figure out what to do."

He did not have the luxury of time. His doctoral defense was fast approaching, and an offer from a private school in Texas for headmaster was entirely dependent upon his earning that doctorate. He could not drop everything to help the Thuringi, no matter how much he wished he could. What they had to learn about Earth, they needed to learn for themselves. The best help Michael could give them was for himself to be gainfully employable so he could afford to buy supplies or whatever they needed.

The Thuringi cleaned the interior of the house and scraped the peeling walls until they were smooth. Gareth and Stuart got the water well in working order and they all quickly figured out the fixtures of the bathroom. It was a fundamental bathroom with a sink, a toilet, and a large claw-foot tub. The toilet was primitive, but they had faced far worse conditions on other worlds. The two broken chairs they found were a challenge. They decided to encase the frames in crystallized sand and fibers using one of their laser pistols. They needed the frames; Darien sat on an all-crystal chair to test it and ended up on the floor a split second later, surrounded by clear glittering shards.

They cleaned two old mattresses found in the bedrooms as well as they could. The mattresses were re-stuffed with dry grass from the nearby fields. One mattress went in Carrol's bedroom, the other in Stuart and Darien's room. Darien preferred to sleep on a floor pallet made from flight blankets, as there was only room for Stuart on the full-size mattress.

Glendon and Gareth fashioned hammocks in their rooms. After testing them out, the others agreed these were probably the most comfortable of all. Darien made one for himself and put his pallet in that. Brent took command of the bathtub and filled the porcelain fixture with warm water. He did not care if the water was cold the next morning. Brent was comfortable at last. The only inconvenience was his being rousted out of 'bed' early every morning so others could use the room.

Carrol surveyed her room from the doorway with satisfaction. The walls were covered with white paint found on the back porch, and the mattress sported blankets from her ship. A small bag of clothing was unfolded and neatly hung in the closet, and a tapered bottle with flowers and water in it sat on the windowsill. Beside the bed on a little table was a time-worn book.

Gareth stole behind her and rested his chin on her shoulder. "Are We pleased with Our royal quarters, Your Nibs?" he asked in his playful, upper-octave "Royal We" voice he occasionally used to imitate the lordly nobles of Thuringa.

"Yes, We are. We especially appreciate the decorative flowers." Without turning around, she reached up to ruffle his hair.

"We thought We might like Our offering," he said in a normal voice as he placed his hands on her waist. He pressed his mouth against her shoulder, not quite a kiss but certainly a sign of affection.

"None of that," Glendon called from down the hall. "I am still your Naradi, Princess, and responsible for you to your father."

"Are you my father, as well?" Gareth shot back.

"If I have to be."

Gareth reluctantly removed his hands. "He is more like a wizened old grandmother," he whispered to Carrol.

"I heard that," Glendon intoned.

"So, you like the flowers?" Gareth asked her.

"Yes, they are wonderful. Where did you find them?"

"Why, they are everywhere you look. Those little blue fuzzy ones are right next to the strands of the prickly wire fence. The yellow ones with the black centers are out along the front near the road."

"They are so beautiful, all the little petals look like little fingers."

"Even better are the ones at the corner of the house." Seeing that neither Carrol nor Glendon recognized the reference, he led them outside to an overgrown domestic rose bush. He carefully snapped thorns from a flowering stem and cut it with his hand knife for her.

"Oh my! Smell this, it is grand!" she declared. The men agreed it was a fantastic scent, so Glendon helped Gareth gather more blooms. The roses reminded them of Thuringi scannia in appearance, but the scent was thicker and rich on these Earthian flowers.

"I wonder what Janis and Echo will say when they see these," Glendon mused. "Why, I can just see them both planning flowerbeds for when we reach Farcourt. I think Echo has the same love of flowers as her mother."

"Likely she will have all manner of young men bringing her flowers on their own accord," Gareth pointed out. "I look forward to watching you and Janis struggle to keep them at bay."

"You saw her at the cadet review during Festival," Glendon said proudly. "I daresay she will be able to keep them at arm's throw distance all by herself."

They sat on the steps of the porch and Gareth looked all around. "This place reminds me of my boyhood in Carzon," he said with a trace of wistfulness in his voice. He gestured to the wheat field across the road from the ranch. "We had a field near our house like that, and alongside the house yard was a pasture where we kept our gakkis. There were little flowers everywhere but nothing quite like these."

The other three Thuringi came out to join them. Darien sprawled out on his back on the porch and pillowed the back of his head with his hands. Stuart sat on the porch swing they found in the barn, repaired, and put back in place.

Brent went out into the yard, where he turned on the water hose to soak his head and neck. He asked Gareth, "Wasn't Carzon the city in the middle of the Thuringa land mass?" Like many Aquatics, Brent never paid much attention to the interior of the land.

"It was near the center. Just a village, really, but it was a wonderful place." Gareth turned to Carroll. "After the Massic Surrell your parents called me in for questions. I suppose they wanted to know more about this odd man who fought for their daughter's honor. In my non-too-genteel way, I told them exactly what I thought about a lot of things, especially what I thought about Thuringi clergy. Your mother is grace itself; she did not faint once."

"What do you think of the clergy?" Carrol asked.

"Well, I recall I said something about our local Carzon bishop being a passage-quoting bastard." The collective gasp echoed in the still of the porch. "They asked me about my large family and what became of them, so I talked about each one, and how the bishop told my father my brothers' accidental deaths were punishment for Mother and him for having so many children. I do not like the clergy. I prefer to simply accept what challenges God puts before me and work them out without high-collar interpretation. Your father seemed to like that."

"That is not much of a surprise. He likes ingenuity under fire. How did you get from Carzon to Arne?" Stuart asked.

"After the boys and Father passed away, we stayed on the farm for a while. When I joined the Air Command Auxiliary, I made Mother and brother Clive move to Gallina with me. He had Bran Fitt as Father had, and the sea air did him good. My sister Pattie married, had a pair of children, and moved to Arne. Then I was transferred to Arne with Maranta, so Mother and Clive stayed in Gallina. When I went home on leave occasionally, I brought the general with me. Mother was very fond of him. She made bannon soup for us and liked to tease him about—"

Gareth stopped and turned to Carrol with a grin. "She teased him about a little officer he fancied but about whom he never mentioned details." Carrol shrugged with a smile and bumped her shoulder against his, as if to admit she had been that officer. "Here was the great mighty Maranta Shanaugh of the Royal Thuringa Air Command, easily brought to a bashful blush by the one woman who could scold or tease him as a mother would. She was not even as old as he, but her widow's heart was much older than twice his age. She treated every man like the sons she should have raised to manhood."

"I imagine she was quite the character if her eldest son is any indication," Darien mused. "Did she ever marry again, or is that a foolish question?"

"After Father passed away, she refused the very idea. She just laughed at would-be suitors, rather harshly too. Then Clive was called back to Arne when his theories about Farcourt garnered interest, and Mother came with him. The General once made the mistake of introducing her to some officer friend of his, and she gave them both an exceedingly difficult time."

Stuart broke in, "I recall a story Ganson Renaugh once told of a perfectly enchanting woman who spurned him so thoroughly, he was lovesick for months. Perhaps it was her. He said she was only as tall as a minute and wore rings on every finger."

"That was Mother," Gareth agreed. "She always wore her wedding ring and a ring for every child."

Darien counted silently and said, "I thought there were only six of you."

"She lost one before birth, but she counted every baby she conceived."

Darien rose and went inside. Night was falling, and the stars came out in the darkening star. Darien emerged from the house with two glasses of milk and handed one to Gareth. "To Maribel and Denys Duncan," Darien toasted, "and the answer as to the source of their eldest son's remarkable attributes."

"Thank you, Your Naughtiness; I think," Gareth replied.

Darien let out a hearty laugh. "It is a compliment. For now, we know where you get your ability to toil for hours, your incessant optimism in the face of the impossible, and your instinctive catering to our sister, Her Most Ardent Nibs."

"You should have seen me during consue, I was the Hack and Slash variety of fighter. I decided to serve my king with a wrench and a spanner rather than insult the Air Command by flailing about like a gakki colt," Gareth admitted to their riotous amusement. He offered Carrol a sip of milk and she smiled and shook her head. He shrugged and took another sip. Glendon saw the exchange and went in to get drinks for the rest of them.

Father was right about one thing, Carrol thought as she watched Gareth out of the corner of her eye as he looked out over the lawn, unconcerned about his actions. Gareth honestly did not know when he made a social blunder. To the high born of Thuringa, a man did not publicly offer a woman a sip from his glass unless they were married, or he wanted to be considered by all as her lover. To farmer's son Gareth, offering her a drink was simply a gesture of sharing. Glendon brought out four more glasses, and they all toasted the beautiful evening weather.

Brent decided the stock pond was too dirty for comfort, and the 'cabrett' often wandered up to drink from the water tank. The Aquatic did not care to lay in the same water from which large noisesome creatures drank and spilled drool from their mouths back into the water. As he sat submerged in the stock tank, he watched the cow cautiously extend its head toward him and lowed mournfully, its open mouth like a gaping maw to the alien. Brent Ardenne, who rarely ventured into the interior of the Thuringa continent, was completely unnerved by such an airbreathing beast of another world. He scrambled out of the tank as quickly as he could and hurried to the house. "I am going back to the Great Water, Stuart!" he half-suggested, half-demanded. Stuart agreed he should, unaware of the reason behind the statement.

Glendon accompanied Brent in his own ship, and they took a quick orbital equatorial tour of the planet out of curiosity. Brent chose the turquoise waters and white beaches of the Caribbean to stop. Glendon stood guard on the empty stretch of sand while Brent stripped off his clothing and plunged into the water. He explored the underwater area for so long, Glendon paced nervously all along the shoreline, concerned that something was amiss. But Brent treated every ocean creature as a potential predator, and he cautiously explored underwater wrecks. It was a strange world and there were sights and sounds that even the Aquatic Brent had never seen before.

When Brent re-emerged, he figured he was due for a good scolding from the Airman and apologized. "It took me longer than I thought it would; I am still tired from our journey," he admitted. "Perhaps I am not quite ready for this yet."

It was unusual for Brent Ardenne to admit to any weakness, especially in the water, so Glendon decided not to give him the lecture he had prepared. They returned to the ranch mid-afternoon by darting in and out of cloud formations.

Their ships all needed to be hidden. One fit inside the barn and two fit in the little fenced corral next to it. Those were hidden by pieces of corrugated sheet metal. The other three were covered with cut branches, next to a rusty metal object near the back fence.

Gareth found an old push mower and wondered about its engine until he realized it never had one. It was a grass cutter, he exclaimed to the others and proceeded to cut the grass all around the interior yard. It would indicate to others someone lived there and therefore deter idle wanderers. They took turns mowing after they recognized the practicality of clipped foliage around the house.

Darien was especially keen on the idea ever since he stepped on an animal in the overgrown front yard. The creature screeched, clawed at him, and ran away. He high-stepped his way back to the porch at a dead run, swearing violently with each step. For his part, Stuart stubbed his toe on a rock and fell onto the scratchy bush with fragrant flowers. The Phillipi brothers insisted on a lawn they could safely traverse.

Once the front, back, and side yards were mowed, they all gathered in the back yard on their third evening on Earth to lie on the ground and look at the starry sky. Glendon and Stuart tried to get their bearings and estimate where the Armada was. Darien watched for meteors with Gareth and Carrol, and Brent enjoyed the last of the milk and admired the shiny sliver of moon. They heard the fall-off sound of a whippoorwill calling out its mournful call, and it fascinated them. Michael had explained some of the sounds of the night, and they tried to imagine what such a creature looked like.

Gareth saw a movement by the corner of the house and softly whispered to the others, "There is a small creature over to the left." They sat quietly as it approached. It was smaller than a dallah, light-colored with lean limbs and a curious round little face. Long whiskers emerged from its nose and mouth area, and it made a sound much like a baby. Stuart held out his hand, and the creature walked to him and sniffed his fingers. It made another of its baby sounds as rubbed its face against Stuart's hand, and the Thuringi stroked its soft furry body. The creature arched its back in response to the touch.

"It is quite an agreeable creature," Stuart told them, and they all took a try at patting it. It made a rumbling sound in its throat. When Brent reached to pat it, the animal suddenly became quite eager to sniff his fingers and bit him. Brent withdrew his hand quickly.

"Agreeable to you," he told Stuart. "I do not believe the thing likes me." It tried to bite him again, so he swatted it lightly on the nose. It hissed and returned to Stuart's lap. After digging its little claws on Stuart's legs, it curled up in a ball and stayed there.

"Fuzzy little thing," Stuart said with satisfaction. "It is not a dallah, but it is apparently used to people. Domesticated, not wild."

"Which is probably why it likes you better than Brent," Darien said with finality. "You are domesticated; Brent is wild."

Brent raised his glass of luket. "Do not forget that bit of wisdom, either!"

Darien suddenly drew his sword as he leaped to his feet. "What are those lights coming this way?" he whispered hoarsely, and they drew their weapons and got into a defensive circle.

"Where?" Stuart whispered.

"Those, there," Darien pointed with a slight movement of his sword to tiny little lights that glowed green for a moment, then went out. When the light came on again, it was closer to them than where it was last. Two other little lights appeared in the yard with the first. Slowly, the six Thuringi eased toward them.

"They are little creatures," Glendon said aloud in surprise, and quickly shut his mouth in alarm. But the little insects continued their lazy pace in the air and ignored the Thuringi completely. Gareth reached out his sword and caught one on its broad side. They examined it curiously before it flew away. Glendon caught one in his hand and said, "It is not attacking me, no sting or anything. They only glow, that is all."

"Word, look at that," Darien said as he nodded toward the pasture. Little lights floated all over the field. "They are beautiful."

"Will this curious world never cease to bring forth surprises?"

Stuart wondered.

Michael gathered books and items he thought useful and sent them to the ranch by airmail along with the contact lens. The mailman knocked on the door and after one look at the tall long-haired man with yellow eyes, he turned and fled for his pickup.

Brent picked up the package on the porch and came inside the house. "A man dropped this and ran away. Perhaps it is a gift."

"We have no gift givers here. We know no one but...Michael!" Darien exclaimed. They eagerly tore the wrapping off the heavy package addressed to Stuart Phillipi, Route 2 Box 459, Iron Post, Oklahoma.

Three cans of peaches were on top, and Glendon whooped in delight at the sight of the picture on the cans. Tucked beside them were flat paper-wrapped bundles containing smooth brown slabs. Carrol tasted the contents first. They all had a taste after she bounced up and down, her eyes wide and little squeaking noises coming from her smiling lips. It was agreed they must thank Michael profusely for such a delightful treat.

"Word, they have the ability to parse distilled drink into solids," Brent marveled, unaware that chocolate was not alcoholic. To a Thuringi anything sweet had the potential for getting one tipsy.

They tried out the colored eye lens, but Stuart's eyes could not bear them, and Darien could only wear them for a few minutes before his eyes began to sting the way his brother's did. Carrol could tolerate them, but it was a constant nuisance. The other three had no problem but instead of blue eyes they had the most startling shade of bright green. These would be worn only if they had to be among Earthians, and the Phillipi brothers would have to continue to wear their dark glasses.

There were books, some with many illustrations on subjects like plant propagation and vegetables. Inside the gardening books were packages of seeds. Glendon sat down in the floor to study the pictures. One of the books was a science textbook and another, a repair manual for a 1940 Chevrolet pickup. Gareth claimed these. There was an eighth-grade civics textbook in which Michael underlined passages he thought important. He also sent a recent edition of the Boston Globe, the New York Times, and Life magazine. He sent a copy of Gray's

Anatomy and another medical book he found in a used bookstore. Carrol claimed the medical books; Stuart and Darien took the papers and the textbook. Brent got the Life magazine whose cover displayed a picture of the ocean.

"What is this language?" Darien fumed. "Our translators cannot help us with the written word."

"There are pictures on your pages," Stuart pointed out. "Perhaps we can decipher the words through them."

"There is naught but pictures here," Brent said holding up his magazine. "And our friend Michael of Tulsa was right. There are definitely women on this world. Look!" He held up the magazine, showing a photo of an actress.

"She is beautiful," Carrol said. "What a handsome race of people Michael's Taulsans are!"

"This must be the woman he was to have red-hot yjass with," Brent muttered, examining the picture with delight.

Gareth looked over his shoulder. "There is an animal around her shoulders."

"A pet, perhaps?" Brent asked.

"A very flat pet," Darien said. "They eat their gakkis and wear their smaller creatures."

Glendon took a sudden intake of air and slapped his hand over the woman's lower extremities. "Yeep! It is naughty!"

Naturally, Darien and Brent pulled his hand away to take a look. The woman wore open-toed sandals. They all squawked as one and snapped the magazine shut and stared at each other in stricken silence.

"She was deformed," Gareth whispered. "She had a number of toes."

"What? Let me see," Carrol said, and then insisted. "I am a medical officer. I must get a better understanding of their physiology." The men shook their heads firmly, so she turned to Gray's Anatomy. "Oh my. According to this textbook, these people really do have more than two toes on each foot."

"Well, since it has scientific merit," Stuart decided, so they looked at the book's illustration. "Well, what do you know."

"Like little fingers. Ugh. Unfinished fingers," Darien said as he crinkled his nose in disgust. "They are deformed."

"No webbing, either," Brent pointed out. "Can you imagine what their stockings look like!" With that, curiosity about Earthian feet was accomplished and put aside.

"I intend to plant some seeds," Glendon decided. "We will be able to eat more than rations if I have an area to plant seeds. All they use is a clear spot of common ground. If they can grow food, I can. And I will grow peaches, too... if I can get some peach seeds."

Gareth took his new books out to the front porch swing. Soon Carrol wandered out and sat with him. "Well, we have some things we can at least look at and try to decipher," she noted as she opened the anatomy book.

"I will attempt to master the indigent people's ground transportation," Gareth said, flipping through the repair book. "I wonder if perhaps I would be better off simply putting the shell of the truck over an engine of ours."

"One of those lumpy things going down the roadway at trace speed?" Carrol laughed at the thought.

"They are all so slow. Look at that one on that roadway over there. No wonder these people are no more advanced than they are. They burn wood to keep warm, and they travel slower than I can trot."

"Do not be so judgmental, Major Sword-and-Fist. You cannot trot quite that fast." He conceded with a shrug and a smile and stretched his near arm out along the back of the swing. She leaned against it to pillow her head, and they concentrated on their reading.

"And have you any questions over the material I left for you to read en route?" he asked at length, still studying his Earthian book.

"Is there supposed to be a test over it later?" she asked as she also pretended to be engrossed in her book.

"Well...lectures only go so far; lab work is far more instructional."

"You are twisted," she told him with a happy smile.

Glendon sauntered out on the porch. "I am going out plant some seeds," he announced. Gareth waved without looking up or moving his arm off the swing. "My secondary gifted task is growing things," Glendon observed airily. "Gareth's must be to navigate books he cannot read and pillow heads brighter than his own." He chuckled as he dodged the book thrown his way.

The mailman came again the next day, cautious. Stuart had Carrol answer the door wearing sunglasses, and the mailman was friendlier. "Nice day, ain't it? Y'all just move here?" he asked with a tip of his hat to her. Carrol smiled.

"(Thank you for leaving the parcel for us)," she said.

"Well, that's my job," the mailman acknowledged proudly. "Did you buy this place from Darryl, or are you renting?"

"(We are staying here for a time)," she replied easily.

"Well, you've got another package from young Mike. I hear he's back to his Ivy League college for his doctorate. He sure could play football in high school. Wish he'd a-gone to Tulsa, or O.U."

"(Yes)," Carrol agreed, having not the slightest notion of what the man was talking about. "(You said you have a job? What is that)?" She meant it as a query of what a job was, but he did not interpret it that way.

"I'm a mailman, m'am. Say, are you from overseas? Like one of those war brides?"

"(I was)," Carrol replied quietly.

"Oh, well, I'm sorry," he said quickly at the sight of her suddenly solemn face. "Here's your mail. You've got two boxes from young Mike. Y'all take care, now. If you need anything, just ring." With a friendly wave of his hand, he went on his way.

One of the packages contained more canned goods and several large size articles of clothing. Darien pulled on a shirt. It was too small for him, but slender Glendon could wear it. There were pants there, too, but only Glendon could fit into them. "Glendon will be the one to do our trading for us, then," Stuart decided. "It will be easiest for him to assimilate wearing those articles."

"I am not terribly eager about this. They eat their ugly gakkis, you know," Glendon pointed out.

Gareth opened the second box. Inside there were more books, many without the visual aid of illustrations to even give them a hint as to their content.

"What does this mean? How do we do this?" Gareth wondered, eager to understand the printed word.

"We will have to go and get Michael to explain," Stuart sighed.

Darien promptly headed for the door. "I will be back with him," he announced and was gone.

"Darien, no! You cannot just 'go and get him', like – oh, why is he so incautious!"

"He has always been that way," Carrol shrugged. "You know that. Besides, there is much here we do not understand, and we have only Michael for help. Oh.... more flat sweets!" she said as she looked deeper down in the second box.

"And more books. What do they all say?" Glendon wondered, frustrated.

Darien toyed with the com controls until he heard mention of the word 'Massachusetts', and he followed the signal to a primitive signal tower. He boldly landed the ship on the roof of a building and took the package wrapping with him down to the street. He stopped the first person he saw and demanded, "Is there a location on this sheet where I might find Michael Sheldon?" The man looked up into his yellow eyes and squawked in alarm. Without a reply he fled. Darien tried again with someone else, and again did more harm than good. He decided to walk inside and ask a man at a desk in the building lobby.

"(I was sent a package from someone, yet I cannot find his location. Can you help me)?" he asked with care.

The man did not even look at him. He took the wrapping and looked it over. With a bony finger he pointed in the upper left-hand corner and said, "Well, you're going to need to go to Cambridge; that's about three hundred and forty miles from here)."

"(I am a stranger here. Which direction is that)?"

The man pointed. "It's thataway. Just follow the signs; I'm sure you'll find it, sonny."

"(I cannot read the signs)."

The man gave a snort. "Damned English! We saved you from the Huns, but we can't seem to save you from yourselves." He finally looked up and visibly paled at the sight of a frustrated Thuringi before him.

"(You are rude! Had I time, I would remain and take lessons as I am certain you are a master of non-civility)," Darien growled before he stormed away. He took his ship and landing by landing slowly made his way to Cambridge.

Michael stepped out of his bathtub and was in the process of drying when the bathroom door sprang open. Darien stood with one hand as usual on the handgrip of his saber. He cocked an eyebrow in surprise at the sight of Michael in the buff. Earthians were short in height, but this one at least looked muscular enough to put up a struggle if he did not wish to help. Darien would need to be cautious; it would be humiliating to be bested by an error in judgment.

"What the –? Darien! How did you get... where did you... did anybody see you?" Michael said, wrapping his towel around at hip level.

"(I showed the package wrapping to people until I narrowed your living quarters to this location. We cannot translate the books and paperings you have sent. We need a teacher. You must come at once)." Darien explained as he grabbed Michael by the arm. His nerves were frazzled by the search. He did not consider that his bright yellow eyes, large body, and brittle scowl unnerved everyone he met. They willingly helped him find Michael if it meant that this frightening apparition would pass them by.

"Whoa, hey wait a minute," Michael protested, and jerked his arm free. "Look, I'm doing my best for you all, but I have classes to teach and a thesis to defend."

"(We will defend your thesis for you)," Darien declared confidently as he patted his sword. Michael shook his head at his literal interpretation. "(The things you gave us have no use, no meaning. We cannot decipher your writings)."

"What about that decoder thing around your neck? Can't you use that?"

"(It is a language translator; it cannot help with the written word, only the spoken word)."

"Oh. I didn't realize that. Well, I'll try to think of something else." Michael pushed past the tall Thuringi and headed for his closet. He noted the little table in front of the bedroom window was off to one side and the window was fully opened. His room in the stately off-campus house did not face the street and the drainpipe next to the window reached to the ground; Darien Phillipi was enterprising at least. He pulled out clothing and dressed quickly. "I appreciate your problem, Darien, but teaching someone to read takes time. Can't this wait until later? Say, after I finish my dissertation when I'll have some worry-free time to help you out?"

"(How long will it be until you will venture out to our aid)?" Darien paced back and forth in Michael's room, impatience growing with every step. "(I told Stuart it was wrong to trust you. I told him to find someone more capable. You have not the knowledge or skill or connections necessary to aid us. We need a diplomat with power, not a child's teacher)."

"I said I'd help. I've done as much as I can," Michael snapped. "At least I'm trying. You might not find that in a lot of people these days." Darien glanced at the Earthian's feet as he pulled on socks and shoes. Michael was like Darien's own people in every way except his terribly ugly multiple toes, which he encased in singular cloth tubes the way the Thuringi did. The Earthian straightened to face Darien, shorter by several inches, but Michael was able to match Darien look for look. "And by the way, smartass: you might try a little diplomacy yourself by not biting the hand that feeds you."

Darien fell silent as he studied Michael thoughtfully. The Earthian man was not afraid of him. He even turned his back and sat down at a desk to peck his fingers at a graceless keyboard. It made a clattering clack-clack sound Gareth could fix in moments. Why – the Earthian ignored him; he effectively dismissed the Warrior Prince of Thuringa! What impertinence drove him to do this?

Darien peered over his shoulder and watched as Michael referred to notes. At the end of every line, the typewriter issued a loud single ring before Michael pushed a lever and sent a moving cylinder back into its original place. It was a strange device and under any other circumstance Darien would have been intrigued by it.

There was a knock on the door and both men turned, startled. "Uh... who is it?" Michael called out.

"It's me, Travis," a friend said from the other side of the door. "Can you loan me some cash? I found a great deal on a rebuilt carburetor, but it's going to cost me all I have, plus more to get it."

"I don't have any money at all, I'm busted. Go ask Clarence Burton, he's always flush."

"I'd rather eat a bug than go crawling to Burton for a sou," came the belligerent response.

"You mean you already asked him?"

"He turned me down flat, the miser."

"Sorry, Travis. I can't help you."

"Okay." Travis shrugged it off and went on his way.

It dawned on the temperamental prince that Michael had no funds because he gave everything he had to send items to his Thuringi guests. He now turned away even his own people for the sake of strangers. It was as if Gunnar Porteau of Thelan refused to represent his own people in order to aid an Earthian. Such a tall order was what Darien expected of this boy, who already did more for the scouting party than most of the Stellar Council. Darien fell silent and reconsidered his foolish demands.

Michael sighed and turned to his recent acquaintance. He was not doing his world any favors by putting his own selfish wants ahead of it. That would give the Thuringi the wrong impression, and this surly prince would have every right to distrust people of Earth. "Okay, okay. Take me out to Oklahoma and I'll see what I can do. But I can't promise anything."

They went to an overgrown empty lot nearby where Darien left his ship. Darien said nothing during the entire trip to Oklahoma, and that suited Michael. When they arrived at the farm, they saw the Thuringi busy trying to decipher by their own methods. Gareth stood beside his jet in the barn with a number of books open on the flat surface of the ship. He scanned parts of them with a pencil-like tube connected to his control panel. This sight was incongruous when at his feet was a gray tabby cat, rubbing against his ankles and purring affectionately.

Stuart and Brent were at the stock tank, Brent immersed in the water up to his shoulders. They argued over the caption of a picture in the Life magazine Stuart held as he stood outside the tank. "It must say this woman was captured for murder. Look what she has done; she has decapitated a man. All you can see is his head."

"But Brent, where are the Naradi or whatever they have here? She is smiling. Why would they produce a picture of a smiling murderess? Michael of Tulsa said they fought a war against murderers."

"I do not know, Stuart; all I do know is, they should arrest a woman who looks like that."

"What do you mean?"

"Look at her. Would you want Aura to wear something like that in public?" The two looked at each other, and suddenly Stuart grinned.

"The last time Aura wore something like that in private, we had Erich later."

"She has no dignity," Brent sniffed.

"She is your sister," Stuart pointed out.

"I have no dignity, either," Brent said, and squirted Stuart in the face with a double palm of forced water.

Glendon knelt in his bare patch of land in a side yard, diligently planting seeds. From time to time, he referred to the illustrations in the books he set at the end of the rows, but most of his efforts were from experience. Carrol sat on the back-porch steps and wearily flipped through the pages of Gray's Anatomy.

Darien landed his ship in the middle of the backyard, behind the house out of sight from the road. When she saw Michael, Carrol brightened and approached the vehicle, as did the others.

"(Michael of Tulsa, you are a most welcome sight)," Stuart greeted happily. "(Your gifts are bountiful, but we are at a loss to use them)."

"So, I heard," Michael replied dryly. "I have some paper and pencils; let's get down to work and I'll try to teach you something." He glanced out at Gareth's ship. "What are you doing, there?"

"(I was trying to decode this information)."

"There's an easier way. Come on."

"(Good)," Gareth breathed a sigh of relief. "(I was about to dump my files on Borelliat dialects, and they would be hard to replace without the Academy)."

Michael began with the phonics of the English alphabet and went through simple words and phrases. Once they could pronounce the vowels and consonants and blends correctly, their universal translators should be able to handle most of the words when they read aloud. They all caught on quickly and progress was rapid. By midnight they all had a rudimentary grasp of the structure of written English, although different pronunciations of identical spelling eluded them.

"(But tell us, Michael of Taulsa)," Brent said as he held out his magazine, "(What is the riddle of this)?"

"She's burying him in the sand. It's sort of a tradition among beachgoers. You bury someone lying down in the sand while they're asleep, and then when they wake up, only their head is uncovered. They have to scratch their way loose. It's a joke."

"(And where are her garments)?" Brent persisted.

"She's wearing a bathing suit. It's what women wear when they go swimming."

"(Ah! Now do you see why great waters are the wellspring of life)?" Brent intoned to the others, who laughed with him.

Michael glanced around the front room as they prepared a bed for him. It was not like the old farmhouse he remembered; their improvements were marvelous. All the walls were plastered smoothly, no longer the peeling wallpaper-covered gypsum of before. There was a warm, cozy, cocoon-like feeling here. They more than repaired the scarred-up table and the broken chairs; each piece was encased in a clear crystal-like coating. Other furnishings were crystal encased, too – the exposed wood on a couch, several chairs, more tables.

"(As soon as we have mastered the written word some of us will seek a means of providing supplies, and I will decide whom I should contact)," Stuart told Michael. "(Our com has been tuned to your radio waves, and we have heard about a great deal of Earth events. What is Cuba and what is Russia)?"

"They're both countries. Russia is a country that's threatening to take over the world. Say, we could sure use your help."

Stuart regarded Michael gravely. "(Our mission is not to rule others, Michael. Were we to become involved in military action by taking sides in a local struggle, we might become tempted to want to govern the hard-won territory, and the temptation to rule is a danger with which we dare not dally. All we seek is a haven for our kinsmen when they arrive. It will be a few more years yet, and even then, we must continue to Farcourt. Getting involved in the Earth's business is not really the Thuringi way)."

A sudden disgruntled snort sounded from a corner. Darien leaned against the wall; his arms folded across his chest as he gazed out the window. "(So, you finally learned the bitter lesson taught to us by the Stellar Council)?" Darien growled. "(It is impractical to help a weaker world; they only become dependent, and supplicants make poor allies)." His eyes met Michael's. The Earthian man could read the trouble that could come of Darien's displeasure, and no translation was necessary.

The next morning, they were up early. Michael suggested they go into town for supplies. The old truck ran better than Michael had ever heard it run before. Gareth used a can of house paint and a rag found in the barn, and the truck was now marshmallow white. It was covered in that crystalline substance about which Michael had to inquire.

"(It is a covering, a veneer, which we use. If you calibrate a laser pistol to the degree I did and find the right type of vaguno, you can encase weak objects to strengthen them)."

"Vaguno... sand. So, it's covered in glass? Like the windows?"

"(Not as brittle)," Gareth said.

Michael, Gareth and Glendon drove into town for supplies. Michael withdrew more money from his bank. He had lied to Travis. His Earthian friends were capable of getting help from someone; the Thuringi had no one else but him. He knew his family's accountant would question this withdrawal, but Michael saw no other option. The Thuringi needed his help now and he could only hope they would reimburse him someday. His accountant and his father Darryl would just have to believe it was for some fling since he was not about to say he needed money for aliens. They would commit him to an asylum in the belief he had a nervous breakdown.

They went to the hardware store where Michael bought tools, wire, switches, and pieces of pipe Gareth needed. Michael called the principal at his school of employment from a pay phone, to explain he needed a few days of unexpected personal leave. He mumbled something about family problems. The principal agreed to arrange for a substitute until Michael's return.

Michael introduced Glendon to the store owner, Ed Gentry. Ed took one look at the large healthy young man and offered to hire Glendon to load and unload feed sacks. Michael held the same job when he was a kid before Darryl struck oil. Glendon was interested, so Ed Gentry invited Glendon to help out a little to see how he liked it. Gareth waited in the truck while Michael bought groceries at the local store, and then they headed back to the ranch. Gareth practiced reading road signs and billboards.

"I hope Glendon will do all right," Michael mused. "He can't read very well yet."

"(There is no need to worry about Glendon)," Gareth told him. "(He is a veteran Naradi Famede. He can speak with almost anyone quite artfully)."

A bullshit artist! Michael thought. Now there's a handy talent for an explorer!

Several trucks were parked in front of the house. Michael

recognized the emblem of a drilling company on the sides of the trucks. He was alarmed when he saw men standing at the bottom of the porch steps, kept there by Darien who stood on the porch wielding the flyswatter.

"You don't scare us with that thing," one of the men said to Darien as Michael got out of the truck and approached the scene.

"(I do not have to frighten you. I only have to squash you)," Darien said menacingly.

"Put that down, you can't hurt us with it," another man tried to reason.

"(Come upon this domicile again, and I will show you how much it will hurt you)," Darien growled.

"What's going on?" Michael asked.

"Hey, that's Darryl's kid. Mike, who are these guys? What're they doing here?" a man asked.

"Hi, Mr. Forbes. These folks are friends of mine. They're foreign and all their belongings were lost in a storm. I'm letting them stay here until they get back on their feet. Dad knows all about it."

"Oh, he does. Well, we didn't," Mr. Forbes explained. "We were coming over here to pee and wash up, and this big fella won't let us in. Threatens us with a flyswatter, Mike, I ask you! That's supposed to be a threat?"

"(No, this is a threat)," Darien snapped as he dropped the flyswatter and drew his sword with a deadly flourish. He stopped it scant inches from the nearest and most belligerent roughneck. The man backpedaled quickly as they all gave a shout of alarm.

"Stop it," Michael ordered as he bound up the porch steps. He grabbed Darien's sword arm tightly. "Are you crazy, put that thing away! This isn't a military insurrection! It's just a bunch of tired, dirty men who want to clean up a little."

"(They shouted at us, called us insulting names. They threatened violence. And that one disturbed Carrol)," Darien thundered as he pointed at a heavy-set bald black man who was just as agitated as his fellow workers.

"Is she alright?" Michael asked.

"(I am well)," Carrol said quietly, from the shadows of the doorway. "(He did not mean actual harm to me. He only startled me)."

Michael turned back to the crowd of men. "There's the pump in the back yard y'all can use to wash." He remembered the unique way the house interior was now remodeled and added, "The bathroom's not working. That's where we were, to get parts to fix it, so you'll have to find a private spot to relieve yourselves."

"Too much trouble for me," someone said. "I'll just wait 'til I get home. But hell, if I'd known someone was living here, I wouldn't have come."

"Especially people who threaten you with flyswatters and swords," someone else added, and after a pause, the absurdity of his statement made all chuckle but Darien. Michael nudged him and said quietly, "Go inside now. I'll take care of it. This is my element, not yours." Darien hesitated, then turned and went inside. Gareth carried their bags inside, and the roughnecks got into their trucks to leave.

"That big fellow, is he always so bad tempered?" Mr. Forbes asked Michael.

"Well, he's just overprotective, I guess. See, the lady is his sister, and she's been through some pretty rough times lately," Michael explained. "A death in the family."

A subdued chorus of understanding "ohs" rose from the remaining group of men.

"You think he might be interested in roughnecking? They look pretty strong, him and that one you came up with," Mr. Forbes said.

"They might. They've never done oil field work before, but they learn quick."

"Tell 'em to get in touch with me if they're interested." Mr. Forbes shook hands with Michael.

"Have that big one leave his flyswatter at home," one wag added. His companions laughed as the crew trucks left.

Michael went inside to Carrol. "Are you sure you're okay? Where's Stuart?"

"(He took Darien's ship and went with Brent to the ocean again, as well as look at the gakkis over the hill by the stock pond. I am well. That one simply...)"

"(He resembled a Shargassi, in a way)," Darien said. He stood beside Carrol and appeared quite subdued now. He looked Michael in the eye and looked away quickly. "(You are right, Michael of Taulsa. This is not my element. I was ready to strike them all. I am a warrior, not a diplomat)."

"Well, you impressed them enough that Mr. Forbes wanted to know if you and Gareth would work for him. He likes men who are strong and unafraid."

Darien said nothing but studied Carrol instead.

Carrol rose from her chair and patted his arm. "(Thank you for defending me, brother, but little Carrol is a Thuringi. I have not forgotten how to fight)."

"(I feared your will to fight hand to hand died with Maranta Shanaugh)."

She cast her gaze downward. "(That did not kill my will to fight. It only broke my heart)."

Gareth finished bringing in the sacks. "(...and thank you so much for helping)," he grumbled, but to Michael said a friendly, "(You are a good man in a pinch, Michael)." He slapped a hand on Michael's back, and it sent the Earthian stumbling forward into Carrol.

"(My pardon, I ask from you)!" Gareth exclaimed.

"It's okay, I'm getting used to being slung around by guys who don't know their own strength," Michael wisecracked. He did not mind falling into Carrol. She smiled at him, and he found himself smiling back. It gave him hope for maybe something with her.

Darien, reminded by Gareth's former complaints, looked through what they brought back from town. "(Where is Glendon)?" Gareth explained about the feed store job and Darien nodded. "(A logical place for a planter-at-heart)."

Stuart and Brent came in through the back door after shaking dirt from their clothing. "(It is true)," Brent informed the others, "(These are neither gakkis nor cabrett. They are Earth cattle. You cannot ride them)."

"Well, you can but I see you found out what usually happens when you try," Michael said with a grin as they put away the groceries.

He drove back into town to pick up Glendon, who waited on the porch of the feed store. The smiling Thuringi got into the truck with a sack in his hands. He waved at the feed store owner as the truck pulled away. "So! How was work – successful, I guess?"

"(I moved sacks: taking many sacks off a vehicle, putting one or two in other smaller vehicles. I moved articles and implements around wherever they directed. He gave me currency, and his woman gave me this sack of goods)." He dug around inside the sack and brought out a jar of home canned peaches. "(Your world is adept at generous bartering, I am glad to note. I am to come back the day after tomorrow. Am I chattering? I suppose I am. But I enjoyed myself, Michael of Taulsa! I like this job business of yours)."

"Did they ask you a lot of personal questions?"

"(Yes. We have been the subject of a great deal of speculation in the area. Carrol is a war bride from England, I believe it is said, and I am her limey brother. Although I am not her brother, I thought it imprudent to correct them. What is limey)?"

"Limey. It's ... well, it's an insult that ignorant people use toward another group of people, in this case from a country called England which is where you sound like you're from. They are just speaking from ignorance and bigotry, Glen. Don't let it bother you."

"(Then I will not. They were pleasant to me. They were very pleasant after I moved their wood burning apparatus)."

"Oh God. You moved a stove? By yourself?"

"(Yes. They said it needed to go in a corner, so I put it there. The men they sent to help move it did not mind that I did it without them. They smiled and handed me this cold liquid refreshment)." Glendon dug again in his sack and brought out a half-finished bottle of beer. "(It tasted terrible, but I did not want to insult their generosity. I swallowed it. I did not know if perhaps they are as proud of their potables as the Thelan. If it was smoothed a little, it might taste like Thuringi ale)."

"It is Earthian ale, beer. It can make you drunk if you drink too much of it."

"(How much is too much)?" Glendon asked as he peered at the amount left in the bottle with concern.

"I guess it won't hurt to finish it off. I can't tell if you're normally this talkative or whether the beer is helping you. What all did you say to them?"

"(I was careful not to mention our true circumstances. I let them believe we lost our possessions in a storm. They spoke of many things I did not understand: elections, civil rights, eyes and hour, so I said nothing. I smiled and moved things as they told me)."

Michael took the beer bottle from Glendon and took a swig of it himself. "Eisenhower, yeah. Sounds like a good plan to me." They shared the beer on the way to the ranch.

Chapter 3: Hard Work and Sundays Off

Stuart was reluctant to take any more time and help from Michael Sheldon. He knew that the Thuringi scouts were a drain to the young Earthian man's resources and Michael needed to return to Boston to his Academy and work on this doctoral thesis. Stuart did ask for advice on their mode of dress for the Earthian culture. Their Thuringi garments were either obvious uniforms or made of fabric unlike most Earthian goods.

"Well, there's quite a few of you," Michael sighed. "It'll be a heck of a shopping trip."

Stuart brought out a small cloth bag and gave it to him. "(Will this be useful in covering the expense of such a transaction)?"

Michael looked inside and gasped. Spanish doubloons shone golden and glorious from their nesting place in the bottom of the bag. "Where'd you get these?" he asked incredulously.

"(One of your reference materials, the Life one with the pictures, depicted treasures in the sea so Brent and I flew around to investigate while you were gone and found a few of these. Coins for your trade goods, yes)?"

"Well, uh, these are old and aren't used for trade these days," Michael stammered. "But you can take them to a coin collector or a jeweler's and get quite a bit in return for them and then be able to buy all sorts of trade goods."

"(Interesting)!" Brent looked at his find with a new perspective. "(If they are so valuable, why are they kept on the bottom of your seas, covered by sand or depths of water? You said your world has no Aquatics)."

"We don't. The ships sank, and those happened to be on board at the time." Michael whistled. "You've got enough here to set yourselves up for awhile. All you need to do is find a buyer. These antiques will bring a good price."

"(Can you do that)?" Gareth asked.

"Well, I can try," Michael offered. He directed Stuart to fly him to Miami, where they found a collector who was extremely interested in what they had to offer. Michael figured that Tulsa, Oklahoma, might be too inland for someone to waltz in with sixteenth century coins, but Miami, Florida might not be too surprised to see someone with them.

Indeed, the coin dealer assumed they would not divulge the location of their find. It did not keep him from asking and he was not surprised when they answered with obscurities.

The coins they traded garnered a great deal of cash, more than enough to pay for supplies. Stuart also insisted that Michael replenish his bank account which the young Earthian man did gratefully. The whole crowd of Thuringi and Michael went into Tulsa to shop at a store that specialized in big and tall people's clothing. They were outfitted in appropriate attire that appealed to their individual tastes.

Darien bought black shirts, denim jeans and a long gray topcoat while Stuart favored khaki trousers and pullover shirts. Gareth chose denim work shirts and jeans and Glendon chose loose-fitting shirts and close-fitting pants. Brent selected baggy clothing that fit loosely over his webbed suit. As the store personnel scrambled to find some kind of footwear that might fit their large feet, Michael saw Carrol looking through the clothes racks, displeased but trying not to show it.

"Find anything you like?" Michael asked.

"(Not really)," she admitted. "(This is very strange clothing)."

"Well, you're closer to average size for us. Maybe you'd like to look in a regular store?" Michael asked. She smiled gratefully. Once the men were satisfied with their purchases, they went on down the street to a ladies' clothing store. They men took one look inside the store and backed out to wait on benches outside along the sidewalk. Michael went in with Carrol. She looked around at the mannequins and turned to Michael.

"(Females here actually wear this)?" she asked incredulously.

"Uh, yes. Why?"

"(All this cloth! All these undergarments and high thin heels on footwear! How can any woman possibly fight in this)?" Carrol asked.

"Well, the truth is, most of the women on this planet don't actively fight."

"(Why not? You have spoken of so many wars)."

"I guess because here, we would rather make the world safe for women to raise the children."

"(Suppose a woman was better at fighting than childrearing)?"

"Then I suppose she ought to be fighting," Michael agreed. "I just find it hard to believe that anyone as beautiful as you have fighting on her mind. Wouldn't you rather have peace?"

"(Preferring is not the same as having)," Carrol said.

"It's those Shar-gah-say people you're worried about, isn't it?" Michael asked gently. She looked down and made no reply. "Look, you don't have to wear any of this stuff if you don't want to. You can pick anything you think is comfortable. Dame Fashion doesn't rule the world."

Carrol smiled at him. "(I like you, Michael Sheldon)," she told him. "(You have a way of settling a quandary)." She bought some slacks and tops. On the way to the truck, however, she stopped so abruptly in front of a store window that Gareth run into her bodily from behind.

"(What is wrong with you)?" he demanded to know.

"(Look at that)," she gasped breathlessly, looking at the window display with a mannequin wearing a simple but elegant Chanel suit. She looked at Michael, who nodded. Carrol charged into the store like a woman on a mission.

"Well, your sister has good taste," Michael told the Phillipi brothers. She emerged later with another shopping bag.

"(I am done)," she announced.

"(Just like that)?" Darien asked. "(You just see it and decide)?"

"(Yes)," she replied. "(I know what I like)."

"(Brent will explore the seas)," Stuart told Michael after they returned to Iron Post. "(We are building him a ship in the hanger)." It took Michael a minute to realize that Stuart meant the barn.

"Does he need saltwater as opposed to freshwater?" Michael asked.

"(It does not matter to him for the now. He is a water based Thuringi and misses the feel of Great Waters. After so much time in the vacuum of space, he craves any kind of water at this point. Eventually, we will need to be apart from your people so that we might prepare a safe haven for the Armada when it arrives. That will most likely be an island)."

"Have you decided where this safe haven will be?" Michael asked. "There are still a lot of uncharted islands in the Pacific Ocean."

"(As soon as the ship is completed Brent will search for a place)."

Brent took Michael out to see his ship-in-progress. "(It is not unlike my old vessel)," he said as he reached to turn on the lights overhead in the barn, "(although Gareth has to make do with material from discarded vehicles of your world to supplement what my old ship could not achieve)." The lights came on, and Michael gaped in wonder.

Brent's ship was shaped like a killer whale, sleek and black and large. It filled the entire doorway of the barn and stretched to the other side of the building. Upon closer inspection, Michael saw where multiple sheets of metal from castoff cars were joined together by a welding technique Michael never saw before: the pieces of metal were joined as if melted, giving a strange but beautiful smudgelike line that had no weld seam. If metal had not been different colors, Michael would not have been able to distinguish where the seam ran.

He followed Brent up a ladder into the interior of the ship. It was fitted like a travel trailer, the cockpit at the head of the whale and a living area in the center. A sleeping area was located in the back. He wondered about the power system.

Brent shook his head. "(Leave that up to our good lad Gareth. He will cannibalize my star-going vessel for the sake of my seagoing vessel)."

"How will you get to Farcourt?"

"(I will sink into one of the tanks aboard the Freen)," Brent assured him. "(I do not plan to go very far from liquid again)." He invited Michael to sit down on a former auto bench seat, now a comfortable couch. "(I did not wish to alarm my friends, but the trip here nearly killed me. My lips were so dry the day we landed, I tasted blood. Another day or two and my skin would have cracked open and eventually I would have bled to death. I saw it happen to my kindred on Thuringa)."

"Oh my God, that's awful! How many of your people are like you; water based?" Michael asked.

"(Most Aquatics perished as the ecosystem of Thuringa collapsed. Our waters became lifeless as the food chain broke down. Pollution from the bombardment poisoned nearly fifty thousand of us; two hundred thousand Thuringi perished in all. There are perhaps, oh... five hundred surviving Aquatics)."

"Five hundred!" Michael exclaimed. "What a holocaust!"

"(Yes)," Brent said. "(I think it fortunate that my parents, my wife, my son, and my sister are among the survivors, heading here with the Armada. Whole families were wiped out; most of my wife's

Aquatic family is gone but some of her Airman kindred survived)."

The hatch opened, and Glendon stuck his head in through the opening. "(There is nourishment available)," he announced with great anticipation, and the two conversationalists leaped to their feet and followed him back to the house. They ate a filling meal consisting largely of fruits, including Glendon's peaches from the Gentrys. Michael glanced at his watch.

"I'm glad that you're doing so well now," Michael told the group, "but if you don't mind, I really ought to be getting back East. I am due to defend my doctoral thesis and I'm sure my associates are wondering where I am."

"(I am sorry for the inconvenience, Michael)," Stuart said with regret, "(but we are grateful for the knowledge you have brought us. I will take you back)."

"Oh no no," Michael replied, "I'm sorry I'm not able to help you more."

"(Academy work is important. I know that as well as anyone)," Stuart said warmly. "(My wife is always very busy with her tasks for the Academy on the Armada)."

"(I can take him back)," Carrol said as she entered the room. She wore her Chanel suit and was a stunning sight. Michael could not take his eyes from her; neither could Gareth.

"(Perhaps one of us should return him)," Darien grunted. "(You are not dressed for the occasion)."

"(Well, where else will I wear this, if not now)?" Carrol countered with a flippant air. "(You do not believe I will wear this here among the lot of you)?"

"(I believe we are being snubbed)," Darien declared. "(Go on then, take friend Michael back to his studies. We undeserving few will remain here, alone, and unappreciated)." He tossed a peach pit at Gareth.

"(Oh, be hushed)," Carrol told her brother in amusement. "(It is simply an opportunity to wear it)."

After Carrol and Michael left in her aircraft, the Thuringi men all fell silent. Finally, Brent spoke up. "Well, he is just an Outlander of no particular station," he ventured. "She is simply sticking her tongue out at you, Gareth."

"Yes, she is," he agreed. "Why are you looking at me like that?"

"Our Carrol may only wish for a chance to wear her outfit, but I am unsure our friend Michael is aware that it might not be for his benefit."

"And why should this concern me? Your father has made it plain that I am not to approach Her Highness for myself. She is a grown woman. She can handle herself." Still, he went out the back door and stood on the porch, deep in thought.

She landed the craft quietly in the shadows next to Michael's outlaw fraternity house. "I'm just staying here while I teach and work on my doctorate," he explained. "I graduated from here years ago but as a former I Phelta Thigh, I have on-site living privileges. Won't you come in for a while?" Michael asked.

"(I should return to the outpost)," Carrol replied hesitantly.

"You know, on Thuringa I'm sure your culture is more refined and sedate than our own. But here on Earth, an attractive woman in a Chanel suit usually doesn't mind showing it off for the appreciative," he commented.

"(Well, perhaps we are not so different after all)," she admitted. "(I do like this dress, and I wonder what the reaction might be)." Michael took her by the arm and led her into the house. His fraternity brothers all sat upright, their "beautiful woman" radar on and running at full power. These Earthian men were much younger than Carrol. They were like appealing dallah puppies, young and eager to make her feel welcome. They had no notion about her and her past; of Thuringa, of anything. All they knew was Michael Sheldon disappeared for a couple of days in the middle of his final push for his doctorate and returned with a blonde beauty they assumed to be around their age, adorned in haute couture. She was amused, flattered, and charmed by all the attention from these Earthian men. She glanced up to see Michael as he leaned against the fireplace mantel, a drink in one hand with a look of quiet contentment on his face. He lifted his glass in silent salute to her. Travis Hicks caught the exchange and herded his fellows out of the room. "We ought to leave Michael and his friend alone for a little privacy."

"Who put you in charge," someone objected, but Travis shut the door behind them as they reluctantly left. Carrol rose to her feet and joined Michael at the fireplace.

"(You have very entertaining companions)," she observed.

"They have their moments," he agreed and for a long minute, they regarded each other. Michael stroked her cheek with his fingers gently. He brought his hand back up to link with his other hand, around his glass, and continued to gaze at her. She studied him for a moment and placed her hand over his. His fingers claimed some of hers in a snug grip. She was enchanted by the intriguing novelty of gray Earthian eyes. She did not realize that he could not think of anything to say to her that would not sound foolish. She was not a contemporary of his; she was decades older, the most mature woman he ever knew. He cleared his throat and spoke. "What will you be doing, now that you're settled in?" he asked.

"(We will look for an appropriate spot for our Armada. Then we will work on arranging diplomatic treaties with your people)."

"No, I mean what will you, Carrol, do? Say, in the next few weeks? You don't mean that your every waking hour will be spent looking for a place to land?"

"(Oh. I am not certain, Michael. I have been admiring your homeland. It is very beautiful)."

"Yes, it is. I guess that until you landed here, I pretty much took Earth for granted," Michael said, and the look in his eyes said something other than what he said.

"(It is easy to become complacent when things are going well)," she agreed. She leaned closer. "(How is it that your eyes are that color, and the other people of your race have different colors)?"

"It's genetics," Michael replied, also leaning closer to her. "Don't other worlds have different colored eyes?"

"(I suppose)," she said. "(I never really noticed anyone's eye color before, really. It has never been an issue as everyone knows Thuringi have yellow eyes)."

"Well, I've never seen yellow eyes before. Yours are wonderful, so different than anything we've got here on Earth," he told her. She was so invitingly close. He decided to take the chance; if she objected, he would call it quits. But the chance that she might not object spurred him to lean further and kiss her on the lips. It was not a surprising development for her, and she reacted calmly.

"I'm glad I met you," Michael whispered. She made no reply but did not draw back. Instead, she studied him curiously. He was thoughtful and considerate and attractive, someone who could stand side by side with any ordinary Thuringi and not be found wanting. But he was not Maranta Shanaugh nor was he Gareth Duncan. It was unwise to let Michael Sheldon believe she was available for his private regard; he was their host here on Earth and it would be foolish to endanger their haven for the sake of reassuring her own ego. In the end, the man for whom she chose the beautiful suit to admire was in Oklahoma waiting for her.

"(I am grateful we have met you)," she assured him. "(But now I must return to the farm)." She started for the door, and he caught her by the arm.

"Did I offend you? I'm sorry, but if you're going to live on Earth, you'll need to understand certain customs. I wasn't assuming anything with that kiss—"

"(I know that Michael)," she said.

"When we find someone, we're attracted to, we try for a kiss sometimes."

"(As do we)."

"Then you understand?"

"(Yes, I do. And now I must go)."

"But why?"

"(It would be unwise if it were to go badly)," she told him, not willing to mention Gareth's name. If things did go badly and if Father should ever find out that Gareth's name was involved, he would never forgive either of them. "(I have too much for which I am responsible to indulge in personal quests)."

"Oh," Michael said as he released her arm. "In that case I'll walk you out to your car – er, your plane."

"(No, it will be all right. Thank you, Michael, for everything)." She let herself out. He returned to the fireplace, his hands jammed in his pockets, when he noticed the little purse on the couch. She was a Thuringi and not used to remembering to take a handbag with her.

She was about to get into Her Nibs when she heard something rustle the foliage nearby. She jumped back with a gasp and scrambled to grasp the weapon that was not at her side. "It is all right, Your Nibs," Gareth said as he emerged from the shadows. "I will not shoot."

"What are you doing here?" she demanded.

"Taking the opportunity to be alone with you; like your friend

Michael," he said as he came to stand before her.

"Jealousy does not become you," she told him.

"It's not jealousy," he contradicted. "It ... Well, perhaps a degree of ... oh, all right, then. Do you think it fair that I must stay at arm's length from you, yet this Earthian has the right to be in your company, can be close to you because he is what, indigenous to this world?" Gareth asked her unhappily. "You want me to leave you alone with our new friend now in your new gown that you know looks queenly on you? Or ... would you like to dance?" He put his hands on the sides of her waist. She smiled.

"I want to dance," she told him, and placed her hands on his shoulders. They slowly swayed from side to side.

"It is not proper form; we would be scolded by the Bishop," he warned. He also made no move to change anything.

"Let him scold," she murmured and offered a kiss. He took it gladly and slid his arms around her for a firm hold. They continued to sway. "There is no music," she said quietly in his ear.

"There is for me," he replied.

"And you say you have no gift for gentle phrases!" she said with a soft laugh. She snuggled her face against his neck.

Michael Sheldon saw their silent dance in the moonlight. Without a word he turned and took her purse back into the house. It was all clear to him. He understood a secret love affair as much as anyone and was relieved he had not made a fool of himself.

"We will not be able to stay gone long," Gareth reminded her at length. "Guardian and Good Boy have sharp eyes."

"Just a minute more," she encouraged, and he was willing to indulge her. "You were naughty to give me the Tarinade to read on that long trip. I should not be so cozy with you," she said, and gave him a deep kiss.

"I cannot believe you read it! Quote me something."

"We have to get back."

"Something short, then."

She sighed. "I would rather read it with you. That is how it was intended, I believe."

"And just when will we do that, Your Nibs?" Gareth asked in her ear. "While our four guards are asleep?"

"They have to at some point," she pointed out.

He landed behind the barn first and wandered up to the back porch. He was about to step quietly through the back door, when a hand lantern lit up beside him that illuminated Stuart in the glow.

"Out on patrol?" Stuart asked noncommittally.

"Yes," Gareth replied curtly.

"Hmmm." Gareth went inside. Carrol landed her ship a few minutes later and also came back from the barn. Stuart lit the hand lantern just as he had for Gareth.

"Oh! Stuart, you startled me," Carrol laughed.

"And you startle me, sister, at every turn," he replied. "How is our friend Michael?"

"He is well. He is back working on his doctorate now," she told him.

"He seems quite taken with you, not surprisingly," Stuart observed. Carrol did not reply. "Carrol, I do not think you should let our friend Michael believe -"

"He does not. He was genuinely nice but when he became forward and obvious about his interest, I took the opportunity to explain that I was not interested. I did not wish to embarrass him by saying so in front of all of you, and none of you would give me the opportunity to speak to him privately here. He understands, I think."

"And Gareth? Does he understand?"

"Understand what? What are you saying, Stuart?"

"Do not toy with Gareth," Stuart said plainly.

"I have no intention to 'toy' with him," Carrol told him sharply. "I do not believe in toying with anyone."

"Then what are you doing?"

"Very little with two brothers, a Naradi and a bad-tempered waterman always scolding and wagging their fingers at us," she declared.

"Yes, you have certainly picked up on Gareth's way of speaking," Stuart observed with amusement.

"After gintas of listening to the five of you men chatter over the com? I should be ripe for a rousing conversation," Carrol said as she opened the door. "If you do not mind Stuart, I would like to go and change my clothes. Whoever this Chanel person is, did not design for flight. Then I am going to bed. Was there anything else you wanted to say?"

"No," Stuart said easily. "Good night, Princess Nibs." She went on in.

Beside his brother in the dark, Darien chuckled. "I told you. Those two are amateurs."

"We should count ourselves fortunate then, Darien. I cannot image how I would keep watch if they were proficient."

"I have never been on an outpost before," Brent confessed as he stirred from a full washtub on the back porch. It startled the brothers who did not even realize he had been there the whole time, and they felt foolish to have been surprised by an Aquatic in a tub of all things. "Would you say this one is successful?"

Stuart considered their health, their lodging, and their native friend, and smiled broadly. "Oh, I would definitely say so."

Gareth tossed and turned in his hammock all night. He was tired and knew how vital it was for him to get a good rest at night, but his mind would not stop whirling. There was so much to do, so much to think about. For ginta after ginta the scouts bored each other numb with jokes and stories and mind riddles to pass the time in the flight to Earth. They had no idea what to expect from the unknown world and therefore were plagued by the lack of anything to keep their minds busy.

Glendon was the best at making up of silly poems, it was decided; Stuart did a surprising but hilariously dead-on impersonation of Bishop Trapis at the most appropriate moments in conversation. It was agreed that Darien was no singer by any stretch of the imagination, and Brent knew the best naughty jokes. Now that they were on Earth and safely ensconced on Michael Sheldon's old home, there was so much for him to do. Gareth scarcely had time to think in the daytime, only act.

Brent's ship must be finished and finished quickly so he could do further studies of the oceans. Stuart and Darien and Glendon all needed smaller ships than the scouting ships for reconnaissance flights. They all needed better means of intelligence gathering as well as more subtle communicators. Carrol needed a better medical research facility than the farmhouse parlor.

And Gareth needed Carrol, in the most fundamental way. It was excruciating to watch her leave to take the Earthian back to his home. He could tell the man was taken with her, and that irked Gareth so much he followed them despite his resolve. The time until she came out to her ship seemed interminable and he paced back and forth in the bushes until she appeared. Then Carrol Shanaugh de Phillipi was in his arms and Gareth forgot his impatience.

Holding her in his arms was one of the many things he wanted to do for weeks; to wish for more now seemed unlikely with her brothers on the watch. Naturally, he read the Tarinade before he gave it to her and wished he had not. Those tormenting thoughts and phrases had been in his head ever since.

During the flight, Brent decided to quote some of the text from memory and got stuck with a forgotten phrase. "No, no, you fool!" Gareth shouted. "You have mangled the entire phrase!" There was a sudden silence, and he managed to continue with, "Any school boy old enough to go through consue knows that phrase." They all laughed and agreed, and the incident was soon forgotten. But oh God, to hold her and dance in the silvery moonlight brought the entire passage back to his mind. Damn married men: only fellow bachelor Darien understood Gareth's longing. But Darien spent time with a willing lass on the Armada before their flight to ease his needs. The only compensation Gareth had was plenty of work to keep occupied and a cold tub of water. He finally decided to stop tossing around. He unfolded from his hammock and went to the door of the bedroom.

"Where are you going?" Glendon mumbled, sleepy but aware.

"No need to worry," Gareth replied wearily. "I will be in Brent's water tank out by the hanger, if it is any business of yours."

"Whatever for?" Glendon asked, awakened a little more by the odd reply.

"Oh, who cares," Gareth said, angry with frustration. "I will be awake enough tomorrow to do what I am told. Just leave me alone." He was gone, and Glendon heard the back door shut moments later.

Although the water tank cooled his ardor, it also woke him completely. It would do no good to return to bed now; Carrol's bedroom was only a few steps further, and he was just addled enough to petition her if he went back into the house. Instead, he went to the barn to work on Brent's ship. Glendon found him lying across the engine later than morning, sound asleep with tools in his hands. He covered Gareth with a blanket and went back into the house.

"I found him. He is asleep on Brent's engine."

"Why did he go out to work if he is just going to sleep?" Brent wondered. Carrol joined the team in the kitchen. She also had a restless night and did not even bother to brush or re-braid her hair.

"I need to see about this rousting work of which Michael Sheldon spoke," Darien said as he ate an egg. "It may be interesting to see how the average Earthian works with his hands."

"Did you know that Michael said you can cook them to eat," Stuart told his brother.

Darien picked at his teeth with a slim wooden stick. "Well, perhaps it would soften the peeling a little."

Gareth trudged into the kitchen, his eyes heavy and underscored with dark circles. For a moment he and Carrol regarded each other. He gave her a weary smile and poured himself a glass of orange juice.

"Gareth, will I be able to steer that monstrous white thing of yours?" Darien asked.

"I need that to go to the feed store," Glendon objected.

"Well then, Gareth will need to build me one," Darien shrugged.

"When will my ship be done?" Brent asked curiously.

"We will need to go on reconnaissance soon," Stuart murmured in thought.

Carrol watched as Gareth sat down his glass of juice and stared at all four men until he got their attention. The glare in his weary eyes told them of his mood. He turned to Carrol.

"Good morning, Your Nibs," he greeted hoarsely.

"Good morning, Gareth. You look awful." She wanted to kick herself for such a rude reply. She was suddenly aware of her own disheveled state and belatedly reached up to smooth her hair.

Gareth laughed but it held no mirth. He headed for the barn again.

"Stuart, he looks so worn," Carrol fretted. "You must let him rest."

"Carrol, we need his talents now," Stuart explained.

"Then perhaps some of you should help him instead of simply saying Gareth do this and that!" Carrol snapped. "I am going to go help him. Darien, you and Glendon can both use the truck – it is called a truck, Darien! Gareth does not build monsters and do not insult him by saying such! Stuart, you can hold a tool, too. Get up, you lazybones," she commanded as she pulled the chair out from under Brent. "If you want a ship, go help build a ship!" She stormed off to her bedroom.

Brent picked himself up off the floor. "What has gotten into her?"

Stuart shook his head. "She is right. Darien, ask at Glendon's store about the oil man and do not forget to wear your glasses. Brent, we can go to help Gareth. He has been working constantly since we got here and even before, on the Quantid. It is not fair to leave all the toil to him. We can at least do what we can."

Glendon picked up the truck keys. "I am driving."

"You do not know how to drive," Darien protested.

"Neither do you. But I have ridden, and I have watched. You have not." The two debated the issue all the way out to the truck.

Carrol barreled back down the stairs in slacks and a shirt, her hair brushed and neatly braided once more. She found Gareth in the barn, cursing at the engine.

"What did it do?" she asked.

"What? Nothing," he replied, surprised at her appearance at the door. "It is what it will not do, which is move where I need it to go."

"It will not fit?"

"Yes, but I cannot do it by myself."

"Stuart and Brent are coming out to help us," she assured him as she gave him a swift kiss on the cheek.

"Us?" He smiled at her. "Your Nibs, are you going to get dirty with me?"

For a moment she looked at him as if seeing something distant. Then she smiled broadly and gave him a bigger, bolder kiss on the lips. "Would you rather I clean you off?" She was rewarded by his look of sweetly tortured but willing anticipation.

"Verse Twenty," he groaned, and she clapped her hand over her mouth.

"You read the Tarinade," she gasped.

"Before we left the Quantid."

"Oh, poor man!" She laughed and he joined in as Stuart and Glendon entered.

"What is the joke?" Stuart asked curiously, but all he got in reply was another burst of laughter. They moved the engine where Gareth needed it and continued to work on the ship for the rest of the morning at his direction.

Glendon managed to get the truck to the store without grinding the gears too badly or hitting anything important or living. When they got out of the truck, Darien indicated that the Naradi should keep the keys. He wanted no part of a vehicle that growled and lurched and bounced about so.

Darien dwarfed the people in Glendon's store, who told him the oil company workers usually stopped in for morning biscuits at the café down the road.

"They're always taking on help, and they'll give you a ride back here at the end of the day," the store owner said. Darien nodded and went out the door to the café. Ed Gentry looked at Glendon. "Boy, they grow 'em big where you live over there in England, don't they?"

"(Yes)," Glendon agreed. "(I am very prepared to work now)." The owner just shook his head.

"I don't wonder that y'all survived the blitz. Your work ethic just can't be beat." He directed Glendon to re-arrange some heavy items that he could not manage. Glendon did as he was told easily and cheerfully. "Dang," Ed marveled to his wife as they watched him work. "I never saw the like. He's just one great big friendly mechanized crane."

They noticed he did not seem to know much about the retail business. Glendon smiled pleasantly to customers and spoke with a lovely musical lilt to his voice, but despite his polite phrasing he did not have a grasp of the value of goods. The first time he was asked about the price of a box of canning jars, Glendon blinked and smiled wider. "I have only begun my task here," he admitted glibly, "but I am certain Lady Gentry would be delighted to inform you as to the nature of the item." He had no idea what 'price' any item was, but he listened carefully to the conversation that followed and learned. He noticed the numbers on the signs and surreptitiously watched Ed Gentry give change to customers beginning with the price and counting out the remainder.

"That's two dollars and sixteen cents, out of three; all right, four gives you twenty, five makes twenty-five, and here's fifty, seventy-five – three dollars. There you go," Ed said pleasantly. He noticed the serious way Glendon watched the exchange. Ed assumed his new help was converting American dollars into British pounds in his head. After the customer left Ed counted the cash in the till out loud casually, as if he did that sort of thing regularly. Glendon was quick to absorb the information since basic mathematics was something Earth had in common with the Stellar Council worlds.

Darien's appearance at the door of the café made the waitress gasp. "Holy cow, Bobby, we got us a giant," she called out to the cook. She approached Darien cautiously and gave him a good look up and down. "Can I get you something, mister?"

"(I seek the oil man Forbes)," Darien told her. "(He suggested I roust a bout)."

"Oh, Dickie will be along directly," she assured him. "Him and his crew almost always stop by here on the way to the rig. You want some coffee and a donut?"

"(Why)?" Darien asked, and cursed Michael Sheldon privately. He told them all about Earthian history but there were many things they still did not know about day-to-day living. The Earthian did not give a hint on how to answer such incomprehensible questions.

"Well, have you had breakfast?" she asked.

"(No)."

"Honey, you can't go work for Dickie Forbes on an empty stomach. And where's your lunch kit?" Darien shook his head. "You've never worked on an oil rig before, have you, big guy?" she asked.

"(I have not)," Darien told her, "(but I daresay he has never done things I have done)."

"I wouldn't doubt that for a minute," she said, and showed him to a table and handed him a menu.

He groaned. Damn that Michael Sheldon of Taulsa! What is the meaning of this ritual?

"(I am newly arrived here. I cannot read this)."

"Oh! You're a foreigner?"

"(Yes. What did you say, a coffee...)?"

"Coffee and donut; sure, honey." She went behind her counter and brought both out to his table. She watched him sniff the coffee curiously. Before she could warn him, he took a big swallow. Roaring, he leaped up out of his seat and threw the coffee cup away to shatter against the wall. The cook ran out to see what happened.

"I'm sorry, I thought you knew coffee is hot," the waitress fretted.

Darien pointed at the donut. "(And this thing; what will it do? Bite back)?" he demanded suspiciously.

"You ain't never had coffee and a donut before?" the cook asked. "Man, are you from another planet?"

Darien straightened quickly and said, "(No. I am... an English)."

"My brother was over there in the war," the cook said. "Whereabouts in England are you from?"

Darien thought swiftly. "(The place where the drinks do not scald the mouth)."

The cook laughed. "Jenny, clean up Mr. Churchill's coffee for him and get him some orange juice. You just sit back down there, fella. We'll fix you up."

A large work truck pulled up outside, and four men piled out of it. One of them was Dickie Forbes. They came into the café and whooped at the sight of Jenny cleaning up the broken cup and coffee. "Must be a bad cup of beans," one of the men told the others.

"That big guy over there is looking for a job," she told Dickie Forbes.

"Well, hello there, fella!" Dickie greeted him as he shook Darien's hand. "So, you want to work on a rig, do you?"

"(No)," Darien replied. "(I am interested in oil work)."

Forbes laughed. "Boy, are you green. Okay, son: I need some muscles, and you need some work. You come on with me, then. Jenny, let's get a cup to go."

She got them all go-cups and put lids on them. "Let it cool off first," she told Darien. "Then drink it."

"Did you do that to the coffee?" one of the men asked Darien as he pointed to the coffee stain on the wall. Darien nodded. "Where's your flyswatter?" The other men hooted with laughter.

"Pete," Mr. Forbes warned.

Darien remained silent. He went with them to the truck, and they headed for the oil field. The men looked him over and did not know what to make of him. He was by far larger than any of them, but his black clothing, long blonde braid and sunglasses were completely out of place in the Oklahoma oil brotherhood. They waited for him to say something, but Darien did not know what he should say. He was reluctant to initiate a conversation because he might say something that would betray his true origins. A slip of the tongue could be costly. He wished he had Glendon's conversational skills or Gareth's easygoing personality. He had wanted to get out and do something on this world to help his people but now he regretted his haste.

Finally, the man named Pete spoke up. "So, what's your name?"

"(Darien Phillipi)."

They waited. "Where are you from?"

"(I am from Thuringa)."

"Well, where in hell is that?"

Darien pursed his lips together in consternation. This 'hell' place was a familiar notion. The Gollar held a belief that when the wicked die they were consumed by their own evil presence and fated to remain locked away from the presence of peace that the good were promised. The Warrior Prince did not care for the implication that Thuringa should be cast similarly. "(It is not in hell)."

"Well okay, Goldilocks! I didn't mean to spoil your day," Pete chuckled, and the other men joined in. They were baffled by Darien's strange silence and temperament. They decided to leave him alone.

Once at the work site, Darien was appalled to see the green field scarred by the mess and confusion of an oil rig. In the distance he saw pumpjacks working to bring oil to the surface. He could sense it being drawn from the ground and it made him strangely weak and weary. The smell of the oil and grease made him so nauseous, when the sludge and film got on his skin he had to dash away to throw up in private. He scrubbed most of the oil slurry off with a red cloth, but he still felt ill. His co-workers cut him no slack.

"Goldilocks sure is a delicate thing, ain't he?" they asked each other loud enough he was sure to hear.

"Yeah, he don't like to get dirty!"

"Don't let those old boys mess with you," Dickie Forbes told him. "You'll do fine."

Darien was taken completely aback by Forbes' words. Fine in Thuringi meant something far different than it did in American English. To an American, fine meant good, acceptable, approved. To a Thuringi, fine was a term applied to a particular part of a female's body, her extreme charms – her genitalia.

Darien was stunned, wondering what Dickie Forbes meant by

saying Darien was… doing fine? He had not 'done fine' since the night before they left the Armada. This was not a good time to join these people, Darien decided. Their lexicon was still too foreign for his comprehension. But what could he do? He could not simply walk away from the job site. He had no idea where the ranch was, and they took so many twisting roads he was quite confused about direction.

Darien mused over the use of the word 'fine' until another truck of workers came out to the site. Darien stared at one of them. He was the same dark colored man who frightened Carrol when they came to the ranch house and walked inside unannounced. The man did indeed bear a vague resemblance to a Shargassi with his shiny head with sparse hair, round eyes, and wide flat nose. His eyebrows arched when he spoke as multiple wrinkles appeared on his forehead. He was much shorter than a Shargassi. His eyes were markedly smaller, and his nose was not so beaklike that he could be mistaken for one of the enemies of the crown. Still, Darien kept a wary eye on him as well as another man with the same kind of round-shaped head but lighter of skin tone and slicked-back hair.

"How did you like the peaches I gave you, Glen?" Margie asked.

Glendon turned his attention to her, and the fifty-year-old woman was smitten with his sunny smile. "Why, they were wonderful, such a treat! We appreciated it very much, thank you."

She glanced around. "Did you bring your lunch with you, or were you going to go to the café to eat?"

"Is it dinnertime already?" Ed asked in surprise. "Boy, the morning just flew by."

"I did not bring anything. Is it required?"

"No, but you just might get hungry," Margie said with a laugh. "I'll tell you what, you can have dinner with us. I have some fried chicken in the refrigerator left over from last night. Why don't we go have some of that and I'll fry up some okra and heat up a mess of peas."

Glendon's benign smile masked his complete ignorance. "That sounds pleasant."

Lunch was laid out on a small table in the little office behind the cash register. The food was a revelation; it was tasty and after so many gintas of travel ratios, it was a veritable feast for the Naradi. In answer to his question, Margie explained how she cooked it.

"Why, that sounds deceptively easy," he said. "I have never eaten a bird before."

"You haven't?"

"No. We are not meat-eaters by nature."

"Where did you say you were from? Turkey?"

"Thuringa. Thur-ING-gah." The subject was too uncertain for him, and a quick glance at a shelf provided a change. "Is that an image of your son?" The young golden-haired man in the framed picture stood before a tent in a green uniform, smiling proudly for the camera.

"Yes, that's our Gary. He joined the Army right out of school."

"Where is he now?"

Margie took a moment before she replied. "He was killed on duty earlier this year. He was our only child."

Glendon heard similar words from his own people, and his heart went out to the Earthian couple. Unlike Thuringi, Earthians had a limited number of years to bear offspring, and it was obvious this couple would not have a 'late child' as Thuringi in their four hundreds or five hundreds sometimes did. Glendon placed his hand on hers in sympathy, and that gesture and the tender look of understanding in his eyes told them what they needed to know about Glendon Garin. "There is nothing so noble as a sacrifice in the line of duty. I know that may mean little to a mother's grieving heart, but every military man knows it is the ultimate service to one's king ...or country." At that moment, the bells over the door jangled to indicate a customer had entered. Glendon rose and bowed. "I will see to their needs," and with that he left. They heard him greet the customer as smoothly and welcoming as a toastmaster.

"He reminds me of Gary," Margie said with a smile as she gathered up the bowls and plates. "He's got that same sweet way about him when he talks."

Ed Gentry was thinking the same thing. Glendon's soothing tone and elaborate but sympathetic words were remarkable from such a young man. Ed went to the cash register counter and watched as the customer pointed to a stack of one hundred-pound sacks of horse feed. Glendon nodded and, in one swift movement, swung a sack of feed onto his shoulder and walked to Ed at the counter. There was no strain in his muscles and no effort betrayed on his face. It was as if he had placed a kitten on his shoulder and was taking it for a ride.

"Whoo-wee, where's you get this weightlifter, Ed?" the customer called out.

"He's one of Mike Sheldon's friends," the store owner replied. "Pretty strong, ain't he?"

All that afternoon Glendon did whatever was requested and behaved as if he had done it his whole life. No task was too insignificant; no load was too heavy. The sun shone down on his long gleaming braid as he loaded supplies into trucks, much to the amusement of the customers.

"You know, they have a barber shop in town," one man teased him.

Glendon considered his words and replied pleasantly, "I shall remember that when I am in need of barbs." The customer howled with amusement, but Glendon could only tilt his head slightly and wonder what was so amusing.

Ed thought it's as if he just came to Earth like some kind of – Suddenly he looked at the picture of his son on the shelf behind him. Ed was a practical man, but he always harbored a secret longing to see an unearthly being. Maybe it was just his imagination working overtime and mixing with the subject of his late son, but it was a comforting thought.

"I tell you what, that boy sure ain't the sharpest ax in the shed, is he?" the man asked as he came to Ed to pay the bill.

"That boy is an angel sent here to look after me and my wife," Ed unintentionally spoke his notion aloud, but the customer simply nodded in agreement. Perhaps the young man with the British accent was just a foreigner on a streak of bad luck, but Ed would not have put it past his son Gary to be so thoughtful as to send help from the Great Beyond.

The thick black sludge that encrusted the tools continued to nauseate Darien and he bore it with a stoic face. He did not understand why he was sick to his stomach or why his head ached so, but with all the new experiences around him he supposed it should have been no surprise. Many times that day, his hand instinctively reached for his pistol. Darien did not understand the slang, the oil terminology, or the nature of the work but he did know when he was the butt of an ongoing joke. The first time they teased him he reached for his weapon and found nothing there. It was back at the ranch house on his hammock. Never in his life had he ever held his temper as he did that day. Every time one of the men laughed at him or made a comment about coffee or flyswatters or the dark glasses he wore, he had to swallow his pride.

At lunch break most of the other workers took out tins containing wrapped meals. When he saw that Darien had no lunch, Dickie Forbes shared his lunch with the new worker and Darien discovered cold cut sandwiches. His coffee was cold. It was very bitter, but at least he could drink it without being scalded. He was seated near the black man and decided to test him to make certain he was not a Shargassi spy.

"Crita vonn?" he asked. Their universal translators were now tuned to translating only between Thuringi and American, and the Shargassi for "who are you?" came out as pronounced.

"Say what?" the man asked, perplexed. "You talkin' to me?" Darien nodded. "Well, what are you saying?"

"Crita vonn," Darien repeated.

"My name is George, ain't no Critter Von," the black man said.

"Big guy calling you names, George?" asked Pete, the one who took particular pleasure in teasing the Thuringi.

"I don't know what he's talking about," George said. The other men looked at Darien curiously, and the intense inspection made the Thuringi uneasy.

"(I... I ask from whence you came)," Darien said hastily. "(I thought you understood the language)."

"'From whence you came', George," Pete mocked Darien's solemnity. "Hell boy, we don't understand you any better'n you get us."

George shook his head at the Thuringi. "No, I don't know what you're saying. You've been staring at me all morning. You still mad about your sister? I didn't mean to scare her, you know."

"(I understand you meant no harm. But I have never seen anyone like you on Earth before)."

"Then buddy, you ain't been around!" George said, and the others laughed.

Darien smiled frostily. "(Not around here, no)," he admitted. When they went back to work, their teasing did not let up. By the end of the day, Darien was terribly ill from the nauseating black oil and his repeated need to step away and throw up. He only felt marginally better afterward.

By the time he was let out of the truck at the store, Darien was in a white-hot fury. He stalked into the feed store like a man on a mission and looked around for Glendon. Glendon saw the stormy set to Darien's jaw from across the store. "(I am over here)," he said.

Ed Gentry waved Darien over to the cash register stand. "Hello there, big fellow! You look like you could use a cool drink." He reached into a large red box and pulled out a curvy bottle of dark water and handed it to Darien. It was frosty cold, and Darien looked at him with frank suspicion. "Go ahead, it's okay. Oh, wait," Ed said. He took back the bottle, turned to the large box with an attached device on its side and removed the top from the bottle with the device. He handed the bottle back to Darien and said, "It's soda, son; it'll be good for you."

Darien glanced at Glendon, who nodded encouragingly. Darien took a drink cautiously, remembering the morning coffee. It was cold and tingly and sweet, and Darien jerked his head back in surprise. It was the best thing he experienced all day long. He looked at Glendon's boss.

"(You are a good man)," Darien intoned. "(I shall remember this kindness)."

"Well, that's all right," the man said humbly. "We'll see you tomorrow, Glen."

"(I shall be here, Lord Gentry)." Glendon and Darien went out to Darryl Sheldon's truck. Glendon got behind the wheel. "I assume rousting is not a pleasant endeavor."

"The endeavor is not nearly as difficult as the cretins who perform it. I will choke Michael Sheldon when next I see him! I had no idea what I was doing or why they mocked me. Nothing was explained to me, and I stumbled about as a fool all day. I have never felt so helpless in my life."

"It is not Michael's fault. I had no idea what I was doing, but Lord and Lady Gentry have been kindness itself."

"The Dickie Forbes is pleasant enough, I suppose," Darien grudgingly admitted, "but oh! If only I had my sword with me for even a minute with the rest of them." They got back to the ranch house and

Darien promptly went to bathe. The oil and grease on his clothing would not come clean, and his skin was scrubbed until it was red before he was satisfied. Glendon prepared the evening meal, a pot full of a meaty red soup that was spicy and hot and tasty.

"Lord Gentry suggested this," Glendon told the others.

"What is it?" Carrol asked.

"He said it is chili," he answered, ladling it into bowls.

"It is chilly and hot?" Brent asked. "This is a strange world."

"How was rousting?" Stuart asked as he reacted to the taste of chili with delight.

"I do not like it," Darien said told him. "I must know more about the nuances of this society. Did you know, they drink scalding hot bitter water in the light of dawn, and in the hot afternoon sun they drink cold sweet water?" He showed them his soda, only half-full now. He passed it around and they all took a taste and agreed it was good.

"This world has fizz bars," Stuart exclaimed.

"It does not mean they are civilized," Darien muttered, "just handy with liquids. If it were not for the fact that I refuse to be defeated, I would be tempted to stay here tomorrow and find out more of their customs some other way." He peered at Gareth. "What is the matter with our good Major Sword-and-Fist?" he asked.

Gareth had propped his elbows on the table over his bowl of chili and fell asleep sitting up. "He is tired," Carrol said gently. "I am loath to wake him only to send him to bed."

"We should carry him upstairs," Stuart suggested. "He ate a good lunch, and he can always eat when he awakens." He and Darien got on either side of him and lifted. Gareth jerked awake. "Go back to sleep," Stuart said quietly to him. "You've earned a rest." Gareth faded again. They carried him up the stairs, and Darien paused at Gareth's bedroom door.

"We will hang him if we try to put him in his hammock," he said. "He ought to have a proper bed."

"Put him in one of ours."

"Put him in Carrol's," Darien said with a devilish grin.

"You are not funny," Stuart said. "It is difficult enough for them."

"Why make it difficult?" Darien asked.

"She is our sister," Stuart hissed.

"It would make her happy," Darien whispered back hotly.

"Many things that make us happy are not always good for us," Stuart reminded him as they continued to hold the groggy engineer in the hallway.

"Stuart, must you always do the proper thing?" Darien groused. "Can you not go on instinct for once?"

"It is instinctive for me to see to the proper conduct of our dear sister and her admirer."

"Then put him in her bed to sleep and make her sleep in his hammock." In the end they put him on Stuart's bed and Stuart slept in the hammock. He decided upon awakening that beds were a must for all of them.

"Why, hammocks are comfortable," Glendon said in surprise. "I like mine. It is like a lover's arms around me."

"I felt wadded up," Stuart said as he stretched to relieve his muscles.

Gareth came down the stairs the next morning to find only Carrol in the house. She was in her workspace in the master bedroom, making notes on the vegetation samples she had gathered so far. "Where is everyone else?" he asked.

"We all had a nasty reaction to the meal Glendon made, but that has all been handled. Glendon and Darien went to their tasks. Simply put, Glendon is learning much from the store man and Darien hates the oil people." Gareth chuckled and moved closer in order to hold her hands. "Stuart is walking about the property to see what he can find, and Brent is puttering about with the gakkis – er, the cabrett. Or no! They are called cows."

"Why would Brent deal with them?" Gareth wondered.

"He wants more luket, I suspect." She let go of his hands in order to slip her arms around his waist. For a moment they regarded each other solemnly.

"Brent can have his luket," Gareth muttered to her, "this is more to my liking."

"I am entering the house!" Brent's voice warned. "I am moving through the kitchen!" Reluctantly, Carrol broke away from Gareth and went to the parlor door.

"We are in the parlor, Brent," she called out, and explained to Gareth, "He does not want to come upon anything he would have to admit that he saw."

"We should leave the house entirely," Gareth suggested playfully. Brent came to the doorway covered in dust.

"One can elicit luket from those ugly Earthian cabrett," he informed them with a satisfied smile. His hair was wildly askance, and his face bore a dirty smudge across one cheek. "It is not easy, but it can be done." He entered the room as Carrol returned to her sorting. "We decided that we would take the Isador to the Great Waters on a day when Darien will not be in the oil field and Glendon will be at the store only in the morning. Saturday, it is called. Did you have a good rest?"

"Yes, I did," Gareth said.

"And have you had a good awakening?" Brent asked saucily.

"If you would only go elicit more luket, I might," Gareth told him, and Brent laughed. "So, you named your ship the Isador?"

"Yes. She is beautiful, accommodating and hopefully, will respond eagerly to my touch." Carrol's cheeks reddened and a small "yeep!" escaped her lips. Brent picked up on it. "Little sis, I fear all our coarse talk will harm you."

"I shall not be harmed by the likes of you," she said, tossing a cloth at him. "I have Gareth to protect me from your alarming conversation."

"Gareth?" Brent hooted. "Between the two of us, it will be a wonder that your ears are not burned away." He retreated to the front room, grinning to himself as he did. He started to taunt them a little more, but a rumbling noise outside caught his attention.

He went to the front door and peered through the aged brown screen. It was still the bright daylight, but the sky was being overtaken by heavy clouds rolling in from the horizon. Brent walked out the front door as if in a trance.

A strong, steady wind bent the tree branches about and made the grass and leaves swirl in place on the ground. The breeze against his face was exhilarating. As he slowly stepped onto the porch steps, he felt a drop of moisture on his face. He reached the bottom step, looked up to the sky, and stretched out his arms. The clouds opened up and the rain began in earnest, pelting him with fat drops of clean, life-giving moisture. Brent stood with his eyes shut to the skies, his head lolled back with a look of bliss on his face.

This was no tank of water that the cattle drank from; this was not a nearly stagnant stock pond half full of mud that almost twisted his feet from his ankles. This was pure water and Brent reveled in it. A water planet, a planet teeming with life, a planet he could bring his five hundred surviving watermen for a renewal. Perhaps, just perhaps, they could thrive and grow since this planet Earth supported millions of people. He loved this world; he loved the hope it gave him. It was impossible to tell which were raindrops or tears of gratitude on his face.

Gareth and Carrol stood at the window to watch as Brent continued to stand with his arms outstretched, catching some rain in his mouth as it fell. "He seems content," Carrol murmured, then realized with a start, "Oh! Stuart is out in this rain!"

They went out onto the front porch and saw him in the distance, running at a comfortable pace back to the ranch through the field next to the fenced yard. He jumped and cleared the fence easily – a four-foot fence was hardly a challenge for a Thuringi. They saw as he neared that he was soaked to the skin and laughing.

"Have you no more sense than to stand in the rain?" he hooted at Brent.

Brent regarded his question with disdain. "Where the rain is, there am I," he said proudly. Stuart stopped and thought for a moment before he lifted his own arms and stretched upward to call upon his unique gift. Among the Thuringi, only the Phillipi line had the genetic ability to use the fabled Arda liquid of their home world. The liquid was a powerful source of energy, and each Phillipi had his or her own particular talent through which that energy was channeled. Little blue sparks danced on the tips of Stuart's fingers, and Brent found himself in a three-foot-wide circle of clear dry air, surrounded by the heavy rain.

"Stop messing about, Son of Thuringa!" Brent protested. "This is my time." Stuart lowered his hands suddenly, and rain smacked against Brent's face like a wave. Brent jumped at him and chased his brother-in-law around the yard. They both slipped on the slick wet grass, and Stuart made it up to the porch just ahead of Brent.

"A base!" he called out the time-honored child's claim.

"And Father supposes these two are among the hopespring of the Thuringi," Carrol told Gareth dryly. He leaned over and kissed her briefly on the tip of her nose.

"Take heart, Your Nibs," he said blithely, "sometime in the not-so-distant future, they might grow up." She laughed.

Darien's next day in the oil field was no more pleasant than his first, with two exceptions. One, he was assigned to handle the pipe joints for the drill unit and this physical work gave him an outlet for his anger. Two, Darien Phillipi made a friend.

He was a slightly built, sandy-haired man named Lloyd Martin. He spoke in a soft voice from beneath a sandy-colored mustache. Darien, whose people never grew facial hair, was amused by the sight of it but said nothing aloud. Gharadee men grew beards, and the Hunda favored the occasional mustache with their thin white hair, but Darien never saw so much variety in one place until they came to Earth.

It was no chore for the Thuringi prince to move the heavy pipes from where they were stacked to the hole being drilled, but he noticed Earthians were not as strong as Thuringi, so he used their machines rather than his own strength as he could have. They could tell he was not straining but some of his co-workers thought he was lazy rather than simply bored.

He neglected to bring a lunch with him again. Half the night was spent waiting for bathroom availability; the meaty chili did not sit well with Thuringi digestions. He had not given another thought about meals until late that morning. Lloyd drove his own truck to work so when he saw Darien without a lunch bucket again, he took him into a nearby diner and offered to buy his lunch.

Darien ordered what Lloyd ordered, a hamburger and fries with a side order of soda. All three pleased Darien very much. The day was more pleasant because of the tasty lunch and the friendly encouragement of quiet Lloyd.

"Pete's not an easy man to work with, I'll grant you that. I take it you've never done roughneck work before?"

"No, but it is a task that will garner needed wages, and I shall not be deterred," Darien replied firmly, and bit into his hamburger with gusto.

"You'll be all right. Don't take anything Pete says seriously; consider the source."

That phrase got Darien through the rest of the afternoon as he dismissed the miscreants' comments privately. Lloyd gave him a ride to Gentry's store. "I'll pick you up tomorrow at the diner," Lloyd offered. "It's not out of my way, and I know those guys who ride with Dickie are a pain in the ass."

"Thank you," Darien said with relief. He bought a fizzy drink from Ed Gentry and offered to pay for the one from the day before.

Ed declined. "No, I was proud to do it. You looked like you needed it."

Glendon had another jar of canned peaches from Margie Gentry to bring home. "You see, Darien, there are wonderful people here on Earth," he told him in the truck as Darien inspected the jar in one hand and held the soda in the other. "I hope to bring Janis and Echo here to meet the Gentrys when the Armada arrives. I would like them to meet kind Earthians like them." Glendon's driving was a little better today, and Darien did not have to clutch at the dashboard to maintain his balance.

The brother princes were on the front porch in a rousing debate as evening approached. Stuart rocked in the porch swing as Darien leaned against a porch roof post, his hands shoved into his front jeans pockets. The intermittent rain of the day was now gentle and steady, the breeze bracing and pleasant.

"This young President Kennedy needs help against his enemies. I do not see why we cannot help him along," Darien declared. "Is that not the Phillipi way, the altruistic thing to do?"

"What do you have against altruism?" Stuart asked. "You speak of it as if it is a personal offense."

"Four-fifths of our people are dead and none of those whom we have always aided lifted a hand to help prevent it, that is what I have against it. Doing a good deed for an individual is one thing. It is a kindness, pure and simple. But to continually rush to the aid of others who only care whether your blade is sharp enough to defend them, so they do not have to do it themselves, is stupid."

"Then why are you promoting the idea of helping President Kennedy in a military gesture? You know full well that Father will not approve of it, and it goes against our plans, and any other way would smack of the very altruism you abhor," Stuart demanded.

"It is not stupid if we can profit by it." Darien rolled his eyes as

Stuart exhaled in a sudden gust of disbelief. "Oh, do not be so offended. How can we hope to promise our people a safe haven in which to rebuild our strength for the final journey to Farcourt? We cannot! As long as these people are in open war with each other, we will not know whether or not they will turn on us or even whether they will let us land! Or whether they will not destroy themselves and take this planet with it."

"What do you propose we do, Darien? Aim our weapons at them and force them to capitulate to our demands for peace? And then what; turn our guns on every country and demand peace? Darien, this world is so much more than Thuringa, so many more people and more land and factions against the other that our few scout ships cannot possibly force peace upon them! We are the ones who need aid. All they would have to do is band together in their United Nations and vote against allowing our people to rest here. Then what? Start a war with Earth when the Armada arrives? Become like the Shargassi, and take over planets that have something we want for ourselves?"

"Of course not," Darien snapped, annoyed that Stuart would even suggest such a comparison. "But if America is the most powerful country on this world and we need powerful allies, then is it only sensible to collect them through helping them?"

"How can we convince these people that we only desire peace and that we are not monsters from outer space, when the first thing they are aware that we do is pull out weapons and make their decisions for them?" Stuart countered.

"Well, how do you propose we introduce ourselves to Earth, then? Do you plan to accidentally slash open the legs of every leader in the world, then treat his or her leg?"

"You need not be such an istay," Stuart came back, and Darien's eyebrows rose in surprise.

"Why Stuart, I did not realize you even knew how to pronounce that word."

"You might be surprised at the kind of words I know how to pronounce," Stuart told him shortly. "The trouble with being compared to you, Naughty Boy, is that I am constantly assumed to be the perpetual Good Lad. It never occurred to you or anyone else that what I do and what I think are not always for good."

"Oh?" Darien perched on the edge of the porch rail. The problems of Earth would have to wait or be solved by Earthian means, now. For Stuart to make such a statement was tantamount to a confession of something darker. "Just what might you think that is not good? Of what naughtiness might you be capable?"

"I can curse just as vile, I can threaten just as cruel, and I can wegodgoe with just as much lust as you," Stuart told him. He sat in the porch swing and stretched out his legs to rest his feet on the porch rail. "The main difference is, I pick and chose my battles carefully. When you curse, people take it as a matter of course. When I curse, people are rocked back on their feet with the notion that I even know the words. When I threaten, the very notion is as unnerving as the hideous promises I make, instead of expected as a matter of course."

"And do you wegodgoe better than I?" Darien laughed.

"No, but it would probably make a more lasting impression from the novelty of the suggestion." Stuart grinned, but his grin slipped a little as a thought occurred to him. "The lesser use, I do not know why that is so. She never told me why. Perhaps I am just not that good, after all." The silence was deafening. Stuart's soft, deep voice rumbled out a concern that caught Darien off guard.

"Maybe you are, and Aura is just a chill woman."

"She was not when we first married," Stuart sighed. "What else can it be except disappointment?"

Darien was astonished at Stuart's courage to voice such a thing. Darien would rather lose his arm than even hint that his bed performance was off. "Perhaps you overwhelm her," he suggested. It was certainly what he would have assumed.

Stuart laughed. It was not his usual full hearty laugh, but it was one of amusement. "Ah, Darry," he chuckled. "You were never one to let me denigrate myself."

The knowledge that he was the chief reason behind Stuart's problem made it all the more painful to Darien. Had he not been so careless and cruel to Aura, she might be more open to the gentle, loving Stuart; Stuart, who actually deserved Aura's fiery passion which Darien squandered.

"It is not your fault," Darien insisted.

"Well, perhaps you are right," Stuart said reflectively, "but then if you ever tasted the kind of passion of which Aura is capable, then you would see my point."

Darien was thunderstruck. Good God. Stuart still has no idea Aura and I were once lovers, he really does not know. Darien stammered but before he could formulate a reply or confession of his own, Carrol and Glendon came out on the porch. They carried lemonade in glasses and handed the drinks out. They joined Stuart on the swing. Darien sat helplessly on the porch rail and listened to them comment on the nice evening shower.

"The things that we do can either bolster our convictions or wrap us in damnation," Maranta told him on Stuart's wedding day, "Darien, whatever you do in your life, do as if it will be placed in a book for all to inspect. Even if no one else sees that book, your conscience can see the fact plainly. No punishment is worse than what we do to ourselves."

Darien was simply uneasy at the time Maranta said it, concerned only that the man he most admired somehow found out Darien unwittingly robbed Stuart of Aura's First Night seventy years before the night. He still did not know just to which transgression Maranta referred, but the words haunted him now.

"Why have you two been so intense?" Carrol asked, noting Darien had not touched his drink.

"Nothing important," Stuart said easily. "Just brotherly jesting."

Stuart would confess his imagined shortcomings to his twin brother but would of course not mention such a raw subject to their sister and their Naradi friend. Darien suddenly did not want to argue with his brother any longer. He already wrapped himself in the damnation of his private history with Aura. The Thuringi people had too much at stake to risk following his impatient ideas about diplomacy.

The Elders of Thuringa worried over a future power struggle and warned the king the twin princes would have to be carefully raised. Lycasis saw no need for such concern: Stuart, being the eldest, was the Crown Prince and heir to the Thuringi throne. Darien would be the future Warrior Prince, in charge of his brother's armed command. Properly instructed and correctly taught by their Warrior General, the brothers could share in the glorious apex of Thuringi power. As the years went by, Lycasis was proven right. No two brothers were as close as the Phillipi twins and the Elders agreed it was a remarkable and fortuitous alignment. They had disagreements like any other siblings, but their close bond transcended mere squabbles.

Darien remembered Stuart's strategic abilities during the escape from Thuringa. He had been an able general, much better than Darien; cool under pressure and quick at making sensible decisions. He was also a peacemaker and making a peaceful haven was what a Crown Prince should do. Stuart would have been as good a Warrior Prince as he was a Crown Prince and Darien was not remarkable in either role. The God of All aligned the stars correctly at their birth. Stuart was capable of someday assuming the mantle of kingship and if he needed a hotheaded but loyal Warrior Prince, he had one. It was a shame that Stuart would not have the kind of queen to make him happy in his home.

"I must venture out and get things we need," Stuart had told Darien, and handed him some dollar bills. "We must all remember to carry this currency with us to trade for services rendered. Michael said that we will receive our purchase and any balance due us." Darien stuffed the bills in a pocket and nodded.

Saturday afternoon Stuart opened the gate to the gakki pasture and Glendon drove the truck out into it. It was time to learn to drive an Earthian vehicle properly, Stuart told them, and Darien and Glendon were the first to agree. Once they all understood which pedals did what, it was a matter of who made the truck lurch around the least. Gareth cringed inwardly every time someone grinded the gears, and they all groaned in dismay when Stuart plowed over a little sapling by mistake.

"I did not see it," he protested. "It all but leaped out in front of me."

"Roots and all," Darien taunted.

Gareth also had a difficult time driving. "I can repair them, I never claimed I could master them," he reminded the others. "Let me see what this does," he said, putting it in reverse. He stepped on the gas, let off the clutch, and hung onto the steering wheel for dear life as the truck abruptly roared backwards, scattering the panicky cows that wandered over. He slammed on the brakes, and the resultant dust that kicked up had all six Thuringi coughing and waving their hands to dispel the swirling tide. "I will stick to repairing them," they heard Gareth call out.

"Let us try it again. This is worse than a simulated fighter," Brent groused.

"That is what the problem is for us, at least for me!" Glendon exclaimed. "We are making this too hard! We expect this thing to move like a ship in a three-dimensional area when all it is supposed to do is go back and forth on the ground. All right then, I am ready to think on a simple linear plane." After so many years of flying in space it was true; the more they practiced with a ground vehicle's movement in mind, the easier it was.

By the time the sun set, they had a better grasp of driving an Earthian truck. The dinner that night was Glendon's turn again, and he served peaches of course as well as a brace of cut-up fowl. The instructions on how to cook them were courtesy Mrs. Gentry. His first attempt at fried chicken was well received by the Thuringi, who all hoped what had happened after the chili would not re-occur. Fortunately, it did not have the same affect, but it did weigh heavily in their stomachs.

Michael summoned a telephone repairman out to the ranch house to install a line. The man liked what he saw when he spied Carrol, but the Thuringi men made him uneasy with their height and large muscles and eerie yellow eyes. He worked as fast as he could and left promptly after he explained how to use the phone. Gareth itched to take it apart and inspect it, but Stuart said no. It was not on a party line; Michael paid extra so the line would be private. He knew if he did not, the whole world would be alerted to the aliens by the inquisitive party line operators from the phone company.

At the end of every hot, humid day Darien trudged home and immediately set to work scrubbing the sludge off his skin. He lost considerable weight by week's end and was unnervingly slim, not the robust Darien Phillipi de Saulin at all. He took it with a carefree air, but the others could tell that something troubled him. He would not discuss it until a call came for him one night. Gareth answered it and handed the receiver to Darien. They could all hear the raucous voice on the other end of the line. Darien knew it was Pete.

"Hey, Goldilocks! Forbes said to remind you to bring your lunch tomorrow; we're going out to a field where there ain't no diner handy. See if your mommy'll pack you a nice sammich after she braids your pigtails!"

"(I am well aware of the need to bring lunch, thank you)," Darien replied, tight-lipped.

"Yeah well, you don't seem too awful bright, or the boss wouldn't have to keep reminding you, Dumbass." There was a click and then a dial tone. Pete had hung up.

"Does he taunt you that way often?" Stuart asked as Darien fought to not slam the phone back down on the cradle.

"Yes."

"Why? What is the reason for his actions?"

"I do not know," Darien's reply was terse. "He finds fault with me constantly. I have learned to make a game of not snapping his neck. Fortunately for him, I have won so far." He stood and stretched. "I shall go to bed early tonight."

"Do you want some luket?" Carrol asked.

"No, I do not. Thank you." With that he went upstairs.

Carrol turned to Stuart. "Does that sound like Darien to you? I never thought I would miss his bold improper ways, but this troubles me, Sunny."

Stuart left with Glendon and Darien the next morning and went with his brother to the cafe in order to learn more about hot coffee and other Earthian things. They sat at a booth in the diner, where Stuart spoke softly in their native tongue.

"Darien, I do not wish you to continually be insulted by these people. You are a Thuringi prince. I would not ask you to suffer slights such as you have described, not even for our people. There is always something else you can try."

"No, this cannot be abandoned, Stuart. I must gain the upper hand of the situation." Darien toyed with the handle of the new black lunch box he purchased the day before at the Gentry's store. Inside was an apple and a packet of rations re-packaged in wax paper so it would not look obvious in its original Thuringi container.

"You are a stubborn, aggressive soul," Stuart said with a shake of his head. Jenny the waitress approached them.

"Well, hi there. Y'all must be related."

Stuart rose to his feet politely. "(We are brothers, madam. And to whom have I the honor to address)?"

"Oh my," Jenny exclaimed as she tilted her head back to address him, "you Brits have the nicest manners! My name's Jenny," she said as she pointed to her name tag.

"(I am Stuart, and you have met my brother Darien)."

"Darien, so that's your name." She shook hands with Darien, who was careful not to hurt her hand with his grasp. "Look, I'll bring you some coffee and put an ice cube in it to cool it down, okay?"

"Oh, Kay," Darien replied. She left and returned promptly with two cups of coffee. "Here's cream, and there's sugar right there. You want anything to eat this morning?"

"(A... a cooked egg)," Darien told her.

"How do you want it cooked?" she asked as she pulled out her order pad. She saw his perplexed look, and added, "Fried, scrambled, boiled, over-easy or omelet?"

"Omelet?" Darien repeated curiously.

"You got it. How about you, brother Stuart?"

"(I would like a egg over easy)."

"Bacon and grits?"

Stuart shot Darien a dumbfounded glance. "Perhaps a little," Darien said, and shrugged at his brother. He did not understand her, either.

She left to hand the cook the order. "It all sounds interesting," Stuart told Darien. "I wonder what it is it will be over, this bakenangreets?"

"Their dialect is one thing, but their odd re-phrasing is beyond understanding," Darien said. Dickie Forbes' truck pulled up as usual and Darien grimaced. "And thus begins another bad day." The four men crowded into the diner.

"Hey, it's Marilyn Monroe and Lana Turner!" Pete called out at the sight of the brothers.

"Lay off them right now," Dickie Forbes ordered.

"Our hair is apparently of issue as too long for their liking," Darien muttered.

Stuart got to his feet to face them. Pete took a step backward as the princely figure seemed to keep rising before him. Stuart's unsmiling expression was at once bland and ominous like the dead stillness before a windstorm, and the dark glasses betrayed no hint of his gentle eyes. "(My name is Stuart Phillipi. My brother Darien tells me you are not pleased with his appearance)."

"Well now, no, not exactly," the roughneck said feebly.

"(My brother Darien has done well holding his renowned temper. In our homeland, a man's hair length and other physical attributes are inconsequential as long as he can fight. Darien is well regarded and even feared there. Yet I have overheard taunts toward him from some of you. I shall warn you that my brother has slain many men in war. To insult him further is to invite disaster. Do you understand this, oil man)?" His voice rumbled with all the grandeur and majesty of the Royal Thuringi High Court, imperial and final.

"Uh, sure," Pete replied.

"(Who is this Dickie Forbes)?" Stuart asked.

Dickie stepped up, and they shook hands. "Your brother is a hard worker. Don't worry about these roughnecks, they're just having fun," he said in his easygoing way.

"(At Darien's expense)," Stuart pointed out with regal chill, and the lift of one eyebrow suggested he believed Dickie was lax about reining in his subordinates. Dickie felt the hair stand up on the back of his neck. "(It may prove costly to you someday, and you would not wish to pay the price Darien can exact)."

He sat back down and in this proud unhurried way, royally dismissed them from further attention. There was nothing rude or express in his actions, but the roughnecks and their boss got the distinct impression that their audience with this regally self-confident young man was over. Although he found disfavor with their actions, he was willing to overlook it for the now, but his generosity was waning.

The drilling rig crew sat uneasily at another table. Jenny brought out the Phillipi's plates. The two Thuringi gazed at the food and then up at Jenny.

"(These are eggs)?" Darien asked.

"Yeah; didn't you want an omelet and one over easy?"

"Yes," Stuart said. The brothers picked up their forks, and together they took bites.

"Excellent!" Darien said after he swallowed it. "It does not crunch at all." He smiled at the waitress. "(I must learn your secret)."

"Hey, you're really cute when you smile," she told him. "You ought to smile more often." His smile turned into his roguish leer, and she laughed. "Oh, boy, are you a hot one!" She went over to take the roughnecks' orders.

Darien's friend Lloyd came in and sat with the Phillipi brothers when they beckoned. Darien made the introductions. Lloyd then turned to the waitress and said, "My usual, Jenny." He turned back to the brothers. "I almost didn't make it," he admitted. "Thought I was going to have to take my little girl to the hospital."

"(Why)?" Stuart asked.

"She's running a fever, got a summer cold or something. When fall comes in, she always catches the first cold of the season." They nodded at him, but only partially understood what he meant. "Y'all married, have kids?"

"(I have a wife and son)," Stuart told him. "(Darien chooses to lead a solitary life)."

"Well, there's good and bad to say for both," Lloyd laughed easily. "Some days you want to tear your hair out; other days, you don't know what you'd do without them." Stuart readily agreed.

Jenny brought Lloyd a plate of soft yellow fluff, with two brown wrinkled strips beside it just like the strips on their plates. "Bacon and scrambled eggs," he said, rubbing his hands together in anticipation. "When my wife has a day off like today, I let her sleep in, so I have breakfast somewhere else, like here. Yes, sir! I love bacon and eggs."

The Phillipi brothers paid for their meal and for Lloyd's, since he was kind to feed Darien lunch previously when the prince had no coin on hand. When the oil crew rose to go to work, the Phillipi brothers were ready at the same time. They got to their feet and left the establishment just ahead of the crew. Stuart noted Darien's weight loss and spoke in Thuringi, completely forgetting that his translator converted his words into American. He did not intend for the crew to understand him, but they did: "(Darien, you must eat better and regain your weight. I daresay you cannot lift more than two hundred pounds)."

"(I beg your pardon; I can still toss you across the room, and through the wall too no doubt)!"

"(Perhaps but take it easy on these little fellows. They appear to squash easily)."

Lloyd did not know whether it was Stuart's aloof warning earlier that he heard about, his offhanded comment about squashing the crew, or Darien's nasty snicker of a laugh at that comment that put the teasing temporarily on hold, but he liked it.

Friday evening Glendon returned to the ranch house alone. "Darien's friend Lloyd invited him to a bar. I was not certain about the idea at first, but Darien assured me that he would behave and return to us with no damage to our mission."

"Darien's assurance is not terribly comforting," Stuart said. "His idea of good behavior and mine are radically different."

"To say nothing of the fact that he cannot hold his liquor," added Brent.

"I always thought he did admirably," Gareth said.

"On the surface, perhaps he appears that way. But if he has too much, he cannot recall his actions the next day."

Stuart frowned. "That is worrisome. I hope he will be careful."

"Not to worry," Glendon assured his prince. "Darien is in the good company of his friend Lloyd Martin. Lord Gentry told me he is a trustworthy man and will keep Darien out of trouble. Lloyd Martin feels Darien might make better acquaintances of his co-workers away from the workplace, and Darien asked that I return here. Otherwise, it will only cause more mockery if they believe he must have a guardian like a child, and I agree." Stuart did not argue with the Naradi's decision.

Darien immediately liked the bar Lloyd took him to the moment he stepped inside. It was smoky and poorly lit with glowing signs behind the bar extolling the names of the brands of ale on hand. It was so close to a Thuringi cantina, only infinitely dirtier, that Darien felt a heavy twang of homesickness on his heartstrings. A yowling voice wailed along in time with the tune from the music box extolling cheating lovers and lonesome feelings. Young women in tight-fitting clothing carried drinks and glasses back and forth from the bar to the tables, and everywhere there were Earthians chatting about whatever subjects came to mind.

Lloyd claimed a table for them nearly in the center of the establishment, across from the bar. "My wife lets me go out and whoop a little every Friday night," he explained by shouting to Darien over the music. "I never get more than three beers, and it gives me a little chance to unwind." Darien nodded and sat down.

"You can take your glasses off," the waitress said to Darien as she put paper coasters on their table.

"(Thank you, but I prefer them on)," Darien told her the same story he told everyone. "(Eye problems)." He ordered a beer as did Lloyd. They talked about work on the oil rig for a while. Gradually the conversation drifted to Lloyd's wife and daughter.

"My little Monica's in the third grade." He took a picture out of his wallet and handed it to Darien. Darien saw the resemblance between Lloyd and the face of the child in the picture ring away despite the dark hair that framed her face. She had large brown eyes and a gap in her teeth, as pert and attractive as a Thelan child. Darien was fond of the Thelan race.

"(She looks very charming)," he replied as he handed back the picture.

"She's a good little girl -" Lloyd began but before he could finish, two hands came down on Darien's shoulders from behind.

"It's Marilyn Monroe!" the roustabout called Pete bellowed. "Where's your girlfriend you had with you the other morning?" Darien turned around in his chair.

"(Do not insult me again)," he warned.

"Come on, Hollywood," Pete said. "It ain't sunny in here." He snatched off Darien's glasses and froze in place. The yellow Thuringi irises caught the lights and glowed by the illumination. Darien rose to his feet, grasped the man's shirtfront, and lifted him off his feet with both hands.

"(My brother warned you about making me angry, istay)," Darien declared.

"Uh...!"

"(You are too stupid to suffer, yet too theoretically advanced to kill)," Darien observed as he dangled Pete a foot off the floor. "(I suppose all that is left to me is to hurt you until you scream)."

"Oh God, help me out here," Pete screamed and wriggled to get away from those frightening devil eyes.

"Darien, our beer's here," Lloyd said. He did not jump to his feet like the others in the bar but remained where he sat. Darien let go of his tormentor suddenly, and Pete fell to the floor in a heap. Darien sat back down to address his beer. Lloyd took a look at Darien's eyes and flinched. "Sweet Jesus," he breathed in awe. "What happened to your eyes?"

"I got pissed," Darien intoned a phrase borrowed from Michael Sheldon. Lloyd said no more about the yellow irises. The bar patrons gave Darien a wide berth. When he did not appear to have a forked tail or horns and pitchfork and had nothing eviler on his mind than to drink a few beers with his friend, they relaxed a little but kept far away.

Darien and Lloyd stopped by the latter's house after another round of beer, and Lloyd introduced Darien to his wife and daughter. Lloyd's wife Katie found Darien delightfully mysterious with his large build and yellow eyes. Little Monica Martin took to him right away.

"I'm going to be a princess for Halloween," she told him.

"(A princess, really)," he replied. She walked over and stood by his knee.

"Yes. I'm going to have a beautiful dress and a big, tall hat like princesses have."

Darien recalled a conversation at work. "(This is the festival where children dress strangely and go about extorting sweets from strangers)?" he asked, and Katie Martin laughed along with her husband.

"You hit the nail on the head, Darien," she told him. "I don't reckon you'll have many visitors out there at the Sheldon ranch. It's pretty far out for most folks to go."

"(Good)," Darien said. "(We do not have many sweet things on hand)." He glanced again at Monica, who gazed up at him in fascination. "(What is on your mind, child)?"

"What is that thing on the side of your face?" she asked, meaning the cordlike Universal Translator.

"(That helps me hear the hearts of my fellow man)," he said in a deliberately dramatic tone, and it made her laugh.

"Why are your eyes yellow?"

"(I am magic)."

"I know that," she said with a smile. "Do magic people always have yellow eyes?"

"(Only the very good ones)," Darien confirmed.

Lloyd took him home to the Sheldon ranch. "You have done fired up that little girl's imagination! I don't believe I've ever seen her so fascinated by anyone in her life."

"(How many men with yellow eyes do you bring home on the average)?" Darien asked, and Lloyd chuckled again as Darien got out of the truck.

"You'd be the first."

Each day after he came in from work at the feed store, Glendon tended to his small garden. The royal siblings were not used to gardening ventures; Arne had been a large city that did not host public vegetable gardens, only flower gardens. They were intrigued by the idea and quite impressed that even though farmer's son Gareth was busy in the workshop barn, their very own Naradi Famede was the one who knew how to encourage edible plants to grow.

Carrol and Stuart offered to help. Glendon showed them how to tell the difference between Earthian plants and weeds once he realized the difference himself, how to hoe back weeds and when and how to water the vegetables. Nearly everything was done from illustrations found in seed catalogs and from Glendon's careful listening at the feed store. While it appeared that he was only making polite conversation with customers, he was in fact gleaning information about Earthian plant cultivation from them. He brought this knowledge home and imparted it to his royal companions.

It was hard work. The royal siblings never realized before what it required to get produce to the marketplace. They learned about plants in their science studies but as nobles, they never saw plants on the vine from the viewpoint of a farmer. As warriors of a space-going fleet they came to associate tending plants with grow-lamps and automatic irrigation systems. For the first time in their lives, Stuart and Carrol stood in the blazing sun and dutifully chopped away weeds from growing food plants. They hauled buckets of water or wrestled with a water hose and learned when to pinch back shoots and when to allow new growth to flourish.

Thanks to Gareth's experience on his farm as a youth they learned even more about farming, including all about making fertilizer and using compost to improve the crop yield. From time to time, they peppered him with questions which Gareth gladly answered. They did not ask him to actually work in the garden, since his ship construction work and other mechanical improvements were far more important ways to spend his time. The Phillipi could not contribute very much to shipbuilding, but they could put their muscle into tending a garden, and it made more sense for them to do it rather than take Gareth away from his task or expect Glendon to work after a full day at the feed store.

Stuart was thrilled despite the sweat and effort of farming. He was doing something helpful at last; he was able to contribute in a very real way! While it was important for him to make contacts on Earth, it was also important to be able to provide sustenance for them all. Once the Armada arrived, they would need to provide their own food if at all possible.

He stripped to the waist and after an awkward start, thought nothing of wearing abbreviated trousers called 'shorts' with sturdy Earthian slippers to wear as he tended the garden. His skin turned a golden bronze and his muscle tone improved with every stroke of the hoe. Crops in the area benefited from the presence of a Phillipi with the power of Arda liquid at his command and the gift of wind and atmospheric control. Stuart could coax rain clouds to provide a beneficial soaking with no serious thunderstorms. When storms developed naturally, the storm cells never seemed to trouble the Iron Post vicinity. Stuart was subtle enough not to make clouds travel in an illogical fashion.

Carrol also did her part in the garden. She wore abbreviated clothing and piled her long hair up on her head, and in time she developed a tan as deep as her brother's. Glendon worked in the garden on the weekends for the sheer joy of indulging in his favorite hobby. Gareth helped from time to time since not only did he have the most practical experience at the venture than the others, but he could also not resist being around Carrol Shanaugh de Phillipi when she wore shorts and a skimpy blouse.

Darien would have been happy if all he did was turn over the healthy soil with a rake. Gardening was a relief to him and balanced his oil field work. The entire side yard along the driveway was eventually taken over for several kinds of squash, tomatoes, pole beans, melons, and greens. Darien also liked to go to the nearby creek and fish with Brent, and the two friends brought home a string of fish to grill every time. Once the harvest began, the Thuringi ate well. Glendon brought home jars with instructions from Mrs. Gentry on how to preserve the excess produce. Darien was curious about this aspect and took command of it. As usual, he went overboard, and they ended up with dozens of jars of preserved vegetables and no place to store them.

He marched out with a shovel to the opposite side yard and dug a deep cellar. He lined this with large rocks from along the creek bank and added several rows of shelving. Stone steps lead down to the cellar and he added heavy wooden crossbeams for a roof. He covered the whole thing with dirt from the excavation, and there was plenty of room for the jars.

"I wonder how long harvest season lasts," Glendon said one night as he idly leafed through a feed store calendar.

"It had best last long enough to fill the rest of these jars," Darien declared. "Word! Tomorrow we shall go on a berry excursion!" That was what they did, but they enjoyed the blackberries so much, they ate most of them before they returned home.

Stuart obtained a pair of scissors and one Saturday evening he sat down in a kitchen chair. "If I am to contact anyone on this world, I must appear like them. Would someone shorten my hair, please." Stuart's long mane of hair reached down to the small of his back. In the Thuringi culture, hair was worn at least shoulder length. Short hair was found only on the young and a few exceptions like Gareth and other mechanics. No one thought it important to clip off one's hair; trimming was often necessary but to intentionally shear oneself was an absurd notion.

No one stepped forward until finally Gareth took the scissors from Stuart's hand. "Are you certain, Stuart?" he asked. Stuart nodded. Gareth picked up a handful of hair in the back and lifted it. The others stood fascinated as they listened to the rasp as the scissors sliced into Stuart's hair at the collar line. Gareth placed the cut lock on a nearby table, took another cut of hair, and another. Soon Stuart had a very uneven pageboy haircut. Glendon took the scissors from Gareth.

"Let me try," he suggested, and Gareth gladly turned the duty over to him. Glendon evened up the length, but the hair was still wrong.

"It must be short, as short as... that young Kennedy chap, the president," Stuart said.

"That short!" Glendon declared. "Your ears will show."

"I know," Stuart sighed. Glendon went ahead and cut more. It was an awful sound, and they all cringed at it. Stuart's hair was not looking particularly good. Darien finally stopped Glendon.

"We are soldiers, not clippers," he said. "This sort of thing needs the hands of experience." He drove away in the truck and returned followed by Lloyd Martin and his family. The Martins were awed by the number of muscular long-haired people in the ranch house but were gracious enough not to comment. Darien's astonishing yellow eyes were matched by Stuart's, but the others wore blue contact lens that made their eyes bright green. The contact lens were not very comfortable for Carrol or Brent, but Glendon and Gareth had little problem with theirs. Monica sat nearby in a chair to watch the proceedings, and her hands grasped the chair arms tightly.

"(I asked them if they knew of an experienced clipper, and the wife said she would do it for us)," Darien explained.

"(You must clip me, too)," Glendon told her. "(I am attracting too many odd stares in the Gentry's store)."

"(And me)," Darien sighed. "(Damnation)." Monica giggled, and her mother quietly shushed her. Darien smiled at the little girl.

Carrol offered the Martins iced drinks as Katie set to work on Stuart's hair.

Stuart had slipped off his Universal Translator and could not understand anything Katie said, so he just smiled at her. She worked quickly until Stuart sat before them all with his hair trimmed neatly around his ears and short in the back, a part to the side in front with an even cut all over. It was a very professional, businesslike look from an Earthian point of view but to his kinsmen, Stuart looked like a six-foot-seven-inch five-year-old.

"You have such nice thick hair," Katie observed, running her fingers through it when she was done. "Lord, what some folks around here would do to have hair like this." She looked around at the other Thuringi. "I don't guess anyone cuts your hair where you're from." She patted Stuart's shoulder to indicate she was finished with him. He got up, and Glendon sat down before Katie.

"(No)," Glendon said. "(Most of us never had need of the deed before. Only in the front, for our vision's sake)."

Stuart repositioned the translator as he headed for the bathroom, where a mirror hung over the sink. He felt as if his head might float off his shoulders, it felt so light. "(Oh, God of All)!" they heard him exclaim. "(I am bald)!"

"(If you could, clip me a little longer)," Glendon whispered to her. He slipped off his translator with a smooth motion of his hands and none of the Martins noticed it. She smiled and whispered she would see what she could do. She cut his braid off in its entirety and fastened together the cut braid top with a rubber band to hand to him.

"Now you have a keepsake," she told him, and Glendon took the braid and stared at it as if in shock. She did not take any more length off. She trimmed his bangs and styled the sides to cover the tops of his ears and tapered from the ears back to just above the collar. "There," she said, pleased with the results. "You look your age now." He looked at Carrol for confirmation. Her eyes were wide, and she shrugged and repeated what Katie said, not wanting to agree or disagree. He thanked Katie and went to the bathroom.

"(I am a seven-year-old child)?" he asked forlornly when he returned.

"No," Katie protested. "Aren't you about nineteen?"

Glendon swallowed hard. "(Um, yes. Thank you for cutting me)," he said politely.

Stuart was back downstairs, ruefully scratching his shorn head. "(Well, it is close enough to Kennedy's length)," he admitted.

Darien sat down heavily in front of Katie Martin. "(This is a strange event)," he muttered. "(I am losing my hair in an effort to guard against ridicule. I hate this. I hate it all)."

"I'll try to leave you some length."

"(It does not matter)," Darien told her. "(If my brother can bear the insult, so can I)."

"What makes it so insulting?" Lloyd asked curiously.

"(It is a child's head of hair)," Gareth explained.

"What about you? Your hair isn't as long as everyone else's."

"(I am a mechanic. I must always trim mine so it will not become entangled in my work)." Gareth's hair came down to brush along his shoulders in back and his bangs and along the sides of his face was trimmed so he could see easier.

"(We just braid it or pull it back)," Brent explained, and privately mused, "(This way may not take so long to dry)." Katie cut Darien's hair the same way she did Glendon. Monica approached Darien as her mother worked and patted his hand sympathetically.

"I think you look nice," she told him.

He regarded her through half-closed eyes. "(You are a good-hearted child)." When his haircut was done, he addressed Lloyd. "(Will this suffice)?"

"Well, it's shorter," Lloyd said. "I don't see why it wouldn't."

"Now you look handsome," Monica whispered to him.

"(To an eight-year-old child, I am handsome)," Darien moaned.

"Anyone else?" Katie asked, holding aloft the scissors. She looked at Carrol. "Miss?"

"(No)," Gareth suddenly declared in alarm. "(Her Nibs should keep her locks)."

"(Carrol need not get a clipping)," Brent agreed.

"Long hair looks good on ladies," Lloyd said. "And hers is so long and pretty."

"(Carrol will not need any clip, thank you)," Stuart told Katie.

"(Good)," Carrol said with relief. "(The very sound of cutting unnerves me)."

"(Cut my hair)," Brent said, and rousted Darien out of the chair. "(I shall join my brethren into the abyss)."

"(You do not need to)," Stuart told him, although he was touched at Brent's sentiments.

"(But I will)," Brent said. "(Besides, it will dry faster)."

She cut his hair as short as Darien's, which exposed the diagonal gill slits on his neck under the ears. Katie said nothing but when her eyes met Brent's, he winked at her. Her glance asked the question as her line of sight flickered over to his gill slits briefly. Too late he realized the mistake of exposing them and decided to meet it head on. He whispered, "(Magic)!" Katie managed a smile at his disarming friendliness.

Gareth looked around at all of the clipped heads of hair and nodded. "(All right)," he agreed. "(All as one)." Carrol murmured sympathetically but was pleased he joined the others.

"You won't need much," Katie told him. "I'll just trim it all over." It was much shorter all over, but his change was not as radical as the others. She noticed that Brent was the only one with diagonal slits on his neck, and that he also wore a 'hearing aid'. When she looked at the others again, she saw that they all wore them.

"(You are very good with scissors)," Stuart told her, comforted now that he was not the only strange-looking Thuringi among them.

"Oh, I do this for a living, too," she told him. "My main job is at the grocery store, but I work part-time at a beauty parlor."

"(Beauty parlor)?" Darien asked, in a dreadful voice.

"I cut men's hair, too," she assured him.

"(Then we will happily compensate you for your work)," Stuart said, and would not hear of her protests otherwise. He paid her a hundred dollars.

"Oh, I can't take this!" she protested. "That's twenty dollars a head; nobody charges that much! Two dollars apiece is more than enough."

"(This should be your free time)," Stuart told her. "(To bring you out in the night to cut off so much hair should be worthy of a bonus. We could not do it ourselves, and we would not have felt comfortable with a stranger)." The statement was a gallant one since no one except Darien had ever met her before that night.

"Well, thank you," Katie said.

"(Will you have another drink)?" Darien asked Lloyd.

"No, we'd better go on home. It's Monica's bedtime. Monnie, say goodnight now."

"Goodnight," she told them, and squeezed Darien's hand. "You'll feel better when you see how handsome you look."

"(Thank you)," Darien said, amused.

"Oh Lord, my little daughter has a crush on my buddy," Lloyd laughed as he and his family headed for the door. "I thought it wouldn't happen for years."

"Daddy," Monica protested, embarrassed. The Martins left after promising to return for a feast hosted by the Thuringi. Monica fell asleep on the way.

"Lloyd, how well do you know them?" Katie asked as soon as she was sure Monica was asleep.

"I know Darien better than the others. You know it's strange about him: you can just tell he's holding something back all the time. I've seen him pick up a length of chain that weighed a good hundred pounds and treat it like it was light as a jump rope. He could probably break the necks of every one of those idiots at work with just one finger, but he won't. He doesn't like them, but he puts up with them.

Sometimes I think he's just testing us, or maybe he's testing himself."

"But why?"

"I'm not sure. It's like none of his folks ever met other people before in their lives."

"Should we be afraid of them?" She thought of Brent's unusual gills.

"Oh, I don't think so. I get the feeling that they are more scared of offending us than we should be of them."

"What do you mean?"

Lloyd scratched his head and laughed self-consciously. "I haven't got a good reason really. Call it a gut feeling but the more I get to know him, the more I think Darien Phillipi wouldn't hurt his friends for anything in the world. He might not let his enemies off the hook, but I don't think we have to be afraid. They're a lot nicer than most folks I know."

Katie agreed. Brent did not cause her any trouble at all. He was as friendly and cooperative as she ever met in a haircut client. She had never before met people who all needed strange-looking hearing aids or had yellow eyes. Maybe he was like a circus freak; maybe the Thuringi were all like circus freaks and did not need their differences pointed out to people like Pete any more than they already were.

"Yes, we all look so very handsome in our shorn locks," Gareth said, ratcheting his tone of voice to a high screech he called "the Royal We" voice. It was remarkably similar to the elegant if nasal way some of the noble Elders spoke. "We are ready to take on the world now." They laughed and cleaned up the fallen hair. Darien and Brent retained their braids as mementos, but Stuart only kept a few separate locks. He was philosophical.

"It will grow back."

A cold front came through that night, and they awoke to a chilly house. None of them said so, but the men thought their timing for losing their hair was poor indeed. Michael called that morning and suggested they arrange to get a load of firewood to stock up for the winter and went on to explain in detail how to start and keep a fire going. Glendon decided to purchase firewood from one of the store's customers.

The Gentrys liked his haircut and declared he looked just like their son. The other store customers were equally positive. One woman declared, "You look like a movie star!" She evidently considered this to be a good thing, although he was uncertain why. From what he had heard, movie stars did scandalous things.

Ed Gentry had him drive the store pickup into town for some gas and supplies. Glendon caused a sensation at the pumps. Girls from the local school also gassed up their cars, and they flirted with him so outrageously he almost forgot to pay. He drove back to the store, shaken by their interest. He preferred the former disapproving looks from older people to this sudden and overt attention from the young. The girls found their way out to the feed store as did other girls from their school the next day.

"I never saw so many girls wanting to ask about the price of chicken feed before," Ed Gentry chuckled. Neither had the girls' parents. Many fathers bewilderingly agreed to let their daughters pick up the chicken feed or the cattle salt licks or horse tack and feed. If the girls did not live on farms, then they came by to buy sodas and hang around. They derived a special pleasure in watching Glendon load sacks of feed into truck beds or stack them neatly in the store. One bold girl asked if he was dating anyone.

"(Dating)?" he asked. He was uncertain what it meant but thought it best not to admit it. "(No)."

"Well, would you like to go see a movie at the drive-in with me Saturday?" the bold girl with dark red hair asked.

Glendon did not know how to respond. They were supposed to contact Earth people, but this sounded like an unseemly way to go about it. "(I... I have never been to a drive-in before)," he told her.

"That's okay, you'll like it. I know you will."

"(I apologize but I do not think I can)," Glendon said awkwardly. "(I am too old for you)."

"I'm seventeen," she declared. "How old are you?"

One hundred sixty-one. "(Older than that)," he answered out loud.

"Sharon!" her father bellowed from a car in the parking lot. "Quit flirting with that boy and get over here, we have livestock waiting."

"Well, you think about it," Sharon said, and ran off to her father's car.

Glendon went home that day in a pensive mood. He told Stuart about his experiences. "The Gentrys seem to not mind at all; they said there are many more customers in the store than before, and that fact pleases them. But Stuart, I am a married Thuringi, and these little girls do not see me that way. It is uncomfortable. I do not enjoy being rude, but I do not want to be anything worse."

"It must be difficult to be so admired," Stuart said with a grin. "Well, Glendon, I do not see how a simple decline of invitation could be found rude. You are not encouraging it so she can hardly fault you for honesty."

"She is an adolescent Earthian girl," Glendon sighed. "It is my understanding they can find fault in an Elder for anything."

"But she does not see you as an Elder. She sees you as - what did Katie Martin say? A nineteen-year-old youth. Just show her your ring."

Glendon was visibly relieved, and he fondly twisted the silver wedding ring on his index finger. "Yes, I shall do that."

It did not seem to deter the girl. "How long have you been married?" she asked. "You're even wearing it on the wrong finger! Can't have been too long."

"It does not matter how long," Glendon told her. "Would you want your man to marry you and then dally with another?"

"No, I wouldn't," she admitted. "But... it's not fair; you're so cute." She turned and walked away.

Glendon was relieved and sat down on a stack of feed sacks wearily. Dealing with Earthians could be a struggle. It was fortunate that Thuringi wore wedding rings on their fingers, as did the Borelliat. Thelans wore specifically styled earrings and the Pleonians favored small nose rings. The Sturbin did not bother with wedding rings since such were inconvenient reminders to their lovers.

For the most part, Glendon's task was easy and interesting. The Gentrys were well regarded in the county and their little store was frequented by most of the populace for one reason or another. Glendon listened to conversations whenever he could and reported it all back to Stuart when he returned home. Local politics were hard to fathom since so much of it hinged on personality rather than work ethic.

Glendon paid no attention to local gossip, but he did take note of what was considered general proper behavior and what might cause a scandal. People were attracted to him and charmed by his polite demeanor. No one had a bad word to say about him, except perhaps the local Romeos whose noses were out of joint over having a stranger in town. Glendon attributed their attitude to mystery rather than his looks. Garins did not flatter themselves with self-praise; it was not seemly.

Darien got another round of ribbing from the roughnecks, but it was less than he had previously received. The incident in the bar and Stuart's warning saw to that. He wore his sunglasses only occasionally at work now, and the yellow glow of his eyes kept teasing to a minimum.

Stuart took Brent back to the spot in the Caribbean where the cache of Spanish doubloons was found, to gather more. They took them to Michael in Boston, where he helped sell them for cash. They gave him a generous share in it despite his initial protests. Michael treated them to a seafood dinner at a restaurant on Cape Cod. He was delighted to hear of their triumphs and voiced regret that he could not be there.

"I wanted to come back to Oklahoma, but I had a longstanding obligation up here since last winter. I can't just back out of it; it may lead to bigger and better things."

"One cannot disregard a promise," Brent said. "You should not disrupt your life simply because we wandered along."

"We are learning on our own, with your help on the telephone," Stuart assured him. "It teaches us to be more self-sufficient, I believe. At any rate it is the best outpost assignment I for one have ever had."

One morning Stuart went on into the larger town nearby after Darien and Lloyd went to the oil field. The marshmallow white truck was easier to drive because of their practice, and Stuart felt comfortable with it. Gareth would start work on the smaller reconnaissance planes after Brent's ship was completed, but they still needed ground transportation like this.

The town was like a marketplace on D'tai or Borelliat, only smaller and not as hasty. There was a warm peaceful feeling to the main street, where people greeted each other by name and were polite and friendly to strangers. He found a store with furniture in its display window and saw the beds he wanted.

The owner promised prompt delivery and wondered why this large man never took off his sunglasses. But what did he care, the owner told his equally mystified sales staff. "The guy just walked in and bought five beds and mattress sets and a complete living room set, all in cash. He can wear a turtle on his head and that'll be all right with me."

Stuart drove around town a little more and returned to the store. "(We will need the cold storage unit – refrigerator? Yes)," Stuart told the manager. He arranged for that to be delivered, too. Stuart paused in another area of the store, thoughtfully looking over the televisions. Michael said they were the best way of receiving news.

"Interested in a television? We have color sets, too," the manager said.

"(I am intrigued)," Stuart told him. "(Tell me more)." The salesman jumped into his spiel, and Stuart nodded thoughtfully.

The manager and his assistants loaded a console television into the back of his truck and promised to deliver the refrigerator that day. Stuart was pleased with his purchases and drove away. This manager told his associates, "If we can keep that fellow happy, we'll have a really merry Christmas this year."

Stuart went into a supermarket and bought bags of different fruit and vegetables, a gallon of luket and more chicken meat and eggs. Then he drove home, careful not to let the television slide around in the back by not overreacting with the steering wheel. Gareth was immediately taken with the television and had it ready in short order, complete with the aerial out on the rooftop of the ranch house. They switched it on, and Brent adjusted the aerial until they called out that the reception was excellent. He joined them, and they stood mesmerized by the current program.

The Secret Storm, as the title proclaimed, told the tale of tawdry behavior and manipulation among Earthians in a small town.

"Why," Carrol declared, "They have lifted a page from Brent Ardenne's journal!" He swatted her in reproach.

Gareth turned the channel. A pretty Earthian woman was dismayed over her naughty son's dirty clothes and swore that a wonderful cleaner would brighten her day and, presumably, her clothing woes.

Gareth turned the channel again. "This is a test, only a test. For the next sixty seconds..." intoned a serious-sounding man's voice, while a high-pitched noise sounded in the background. They all covered their ears.

When it was over, Stuart picked up the television guidebook the store manager gave him. "There will be news this evening," he said. "Until then, it is different stories of amusement."

Gareth flipped the channel again and came upon another serious sounding man droning on about educational television for the public. Gareth turned the set off. "Well, at least we will be able to understand the culture better without actually getting among them at every turn."

A heavy truck came up the drive, and Stuart consulted his timepiece. "That will either be our cold storage or more comfortable furnishings." He turned to Brent. "We will need more coins to trade soon. These items demanded a good deal of scrip."

Brent smiled in anticipation. "I will take one of your ships for the task. I hope the Isador will journey to claim a great deal of them soon."

The truck delivered their furniture, and the deliverymen were astonished the customers did all the lifting and carrying themselves. "That's okay, we'll do that; it's what we're paid to do," one protested to Carrol, who smiled at him.

"(Quite all right)," she replied as she picked up an oak headboard. "(You brought it out here to us, and that was our main concern)." Before they left, one deliveryman offered Gareth a job. Gareth explained he already had more than enough work to do.

Carrol and Brent tried their hand at frying the chicken, so Stuart drove to get Glendon and Darien. Gareth put the beds together and returned downstairs.

"Stuart neglected to get bedding," he told them.

Stuart slapped his head in self-remorse when told the news upon their return. "Oh, it does not matter, Stuart," Darien declared as he threw himself on his bed in delight. "It is a soft flat surface, and I am quite willing to do without superfluous sheeting for one night." He had never complained about his auto seat or his hammock, but his relief at having a real bed humbled Stuart. Since Darien actually complained aloud about the treatment of the oil workers, the hammock must have been even more excruciating for him than he let on.

That evening they watched the news and an entertainment show until they voted to turn the set off. "If she is that silly and obstinate, I believe I would do more than just tell her she has some explaining to do," Glendon grumbled about a character on the popular comedy. "If he were I, I would shut the door and tell her to get herself out of her own mess."

"But then she would bellow in that maddening squall, most likely," Darien remarked. "She is perhaps a good example of why some people should never marry and procreate."

Carrol went to her bedroom and found a fresh collection of flowers in her bottle vase. She peered out into the hallway and caught Gareth as he was about to enter his room. She smiled at him, and he winked at her. It was all they conveyed, but it would have to do.

Carrol went with Stuart into town and was surprised that several people called his name and waved at him. He waved back and chuckled at her expression. "These are very nice people," he explained. "Very nice, indeed."

They purchased sheets and blankets and pillows for the beds. They went home to discover a package from Michael Sheldon. Brent was impatient to open it and told Stuart and Carrol the beds would have to wait.

Inside the package was a rectangular box with two circular disks on top, connected by a flat thin strip of flexible material. A sign on one of the buttons along the top said, "Push Me" and that is what Gareth did.

"Hello there," Michael Sheldon's voice said through the speaker. "This is, um, kind of unorthodox, but I thought this would be easier for you than trying to read and translate my writing. This is a tape recorder, and I thought I ought to fill you in on some of the customs that are coming up." He went on to explain the other buttons on the machine, and Gareth pushed Stop.

"We should wait until the others are here," he suggested. "Darien complains that Michael Sheldon did not tell us everything we needed to know, and he should hear this proof that Michael is trying." Stuart agreed, and they went on about their business until Carrol fished around in the box and came up with more flat sweets.

"It is chocolate," Stuart told her. "The woman in the food store told me."

"It is good," Brent said. "I think we should plant some of it, instead of vegetable seeds in Glendon's garden."

"Aquatics," Gareth drawled in an excellent imitation of Brigadier

General Hartin Medina, an Air Command officer known for teasing Brent's father, "They could not farm their way out of a paper net." Brent snorted in amusement.

When Glendon and Darien came home, they all ate a large dinner of fruit. Afterwards they enjoyed their new furnishings in the front room and listened to Michael Sheldon's recording. He explained the seasons of the year, the holidays, the days and weeks of special note, the requirements of the government and the American monetary system. "At some point, you will need birth certificates, proof of birth. I know your mere existence should be proof enough, but the government wants proof on paper, a way to trace you. This might be difficult and possibly not what you need right now. Working usually means getting a social security card, but you have to be a citizen of the United States for that. You need to have a passport as an 'alien', a foreigner. As it is, you have no proof of who you are, so you can take one of two roads: either lie or forge false documents which I wouldn't recommend; or the rest of you, don't – do not - get jobs."

"Too late for Darien and me," Glendon declared to the air.

"I do not recommend lying, because if you want people of Earth to believe your story about the Armada, you don't need to start out with an already fantastic story and then lie about something. Everything will be seen as a lie then. Just stay as out of notice as possible. If you have a chance, get a radio or television." Stuart nodded, pleased he had accomplished this already. "I can call more often now that I'm in a steady schedule. I can still answer questions you might have if I can't be there, and you can later use your telephone to make arrangements for meetings with people you want to contact."

He went on to briefly describe the upcoming holidays. "In America, families often gather for a big dinner together in observation of the early settlers of this country surviving their, er, their outpost. Christmas will occur the next month, and there will be a big celebration in which people give other people gifts and pray for peace on Earth. It's to celebrate the birth of Jesus I told you about. Now, you don't have to join in any of these holidays if you don't want to, but it's generally a nice gesture if you do." He continued with similar thumbnail sketches throughout the year, what kinds of activities to expect and what might be expected of them.

After they listened to all of the tape Darien sat back, contented.

"So, I was wrong about friend Michael. He does care to guide us in our uncertainty."

They all made their beds in a flurry of activity, especially after Brent tested a pillow against Darien's head to test its sturdiness. There ensued a rousing quasch. Glendon still preferred his hammock, so the Phillipi brothers squeezed his bed into their room to give Brent a place to stretch out and sleep. He was well hydrated now and liked the warm feeling of covers over him. It also freed up the bathroom for anyone to use at any time during the night without disturbing him.

A week later, before the break of dawn, they rolled the Isador out of the barn/hanger and attached guides to it. Rather than tear the ship completely down, Gareth succeeded in encasing the spaceworthy ship in the Earthian sheet metal shell and refitting it to travel underwater. It would have taken far too long to cut through a Pleonian steel hull and Brent needed the ship now. Gareth's next project would be to cut down at least two of the other scout ships and create smaller fighter-sized ships. It would not be an easy task.

Suspended between four scout ships, the Isador was lifted into the air and flown to the Gulf of Mexico. UFO sightings were reported in a straight line through Texas. Once the Isador settled into the water and Brent and Gareth checked to make sure all seals were tight, they took her for a test run. The other four ships sat down on the island beach of Galveston, stunned at the expanse of sand and surf. Carrol eagerly gathered samples of sea life she found washed up on shore and put them in her ship to study later.

The Isador was smooth and trim, easy to manage despite its power. Brent took Gareth out until they reached the edge of the Continental Shelf, and he gingerly approached the edge. Gareth pressed forward. "If it leaks it would have done it by now, and if the engines fail you will be able to swim outside and perhaps drag it back to the edge. I have enough confidence in my work that it does not alarm me."

Brent was pleased with the Airman's courage and confidence. The Isador performed ideally. They sailed back to Galveston, Gareth testing the Isador's speed and responses along the way. They finally came ashore where the other scouts waited.

"On the weekend days, we will come and get you," Stuart told

Brent. "But on the weekdays, you can explore the Great Waters to your heart's content. Just be careful and check in with us as often as possible. You are the first Aquatic to scout a world, and we have no idea what is in store for you." Brent agreed readily. "For the now, you can go on out and explore. Your com is coming in quite clearly for us."

"I am ready," Brent said, and saluted. "Into the deep!" he cried out with enthusiasm. He boarded the Isador once more and took her back out to sea.

"Let us return to the ranch and we can monitor his progress," Stuart suggested. He, Darien and Glendon got into their ships and left. Gareth looked at Carrol, who climbed into her ship.

"Well come on," she invited, "before they realize what they have done." He climbed in after her. After a bit of testing out the logistics, he finally sat in the pilot's seat, and she sat on his lap. He put his arms around her waist, and she grasped the controls. "This should be interesting," she said, and they took off. They went over the least populated areas of Texas and Oklahoma they could in order to get back to Iron Post and the Sheldon ranch. He kissed the back of her neck playfully.

"You are wicked!" she exclaimed as she flew the ship.

"I am not," he told her. "I am simply sitting closer to you than normal."

"Normal; something you are not." She shrieked as he poked her in the ribs.

"Are you glad it is not a boot?" he whispered in her ear, and she settled back in his arms.

The overhead sun made it difficult for them to fly high unnoticed, so they meandered for some time through the sparsely inhabited countryside. They were in no real hurry to get back; they were comfortable as they were. His arms held her snugly around the waist, and she remembered the times she and Maranta flew in a similar way. His hands had been much busier with naughty applications; things that she wished Gareth could be at liberty to do. But her brothers and her Naradi waited for them, and she could only take comfort in the fact that Gareth enjoyed the situation as much as he might be allowed. Upon their return to the ranch, they found the other three ships in the back yard but the Thuringi nowhere in sight. They heard Brent's voice coming in over the com from inside the house, so they went into the front room.

"These are indeed great waters. There are marvelous creatures here, colorful, and tiny, great groups of them! There are large clear bulbous things atop the waters with long strings attached to them, the like of which I have never seen! I like this Earth, these waters! If I could fly and venture over quickly to the other great ocean, I wonder what I might find there! Gareth, is there any way I could do that? Is the Isador still capable of flight?"

"No, she can either swim or fly, as I cannot master both with the primitive tools and supplies that I have on hand. Patience, my friend; patience. It is a lesson we all have to suffer," Gareth told him.

"Master Sword and Fist; how good of you to join us!" Darien exclaimed, patting Gareth on the back. "Did the two of you get lost?"

"No, but it is nearly impossible to land a Thuringi scout ship at the front door of an Earthian bar, no matter how hard you try to be inconspicuous," Gareth replied. "We had to settle for returning here in hopes of snatching the keys to the truck away from Glendon."

"A bar? You two went searching for a bar?" Brent exclaimed over the com. "Gareth, you treasure potables over fair company?"

"I did not say that," Gareth said wryly. "But two brothers and a Naradi would tell me to."

Brent laughed, and the other three joined him. Carrol came to stand next to Stuart, who hugged her companionably. He glanced at Gareth and saw him absorbed in Brent's conversation, personal interest in the Thuringi princess set aside for the moment. They spoke a little more with Brent until the signal became weaker. He was far out into the Gulf now and the com broke up. He signed off.

"I have little faith in Earthian satellites," Gareth admitted. "They are unhandy."

"That is the most cheerful Brent has sounded in a very long time," Glendon remarked. "We should have thrown him in the ocean a long time ago just to shut him up."

"All hail the master builder, Gareth Duncan!" Stuart declared. "I think a visit to an Earthian bar is a grand idea to celebrate the triumph of our engineering marvel!"

"I certainly have racked up the hours for it. Well, not that it matters here."

"I have currency from Lord Gentry," Glendon announced. "I believe we should all go out and become... what was it you said once, Gareth? Wildly, splendidly, foolishly drunk."

"Just splendidly drunk. Wild and foolish is not a good idea here," Darien recommended.

"How says Darien this, the man whom no law binds?" Carrol asked in surprise.

"We are not royalty or Naradi or recognized geniuses on Earth," Darien said. "We are only foreigners with yellow eyes. Our purchases have alerted the local populace to know of our accumulating fortunes, and they might encourage wild spending. From what I heard in the bar, rowdy drinkers are often jailed for over-abundance of enthusiasm and over-indulgence of libations." He looked at each of them. "I for one would not care to be jailed with the type of people I work with. Murder of such in a cell is a charge too tempting to garner. Remember the lessons taught by the Gunsmoke and the Bonanza: their Naradi will place us in a barred room full of nasty people with foul habits, and someone will be shot or struck on the head with an object."

"Then we must not over-indulge," Stuart said. "They have all seen your eyes; they know we are different. We shall keep to ourselves and quietly celebrate."

Darien brightened. "Then, let us dress in our best and do it!"

With Glendon driving and Darien riding beside him to navigate, the other three Thuringi rode in the back of the pickup to the Anchor, the bar Darien visited with Lloyd. When they arrived, there was hardly any place to park; it was Saturday night, and the locals were ready to unwind. The Thuringi parked down the street and walked, making certain their translators were all switched on along the way. It was not their size or their number that made people turn to stare at them when they entered the bar. Too late, they all realized that none of them wore dark glasses and in their excitement to celebrate, neglected to wear their contact lens.

"Well," Darien muttered in an aside to them, "Now we shall learn our true measure." Gareth spotted an empty table, so he walked over to it and moved the empty glasses to the middle of it. The others followed him. They all sat down, as if they were not all well over six feet tall and possessed yellow eyes. Darien gestured to a waitress; conversations started up again and the jukebox kept playing its songs.

"I'll be with y'all in just a minute," the waitress promised. She cleared their table as fast as she could, with hardly a look at them.

"(It is quite all right)," Carrol told her kindly. "(You have many patrons here; we realize you are very busy)." The waitress looked at her then and saw no reason to be afraid. They did not seem like devils in person.

"Y'all ain't from around here, are you?" she asked, and Carrol shook her head.

"(No, but we thirst the same)," Darien told the waitress. "(We would like a round of beerz at your earliest convenience)." His way of saying beers seemed to amuse her.

"Okay, big fella." She carried away the empty glasses to the bar, where she was immediately swamped with questions by the bartender and several customers. She came back with five bottles of beer. "Everyone's kind of curious about you folks," she explained. "I guess you're all related?"

"(We are from the same village)," Stuart said, truthfully enough.

"In England?"

"(Y... yes. We are from that direction)." The other Thuringi smiled knowing how Stuart could not bear to tell a complete lie, yet reluctant to speak the bald truth in this situation.

"Well, I guess I can serve you boys," she said with a nod at Darien and Gareth, "but you other three are going to have to show me some I.D. before I can serve you."

"(Why)?" Glendon asked in dismay.

"Honey, you have to be over twenty-one to drink beer in this state," she said sweetly.

"(But I am well over twenty-one)," Stuart protested belligerently.

The waitress fixed a knowing look on him. "Honey, please. I can tell a kid with a fake I.D. from a mile away, so don't even haul it out." Darien laughed at the look on Stuart's face and spoke up.

"(No, my dear, he and I are twins)," Darien offered, and she smiled at him.

"Then I guess I can't serve you, either."

"(Well, I tried, little brother)," Darien told Stuart in a complete about face, "(And do not go squalling to Mother about it, either. You will get a spanking)." Stuart dropped his mouth open with a biting face. "(Get the boy and his little siblings a wizzar... a soda, and get my friend and myself, a nice cold beerz)."

"Two beers and three Cokes, coming up," agreed the waitress, and she went away.

Darien looked at the three soda drinkers impassively. "We are here to celebrate, are we not?" he asked. "Here to celebrate our good Major Sword-and-Fist's great triumph."

"You are only happy because you will get a beerz," Glendon laughed at Darien. "You would be in as bad a state as Stuart if your hair was shorter."

"I am more dignified."

"You are more worn," Stuart finally said, disgruntled but accepting. They paid for the drinks when they came, and Gareth tested his beer.

"Are these people as testy about their potables as the Thelan?" he asked Darien.

"No, I do not believe they are."

"Good then. Phew!" He made a face but went ahead and drank his beer. "They are inadequate in everything, but perhaps in time they will improve."

The waitress approached Stuart again. "Are you really over twenty-one?"

"(I swear by all that is holy to me, I am aged beyond twenty-one years)," Stuart said solemnly. She handed him a beer and winked.

"Don't tell where you got it," she whispered, and he favored her with a broad grateful smile. "But the kid there," she said, indicating Glendon, "is going to have to drink his soda, and your sister, God; she shouldn't even be in here. Do you have a driver's license, miss?"

"(No)," Carrol answered honestly.

"Not even sixteen; that's what I thought," the waitress sighed.

"(No, I simply do not have a license. How can I when no one lets me practice)." Carrol pretended to glare at Glendon, who gave an exaggerated shrug. The waitress shook her head in amusement and returned to her work. As long as they did not look anyone in the eye no one was bothered by them as the evening progressed. They were able to toast to Gareth's success and future successes with gusto.

"Do you mind if I have a dance?" an Earthian with a wide brimmed hat on his head and a checked shirt and denim jeans asked Carrol.

"(No, go ahead)," she replied, and realized when he took her hand, just with whom he intended to dance. She looked worriedly at Stuart and Darien and glanced at Glendon and Gareth as the man led her out to the dance floor.

"Even strangers may dance with her," Gareth noted, a trace of melancholy in his voice.

"Look how closely these Earthians dance with each other. God of All, Stuart, what would Father say about this?" an annoyed Darien asked his brother. "Oh, let her be handled about by some istay in an outpost cantina, is it perfectly all right? Well, not to me," he said, and turned to Gareth. "As your Warrior Prince, I order you, Major Duncan, to re-capture our Carrol immediately and guard until further notice."

"I am her Naradi," Glendon said as he rose to his feet.

"Sit," Darien ordered. "You are her 'brother'." Gareth looked at Stuart, who nodded. Gareth rose and approached the couple.

Carrol was displeased by her treatment. This strange man who smelled of the abominably brewed beerz and of burned leaves, held himself against her with one hand holding one of hers out to the side and the other hand around her waist to force her closer to him. She kept her gaze down and away so as not to meet him eye to eye. "(Stop that, sir, you are far too disgusting for words)," Carrol said bluntly.

The man just laughed. "I love to hear you British gals talk. Say something else to me, like... what's your phone number?"

Gareth put a firm hand on the man's shoulder. The dancer turned around ready to say something, but the look on Gareth's face and the blazing yellow eyes convinced him to stay silent.

"(The lady is mine)," Gareth told the man in no uncertain terms, "(and you will release her to me at once)." The man did exactly as he was told and eased away. Gareth took his place with one hand on Carrol's waist, and the other held her other hand out to one side. "How interesting a stance. Perhaps your father would not object to such as this." He looked her in the face and smiled. "Hello, Your Nibs. Are we enjoying this little Festival?"

"We are now," she assured him. "What a disgusting man he was. The smells were hideous."

"One must learn to tolerate such behavior if one is to look the way you do, Your Nibs."

"And what way is that, Royal We?"

He smiled. He was not even using his Royal We voice. "We believe Your Nibs looks quite irresistible." They inched together a little more as they danced.

"And what are we resisting, sir?" She enjoyed the look on his face when she asked.

"We are resisting our impudent thoughts and unseemly musings of late," he replied, and glanced at the other dancers. "There are others who dance more daring than we and think nothing of it. I am uncertain our people will feel comfortable in such a freewheeling society."

"I want to be first in line to see the Bishop's face," Carrol snickered, and they both laughed. He found her body against his own solidly. He pressed the side of his head slightly against the side of hers as he saw the other couples do. She closed her eyes happily.

"It is a custom of dancing, here," Glendon observed from their table, "yet it does not seem wrong, does it?"

"No, it is rather appealing," Stuart said. "Older persons are doing the same, with dignity," he noted with a look around at the rest of the crowd. "Can you imagine Mother and Father dancing that way?"

"Why, they more or less do anyway, largely because it is the only way Mother can. Can you imagine, say, Hartin Medina squiring Lady Melina about like that?" Darien chuckled as he said it.

"Yes," Glendon said. "I believe they experimented a bit at Festival, after our Gareth and Carrol's unheralded moment. I can see that, yes. I can also see the same with Janis. In fact, I intend to teach it to her the minute we reunite." The Phillipi brothers were greatly amused by this.

"So much for the stalwart guardian of the Princess," Darien snickered.

"She is a grown woman; against whom does she require a guard?" Glendon asked. "If you want my humble opinion, all your father needs to do is give Gareth Duncan free rein. Look at him; deterring all comers!" It was true. Men came up to cut into the dance, and Gareth firmly shook his head like Carrol. The men were turned away, and the happy couple resumed gazing into each other's eyes. "The man is a one-woman Naradi."

"Can you see your fair Aura dancing like that?" Darien teased his brother.

"No," Stuart said flatly. "Not unless a pistol was pointed to her head by the Bishop himself." The comment did not have a jesting tone to it, so Darien decided to let the subject drop. He glanced at Glendon, who gave the naughty prince a thoughtful nod.

The Princess Aura does seem to have a rather stiff neck, Glendon thought. It cannot be easy to be married to such a difficult woman. I must remember to keep my own private life pleasant for Janis's sake since I must belabor under my own clan's expectations.

The song ended and Gareth and Carrol returned to the table. "Your Highness," Glendon said to her, "I have decided that I am going to persuade my wife to dance in Earthian style at the next Festival we attend. Would it be a disgrace to practice this with you for a tune? I promise I will not behave familiar. I am your Naradi," he explained.

"Yes, you may practice with me," she agreed, and they went out to dance. Glendon was awkward about the outheld hand, and they laughed about it while he experimented with the bend of his elbow.

"So that is why you enjoy dancing so close with our sister," Darien said to Gareth. "You are not bold; you are merely far-seeing." Gareth nodded as he watched Carrol with complacent delight.

"Gareth, you are indeed a breath of fresh air," Stuart told him. Gareth looked at him curiously, and the crown prince said further, "There is no telling what that imaginative mind of yours will come up with next. You are already able to blend in with Outlanders." The dancers returned to the table.

"Perhaps we can practice at the ranch," Carrol offered. "A public place is a difficult rehearsal hall." The sound of an argument was heard over the din, followed by the sound of fists striking flesh.

"A quasch!" Darien leaped to his feet, his eyes bright with anticipation.

"Oh no, this is a cantina fight, and you will not get into it," Glendon objected with a cautious hand. "The Gunsmoke has cautionary tales of these, as well."

"We had best be on our way," Stuart suggested, and placed a folded bill on the table. "We do not need to get in an outpost fight." They left quickly, and Darien gave one last look of longing toward the sound of a promising fight.

The waitress picked up the folded bill after they left. All this for a few beers and sodas? What a tip! I'll be sure to welcome anybody with spooky eyes from now on, she thought.

"What happened then?" Stuart heard Darien ask Glendon the next morning.

"You know perfectly well what happened."

"No, I do not. After Gareth danced with my sister, the evening became misty for me. Did we have that quasch?"

"No," Glendon laughed. "It was hardly the proper course of action, Darien. We came home instead."

"Oh, you always find the proper course," Darien grumbled good-naturedly.

"You do recall the quasch just before we left, correct?" Stuart asked in amusement. "I should think you would know we did not join in it. We returned here."

"Why would I wish to recall something as forgettable as going home? I would rather remember a good fist fight."

Chapter 4: Earthian Ways

Brent's initial excitement at exploring the Earthian oceans was tempered by his first good look at a Portuguese man-o-war and noticed the number of fish entangled in its extensions. He recognized a predator when he saw one and as the Isador moved along in the water, he realized how fortunate he had been. Sharks and barracuda and sea snakes were beautiful creatures, but he was completely ignorant about them until now. They were as bad as the parmenters and scorrups of Thuringa. He told himself to be more cautious when exploring outside the Isador. He was the only Aquatic scout, and it would be quite easy to be killed on this alien world, and his airbreathing kinsmen might never know what happened.

Still, he was not afraid of anything except being caught by Earthians. He had the Isador to protect him while he slept; he had a laser pistol and a sword for hand-to-fin fighting and his ship resembled an Earthian killer whale so much, no human could tell from a casual glance that it was made of metal. It would take a good hard inspection up close to tell and Brent did not plan to get close enough for anyone to discover his secret.

There was so much to see, so many places to go! These were not like the Thuringa seas which his ancestors mapped and explored until there was little to discover any more. This was all new to him and even a mystery to the Earthians who lived on this world! Brent started his exploration log and made notes, charts, and captured images, and knew he would never be able to thoroughly cover everything. He would have a good time in the attempt, however.

He was curious about a world with such a grand series of oceans and no Aquatics to live in them. Thuringa had only one ocean that covered much of the world's surface. Technically, Thelan had no oceans, only millions of large freshwater lakes. Senga's ocean covered forty percent of its surface, but their beaches were rocky. There were very few deep natural harbors on Senga. D'tai's two oceans were the only things left on its world that were not thoroughly mapped, regulated, and utilized efficiently, but Father said it was only a matter of time before every fish on D'tai was tagged and registered like the rest of the planet.

Earth was seventy percent ocean, full of variety and color and beauty. Brent busied himself with mapping the oceans with the help of the Wet Dream's computer. He cataloged points of interest he discovered: undersea volcanoes, shipwrecks, coral reefs, drop-offs into the abyss. He had so much to study in the tropics that he did not venture anywhere close to either pole. He observed human behavior at sea and was appalled at their relative lack of seamanship. "Oh, you fellows are just begging to have Father give you a scolding," he laughed aloud as he watched fishermen dragging in a net.

Brent Ardenne was accustomed to peacetime Thuringa, where Aquatics lived in relative harmony with Airmen. When he came across a 40-foot yacht drifting with the tides, he became curious. There was no activity or sounds after two hours of observation. He boarded the yacht at its aft deck cautiously, keenly aware he would have to leap over the side at once if anyone discovered him. He noticed at once a sickly odor, but he recognized what it was only a second before he saw what caused it. He was so repulsed that he immediately threw up his latest meal.

A man and a woman lay side by side dead, their bodies swollen grotesquely in the tropical heat. Brent had no idea when or how they might have died, but from the haphazard way their limbs were positioned, theirs were not peaceful or willing deaths. Blood had pooled and dried beneath the bodies where they fell. Brent Ardenne was unfamiliar with homicide at firsthand, but this was surely it.

He staggered back to the end of the boat and leaped back into the water, aghast at what he had witnessed. He boarded the Isador once again. He steered it away for a few lengths and then sat and brooded for a while.

What should he do? It was pitiful to simply leave the couple there, but he could not bear to board the ship again. He saw enough of the dead and dying on Thuringa. At last, he adjusted his universal translator and turned the com to a frequency he had discovered was used by the American Coast Guard. Not knowing radio protocol, Brent's contact with Americans was remembered for years after by the Coasties:

"(Ah, yes. You coastal chaps need to come see to the dead people on the vessel The, ah, The Scurvy Mate. They are in a dreadful way, you see)."

"Copy that. What is the location of the vessel?"

Brent was stumped. He did not have access to Earthian sea coordinates; he used his own Thuringi methods for determining locations. "(I am east of the island of Pewerto Rico)." He was proud to be able to identify that much.

A pause. "Roger, how far east?"

"(I do not know. I have no means of determining the distance for your use)." He almost added, What cheek you have to assume my name is Roger, but he was asked another question.

"Sir, how is it you are asea without proper instrumentation? Do you at least have a sextant?"

"(Do I what)?"

A different voice came over the com. "Unknown call, please identify yourself."

"(I am the man who came across two dead people in a large white ship)."

"Your name, please."

"(Oh for the pity of it! What does it matter what my name might be; there are dead people out here! Now you chaps ought to come and fetch them and give them a suitable burial; your society does that sort of thing, do you not)?"

The American tried again. "What is your port of call?"

The unfamiliar terminology coupled with the horrific sight he just witnessed stretched Brent's nerves to the edge of breaking. "(I cannot understand a single thing you mean! What is a portovcall)?" his voice rasped into the com.

"Sir, could you at least give the name of your ship?"

Finally! "(At last, a chap who does not speak in riddles! Yes, this is the Isador)!"

"And what port did you sail from? Where is your ship registered; your home port, your city?"

"(I have no city and I have no register. You know if you do not wish to retrieve these people I understand. They are quite disturbing a sight, but you should know right now, I am certainly not going to do so)." He switched off the com in disgust. "How cheaply is life regarded here; just leave bodies to fester in the cruel sun at sea! Ugh!" He decided to leave the area. Sooner or later a storm would swamp the yacht, or it would eventually wash up on a shore somewhere. Brent did not want to sink it himself since there was bound to be identification on it somewhere and the families of the deceased deserved closure if possible.

The Isador had not gone far when a Coast Guard cutter appeared on the horizon. Brent dropped his ship to just below the surface so he could see what would happen, and he turned on his com again to listen in.

"...I repeat, we have a ship in sight, one ship. Over."

"Not two?"

"Negative."

"But they can't have left the area that fast! Is that the caller's ship? Over."

"No...no, it's the Scurvy Mate, out of Miami. We are preparing to board her."

"Roger."

Word, they name everyone Roger here! Brent thought with annoyance.

Some uniformed men leaped aboard the Scurvy Mate, searched topside and then went below. They returned topside and radioed in what they found. "Base, there appears to be a triple homicide here, a man and a woman at the wheel and another man below deck with a fired weapon in hand. All three appear to have died execution-style. Just offhand I'd say smuggling."

Despite the gravity of the situation, Brent had to stifle a snicker. In the Pleonian language, to smuggle was to be caught with one's pants down during something private or embarrassing, as if suddenly being seen by the public while defecating or pleasuring oneself. These Earthians had peculiarly similar words to Stellar Council worlds even if the definitions differed.

"We'll send out a team to investigate and bag the bodies. You don't see any evidence of the Isador in sight, over?"

"Negative! It's downright creepy. Over."

Brent could not resist addressing them on the com. "(You simply do not know where to look)." He took the Isador deeper before he turned off the com and left the vicinity and the Coast Guard crew, who scrambled all over the place trying to figure out where he was.

Curious about this quarrelsome race of "Communiss", Stuart took the Good Lad to the U.S.S.R. to investigate. "If we had landed in their country instead of Michael's, we might have a completely different way of looking at Earthian matters," he told Glendon one evening. "I will see these powerful people and try to determine how large a threat they are to us. But do not let Darien know I am going! I will go during day hours here for the cover of dark there, and Darien will not come with me and perhaps cause unwarranted mischief."

"I should come with you. This is a dangerous outpost at times," Glendon said with concern.

"I would rather you remain here in case Darien or Carrol have need of you. I am an Air Command Warrior, and I will take extreme caution. I only wish to observe what I can."

"I am not much of a Naradi Famede."

"We are all scouts on this world, Glendon. It is true we need protection in the scope of our roles as members of the Thuringi Royal Family at times, but there is so much to learn that having a Naradi Famede is more of a luxury for the now. Your task at the Gentry store is extremely valuable and we need you there very much. I am not toothless; I will take full responsibility for my well-being and Father will be made aware of it."

"Yes, but if anything happens to any of the three of you, I will have to answer to your mother! Trust me, Stuart; no one wants to tell Oriel Phillipi de Saulin such a thing. She is a lovely soul, but her wrath would be terrible!"

"For your sake, Glendon, I will take the utmost care," Stuart promised. "I would not want to cross Mother, either."

He took the Good Lad after Darien and Glendon left for work. He flew close to the treetops until he was in a safe enough area to lift off without being detected. He then flew the ship to the center of the Soviet Union. Since the ranch in Oklahoma was in the center of America, he thought he might see how the Soviet counterparts lived.

To his astonishment, he found a vast forested land, far different from the highways and towns of Middle America. He came upon a small village and studied it carefully with both his eyes and his ship's sensors. He followed the rivers until he came to other villages, each as humble and nondescript as the first. He flew east in search of other cities. The country was so vast it took him all day to explore it even simply flying in a straight line. When the sun rose over the land, Stuart got his first good look at the Soviet Union.

He was dismayed at the lack of modern equipment and goods. The ordinary people appeared to live quite different, very difficult lives than their American counterparts. Their farming implements were cruder and less efficient than the sleek American tractors, and he saw little of the sights he saw on expeditions in America – where were the ball game fields? Where were their grocery stores and livestock auction houses, where were the gleaming automobiles and motorcycles? Many of the people dressed in all manner of clothing to keep warm but had little of the flair Stuart saw in other countries. It was a bleak place. Why were Americans so concerned about this country? he wondered. They cannot even look after themselves.

Even in the sleek modern large cities, there was an undercurrent of need. Goods similar to America's bounty were available as long as the citizens had the scrip to obtain it.

It was power, he realized, the power of threat and intimidation that fed the Communiss reputation. Like the Shargassi, the Soviets relied on their reputation to pave their way for them. Their weaponry and ruthless willingness to use it kept them in power. As long as they were a secretive nation that did not reveal its secrets, that power would go unquestioned. Stuart found himself challenged by Soviet aircraft over Minsk.

"Unidentified aircraft, identify yourself!" a stern voice commanded over the com. They even spoke similarly to a Shargassi accent, and a cold chill ran through the crown prince of Thuringa. The only comfort he had was that those were definitely not Shargassi ships.

"(Why)?" Stuart asked. It was translated into Russian, and the Soviet pilot grew irritated.

"Identify yourself or be shot down."

"Not this day, sir, nor ever in your lifetime." Before the astounded Soviet squadron, the strange triangular ship suddenly streaked away faster than anything they ever witnessed before. Fortunately for the Thuringi, Soviet Russia did not divulge this encounter to the rest of the world thanks to their secretive society, and the alien visitors remained a mystery. Back at the Soviet base, however, a huge uproar took place.

"They sounded British but that was no British spy plane. That was no American plane, that was... that was incredible," the lead pilot told his superiors. "But they spoke in Russian quite fluently!" The

Soviet Air Force was on high alert for several weeks after that and their relations with the British was strained even more. They did not press the point, however. If the British had access to a ship that could fly that fast and that silently and not show up on radar, then it was in the Soviet Union's best interests to stay quiet and increase their spy network. None of their operatives knew what they were talking about when asked to find out about large triangular ships that flew far past the speed of sound.

Stuart returned after dark, and Darien demanded to know where he had been and why no one knew where he went. Stuart shook his head at his hot-headed brother.

"Darien, I have been doing reconnaissance work as is part of my task, and I went to see about the threat of the Communiss. As far as I could see, the only reason Michael's people are alarmed over the Communiss is because they have powerful weaponry. America has far, far more power in its cohesive infrastructure and its network of communications and technology availability to its population. The Communiss have grand land tracts but the people themselves in a territory equal to our ranchland's seem woefully poor. Goods are plentiful here as long as one has the scrip to exchange for it.

"Perhaps if we had come to the Communiss first, we might believe America as a sprawling, prideful nation of greed and excess who does not share with its fellow Earthians. But we can see from Michael Sheldon and the Gentrys that this is not so; there are many Americans who are kind and generous. Perhaps in Communiss there are good-hearted people as well, there are bound to be. For that supposition, there is no one against whom we should raise a hand."

"Then why do they boast of grand military might if their people are poor?"

"You are asking the wrong person, Darien. I do not understand the basic Earthian mindset of miserly living. But I do understand that we are fortunate to be here in this safe house in this land of plenty. Here, I have an idea – come with me." He took Darien to the Soviet Union himself, and Darien saw the great disparity between the simple villages and the bright glory of Moscow. "You see, Darien: America is not the only country with those who have and those who do not. This land boasts of every citizen being of equal status, but we can see for ourselves that it is not. It is like a rotund D'tai businessman looking into a warped mirror and seeing himself fit and trim; they are fooling themselves. We cannot hope to help these people if they will not even help their own."

"I suppose you are right," Darien admitted. "But oh! Such lovely forests, such grand mountains! It is as if they have so much land, they do not know what to do with it. And yet they want to take over even more lands. Bah! They are all greedy people, these Earthians."

Stuart sat in the dark front room, deep in thought. It was late and his fellow scouts were in bed for the night. Everything was still and peaceful; he could at last gather his thoughts. He liked the comforting feel of the rocking chair Glendon got by trading some of his feed store coin. The farm cat was allowed in at night as long as it was not in the same room as Brent when he came home. It now took command of Stuart's lap. Stuart liked to pet it and coax it into purring. Cats were unknown creatures on Thuringa, and they fascinated Stuart. Brent hated them and claimed the cat always tried to bite him.

There was only a sliver of a moon visible, and the night creatures were all in full riotous song. It was a beautiful world. The more Stuart tried to make sense of its people and their behavior, the more confused he became. In a world of plenty there were so many in want. In a peaceful setting like this it was hard to believe that there were wars and strife elsewhere. In a world that had kind generous people like his neighbors, there were also terrible people doing cruel injustices to others.

He was baffled by the Berlin Wall and had a difficult time describing its purpose in his scouting report. The idea of walling half a city in the middle of a country that was divided from the rest of its country was insane. To divide families over politics – madness! Democracy and communism were each convinced of their own greatness, yet neither ideal was capable of working without the right people at the helm.

Voting for those right people had its hazards despite being as fair as it seemed to be on the surface. Placing someone in power simply because of what they said to those making the choice? How was one to know the truth? What would stop them from saying anything whether it was true or not? How could this be better? Communism in theory was a good idea, but it did not work in practice. On Earth there were still the haves and the have-nots. There was no equal access to all goods evenly across the land. Those in power had the power to abuse and they did so with impunity.

There were pockets of wild people on this world, people who knew of no civilization whatsoever, and the thought of these people still in a primitive state unnerved the Thuringi. The disparity between the industrialized nations of the world and natives in grass huts was unfamiliar on the Stellar Council worlds. There were kingdoms on this world, but the teeth of royal power had been filed down by the notion of democratic rule until the beast was nearly toothless.

That kind of news would be of great concern to Lycasis and heard eagerly by the likes of Elder Asa Mennar. Asa had long been displeased with the Royal House of Thuringa. He was always one to fight authority in any form and age bolstered his animosity past merely being cantankerous. He fed upon the power that came with dissension and used his position on the king's council toward that hunger. Lycasis once explained to Stuart that keeping Asa where he could keep track of the troublemaker was more advantageous than booting him out of sight.

Every Phillipi in every rule knew of the awesome responsibilities of guiding the kingdom of Thuringa, and at no time in all those centuries had a Phillipi monarch let the people down. However, there would always be those who could not be satisfied even in the best of times. Stuart dreaded to think that perhaps now, at the lowest point of the history of Thuringa, someone might use the whims of fate to their advantage against the Phillipis in order to chase the empty promises of elected rule. Now that he thought about it, he was anxious to settle the outpost and get back to the Armada in case those sour to the crown chose the dearth in royal numbers to start trouble.

On nights like these, Stuart liked having the rhythmic pace of the rocker and the soothing purr of the cat to ease his nerves and encourage his patience.

Carrol plaited her hair into a single braid and let it hang down her back. She intended to walk to the feed store with a shopping list for Glendon and did not want to fuss with tangles in her hair from the stiff Oklahoma breeze. She glanced out the kitchen window to check on the whereabouts of Stuart and Gareth. The barn doors on both sides had been pushed wide open in order to let in as much light as possible until it occurred to them that the skeletal form of the new ship could be seen from the road and might attract unwanted attention. Carrol went to the barn since the front-facing doors were closed again. Gareth spent months painstakingly dismantling two ships' Pleonian steel hulls. He now welded those pieces of steel to the base of the newer, smaller ship. Stuart held the pieces in place for him.

"I am setting out for the store now," she told them. "Are you certain there is nothing else you want Glendon to bring back?"

Gareth stopped welding and pushed back the dark goggles to rest atop his head. "You can let them go now," he said to Stuart.

Stuart turned to Carrol. "Are you certain you want to walk in? Would you rather just wait until he gets back tonight?"

"That would entail another trip into town for him. I do not think he should do a lot of driving without a proper license," she said. "I will enjoy the walk through the countryside! I might get some good samples of vegetation along the way for my research collection."

"Let me see the list, then," Stuart said, and took it to study. Carrol became aware of Gareth as he stood quietly beside the partially built fighter. He watched her as if drinking in the sight. She shook off the thought; she was being entirely too egotistical. Gareth was fond of her, yes, but he had much more on his mind these days and it was vain of her to think otherwise. She smiled a tentative smile at him and was rewarded with his bright breezy smile.

"Going out among the locals at last, eh, Your Nibs?" he asked as he wiped off his hands with a cloth. "You might want to take a pistol."

"Do you think I should?" she asked, surprised. "But these people are not violent."

"I did not say they were. You still might need protection, though."

"Whatever for?" she asked, unable to imagine why.

He did not move any closer to her but remained where he was. His gaze began at the top of her golden head and made a leisurely inspection down her figure. She wore a light blouse that buttoned in front, and each button seemed to unfasten in the mind's eye of his gaze. He took in the way the snug fit of the jeans clung to her hips and shapely legs. His gaze swept back up slowly and delectably. By the time his eyes locked back in on hers, she felt herself trembling under the caress of his look. Gareth smiled warmly but said nothing, and the sensation of his attention electrified her.

"Do you think I should bring a pistol, Stuart?" she stammered to her brother. Stuart was adding a couple of items to the list and thought her question odd. He glanced at Gareth, then back at Carrol.

"Of course. This is still an outpost for us, Carrol. Just because we feel safe here does not mean we should carry on as if nothing could bring us harm. Suppose there should be an outbreak of violence among the Earthians, and you are caught in the middle? Suppose the Shargassi or perhaps some unknown race should stumble upon this world? Get your pistol and wear it under your garments." Gareth cocked an eyebrow and pursed his lips, then deliberately winked at her and grinned. Carrol snatched the list from Stuart's hands abruptly and went back to the farmhouse. Stuart looked at Gareth curiously. "What did you do to my sister?"

"Nothing," Gareth replied, even as he wondered if he had gone too far with her. She was a princess, after all, not some rowdy who was too far into a bottle in a cantina to think straight. He promised the king he would be worthy of her, and this was not the way to go about it. "Let us get that little piece over there and see if we can fit it in this space," he suggested, heading for a piece of scrap metal. Stuart shook his head and smiled. One moment the erstwhile mechanic was actively flirting with Carrol, and the next he was fully back into his work. That Gareth could compartmentalize his thoughts completely amazed Stuart, who would have had some mental bleed-over.

Carrol tucked her laser pistol into the pocket of a jacket and started down the driveway at a comfortable pace. She took a deep breath of clean fresh air and suddenly thought what a fool Lia Hellick de Neo was. Trapped in marriage with Tomas Hellick in the cold reaches of space was bad enough, but the fool rushed into matrimony after turning down Gareth Duncan! Knowing firsthand how even a few moments of Gareth's appreciation felt, Carrol wondered how the woman could have walked away from him. She had to rush away from the barn lest she threw herself into his arms and beg for something more physical, despite the presence of her brother. No one else made her feel like that since Maranta, something she never thought would happen.

She was aware of Gareth's reputation in the bedroom for the

entire time he looked at her. Even that reputation paled compared to the promise of those passionate eyes. She was hungry for that which no Thuringi woman could openly confess, and she was doubly glad for the walk into town. Physical exertion might put aside her desire for another kind of physical exertion.

She enjoyed the fair morning walk, and the five miles passed quickly. She walked into the Gentry's feed store and saw Glendon immediately. He crawled along the top of some feed sacks stacked in a loft area. He smiled cheerfully and waved in recognition and then continued his way across the sacks to a ladder.

"May I help you?" asked a friendly feminine voice beside her. Carrol turned, startled.

"(Oh! I was looking for Glendon)," Carrol explained.

"You must be his sister. I'm Margie Gentry." The woman introduced herself as she shook Carrol's hand. Margie Gentry was much shorter than Carrol and plump as a sedentary D'tai matron. Her dark hair was streaked with gray, pulled back into a tight bun at the back of her head. "We really enjoy having your brother here working for us. I don't believe I've ever seen anyone as strong as Glen before."

Carrol smiled and nodded, noting the way Glendon's name was shortened. Did all Earthians shorten names that way and if so, why? Were they in that much of a hurry? Did it have anything to do with their rushed way of living or their short life spans? She and her brothers often called Brent 'Brenton' simply to tease him. In Thuringi, brent meant 'powerful stroke', whereas brenton was a Thelan term for a noxious weed.

"You know, I keep meaning to invite you folks over for dinner some Sunday, and I never seem to be able to what with the holidays coming up, and all the rush for winter seed and such," Mrs. Gentry continued, which drew Carrol back to the immediate.

"(That is very kind of you)," Carrol told her. The entry door slammed behind her, and a strong, strident woman's voice boomed out.

"Why, you're that English girl who lives over to Darryl Sheldon's farm," said the tall rawboned woman with thin cheeks and intense birdlike eyes who approached Carrol. She wore a blue hat with a large blue plume attached to it, and forever after Carrol simply thought of her as the Bird Woman. "I'm Agnes Derby; my husband is your mailman. I know you're a long way from home so if there's anything you need you just let him know. We're always happy to help newcomers. But now, you're too young to be a bride from the war – oh goodness! You must be Mike Sheldon's wife!"

"(No, I am not)," Carrol corrected gently. "(I am not married at all)."

"Agnes, this is Glen's little sister," Margie Gentry began, but the angular woman continued on as if neither of them had spoken.

"Mike should have married a long time ago, if you want my opinion, but I suppose better late than never. He's got a good head on his shoulders, but of course, it never hurts to marry an oil man."

"Agnes, she's not married to Mike," Margie said louder than before. "Hush up and listen. She's Glen's sister."

Glendon made it down to ground level by then and approached the trio. "Hello, little sis," he greeted the way Brent did. "What brings you here?"

"(I have a list of things we need)," Carrol said as she handed him the paper.

Agnes Derby craned her neck over for a closer look. "Why, I never saw writing like that before," she said. "That's not English."

"It is a foreign language," Glendon told her. "Our mother is a linguist, and we learned it from her." Carrol admired the glib way Glendon was able to make up a story on the spot, as well as his command of American speech. He did not even need a translator anymore.

"Well, why don't you just write in English like everybody else?"

"It keeps nosy people from knowing all our business," Glendon told her, his expression guileless and his voice friendly. The tip of Agnes's nose quivered slightly.

"Well, I declare!" she stated, and went out the door of the store in a huff.

"I am sorry," Glendon said to Margie.

Margie allowed the grin on her face to blossom out. "You know, it's your charm and your accent that kept her from bellowing at you," she told him, and confided to Carrol, "I think she's taken a fancy to your brother. Can you imagine, a gossipy old cow like her, all moon-eyed over a boy a third her age?" Carrol giggled until she wheezed, and Margie continued in amusement. "By tomorrow morning, she'll have it spread all over the county that Glen gets smart when his kid sister shows up to visit. I say, so what? I think it served her right. It's none of her business what other people do. If not for the fact that it's a federal offense, I wouldn't be surprised if she opened people's mail just to be able to get better gossip. But she doesn't because her husband is an honest man and won't let her." She patted Carrol on the arm as she turned back to her register. "Now, don't be such a stranger from now on; you're welcome here any time! What's your name, honey?"

"Carrol."

"Oh, that's a pretty name," Margie said, and left them alone.

"She is very nice," Carrol told Glendon.

"She is. So, do you need all of this? Very well." He folded the paper and put it in his shirt pocket. "Did you walk down here?"

"Yes. It is so beautiful here. Can you imagine –"

"Hi, Glen," came a trio of young voices from the doorway.

He smiled weakly and waved, but he whispered to Carrol in a fierce, almost panicked way. "Please, please, do not leave until they are gone. Please, sister dear."

"Who are they?" she whispered back.

"A dangerous species: predatory young females." He cleared his throat and announced to the girls, "How pleasant. You are just in time to meet my sister Carrol."

The three teens were obviously as taken with Glendon as the mailman's wife. One of the girls had red hair, a hair color rare among the Stellar Council worlds. Even though Glendon was uneasy in the girls' presence, he could not help but gaze at her hair.

The teens immediately zeroed in on Carrol, and one with the lovely red hair spoke up. "I'm Sharon. Are you going to go to school here?"

"(Me? Of course, not)," Carrol laughed, and would have dismissed the thought if not for the quizzical looks on their faces.

"Well, in America, you have to go to school until you're sixteen," Sharon told her. She blew a pink bubble from her mouth until it popped, and she continued to chew on the pink material. She linked arms with Glendon and smiled at him in a saucy way. "You're full of surprises, Glen. You never said word one about having a sister here."

"I am full of surprises," he agreed, but he looked at Carrol. "I never noticed how young you look comparatively speaking, but it is true. It is astonishing."

"Why, how old are you?" The girl asked Carrol.

"She is sixteen," Glendon quickly told her.

"Me, too," the girl named Sharon said. "Say, wait! If you're his sister, then you can tell me this: where is Glen's wife? He keeps saying he's married but I've never seen her."

"(She is at their home)," Carrol replied. She wondered if it was an answer that would help or hinder her Naradi.

"Oh, yeah? Back home, over in England?" the redhead asked with a broad smile. She cuddled closer to Glendon. He looked away uncomfortably as the other two girls giggled. Glendon's sterling reputation was never in question and Carrol did not like to see him so ill at ease. He was an exemplary Naradi, among the best of the best, yet he could not use a sword to cut himself loose from this predatory female.

"(Oh yes, and she is absolutely gorgeous)," Carrol told the girl. "(I have never seen anyone so madly in love as Glendon and Janis)."

"Then why isn't she here?" Sharon countered.

"(Oh, well because she is back home straightening out the last little girl who tried to divert his attention)," Carrol said with nonchalant ease. It was a simple premise to present and Glendon thanked her with a grateful look in his eyes.

"What happened to her?" Sharon asked, loosening her grip a little.

"(Janis happened to her. She is very territorial)."

"There's always a gaggle of girls around your brother," Margie informed Carrol from behind the counter. "It's those movie star looks of his and those big green eyes. I tell you, the girls here are just heartbroken that he married so young." She drilled Sharon with a piercing look. "But he is married, and I doubt that your mama and daddy will appreciate your hanging around a married boy."

Sharon scowled, but evidently decided the older woman was right. She and her friends left, after singsonging 'goodbye' to Glendon on the way out.

"Janis would be proud of you, brother," Carrol laughed, and gave him a kiss on the cheek. "I believe I will stroll back home now and leave you in the capable security of your superior." He swatted her with a yardstick in reply.

Jay Michael Jones

Carrol walked back to the ranch and gathered samples of plants as she went. People stopped and offered her rides, but she politely explained she walked for exercise.

Stuart and Gareth were on the porch at work on the air pressure ductwork for the ship. Stuart stretched his leg out and nearly tripped Carrol as she passed by him.

"That was suspiciously like a prank," she observed, amused at the impish look the Good Lad brother gave her.

"Would I do such a thing," he said mildly. Gareth chuckled.

"And you put him up to it, I suppose, Royal We?" she asked. Gareth sat back on his heels and grinned at her.

"You are awfully skeptical, Your Nibs," he replied. His shirt was partially unbuttoned for comfort's sake, and the scarf of hers that he wore around his neck was plain to see. She remembered her mother's observation that should a man wear an article of clothing from a woman, it suggested they were next to each other's skin. The thought made Carrol blush, so she hurried inside before she said or did anything to betray her thoughts.

Gareth glanced quickly at Stuart, but the prince no longer paid any attention to his sister; he concentrated on the ductwork. Gareth kept busy as well and wondered if his earlier foolishness overstepped the line of proper behavior. Perhaps she did not approve of his flirtations any longer.

Glendon brought home everything from Carrol's list, as well as some very ugly fish. They were a gift from the Gentrys. Instead of scales they had skin, and their heads were flat with whiskers on either side of the mouth. Carrol screamed in fright when she saw them, so shaken that Darien suggested Gareth take her out to the porch. Darien, Stuart, and Glendon prepared the mysterious creature as Margie had instructed. The first thing the men did was to cut away the heads and get rid of them. The farm cat was eager to help, which explained to the Thuringi why the ugly creature was called a catfish.

"Only a cat is brave enough to look at a face like that and still eat it," Stuart guessed, and the other two cooks solemnly nodded in agreement.

Gareth sat beside Carrol on the porch swing. She still trembled, even as she gave a little laugh at herself. "Can you imagine, I am being so silly," she said shakily. He put his arms around her, and she turned to him and nestled her face against his neck.

"Nibs, you are starting to alarm me," he said gently to her. "I cannot remember seeing you distressed this way over a creature. What is it, dear one?"

"It is just so ugly and slimy and... it looked evil, simply evil," she whispered.

"Do not think about it, then. Think of something pleasant. Think of... think of those pleasant-smelling flowers that grow over there by the corner of the house. Think of how bright blue the sky was today. Did you have a pleasant stroll into town? You did not say when you returned." She nodded and felt the hard strength of his arms around her. Her racing heart slowed its rapid pace and she snuggled more comfortably against him. He could not withhold a gentle caress. "Ssh, it is all better now," he whispered.

"It was a pleasant stroll," she ventured at last. He made the swing rock back and forth with a gentle push of his feet.

"Nibs, I feel an apology to you is in order."

She turned her head in order to look at him without lifting her head from the comfortable cushion of his chest. "Whatever for?" she asked, stumped.

"I think perhaps my behavior earlier today has set you on edge somehow. I was completely out of line in the barn this morning. You are someone I respect more than any other living soul and I had no business behaving so commonly towards you."

"You have always shown me the greatest respect, Gareth, and it is not as if we have had no other encounters with each other. We are so closely guarded now; it only accentuates that which is forbidden to us." She curled up snugly to him. "You have the most mischievous eyes."

"Mmm. They are appreciative, I will grant you that." They could hear the three men inside the house tease each other as they prepared the meal. He was uncertain how long that would take so he was reluctant to reveal his heart's truth in any further detail.

"Gareth, tell me a story. A lovely story," Carrol requested.

"I am not a very good tale spinner, Your Nibs," he warned, and kissed her forehead.

"Then tell me how your parents met."

"Oh, they knew each other all their lives and grew up in Carzon only a few miles from each other. They attended the same poddack, attended services at the same hour, attended the same Festivals, everything. He was granted a farm to tend when he was still quite young and worked hard to develop it. Mother went to Gallina to attend a special weaver's academy in her twenties, so they did not see each other for nearly thirty years. He farmed and ranched in the interior, and she learned to weave by the sea. She traveled to Arne and Fellensk to learn more of her craft before she finally returned to Carzon. Father told me he was half-heartedly courting a lady at the time, just to keep from boredom, really —"

Denys Duncan was torn between being lonely on his ranch out in the wilds of the country and so busy with newborn livestock and burgeoning crops that he could not sit down without falling asleep. He was considered a 'town Duncan', since the majority of the clan lived all throughout the mountains of Thuringa as wildlife managers and vegetation specialists. Denys did not even like a town the size of Carzon and purely hated a large city like Arne. There were too many people and not enough gakkis for his liking.

The local medical warned him not to work so hard and to get away every now and then to relax a little and clear the bran dust from his airways. Denys went to Festival with his parents and attended church services when life on the ranch permitted, and every ginta or so he visited the Bale, the local cantina. Life was slow and sure, and he kept himself busy.

He was seated on a bench on the village square to cool off after loading his wagon with seed grain. He chatted with passersby since he knew everyone in the area, and they all liked him. The early morning bustle of the village slowed down as the rhythm of the day bowed to the effect of the warm sun. The breeze made the tree branches in the village square dance overhead, and the scene was as idyllic as any could be. A former neighbor tugged at Denys' hat as he went by. The neighbor wore an Air Command uniform and Denys almost did not recognize him.

"You remember my sister Maribel?" Slate Gordon asked. Denys shrugged and nodded. "Well, she returned home this past ginta from her studies and feels a little out of sorts after so long away. If you see her go by, be a good chap and give her a hello to make her feel welcome, will you?" Slate hurried away to return to the Carzon Air Command base in time for inspection. Denys was about to climb onto his wagon to go home when he spied a woman down the pathway walking toward him. She was a short Thuringi at five-foot-seven and her disposition was so cheerful it was as if every moment was a newly opened gift. She saw him and slowed her pace ever so slightly the closer she drew to him. She had an inner confidence just on the edge of brash. He thought he had never seen such an appealing face: oval shaped with high rosy cheekbones and a pert little nose. Denys stared and remembered her from years ago when she was a tiny imp in braids scampering about the cathedral steps before services. He would never have guessed she would turn out to be such an alluring little thing.

Likewise, she remembered him from when he was a laughing, singing consue student, always surrounded by friends. She used to climb a particular tree at their farm's fence line as a girl in order to glimpse him as he rode by. He was so busy checking the fence for needed repairs that he never noticed the admiring little girl in the tree. By the time he returned from Agricultural Academy, she was already away to her studies in Gallina.

Her gaze never left his as she approached. Finally, she stopped abruptly a few feet away from him. For a moment neither said a word. Finally, Denys spoke. "I attend the tenth hour Atest at the top of the ginta," he said as if they were already in the middle of a conversation.

"I will be there," she replied. He got in his wagon and drove away. He looked back at her once or twice. She continued on her way but also glanced back at him.

At the top of the ginta on the tenth hour, they met at the base of the steps leading into the Carzon cathedral. "I am Denys," he said without preamble.

"I know. I am Maribel."

"Are you living with your parents now?"

"Yes, until I find a place of my own."

Denys smiled. "I plan to call on you, you know."

"You had better," she replied saucily. They went inside the cathedral and sat beside each other. After services he took her home, and they were practically inseparable after that. Denys told the woman he was seeing that another heart called to him, and he could not deny his interest in the call. He got a slap and a scold, but ultimately the woman recognized he had always seemed reluctant to call on her, anyway.

Denys and Maribel courted slowly, for Maribel was often recalled to Arne or Fellensk for special weaving work using her special talents to repair old tapestries. Denys had several problems in back-to-back years, including flooded grain fields, wildfires, runaway gakkis, and an experimental aircraft that plowed up and burned almost half of his crop one year. Except for the aircraft incident, everyone in Carzon had the same problems so none was a reflection on his ability to farm. Things settled down. As the ranch improved his grant was finalized, and he could court Maribel in earnest.

He added a large room to the farmhouse for Maribel's looms and machines and materials. They married at an extremely early age to Maribel's brother's way of thinking since Thuringi waited at least a century before marriage, but her parents approved of the match. Denys, the common-born civilian, did not believe in making his heart wait any longer and neither did Maribel. They married in the cathedral they had attended as children on the day after Maribel's seventy-fifth birthday.

"Fifteen years later, she gave birth to a perfectly obnoxious little boy who could not be kept from tearing things apart to see how they worked," Gareth chuckled. "They had fifteen quiet personal years, anyway."

"And she knew all along he was the one for her?" Carrol asked dreamily. As his story unfolded, she laid her legs across his lap and her fingers toyed with the scarf around his neck. All earlier fears of ugly fish were purged from her mind, replaced by Gareth's warm reflective voice and a tale of everlasting love.

"I suppose she did, at that," Gareth said. He had the feeling that they were being observed. He looked over his shoulder and saw Darien, Stuart, and Glendon listening at the doorway.

"Do not stop," Stuart objected. "It is a fascinating story."

"Oh, that is mostly it," Gareth told them. Glendon cleared his throat, a Naradi at the ready. Carrol reluctantly brought her legs around in order to sit properly in the swing.

Darien grinned at his sister. "We have managed to prepare what we believe to be a remarkably able meal," he told her. "Unless of course, you prefer to dine solely on the rising light of the moon and a delicious love story."

Carrol stood up with determination. "I am not going to let some hideous creature dictate the terms of my life," she said. As she walked past Darien, she reached up and pinched his nose. "Or allow a fish to frighten me, either." He swatted her on the seat, and they had a brief quasch match as they made their way into the kitchen. "Where is it?" she asked with a trace of dread toward the set table.

"It is the little brown slabs on the plate there," Darien said as he held her chair for her. The meal did not look dreadful at all, and after a tentative taste Carrol discovered the ugly fish made tasty fillets. Every meal was a new experience in the variety of life on Earth. They also had boiled rice that evening, which the Thuringi found to be wonderful, a very Thuringi kind of dish.

The rest of the evening was fairly uneventful. Darien washed his oil field clothing as he did every evening. The odor of petroleum was strong, and it made all three Phillipis nauseous. Glendon and Gareth did not like the smell, but they were not affected as adversely as the royals. Stuart always bought more clothing for his brother since they could not bear the oil smell to stand even overnight on Darien's clothing. It was a sad smell and reminded them of the final days of Thuringa.

Glendon and Stuart worked at mastering the American language as diligently as children in a poddack. Darien told them about a man at the oil field who could not read either. "His own language and he did not take to schooling in it," Darien said. "He does not seem incapable of learning, however, so you would not be the only persons here who cannot read." Gareth helped Carrol prepare some of her vegetation samples for research until bedtime.

In the wee hours of the morning, they heard muffled cries from Carrol's room. All four Thuringi men tried in vain to fit into the doorway to her room at once. Stuart got in first and turned on the light. Carrol was asleep but she was flinging at her arms at some unknown enemy in her dreams. The sudden light woke her. She gave a squeak and scrunched herself up, her bedding pulled up around her.

"What are you doing?" she asked in confusion.

"Dear one, you were having a fright in your sleep," Stuart soothed. He sat beside her on the bed.

"I was? I was," she realized. The men were relieved to know it was only night fright and not a physical grievance. "I saw myself swimming in a grain field, and it became water and all of a sudden these parmenter were heading for me, and they became those ugly fish—" her words became more rushed as she described her dream, and Stuart patted her hand soothingly. She caught her breath and looked sheepish.

"I was afraid this would happen." Stuart turned to the others. "I will sit up with her for a while. You should all go on back to bed." Darien and Glendon saluted her and trooped out since she was calmer, and her older brother looked out for her. Gareth smiled at the sight of her tousled hair and wide-awake eyes surrounded by a blanket.

"One would assume you have mastery over the beasts, Your Nibs. After all, it was you who ate them last evening," he told her.

"I know," she sighed. "Dreams seldom make sense."

Gareth went back to bed. Stuart turned on a small lamp by Carrol's bedside and turned out the overhead light. He sat back down on the bed and took his sister's hand. She lay back on her pillow.

"I am afraid I have no charming, comforting stories like your Major Sword-and-Fist tells. You will have to be content with – why, what is this?" He saw the copy of the Tarinade on the table under the lamp.

"Nothing," she quickly replied.

"Carrol Shanaugh de Phillipi, you have a naughty book," Stuart chided. "Well, I will not read you any bedtime stories from that! Where did you get it? Oh," he chuckled, as she gradually brought the covers up over her head. "From an admirer. You had best put that away, little sister. Father would not approve of your possession of a banned book, nor would it be wise of you to read from it any more than you probably already have. Er... you have not shared it with anyone, have you?"

"No. He gave it to me as a prank, to torment me on the trip here. And we have never had opportunity to share it, thank you for being nosy."

"Carrol, I do not ask you out of nosiness. I ask you out of concern. He is very attracted to you, that much is obvious. But at the risk of sounding like an Elder you must take this relationship with caution. Many, many eyes on the Armada will inspect this mission and some of them are already hostile to the idea of you and Gareth's interest in each other. If they perceive any impropriety between you, it will not fall equally upon your heads; they will likely put the entire blame squarely upon his shoulders. I do not want to see that happen. God of All knows the struggle you already have with the Elder's List. Do not let it ensnare you as it did – well, just try to maintain decorum between the two of you."

She nodded. "Stuart, do you approve of our interest?"

He smiled gently. "Of course, I do." He kissed her forehead. "I approve of anything that makes a good soul like you happy." He picked up the medical textbook Michael sent. "I will practice my reading skills if you promise not to dream about Earthians reading naughty books." She giggled and closed her eyes as he struggled to interpret American.

While exploring the area around the ranch, Gareth and Brent discovered a spot in the nearby river where the water was deep enough to accommodate a swimming Thuringi. They brought the other four to it and spent a delightful weekend day swimming and fishing and enjoying the summer breeze together. That evening they brought home a string of fish to grill. The swimming spot became a favorite place for any of them to go for decompression, a necessity as the days grew hotter, tempers grew shorter, and patience was tested by ill-timed pranks.

Glendon saw no amusement in the girls who came to flirt with him at the store, and their skimpy outfits and sandals left him embarrassed by days' end. He preferred to take a quick refreshing swim in the river before he got home, since Carrol Shanaugh de Phillipi's Thuringi beauty only served to remind him of his wife Janis, which in turn reminded him that Janis was billions of miles away and he was lonely. His nerves were often jangled by the curious questions of townspeople, and he was uncertain just how to answer some of the more detailed queries. He knew nothing of England and could not name any of the towns he supposedly 'lived near', and he was constantly concerned about being caught in a lie. It was a relief to unwind at the river and not have to be on the spot at every moment.

Gareth felt like a little boy again as he shimmied up the large trees and leaped from the overhanging branches into the water. For a brief time, the cares and responsibilities of constant work were gone, and he could frolic as he did as a child in Leiff River back on Thuringa. He did not have to listen to the Phillipi brothers argue politics or listen to Brent tease him about Carrol. He could also swim with her and as long as he remained in waist-deep water, he did not have to guard against physical reaction to her allure.

When Brent set out to explore the seas again, he and Stuart went deep into the jungles of the world to collect samples of plant life and organisms uncommon to their outposts' environs. It was one of the few times Stuart ever knew of Brent being cautious, but once he learned of the kind of damage that jungle creatures like piranha or snakes could do, he was glad his friend asked for help. Stuart thoroughly enjoyed exploring Earth, particularly where humans did not go. They were never so far away that they could not be summoned back to the ranch in case of emergencies and were able to bring back many things that interested both Carrol and Darien. Carrol wanted to catalog and investigate the samples, and Darien was interested in seeing how useful the plants were.

Occasionally Darien went on the expeditions with them. To Stuart's relief, his brother did not need to work every day and was usually so fed up with his oil field co-workers he did not want to visit the local Earthian bars. Instead, he went to cities around the world and bought liquor with the help of his universal translator. These bottles he brought home so they could all enjoy a leisurely drink without having to leave the ranch.

Chapter 5: Winter

Gareth shivered as he came down the stairs early one Sunday morning. It was unusually cold in the house, and he opened the door to the front room wood stove, expecting to see it dark. To his surprise, the embers glowed red hot and the area immediately around the stove was comfortable. It was the rest of the house that was cold. He added some logs and soon built a roaring fire. He adjusted the flue and went into the kitchen to start up a morning meal. At first, he merely glanced out the window, then snapped back in surprise and stared out.

"Stuart!" he yelled as he ran into the front room and up the stairway. "Stuart! Darien! Everyone, up! Look outside!" Querulous voices from all over the second floor sleepily wondered what all the shouting was about. He stuck his head into the Phillipi brother's room.

"Get awake, Your Brotherly Nibs! I have never seen anything like this. Glendon! Get up, reprobate! Guard your window!" he called from the hallway to his roommate. He went to Carrol's door and knocked.

"What is it? What is happening?" Carrol called out. He entered, went over to her window, and motioned for her to come. As she did, she rubbed her arms against the cold. He embraced her from behind and covered her arms with his.

"Look, Your Nibs." They faced the window. "Is it not a wonderland?"

The tired brown landscape from the evening before had been transformed overnight. In the early hour of the rising dawn the earth was blanketed with a soft mantle of white as far as they could see. The black trunks and limbs of trees were topped with a white icing. Millions of little white flakes fell from the sky in a whirling dance with the whims of the wind.

"Oh," Carrol gasped. "It must be snow; I did not realize it would come here. How beautiful it is, Gareth; like magic."

Glendon came in to stand beside them at the window. "I thought it was a picture painted on my window glass, but it is all around. They will never believe this back on the Armada."

It was true. Thuringa seldom had snow except on the highest mountains, and that was mostly ice. It could get bitterly cold elsewhere, but the scouts and much of the Armada had never experienced snow where they lived before. The ice and snow the Armada harvested to replenish the water supply was taken from icy worlds by fully automated ships.

"Why is it so blasted cold?" Brent asked and stopped short. He exhaled a concentrated breath, and his voice squeaked as he said, "Look, the very air is seen."

"The fire in the stove is raging," Gareth told him. "It is just that cold."

Stuart laughed with anticipation. "I am going out to investigate this snow. Who is with me?" They all scrambled back to their rooms to get dressed.

Darien was already downstairs at work on the stove by the time they descended. The front room was cozily warm now and the windows fogged over. They wore as many layers of clothes as they could find, and their most recent purchases of heavy coats were treasures now. They gathered at the front door and opened it. The frigid air struck them like a blow. In one accord they all exclaimed in dismay and shut the door.

"Last one out is an istay," Darien dared. He opened the door and hurried out. They followed him into the wonderland.

He leaped off the porch into six inches of snow and stepped high out of his own footsteps. He forayed a few yards before he stopped to look back at his progress. The others did likewise. Glendon fashioned a ball of snow he saw a person do on a television show. He threw it and it made a satisfying smack against Darien's back, sticking to it like a large piece of fuzz. Darien whirled around with a devilish grin. The battle was on.

For the next thirty minutes, the front yard of the Sheldon ranch was alive with the tall, powerful alien warriors who screamed and yelled and laughed like little children, each trying to hit the other with snowballs. It was a romp the likes of which the onlooking cattle never saw before. The cold finally convinced the happy scouts to go back inside to gather around the stove and laugh about their play.

"We will have a distinct advantage if this is included in a future Festival," Stuart whooped. "What a time!"

"Look how it melts around the stove," Gareth noticed. He knocked a little off his coat sleeve to observe the sizzle on the hot metal.

"Your nose is red," Carrol laughed at Darien.

"So is yours, and his, and his," Darien pointed out.

"It is not like this everywhere," Brent told them, and the weather bulletin on television confirmed his words. "I like this planet more and more. The variety is astounding. It was warm down in the Gulf on the Isador."

"Glad you came back now?" Glendon asked him.

"Oh, yes. Are you glad it is the week's end?"

"Sundays-off at that! The entire day to play in cold white!"

When the snowfall abated and the sun crept out at mid-morning, it looked new all over again. The sunlight made the blanket of snow shimmer in its icy glory, and the icicles along the edge of the roof were like crystal swords. Darien broke some off and brought them in for inspection under Carrol's analyzer. Glendon made the morning meal and from time to time that day they went back out to play and explore and get cold.

Gareth finished installing a heater upstairs in the bathroom. It was a unit taken out of his scout ship that he intended to install earlier but something more important to work on always took its place. Now, this was the more important deed.

"How difficult will it be to make more of those using Earthian materials?" Stuart asked, handing him tools as needed.

"If I could get my hands on the right things, not difficult at all," Gareth told him. "We may need to go on midnight foraging runs, but it can be accomplished."

"You mean we need to steal a few things," Stuart clarified.

"Well, not steal, I suppose. We may need to borrow a few items from their metal refuse locations. I was thinking about arranging for another vehicle from one of them; one that is not too damaged. We may be able to exchange a nominal amount of folding coin for it. While we are at it, we can get some vehicle heaters from them for the rest of the house. I can fix up something for us."

"What did we ever do without you, before?" Stuart marveled.

"You mostly led dull, boring lives, Your Crown Nibs," Gareth said as he finished up and put his tools back in his portable kit, "punctuated occasionally by the odd Kellis match." Stuart chuckled, and Gareth turned the heating unit on. They warmed themselves.

"You seem to have a positive impact on Carrol," Stuart said in contemplation.

"And she on me," Gareth replied. "I may very well be able to hold a proper conversation with almost anyone when we return to the Armada." He cleared his throat. "Perhaps even with your father."

"From what he has indicated to me, he likes your somewhat improper conversations," Stuart assured him. "Whatever you choose to say to my father concerning Carrol, you will have my backing."

Gareth looked at him and smiled gratefully. "Because I am handy to have around?" he asked in jest.

Stuart stretched as he rose to his feet. "Well, you seem to have a knack for repairing broken hearts as well as broken machinery." He ruffled the hair on top of Gareth's head as he went out of the room. Gareth closed his eyes and sighed with happy hope in his heart and took his tool kit back to his room.

It was dark earlier now and the warm cocoon of the house encouraged them to stay indoors for the evening. They ate a satisfying meal of vegetable stew and slices of thick bread that Carrol accomplished in the oven. The smell of the bread was a delight to the nose, and they laughed remembering their first day on Earth, when the idea of biting into dry bread was unpleasant.

Michael Sheldon called them nearly every week to check on their progress and answer questions. He would be home this Christmas, he told Stuart on the phone that evening. Stuart had many questions about democracy and the electoral process, having learned about the Kennedy election.

Darien cleaned the dishes not because he liked to, but because it was his turn, and he was unable to talk anyone into trading with him. When he was done, he joined Glendon in front of the television to cater to their weekly indulgence, a western series.

"Sad that a man loses three wives, yet retains three hard-headed sons," Glendon remarked.

"Better than the other way around," Darien pointed out. "Would you want three hard-headed women, when even one might be a trial?" Glendon threw his head back and laughed.

Brent was usually aboard the Isador by this time, but the weather encouraged him to stay and watch the show with them. He wrapped himself up in a blanket and sat before the console television. "I like the gakkis," he declared. "The spotted one is a beauty. Michael

Sheldon should get one like that, here."

Gareth and Carrol sat on the couch and shared a blanket. It could be successfully argued that they sat so close together for the sake of keeping warm, and no one could object to entwined fingers on hands which could not be seen. The occasional stolen kiss was appropriated at delightfully frequent intervals, as avid western saga critics Darien and Glendon caught Brent up to date with the stories from an alien planet's past. The crown prince/head chaperone was busy discussing politics on the phone with his Earthian friend. When Stuart finally ended his conversation with Michael, he asked, "Is this not a grand evening? We are cozy and warm – some especially so," he said, letting the couple on the couch know he was aware of their activity, "all in the happy comfort of what must be one of the most pleasant outposts I have ever served."

"What did Michael say?" Glendon asked.

"He will be out to visit on the twentieth of December, in time for the celebration of the Jesus birth."

"I am to attend a celebration at the school on that night," Darien informed them. At their surprised response, he explained. "Monica Martin made me swear a solemn promise to view her portrayal as a sheep in a child's pageant at her poddack," Darien said with a sigh.

"You do not sound very happy about it," Glendon told him.

"I was coerced by a slip of a child, and I could not back out without serious repercussions."

"She would have cried?"

"Like a rainstorm. It is unreasonable pressure."

"I fail to understand why you let that furry creature inside when I am here," Brent declared as he wrapped his blanket around him tightly in order to discourage the yellow tabby cat nearby. "He bites, and it is always only me."

"Leave him be, he is a comforting thing when he makes that rumbling noise in his throat," Carrol protested.

"Foul beast," Brent threatened the cat, "I will smack you well if you try for me again."

"You are imagining things," Stuart told him. "I shall take you back to the Isador tomorrow. The two-seated fighter Gareth crafted is just right for the task."

"I like it," Brent agreed. "I want one."

"Greedy! You already have the Isador," Stuart protested, and changed the subject so Brent could not put in another demand for a two-seater. "This Kennedy is a handy ruler in the American office. I should contact him," Stuart returned to the conversation with Michael. "Kennedy is interested in space travel and by a coincidence, so are we."

"Time for bed for me; I am interested in sleeping," Darien declared as he rose and stretched. "Is that heater in the bath in working order?" Gareth assured him it was, so Darien went off to bathe. Glendon said goodnight and went upstairs. He preferred morning showers to awaken better. Darien did not like to begin his day outdoors with a shower so his was always at night.

Brent turned off the television and swatted the cat away from his arm. "I am not greedy, I just speak up more often about what I want," Brent explained as he went to bed.

"Coming?" Stuart asked the pair on the couch.

"We were waiting for the program after the gakki one," Carrol said. "Would you turn it back on for us?"

"Yes, I shall," Stuart said. "Would you rather sit closer to the set?"

"We are warmer here," Carrol told him. He eyed her speculatively but made no further comment. He turned the set back on and went upstairs.

"We are getting to be quite scandalous," Gareth whispered to her. "We dance, we sit close to each other, steal kisses –"

"What will we not do!" she laughed. He put his arm around her shoulders.

"That is entirely up to you, Your Nibs," he told her. She gazed at him, and as they began to embrace, they were stopped by the sound of feet coming back downstairs.

"We are going to view the program with you," Brent told them and without further ado, flung himself across both their laps. Glendon leaped on top of Brent, and Gareth and Carrol groaned in protest.

"We will all become knowledgeable," Stuart intoned grandly, and sat on top of Glendon. The resultant weight was too much for the sofa, which was not made of Dorea wood. The legs all gave way at once and sent the furniture piece and its users crashing to the floor. For a moment they were stunned into silence.

"See the trouble that ensues when you choose to sit with my sister," Stuart complained.

"It was not my weight that did the deed," Carrol objected.

"Oh yes it was," Glendon countered. "I sat on this settee just yesterday and had no trouble with it."

"And I had no problem with it," Stuart promised.

"Get off of me before I die!" Brent wheezed. Stuart and Glendon rose, and Brent clambered off the couch unsteadily. Gareth and Carrol reluctantly followed suit.

"Bedtime is a good idea," Gareth acknowledged resignedly, and Glendon slapped him on the back.

"There is a good fellow. Come along, Carrol, time to visit a dreamland."

"You istay. I never gave you any trouble with Aura," she whispered to Stuart.

"I needed none, I had plenty on my own," Stuart whispered back.

Darien drove the truck to the school auditorium as per Lloyd Martin's directions. He promised little Monica Martin that he would attend this 'Christmas pageant' thing of hers, and Darien disliked breaking any promises he made to children. Michael Sheldon drove out to see the scouts and assured Darien that a school Christmas pageant was a treat. He stayed at the ranch with the other Thuringi while Darien drove into town, properly dressed in his Earthian suit and tie and hat. His overcoat covered his pistol well.

Darien was familiar with the Christmas story from hearing Michael Sheldon relate it but did not understand the excitement connected with it. He made his way through the milling crowd of people gathered at the school and found a seat near the front on the aisle of a side section of seats. He glanced around and noted that the other men removed their hats, so he pulled off his.

There was an abundance of red and green decorations all around the auditorium, and an evergreen tree stood off to a corner festooned in large colorful lights and ornaments and strings of sparkling tinsel ribbons. Upon further inspection Darien saw the tree was not growing inside the building but had been cut down and placed in a strange metal holder. Evidently the tree was part of this odd annual ritual but mystified Darien as to its role in the proceedings.

The lights dimmed as a musician played an instrument similar to a Thuringi melator with keys that each struck a particular note when pressed. The musician was very well rehearsed. Darien sat back to watch the pageant.

Two children named 'Mary' and 'Joseph' dragged along a painted wooden representation of a small gakki on wheels across the stage. They were met at an inn by its quarrelsome owner and were brusquely turned away. The next scene found the unfortunate couple in an animal shelter surrounded by the wooden gakki and a wooden cabrett. Little Mary smiled down on a brightly lit baby doll in a trough while children in white gowns and fanciful paper wings attached to their backs portrayed angel spirits. At occasional junctures, a large herd of children on a set of risers directly in front of the stage sang little songs that described the scenes in lyrical detail.

The curtain closed, and three more children in robes with towels wrapped around their heads marched out in front of the curtain and sang. Other children in fluffy white costumes with black arms and legs accompanied them. Darien recognized one of the fluffy ones as Monica Martin. He sat back in his seat and grinned widely as she put forth a valiant effort and sang of shepherds and their flocks by night. The curtains opened, and the shepherds and sheep gathered around the royal couple and their brightly lit infant doll. They sang another song, and the curtain closed again.

Three stout boys came out in front of the curtain in the company of hideous looking creatures with misshapen backs, made from the same material as the earlier gakki and cabrett. The boys wore crowns and fancy robes and carried strange jars and boxes. They claimed to be 'three kings from Orientar.' The curtain opened at the end of the song, and the kings joined the tableau around the bright doll. All the children sang of a silent night, which amused Darien greatly. So far nothing had been silent; either the children sang, or the instrument played, or members of the audience coughed or whispered among themselves.

The children suddenly burst into song to proclaim, "Joy to the World." It made Darien jerk upright in his seat, startled at the sudden switch of mood. At the end of the song one of the boy kings stepped forward and wished everyone a merry Christmas, and the audience stood and clapped their hands in approval of the performance. Darien also applauded as the house lights came on and the children could see the audience. Monica Martin saw her parents, who sat where they told her they would. She glanced around and saw Darien's tall figure. It was not hard to miss him. He was the only six-foot-seven-inch-tall blonde man with yellow eyes dressed in an expensive three-piece suit and topcoat in the room. He observed other adults approaching the stage to collect their children, so Darien went to the stage edge. Monica ecstatically pulled at her friends' sleeves and costumes.

"See? My Uncle Darien has come to see me, just like he said he would! Hi, Uncle Darien!" As she hurried toward him, she tripped over a prop piece that fell from a boy king's costume. She pitched forward off the stage. With a mighty leap, Darien threw himself forward and caught her in his arms and turned in midair before crashing into the wall of the stage front with his back.

The sound and action made the auditorium fall silent, as all heads turned to see what happened. A teacher hurried to them. "Are you all right, Monnie?" she asked. Monica nodded. "My, that was quick!" the teacher told Darien. "You must have been a star football receiver in school." Darien smiled at her but said nothing. Lloyd and Katie rushed to them as the people in the auditorium resumed their hubbub of post-show activity.

"Man, that was fast," Lloyd sighed with relief. "Thanks, Darien."

"(It would not do to let such a noble portrayer of a fuzzy white creature get injured)," Darien replied. "(Would it, child)?" he asked Monica, who hugged his neck in delight. He stepped away from the wall and the teacher stared at it in concern. Darien turned to see what caused her concern and noted the large indentation in the plaster wall. The teacher checked his back. It was covered in plaster dust, but he did not appear injured.

"Are you sure you're alright?" she asked him.

He shrugged. "(I am better than your structure)," he replied. He put Monica down on her feet to talk to her, unconcerned and unharmed. "(And just what is the significance of a fuzzy creature as pertains to this Christmas pageant)?" he asked.

"What?" she asked with a grin.

"(What are you, what is this costume)?" He squatted down in order to speak to her without putting a strain on her neck to look up at him.

"I'm a sheep," she told him. "I'm with the shepherds."

"(I see)," he said thoughtfully. "(And the shepherds came to look at the child)."

"Yes, because he's the baby Jesus," Monica replied.

"(Well, it was a very nice portrayal)," Darien said. "(I thoroughly enjoyed it)."

"I'm so glad you came!" Monica said excitedly. "I told all my friends that you would."

"(If it pleases you)," Darien replied, and wondered what made the sudden flash of light nearby. It was Katie with a flash attachment on her camera. Darien straightened and Monica took his hand.

"Will you come to Christmas Eve services with us? And Sunday, too? And bring your family?" she pleaded.

"(I cannot speak for the others)," he said doubtfully. "(And truly, child, I doubt I can attend this service with you) –"

"Oh, please, Darien!" Monica jumped up and down and held his hand in both of hers. "It'll be really nice at our church, and grown-ups sing a lot better than kids. Please? Miss Evans will be there, too. She goes to our church." She indicated her teacher. Darien glanced at the attractive teacher beside him and smiled at her.

"Persuasive, isn't she?" Lloyd commented with a grin.

"(Like a rapid river)," Darien replied. He turned back to Monica. "(Very well, child; I will attend your service. One service and it is only because your charming presence is too compelling to ignore)."

"Are you all right, sir?" asked the principal, who saw Darien catch Monica and run into the stage earlier from across the auditorium and only now was able to get to them. Darien nodded. "There are refreshments set up in the cafeteria. You're welcome to come and have some punch and cookies with us. Hello, Lloyd; Katie."

"I'm Melinda Evans," Monica's teacher introduced herself to the mysterious stranger before her.

"(Darien Phillipi)," he rejoined.

"How long have you been in America?"

"(Not long)," Darien replied.

"I wonder if you might come to our class and tell the children about growing up in England," Miss Evans said, and he suddenly felt uncomfortable. Michael Sheldon warned about the Thuringi need for proper identification, and visas, and other things Darien never thought necessary until that moment.

"(I am not a good speaker. My language is far too salacious to expose to young children)."

She looked surprised and amused. "Mr. Phillipi, I would be willing to bet that any man who uses a word like 'salacious' so casually in conversation in the middle of Oklahoma, would be worth the risk of exposure." He laughed. "Monica speaks so highly of you. I'm glad to meet you at last." Monica joined her parents, and they all made way through the crowd to the cafeteria with the principal.

"(What has she told you)?" Darien asked, and hoped he sounded merely curious and not as concerned as he felt. Who knew what a small impressionable child might say?

"She told us that, well this sounds funny I guess, but she told us that in your home village, your people never cut their hair."

"(Well, that is generally true)," Darien agreed. "(It is a local custom, so we adapted to yours. What else)?"

"Oh, nothing specific; she just said you were tall and strong and ... well, I think she has quite a crush on you."

"(A what)?"

"A crush. You know."

"(I am unfamiliar with the term)."

"She's... she has a little girl's affection for an older man."

"(Oh)," Darien replied, and laughed. "(She obviously has only the most rudimentary knowledge of my actual personality. She is only a little girl, after all. My nature is drawn to mature charms)."

"Well," Miss Evans replied with a bright smile, "she left out the part about how well you flirt."

"(One cannot relate what one does not know)." The cookies were sweet confections covered with even sweeter icing that made Darien sick. The Thuringi sweet tooth could not handle such an overload; it was like getting drunk without the amusement. The punch he used to try to wash it down only made it worse. He excused himself to the Martins and the fair Miss Evans. "(I am not prepared for the ingestion of such fare)," he told them. "(I must make my way homeward now. You were delightful, child)," he addressed Monica. "(I have never witnessed so insightful a presentation as that of you as a woolen sheep)."

"And you'll come to Christmas services?" she persisted. Darien grimaced for a moment and then smiled.

"(If it is your pleasure)," he sighed. He looked at Lloyd. "(She has all the makings of a general)," he said, then bowed to the ladies and left.

"What an interesting man," Melinda Evans said.

"He's not much for revealing a lot about himself," Lloyd told her. "He will talk all day in that big wordy way of his, and not really say a damn thing."

Darien returned to Sheldon ranch, stopping along the way to throw up the sickly-sweet contents of his stomach. Michael Sheldon was with everyone else in the living room. They fitted him with one of their translators, and he was happy to use the handy device. He brought some Christmas cheer in the form of good, imported beer, which was voted as the best Earth had to offer. Michael made a concerted effort not to look too long at Carrol. He was terribly smitten with her still and wondered how to get her alone.

"We are invited to attend a service on the Eve of Christmas," Darien told them, "And you must all join me."

"Oh, is that so?" Stuart laughed.

"Yes," Darien said decisively. "Tonight, I witnessed a confusing display, and I would like our friend Michael to explain it, please." He described the Christmas pageant exactly as he saw it, and Michael Sheldon nearly rolled on the floor with laughter.

"(I think you'll get a better impression of the true meaning of Christmas at the church service on Christmas Eve than at a school program)," Michael finally said though his gasps for air.

"Will they have real sheep there?" Glendon asked.

"(No, no, sheep are just incidental)," Michael said. "(I think it's because Monica played a sheep that Darien's put so much importance on it)."

"I think it is vital to attend this service," Darien told Stuart. "This is a high holy day to these people and understanding it may bring us a better understanding of their method of worship."

Stuart agreed, and added, "No doubt it will guarantee you will not have to do it alone." He handed Darien an imported beer. Darien took a tentative drink and smiled broadly.

"Much better than fizzless wizzar and confections," he told them.

Michael was persuaded to stay the night and go back to Tulsa the next morning if he must return at all. They made a comfortable bed for him on the sofa. The next morning, he awoke to discover Carrol alone in the kitchen making breakfast. He took the opportunity to have a private talk with her.

"(I'm glad you're feeling more comfortable here)," he said as she scrambled eggs in the skillet.

"It is a nice world you have here, Michael," she told him. "I cannot wait for my parents to get here! They will like it very much."

"(Speaking of parents, how about coming to Tulsa with me to meet my family)?" Michael asked. "(It's only a couple of hours from here. I could have you back by five this afternoon)."

"Why?" she asked. He reached out and stroked her hair.

"(It'd be a nice time for the two of us to get away and talk)," he said.

"About what?" she asked. "We can talk now."

"(Are you still involved with your mechanic friend)?" he asked directly.

"What do you mean?"

"(I saw the two of you up in Boston when you took me back after the reading lessons. I just wondered if it was still a factor in not giving me a chance)," Michael said.

"Michael," Carrol sighed, but said no more.

"(So, the answer is yes, you are still involved with him)?" She nodded at his question. "(May I ask, if you are still involved with him, then why don't you and he show each other any affection)?"

"We cannot," she told him quietly. "Father does not wish for us to be either hasty or blatant as we explore furthering our friendship."

"(So, you're just friends, then)," Michael said. "(Do you have any objections with being a friend to me)?" he asked and moved a little closer to her. She turned off the fire under the skillet and regarded him seriously.

"That depends upon to what degree of friendship you seek," she replied.

"(Is it that hard to figure out)?" Michael chuckled. "(You weren't born yesterday. I would like to be very good friends with you, as I'm sure you realize)." He turned her to face him. "(I'm not Thuringi, but I certainly do appreciate an attractive woman when I see one)." He kissed her, and she trembled. "(Maybe you'd like to explain the degree of friendship that's making you shake like this)," he murmured to her.

What could she say to him? This was the situation she dreaded. If she spurned him, he might retract his aid to them or expose them to warmongers of his world. But if she encouraged him, it would be a lie.

"Please do not make me speak of this," she pleaded. "It is difficult to explain, Michael."

"(No, it isn't)," Michael told her as he held her closer. "(How difficult can it be to admit you're attracted to me)?"

"How difficult is what?" Gareth's sharp voice came from the direction of the doorway. His unexpected appearance startled both Michael and Carrol. Gareth was dressed to go outside, his toolbox in one gloved hand and a hat in the other. He looked from Carrol to Michael and back again, his face a study in frustration and barely controlled anger. Pulling on his hat with a quick jerk, Gareth glared at Michael before he spat out a string of oaths as he headed for the back door.

"Gareth, please wait," Carrol called out to him.

"For what purpose?" Gareth snapped. "A man knows when he is outranked."

"It is not that," she said. She hurried to him and touched his arm in appeal. "You are not outranked."

"No? Then would you like to explain to me, why an istay Earthian can presume to plead his case for your heart, while I must remain silent? If that is not being outranked, then what is?" He forgot that Michael wore a translator and understood every word. "Not a day goes by that I do not struggle just to win an unguarded glance from your lovely eyes, while this boy speaks however he may wish to you! If I could own a piece of land, would that perhaps make me of some worth?"

"You are not being fair," she protested. "I never denied you my glance or my heart. I do not care if you own but a stone."

"Well, it is not up to us, is it?" Gareth remarked. "But I suppose it is safer to keep my mouth shut and say nothing about his embraces, lest I cause us all to be cast out." He went on out to the barn. Carrol wiped her eyes with her shirtsleeves before she turned to the stove. Michael saw the misery plainly written on her face.

"(Is that it)?" Michael asked. "(You're putting up with me and my clumsy come-ons because you're still afraid of what I'll do if you reject me)?"

She was alarmed to realize he understood the conversation. She put the scrambled eggs in a bowl and set them on the table before she turned to him. "We are well aware of our uncertain position on your world," Carrol said shakily. "I do not know how to explain without risking harm to your feelings or jeopardizing our mission. I am at a complete loss."

"(No, no, you're not jeopardizing anything)!" Michael protested. He took her hands in his. "(I mean who am I, anyway? I'm just a guy with a little old farm; I'm nobody powerful. All I've done is give you a place to stay and it has nothing to do with how you react to me, Carrol. If you aren't attracted to me, then okay! Just tell me so and I'll back off. I told you before, I'd never dream of kicking you guys out of here just because my ego's been sacked. Honey, don't be so upset)."

"What is wrong?" Stuart asked as he entered the kitchen with a worried look on his face.

"(Nothing, it's just a big misunderstanding that's getting cleared up)," Michael assured him. He put a hand under Carrol's chin and coaxed her to look at him. "(Maybe you ought to go out and talk to your friend. I wouldn't blame him a bit if he came back in here and flattened me. Of course, you don't have to tell him that)."

Carrol smiled shakily. She got her coat and left for the barn.

Michael sighed and poured himself a cup of freshly brewed coffee. "(You have a beautiful sister, Stuart)," he told the prince, who stood by silently. "(But as God is my witness, I never intended for her to believe that you all are living here conditionally. Sure, I would be happy as a clam if she were interested in me, but she's not and it's like I told her, that's okay)."

"There was a time, Michael, when Carrol was put in such a position with a Scodan chieftain," Stuart explained as he watched his sister go to the barn. "It was very trying for Carrol to walk the delicate balance between keeping peace with the Scodan and keeping him at bay. Father was furious when he discovered what the chieftain had in mind – he called it extortion of the vilest kind – and Maranta Shanaugh was beside himself." Stuart let out a sharp sigh. "Of course, now I know just why he was so beside himself; he and Carrol were secret lovers, and he was not at all happy to see her in such a precarious position."

"(What did he do)?"

"He stormed in with his men and scooped her up under the cover of darkness. Maranta was not the kind of man a Scodan wants to wage war against, and they did not pursue it."

Michael sipped his coffee and then nodded toward the barn. "(Didn't you say once that this Gareth fellow fought for her in a dual)?"

"Yes, he did."

"(And he worked for this General Shanaugh at one time)?"

"Yes. Gareth was his chief mechanic, as well as a numbered kinsman."

"(A what)?"

"I believe he is a sixth or seventh cousin to our late general."

"(Jeez. I think I just dodged a bullet)," Michael said with a smile. "(He was pretty mad when he left. Why isn't he allowed to date her)?"

"To –? Oh. It is long and complicated, but essentially, he is a commoner whose approach to my sister was seen as unorthodox and unseemly to our Elders. My parents like his honesty and directness as do I."

"(Then why don't you loosen up here? Or is one of your scouts an Elder)?"

"No, but it is a little more complicated than that."

"(Does it have to be)?"

Stuart thought for a moment. "No, it does not have to be," he said softly.

Gareth furiously banged on a piece of metal with a shaping hammer. Covering her ears, Carrol went to his side. He stopped and looked at her.

"What?" he asked.

"Why are you angry at me?" she asked.

"I am not. I am just angry, period. Can I still not get angry? Is it against some ancient royal custom that I cannot be jealous?"

"No," she said. She removed the hammer from his hand and stroked his hand tenderly. "It is flattering."

"What good does it do," he muttered.

"We are not in danger of any retaliation," she told him. "Michael assured me the mission is not endangered by my turning him away."

"Oh? You did not admit you are attracted to him?" Gareth muttered.

"What are you saying, why should I admit to something that is not so? What has gotten into you? Gareth." She reached under his collar to fish out the knotted scarf. "Do you have any idea what this means to me?"

"No. What does it mean?" he asked as his belligerence faded.

"It means everything. No one, certainly not an outlander, has command of my attentions and affection as you." With a tug of the scarf, she drew him closer. "The day you took that out of its drawer and put it around your neck sealed your fate with me, Master Sword-and-Fist."

"The day you put it around my neck in the Freen was your undoing," Gareth said. "I hoped you would not come back looking for it. It gave me comfort. I cannot explain, except this way." He gathered her in his arms, and they kissed, their frosty breath enveloping them in mist. "I did not always used to be such a quarrelsome jealous fool, you know. I do not wish to be."

"I am not trying to make you one, either," she assured him. "Let us go back inside where it is warm. My feet are beginning to numb." They returned to the house where the rest of the scouts were eating breakfast.

Michael Sheldon prepared to leave. "My parents were pretty testy about my spending so much time and energy out here, and they expect me to be home at Christmas. If I'm not, then my dad will be out here to find out why and God knows what he'll do when he sees the ships and whatnot. I'll be back out when I can." He hesitated and then held out his hand to Gareth. "(No hard feelings)?" he asked.

Gareth shook his hand. "None," he answered.

With a wave of his hand, Michael went out the door. "(You'll really enjoy Christmas)," he told them as he left.

"What hard feelings?" Glendon asked Gareth. "What was all that about?"

"It was about two points past your need to know," Gareth replied, and the others whooped at his comeback.

"Do not mess about with Major Sword-and-Fist," Darien laughed.

On the Sunday before Christmas, Darien prepared to go to the little church Lloyd Martin's family attended. The other Thuringi, curious to get a first-hand glimpse of the rituals of this strange Christian religion experience, piled into the pickup and went with him. Monica Martin waited by the front of the church. She led the group inside and they filled an entire back row pew on one side of the church. His peers followed Darien's lead and removed their hats and quietly observed the activity around them.

There were many candles lit all around the sanctuary, and boughs of evergreen, decorated with bright red ribbons, festooned the altar and other areas of the church. There was a wooden nativity scene over to one side of the pulpit, and a large cross hung in the central part of the wall with a painting of a long haired, bearded young man beneath it. He had a kind face and a distant look in his eyes.

Likewise, they were observed. Five tall, broad-shouldered, yellow-haired young men and a tall slender girl all dressed in fine clothes sat polite and reserved on the back row. Three had strange yellow eyes but beyond that, they were a pleasant group of young people. Glendon picked up a hymnal in his hands and flipped through it curiously. Lloyd Martin came to shake Darien's hand. "Y'all can sit up here with us," he invited, but Stuart declined.

"(We should sit back here, unnoticed)."

Lloyd laughed at the thought. "Stuart, the last thing you six are is unnoticeable." He returned to his seat after he agreed Monica could sit with Darien. She sat on his lap. As the pianist began a song, they noticed everyone else stood and held the books from the little holders in front of them and sang from notations on the pages. The Thuringi also stood. Glendon recognized the songs from hearing them played over and over on the radio at the Gentry's store all month and could sing along. Stuart and Carrol recognized the tunes but did not sing out. At the conclusion of the songs, everyone sat down. The man the Thuringi assumed to be the church vicar stood up to address the crowd.

"We are so fortunate to gather together here," the preacher said. "We are gathering to give praise to the Infant Jesus in this holy season. I'd like to welcome all our church family, as well as all our visitors," he said, indicating the back row with his hand. As with the usual dictates of the curious, all heads swiveled around to get a look at their visitors.

All were startled at the yellow eyes. As they turned back around the Earthians whispered to each other. The preacher launched into what he later considered one of the most inspired sermons he ever gave. Katie Martin had told him she and Lloyd invited a group of friends who had never been exposed to Christianity before.

"They are kind, intelligent, friendly people who just simply never heard the story of Christ. This is your chance to preach the gospel like a missionary, Reverend McDaniel, and you won't even have to leave home to do it."

The good Reverend McDaniel gave it his all, leading the hymns with fervor his parishioners had not heard from him before. His enthusiasm fired up the choir; the choir fired up the crowd, and the Thuringi were impressed by the strength of their convictions. His sermon was inspired. He preached as if no one in his flock had heard the Good News, and one corner of the church was busy with the older men calling out the occasional "Amen!"

Brent had returned to the ranch for this Christmas occasion and was especially amused by these men. His arms draped along the back of the pew, and he grinned widely every time one of the elders burst out into an "amen!"

"What does it mean?" Glendon whispered to him.

Brent shook his head. "I do not know, but they take their exhortations seriously."

Gareth and Carrol held hands and nudged each other when they noticed something each thought the other might want to see: the amusing restless children; the woman who kicked her shoes off and on; the man who looked so terribly bored and chewed on something continuously. Carrol thought the candlelight gave a romantic feel to the proceedings. She leaned against Gareth with her head against his shoulder. He sat contentedly and stroked her fingers. Perhaps Denys and Maribel Duncan were right to begin their courtship in a cathedral, where love and kindness abounded.

Stuart paid attention to the sermon and remembered Michael's explanation of the religion the night of their first arrival. Stuart understood the basis for this religion and thought it was a sweet sentimental tale of hope and humility of service for good.

Darien paid more attention to amusing little Monica Martin with feats of slight-of-hand, than to the preacher. "How does a baby save a world?" he asked Stuart.

"He grows up to be that chap in the portrait." Stuart nodded to the picture below the cross. "He saved it through peace, without calling on military intervention."

"Well, it did not last long," Darien pointed out. "There does not seem to be a great deal of peace left in this world." The people in front of them turned to look at the brothers, curious about the unfamiliar language with its musical lilt, then back around to face the preacher. At the end of the service, the preacher walked down the aisle to the back of the church to greet the people as they exited. Lloyd caught up with the Thuringi, who found themselves surrounded by friendly Methodists.

"We're sure proud to see you here," one elderly lady told Glendon. "So nice to see young folks turn out for services."

"(Thank you)," was the only reply Glendon could think to give.

"(Amen)," Brent intoned, and Glendon gave him a small kick with his foot. Brent just grinned wider.

"They sure grow 'em big, wherever you're from," said a man to Gareth, who simply smiled.

"Reverend, this is my friend Darien Phillipi and his family," Lloyd introduced.

"I hope you enjoyed our service," Reverend McDaniel told Darien, and craned his neck back in order to get a better look at the tall visitor. "I understand you have not attended a Christian service before?"

"(No)," Darien replied. "(Tell me, vicar, just why and how did a child save your people)?"

"Why, he died for our sins," the reverend said, astonished that Darien did not seem to know.

"(Died)!" Darien roared. "(A child's death saved your people? Just how weak are you vessels, to demand the lifeblood of the helpless)?"

"No, he was a man when he died and rose again."

"(Rose again)?" Darien was confused. "(Did he die or not? And who is the king of whom you speak, the mighty counselor? Why did he not) –"

"(Perhaps if my brother listened to your complete sermon, he would have garnered some important points)," Stuart explained to the minister as he urged Darien forward. "(Darien, we are holding up the line. Go on; we can question the good vicar at a more convenient time)."

"(Good, I would like to know more about virgins who give birth, and kings who slay babies)," Darien said rancorously. "(Some religion; it is a story of fantasy and war, not of peace)!"

"(Would you move along)," Stuart muttered as he pushed Darien forward.

"(Well, this is a confusing religion)," they all heard Darien fume as Stuart pulled him toward the pickup. "(Singing angels of God, and shepherds and wise men who worship an infant one moment, then leave him to the whims of fate and a murderer of innocents the next! And where is the young chap who dies for them? They did not even mention that part)."

"(No wonder the Bishop called you recalcitrant; you do not pay attention to a sermon any longer than a blink)!" They were soon mercifully out of earshot after that.

"Is that your brother?" Reverend McDaniel asked Gareth, who was next in line.

"(No, they are her brothers)," he said, passing the buck to Carrol.

"(I am terribly sorry, vicar)," Carrol apologized, "(I am afraid Darien is ill at ease concerning stories of children in peril)."

"You, ah, you do recognize God?" the reverend asked.

"(Oh yes, we revere the God of All)," Carrol assured him. "(We have never attended American services before. I thought it was remarkably interesting)."

"(Amen)!" Brent thundered enthusiastically behind her. Gareth and Carrol went on out, and Brent shook the reverend's hand with a mighty series of pumps. "(Vicar, what does 'amen' mean? Your Elders like to say it, and your songs like to say it)."

"It's... it means you agree," Reverend McDaniel replied, and Brent let out a healthy laugh.

"(I like a people who weave an amusing tapestry of tales and punctuate it with song! And I understand a large man in red will be flying in a ship overhead. This is also a part of this tapestry, correct)?"

"No, that, er, that is Santa Claus, and it has nothing to do with the story of the Nativity," Reverend Daniel said with a helpless feeling. It was his best sermon, and it still went over some of these people's heads. Good heavens! They were friendly and handsome, but they were also dense.

"(Oh, good)," Brent remarked. "(I would not trust anyone flying about in the middle of the night while people are trying to sleep)." He joined the others out by the truck. Glendon looked at the reverend's hand the preacher gingerly massaged, sore from Brent's strong grip.

"(We will not disturb you again, Your Excellency)," Glendon offered. "(I am sure we have been a trial to you this day)."

"Oh no, on the contrary, I'd love to talk to you again. Please come back for Christmas Eve services." Glendon considered this and bowed.

"(As you wish, Your Excellency)."

"No, I'm just a reverend. Do come again," the reverend repeated.

"(As you wish, Your Reverence)."

Darien calmed down after Lloyd managed a rapid recap of the overall picture of Christian beliefs. "(This is a violent society)," Darien told him. "(It has apparently not improved in two thousand years, despite this savior of whom they speak)."

"(We have been invited back. I think His Reverence wants to explain himself in clearer terms)," Glendon told them.

"Are you alright?" asked Monica's teacher, Melinda Evans, to Darien. "You were awfully upset."

"(You are a charming people with some odd beliefs)," Darien told her. "(Completely confusing in all respects)."

"(You simply did not listen)," Carrol said. "(I understood the story)."

"(Despite the fact that you were distracted by Major Sword-and-Fist)," Darien came back.

"Well, we've got to get home and finish decorating the tree. Santa Claus is coming soon, isn't he, honey?" Lloyd asked his daughter.

"Yes," Monica said, clapping her hands. "Darien, do you know about Santa Claus?"

"(No)," Darien told her. "(I am not familiar with the man)."

"'He sees you when you're sleeping, he knows when you're awake, he knows if you've been bad or good, so be good for goodness' sake'," she sang.

Brent roared with laughter. "(He knows when we are bad or

good? Name of All, Darien, we are lost with this fellow)!" He gave Melinda Evans a speculative look. "(But I am told when Darien is bad, he is at his best)." She looked at Darien for confirmation and Darien smiled his wicked smile, which quickly became benign when he realized Monica was present.

Katie edged over to Carrol. "Your friend Brent. He's... he's quite a bit different from the rest of you, isn't he?"

"In what way?"

"Well, in the way that he's got slits on his neck and webbed fingers."

Carrol glanced at Katie to determine if she asked out of curiosity or fear. She decided it was the former more than the latter. "Yes. He was born that way," she replied easily, as if it was a question she answered often, drawing from what she read in the medical books from Michael. "Some people are born with six fingers on one hand, and some are born with extra limbs. Brent happens to have slits and webs. They do not bother him, but it does vex him when people stare too long."

"Oh." Katie was satisfied with that. It was perfectly understandable for someone born with birth defects to be defensive, and admirable that Brent was so calm when she discovered his secret. She had wondered this whole time but never had the chance to ask until now.

"I think you boys should come over to the community center for Christmas dinner," a sweet-faced elderly lady said as she approached fearlessly.

"(You are very kind to extend the invitation)," Stuart told her.

"Well, Reverend McDaniel said you weren't Christians, and you might want to be saved."

"(Saved)?" Stuart said. "(Oh, yes. Michael mentioned that. Well, we will speak again to His Reverence and learn more about your beliefs. Thank you)." She nodded and went on her way. The Thuringi got into their truck, and Katie Martin invited them to Christmas dinner at her parent's house.

"(Is this an important event, this Christmas dinner)?" Glendon asked her. "(This is the third invitation we have received, including Michael's)."

"Well, it's just a kind of tradition," Katie told him. "Most

American traditions seem to revolve around eating. And at our house, you're not going to get a little old lady trying to save you all throughout the meal." Glendon laughed with her. The truck full of Thuringi pulled out for home.

Where are they from that they've never heard the story of Christ, thought Reverend McDaniel.

I wonder just how good at being bad Darien Phillipi can be, thought Melinda Evans.

Boy, if they didn't turn this little church on its ear, thought Lloyd Martin.

My gosh, but that Glen fellow sure is good looking, thought Katie Martin.

The devil's got that family; just look at those yellow eyes, thought the elderly lady.

"They are a strange collection of people, these Earthians," Stuart remarked on the way home.

On Christmas Eve night, Darien went to Lloyd's house. Lloyd only intended for Darien to shake a set of sleigh bells outside the window for Monica to hear. Darien decided to go one better. At the pre-arranged time, Darien dutifully shook the bells. When he saw Monica's little face appear in the window, he ducked out of sight. He had liberated a plastic Santa and reindeer display earlier from atop a store building in town. He placed a remote device from one of the dismantled ships inside the sleigh and attached a small engine and a small thruster he lifted from Gareth's toolbox. He removed the control from inside his coat and made the display soar across the sky. It was just enough out of range not to betray its origins, but close enough for Monica to see it. She squealed and screamed for her parents.

"It's Santa Claus, I saw him, he's here, he's here!" she jumped up and down on her bed.

"Monnie, you have to go to sleep now, or Santa won't come," Darien heard Katie tell her.

"But he's come, he's here, I saw him, he was right outside the window! And his reindeer; Mama, they flew!"

Lloyd went out on the porch and motioned to Darien frantically. "Did she see you?" he whispered.

"(No)," Darien said, straight-faced.

"Well, something's set her off. She's going nuts and I ran into a problem putting her doll house together. Thought I'd be done by now but I'm not even halfway though yet. We'll have to open presents in the morning. Say, could you read to her or something? She might stay put long enough for me to finish."

Darien agreed and went back to Monica's room, where he sat beside her on the bed. "(Your shouts and declarations woke me, child)," he teased her. "(You should be asleep)."

"But I saw Santa, I saw him," Monica said excitedly.

"(I know; I saw him as well)."

"You... you did?" she asked, her eyes wide. "Oh, you really are magic."

"(He told me to tell you to return to sleep with the other good children until morning)."

"What did he sound like? What did he look like?" Monica asked as she crawled back under the covers. Darien adjusted them over her as he thought of a reply.

"(He was as large and mighty as you might imagine)," he told her. "(Now, then. Are you settling down)?"

"Could you tell me a story? I'm not sleepy, not at all," she said.

"(Er... all right, then. There was in a far away land... a fair princess with golden hair)."

"Cinderella, and she wasn't a princess yet."

"(This is my story, child, from my homeland)," Darien told her. "(Be hushed and you will hear a new tale)." She smiled and snuggled under the cover further in delight. For the next hour he spun a fanciful tale of a beautiful princess who was loved by a wild rascal. This rascal was clumsy of speech and manners, but he could wield a wonderful magic sword. He went on many missions for her, sometimes taking her with him to different worlds of wonder. He flew a powerful ship called the Solenil and fought many great battles with ship and sword. The royal lady was a young girl, just a little older than Monica, with the name of Echolinnea, which according to Darien, meant 'dignified daughter of the brave.'

"And when she grew up, did she marry him?" Monica asked.

"(Why, of course)," Darien assured her smoothly. "(As you know, all fantasy tales must have happy endings)."

"What else did they do?" Monica asked, but Darien shook his

head.

"(I believe they put their children to bed)," he told her. "(Now, off to sleep with you, small bones. There will be time for tales on another day)." He kissed her forehead, and he went to the door where Katie and Lloyd stood, listening.

"What was the rascal's name?" Monica whispered loudly.

"(Why, Darien, of course)," he said with a soft laugh. "(Sleep now, little one)." Monica giggled, and they turned off her light and closed the door.

The Santa gifts were all set up and ready. Darien hesitated, and then asked his hosts, "(And just why it is that you perpetuate this hoax upon your child)?"

"It's like a fairy story, like the one you just told," Katie told him. "There's no harm in firing a child's imaginations and making a few humble wishes come true. That story of yours was a wonderful story. Where did you hear it?"

"(Oh, it is partly a story from my homeland, partly from my imagination)," Darien passed off, "(just a silly tale with which to amuse a restless child. Goodnight, good people, and may your Christmas be happy)."

"Merry Christmas, Darien," Katie said, and kissed him on the cheek. Lloyd patted him on the shoulder.

"I sure wish I knew what set her off," he murmured, and Darien hid his grin. He found the plastic Santa and reindeer where it crash-landed and took it back into town. He removed the engine and the thruster and replaced the display on the store roof. He went home with a cheerful heart.

The next morning, the Thuringi turned on the stereo and listened to Christmas music as they prepared their breakfast. It was a pleasant bonus for the working Thuringi to have the day off, so Stuart declared a holiday for Gareth and Carrol and himself as well. Darien brought out six chocolate bars for them all and explained the Santa myth of bringing gifts and sweets, and his role the evening before.

"No one saw this flying Santa but the child?" Stuart asked worriedly.

"Of course not," Darien assured him. "Even if they did, they may have accounted it to drink or weariness. They account for nearly everything to drink or weariness. Or to flying objects no one believes exist. Now stop your fret, brother. It is Christmas, and time to make merry."

The Martins stopped by at mid-morning, bringing a gift basket of fruit. Monica rushed in and immediately threw her arms around Darien and showed him her new doll, a shapely blonde doll ten inches tall. "I named her Echolinnea," she told him. "Oh, will you please tell me more stories about the princess and the rascal? Please?" she asked.

"(Some time I will)," he said, "(But for the now, I am all spoken out)."

"The princess and the rascal?" Carrol asked. "Anyone we know?"

"Not as well as you think," Darien told her in Thuringi, after he adjusted his translator for the moment. "I just made something up."

"Oh, I have something for you," Katie told Carrol and reached into her purse. She brought out a small piece of greenery with small white berries and held it up over Carrol's head. "See, we have a tradition that if you stand under the mistletoe with your sweetheart, you get to kiss each other."

Brent took the mistletoe from her and dangled it over Gareth's head. "(Oh, what have we here, a lonely soul in need of attention from the toes of mistle)." They all laughed and whooped in raucous delight when Carrol stepped up to kiss Gareth. Gareth took it in stride and especially liked it when Lloyd suspended the mistletoe from a nail over the doorway to the parlor for possible later encounters.

Monica looked around the front room. "Oh, you don't have a Christmas tree or stockings, or anything!" She gave Darien a kiss on the cheek and a hug. "I'm sorry I didn't get you anything for Christmas, but Daddy said you didn't know anything about it."

Darien gave her a gentle hug. "(Child, you have given me a sweet little buss and a warm embrace. It is all that a man could ask)."

His throat felt tight, and he had to clear it several times before it felt comfortable again. Her sweet gesture flooded his emotions as an Arda-powered gift within him quietly strengthened. For the first time since he felt the anguish of his dying world, Darien Phillipi's heart felt a measure of healing from the girl's genuine goodwill.

The Martins went on their way to Katie's parents' house after the Thuringi gracefully declined their thoughtful invitation to come with them. They had a grand feast just the same at Sheldon ranch: Glendon fried some chicken and Brent roasted potatoes as he would friaks.

Darien brought up jars of canned vegetables from the cellar and Gareth opened and distributed the fruit from the Martin's basket. Stuart contributed a chocolate cake he purchased at a bakery the day before. Michael drove out from Tulsa just in time to add his contribution of several bottles of good wine and stayed at their invitation.

They sat down to their first Christmas meal. Bowing her head, Carrol quoted from the Thuringi Book of Prayer, and they all closed their eyes and followed the words in their minds. "Oh God of All, we trust in the unseen, unheard guidance of your wisdom. We are grateful for your many gifts and are mindful of our responsibilities in their use. Lead us onward along the journey of life and guide us on the great Path at our journey's end." Carrol paused, then added, "and thank You for bringing us to this wonderful world. Your wisdom endures forever."

"Amen!" Brent exhorted cheerfully, and they all laughed and feasted. They sang their own culture's songs from different festivals and events, and in their own way celebrated without having to observe a foreign holiday or understand a strange belief.

Chapter 6: Layoff

Brent decided to take the Isador to the Pacific Ocean one fresh Monday after a weekend of rest at the ranch, and he set off for the Strait of Magellan right away. On the map the trip looked interesting but not all that remarkable, but in reality, it took much longer so he sped his ship up a little. The sea was rougher than he realized it would be. He went further south toward where the map showed only a space of white. Brent thought perhaps the mapmakers arbitrarily picked the color for that country the way they chose the colors for other countries.

The air was freezing cold, but he noted there were small animals on the snow-surrounded, pebbly shores: little black birds with large white breasts that waddled and slid onto ice and on into the sea. He sailed the Isador up against the ice and stepped out on its fin with the intent to go ashore.

"Oh, My Horror!" he shouted in surprise. "I will freeze my zenda off!" He hurried back inside the ship and dressed in warmer clothing and thick boots. He returned to the fin and gingerly stepped out onto the ice. He carried his pistol and sword, for he read wild beasts were everywhere on Earth, even at the far reaches, and he was not going to take a chance.

He trudged across the ice and snow with nothing in sight but whiteness and sunshine. He was glad he had sunglasses in case he came across humans, since they also cut the glare to his eyes. He headed for the area where he saw the sliding birds. When he topped a ridge and looked down at them as they marched to the sea and leaped in, he sat down to observe.

They did not fly, although they did possess little wings that thrust out from their sides as they hurried along. He laughed at the sight and continued to laugh at everything the little birds did. The land was not all snow, he noticed. Many exposed rocks let him know there was land somewhere under all the cold white cover. He took out a small flatscreen and recorded his impressions on it, and included the lovely light show in the sky that resembled colorful dancing ribbons or curtains. He took a deep breath – and suddenly he noticed an unpleasant odor of rank raw fish in the air. He heard a flopping noise behind him, a noise that had crept up but now commanded his attention. He turned around and stared at a sizable bloblike creature twice as long as the Thuringi, with an unsightly large nose, large whiskers and two long sharp tusks in its mouth. It roared at him and moved with startling swiftness. Brent scrambled to his feet and rushed away from it, down the hill and toward the birds.

"Run, you fellows! There is a Bulbous Tusked creature behind me!" he shouted, as if the birds could understand him and as if they could not see it for themselves. In his panic these things did not occur to him. He continued to run until he stumbled, rolled down the incline and landed heavily at the bottom. The birds were not helpful, but they had sense enough to run away from the approaching sea lion and the man. The elephant seal roared again and continued to chase after Brent, eager to taste this likely dinner.

"Wait, you!" the Thuringi declared as reason dawned on him, "I have weaponry!" He drew his sword and pistol. After a brief moment's consideration, he sheathed his sword. There was no sense in letting this huge creature get that close. As the elephant seal advanced and there was no place left to run, Brent shot it with his sidearm.

It fell the animal abruptly, but the forward momentum brought it to land on the ice at Brent's feet. He uttered a squawk and leaped back a step. It groaned and grunted, so he finished it with a mercy shot to the head. He slowly walked around it, staring in awe at the massive bulk. It was ugly, far uglier than most other creatures he ever saw. It had attacked him without provocation and with deadly intent. He did not regret defending himself, but Brent was saddened by the necessity of taking a life just the same.

After he recorded pictures of the creature on his flatscreen and some shots of the amusingly solemn-looking penguins, he returned to the Isador. Word, this was an impressive continent! He checked his location and shook his head. No, this was not the Antarctica. This was only an island called Elephant Island, although the creatures he saw looked nothing like the elephants he saw on the television and in Michael's books. The large continent was further south, so he set sail for it.

He reached a shore where, to his everlasting astonishment, he saw the staggering territory in all its ice-locked glory. Brent Ardenne was speechless. He stared out the window of the Isador with a singular thought in mind: Father will never believe me about this.

The water was cold, but he swam in cold depths before on

Thuringa and on Earth. He decided not to take any chances, however: cold water slowed his reaction time, and he did not want to face something like a Bulbous Tusked Creature in it. Instead, he made his way to shore and walked around a little, staring out across the endless snowy landscape in awe. It was far more snow than even the impressive amount they had at the ranch in Oklahoma. Everything about the Earth was larger and grander than the relatively limited number of things on Thuringa.

But Thuringa was more structured, he told himself. Thuringa did not have so many confusing choices, and there were not so many dangers at every turn by our generation's time. Thuringa was small and our population low, we shared, and no one went hungry or without. Earth is impressive but it would be more impressive if it were not so...so... careless. Feckless.

Unseemly.

He laughed aloud at the thought. Oh, if only Bishop Trapis could have heard that, and from Brent Ardenne too! The old scold might have passed out from shock.

When the snow melted, the Thuringi were saddened because it was so delightful to frolic in it, even though the air was cold. The driveway was muddy and slippery and the dead grass in the yard was a sad sight. Darien was always impatient to see green grass again. In no time he got bored so he either helped Gareth work on machines or engines or ships, or he set out across the pasture to find something to do. He saw deer at every turn and was appalled to learn these creatures were killed for food or trophies. "They slay illini for their horns! Word!" he roared. "What, they cannot merely admire horns on a living creature; they must kill it and display it on a wall? What appalling manners!"

"It is quieter around here when he is at work," Stuart grumbled.

One day as he and Darien went out to look at the cattle, they saw snow falling again. They whooped and ran back to the house to get the ax. Michael showed where they could cut down trees for the stove, and the brothers eagerly set about getting their own wood. It was a satisfying way to release their energy and admire the snowfall at the same time.

They stacked a cord of wood by the time Glendon came in from town with news. "The Gentrys said to watch the news report for weather conditions. It is to be a blizzard." And blizzard it was: the snow piled all around the northern front side of the house so high, they could not tell the porch from the yard, and the drifts completely covered the porch floor.

All they could do was eat, sleep, and keep warm. Stuart did not object when Gareth put his arms around Carrol since she was prone to shiver easily, and his warmth was a comfort. Of course, Darien did not object and instead took the opportunity to make kissing noises at them. He cheerfully baked bread and pies of all kinds from the canned goods in the cellar. His apple pie was a rousing success, but Stuart drew the line at green bean pie.

"No good comes of sweetened green beans." After tasting it, Darien had to agree.

One rare occasion when the Phillipi brothers were in the cellar and Gareth was in the barn, Glendon noticed Carrol shivering in front of the stove, waiting for the freshly added wood to get her warm. He picked up a blanket from the couch, wrapped it around himself and then stood behind her and enveloped her in his arms. She was startled as he bent over and burrowed his cold elegant nose against her warm neck. She was about to comment on his unusually forward action until he said, "Forgive the presumption, my dear princess, but it will not do to have our fair Carrol shivering from the cold. Allow me to warm us both until the fire does its task."

He was not seeking romance; he was simply trying to warm his nose. It was not the worst way to get warm, she told herself and enjoyed the unfamiliar embrace of a most proper Garin. Once the room was warmer, he kept his word and left her with the blanket so he could go about his business.

Brent brought back tales of a land where there was nothing but snow and ice for thousands of miles, and they were fascinated and horrified at the thought. "It is as frosty there as Aura's glare." Stuart smiled but said nothing.

The weather reports on television fascinated them. It was downright barbaric to guess at weather this way and the Thuringi were merciless at mocking the weathermen. "They have been wrong more than they have been right," Gareth noted.

"I do not understand why you persist on living this way," Brent scoffed. "In my travels, the other half of this planet is much more pleasant. You should come with me; none of this constant cold until the seasonal exchange. But no, you insist on staying where it is miserable. Airmen!"

"Oh, Watermen," Carrol shot back, "You insist on owning a wandering fin!"

The name of the city was New Orleans, and Brent Ardenne was fascinated by its sheer audacity. For weeks he heard nothing but mardigraw, mardigraw over the com, and apparently some sort of revelry was to come to a head on a specific night of obesity. The Isador slipped into the Big Easy's harbor on Fat Tuesday, and Brent emerged filled with curiosity. He took care to wrap a scarf around his gills, but it quickly became clear that his precaution was unnecessary.

Not only was there a city-wide party under way, but it was also a costume party as well. He could have appeared as a gigantic parmenter and not have stood out in the crowd. Boisterous crowds drank and sang and partied at every turn, so Brent hid in plain sight and enjoyed a rare uninhibited time among Earthians.

Women kissed his cheeks and vowed he had the most wonderful costume they ever saw. He was appalled at the unseemly way some of them exposed their breasts to people on decorated vehicles, but it garnered them colorful necklaces thrown from decorated wagons. Brent saw no need to behave the same way; all he had to do was smile and wave at the vehicles and soon he was festooned in colorful bead necklaces and party hats.

He wandered into one of the many bars open to the revelers and ordered a beerz. He drank and sang in American with the other party goers, and at one point one of them drunkenly commanded him to sing a song. He thought for a moment before launching into The Seagoing Maiden, a ribald song that was a standard in every Thuringi cantina. It was about a lass who offered her favors far too freely to be anywhere close to reality on Thuringa, but it suggested a delightful way to imagine it. It did not matter since it was well received by the hard-partying crowd and won him another round of drinks.

He found himself staggering toward the docks with one arm wrapped around the shoulders of a young woman named Elizabeth and the other hand securely holding a bottle of Guinness. Elizabeth was from Clemson wherever that was, and she was curvy and warm and giggly, all the best traits an Ardenne could want in a woman.

But wait; those were traits that a single Ardenne man wanted, and Brent was no longer single. "(You realize I am a married man)," he told her.

"That's okay, I won't tell her if you won't," Elizabeth giggled.

"(No no)," Brent protested as he stopped abruptly and planted his legs firmly where he stood. "(I cannot dally; I made a vow before the God of All to be true to my wife, and I cannot break it. But, but, but; you are a very lovely girl my dear Lady Elizabeth, and it is no reflection on your allure)."

"I don't know what you just said, but it sure sounds wonderful," she told him.

"(That is what they all say just before they realize I mean it)." She sputtered in amusement, and he joined in. "(Tell me where I must take you)."

"You said you had a ship!"

"(But I cannot take you to it. It would not do)," he intoned as he leaned his forehead against hers.

"It would not do," she repeated, and sputtered again.

"(No, no it would not)!" he chuckled.

"Then I'll just go home, damn it all anyway!" she giggled.

"(Home to your Clemson)."

"Home to … yeah no, somewhere here."

"(It must be somewhere around here)." They headed back up the street, only to find their way blocked by a pair of men of dubious purpose. "(I say, where is Clemson)?"

"Give me your wallet," one man said without preamble.

"(My whatet)?" Brent asked, and he and Elizabeth chortled at the same time.

"Your wallet, man; give me your dough."

"(You speak in riddles)!" Brent exclaimed, "(and I cannot bear it when you people speak in riddles)!"

"Give me your goddamn money," the second man commanded.

Elizabeth was not so far gone that she did not recognize a mugging, and she shook Brent's arm as sobriety rapidly gained a foothold on her. "He's not kidding, he wants your money."

"(Oh, he does. Well)," he said, pushing her to one side and

drawing his sword, "(He is not going to get it, is he)!"

"I have a gun, you asshole," the second man said even as Brent drunkenly swung his body around to face his assailant. The hand with the blade followed the motion, and the Pleonian steel nearly sliced the mugger's hand off.

"(...and now you do not)," Brent breezily observed.

"Augh!" the mugger shrieked. He seized his wrist and fell to his knees in agony. The first man scrambled for the dropped gun, but Brent brought his sword around again and the man stopped just in time to prevent his own decapitation by the blade held closely under his chin.

"(Now I was having a grand time on this most obese day with drink and beads and Elizabeth and her Clemson, and you have to spoil it all with your demand for coin)," Brent scolded. He swayed a little, but his sword remained still as he began a lecture to his panicked adversary. "(I want you to go away, little man, and – oh hush that wailing, you are noisy)!" he bellowed at the blubbering injured man. "(Word, you should not argue with a sword, it is never a good outcome)." He kicked at the gun, and his foot sent the weapon clattering across the street and into a grate. "(Come, fair Elizabeth, we must go to Clemson)." Unmindful of the two thugs, he threw his arm around her shoulders again and continued on to the brightly lit main thoroughfare.

Once there, a policeman stopped them. "That's a pretty realistic sword you have there."

"(It most certainly is. I say, we cannot find Clemson and she must be there)."

"Uh...huh. Where is your hotel, miss?"

"It's the Hotel Monte...Monte..."

"Monteleone?"

"Yes."

"It's the next block over."

"(Thank you, my good man. You are a credit to Naradi everywhere)," Brent praised, and after resheathing his sword, he staggered off with Elizabeth.

After the Thuringi and his friend disappeared into the crowd, the policeman heard the wounded mugger wail again as his partner in crime helped him into the circle of the streetlight. The wound was hastily bandaged with a sleeve torn from his shirt, and blood saturated the cloth. "He coulda killed us, he nearly took off my arm! You gotta arrest that sumbitch!"

The policeman whirled around, but Brent was nowhere to be seen. The cop blew his whistle. When backup arrived, an ambulance was summoned, and the police set out in search of a tall blonde man with yellow contact lens dressed up in some sort of fish costume and in the company of a leggy brunette with hoop earrings.

They never found him. Once they arrived at the hotel, Brent and his new friend ran into some of the group she accompanied to New Orleans, so he turned her over to them. He kissed her goodbye and took the taxi her friends hailed for him back to the docks. It took him unnoticed past the searching policemen and the ambulance that took the injured mugger to the hospital. Brent dove into the water, swam up under the dock where the Isador was tethered, and secured the hatch once he was inside. He peered at his hand that still gripped the bottle and roared in outrage. It was watered down with the undrinkable New Orleans harbor water.

Darien heard a great deal about a 'Strip Club' that some of the oil field workers attended in another town. He could not figure out what it was. He learned not to ask questions since they only left him open to mockery for his ignorance. He mentioned the club to Stuart one evening. "I have no idea what kind of club it is, but it seems to be some sort of place to relax," Darien told him. "Apparently, the membership is open to visitors."

"Perhaps it is some sort of council," Stuart mused. "We might investigate it. Perhaps it is like the organizations Michael mentioned, the Red Cross and the United Way. If it is a place to relax, you should attend it. You have been working so awfully hard, Darien. You deserve to rest. You and Glendon and Gareth should all go to this place."

"What about you and Carrol and Brent?"

"Carrol and I do not work nearly as hard as you three, and Brent is constantly enjoying his work. You deserve a treat. Besides, we can remain here for security's sake," Stuart said. "We will go another time."

That settled, Darien listened carefully to his co-worker's

conversation and cautiously asked where this club was located. He got teased anyway. "Yeah, they'll love you, musclebound," one of the men snickered.

That Friday night Darien, Gareth, and Glendon got into the truck and went to the address he was given, using the directions Lloyd wrote for them. It was quite a long way from the ranch and Gareth was uneasy about the distance. When they pulled into the parking lot of the establishment, they all relaxed a bit. "Why, it is a cantina," Gareth said with relief. "What better way to relax than with a beerz?"

They were stopped at the door by a larger-than-average sized Earthian man who demanded money. "What is a cover charge?" Glendon asked politely.

"Bucks, man; nobody gets a peek for free," the man replied gruffly.

Darien shrugged and gave the man the amount specified. "I suppose it covers the scrip for beerz ahead of time," he surmised.

The three Thuringi walked around a wall into the bar and were struck dumb at the spectacle before them. A nearly naked Earthian girl writhed on a platform to the rhythm of a song, and the cantina was filled to capacity with men who drank as they watched her performance.

Glendon uttered a "Yeep!" and a roar of disgust and quickly turned to face the wall. Darien glanced around at the patrons of the bar, appalled to see they evidently enjoyed the spectacle. Gareth shook his head and reached for the pistol he thought was at his side.

"She is obviously being forced to perform this disgraceful act," he told the others. "She must be some sort of captive. Perhaps we should free her."

"We will need to go back and get the others, and weaponry," Darien agreed. "Name of All! How disgusting! I thought these people were good people."

"Hi, y'all," greeted another Earthian girl wearing an apron and little else. She carried a tray of bottled beerz. "What'll you have?"

"(What will – young lady, are you forced to work here)?" Darien asked as he quickly pulled her to one side. Glendon and Gareth took up defensive positions on either side of them. "(And that poor creature on the platform)," he indicated the dancer with a jerk of his head in order to avoid looking at her again, "(how long has she been enslaved thus)?"

"Huh?" came the plain reply. "Buddy, I have to work here. I got a kid at home to take care of, and this is the only work I can get. And if you're talking about Mary Lynn up there; shoot, she's a headliner. She brings in the best cash. Nobody's a slave around here. It sure beats working at the Dairy Queen."

"Do you mean that young woman is intentionally exposing herself to this crowd, rather than toil for royalty?" Glendon exclaimed, astonished at the very idea. His voice carried and several patrons turned to glare at them.

"Shut up, creep," one inebriated man called out. "Go thump your Bible somewhere else."

"You foul wretch," Glendon shot back angrily. "Have you no pride in yourself or your women? How can you support such scandalous behavior?"

"Look pal, if you want a drink, get a drink, and sit down and shut up. If you just want to complain, get lost," said the man who demanded money at the door. Darien approached him with a dangerous look in his eyes.

"(We did not realize this establishment catered to such foul events)," he said. "(We will not stay. Return our scrip to us, and we will indeed be gone)."

The bouncer sneered with contempt. "You paid your cover; you saw the goods. Now beat it."

"(Gladly)," Darien replied. He picked the man up and proceeded to beat him.

The ensuing free-for-all found all three Thuringi in the center of an enormous quasch from which there was no escape. Beer bottles flew in all directions, as were chairs, tables and the occasional Earthian man. Some of the dancers watched from behind curtains and doors in the back of the club. Word swiftly spread about three big handsome strangers who were tearing apart the bar over them, and it was gratifying to the girls' egos.

Gareth slugged his way through a trio of men, relishing the chance to get back at them for the assault on his eyes that their acquiescence provided. Glendon held a broken table leg and fended off his attackers handily, as if it were consue practice.

Darien was in full riot mode, swinging his fists and throwing anyone he could get his hands on across the room. One of his co-workers from the oil field refused to get into the fracas when he observed the maniacal gleam in Darien's eyes and saw the damage the Thuringi inflicted upon adversaries.

A police siren wailed in the distance and the bar cleared out. A scantily clad girl rushed out from behind the curtain and took Gareth by the arm.

"Come on, it's the cops. Come this way," she shouted. He called Glendon and Darien, and the three ran with the girl to the curtain through the scrambling throng of scattering patrons.

Behind the curtain was a small room with walls lined partway with mirrored dressing tables with many bright lights around each mirror. A dozen barely dressed women were in scandalous costumes, and they eyed the Thuringi appreciatively. Glendon realized shutting his eyes at the sight would not be helpful in the least, so he chose to avert his gaze to the ceiling instead. "Yeep!" Darien put his hand up and pretended to rub his forehead and effectively shaded his eyes from the sight of the women.

Gareth concentrated his sights on the eyes of the woman who brought them there. "(If you are in need of escape, we will offer you a safe passage away from this place)," he told her. "(You need not be forced to perform these salacious acts)."

"But honey, this is how we make our living," one of the women told him kindly. "If anything, you're the ones who need to escape. The cops aren't going to go easy on you for busting up the place. You'd better get out the back way, fast."

"(But you need not live like this)," Darien protested without removing his hand from his eyes.

"Is that a marriage proposal?" asked one of the girls.

"(I am not the marrying kind)."

"None of 'em ever are," she sighed. "Go on, now. Stay out of sight until the cops leave." The Thuringi slipped out the back door and found refuge in the shadows. The exit door closed just before the local police came into the dressing room. The girls all voiced their objections to the intrusion. When he saw no men there, the policeman went back to report to his sergeant. The dancers giggled.

"Isn't that sweet; they wanted to save us from ourselves," one laughed. "How cheesy is that? I didn't think white knights were still around."

After the police left, the Thuringi stole back to the pickup and drove to the Sheldon ranch in silence. Finally, Gareth said, "As the God of All is my witness, I never expected such a thing. Name of All! Even bawdy Borelliat women have better dignity than that."

"Such is life on a jaded world," Darien grumbled. "It is disturbing. Have they no knowledge of the enticement of flowing garments? Have they no shame? Was that a…a stable?" He and Gareth exchanged wary glances.

There were bordellos on some outposts run by scurrilous, unscrupulous Gharadee. When the Ledess of the Chassiren flatly refused their ideas and requests – in fact, she wounded several in doing so – the Gharadee experimented with supplying some of their own Gharadee women to men in exchange for coin. Such ventures did not do well since no one wanted to pay for something the Chassiren supplied for nothing. The Chassiren were more appealing and gracious, and the Gharadee women were perpetually frightened the Shargassi would request their services. Chassiren always filled the need and were infinitely safer to visit than a loose Gharadee woman, as the former were protected from disease and similar unpleasantries.

Beyond that, no one really knew much about the Chassiren, as they seldom disclosed anything. No one saw children on Chassiren, so it was believed they did not become pregnant. If they did no one could tell since children were nowhere to be seen there. A Chassiren had the ability to reflect the preferences of her visitor, so except for the initial meeting in their Grand Hall few knew a Chassiren's identity unless she allowed him to know. It was also a widely regarded opinion that Chassiren preferred Thuringi or Thelan visitors if a preference among the people of the Stellar Council could be made.

Glendon stared out at the highway as he drove, aghast at the whole notion of easily offered gratification. It was not seemly in any direction. A thought occurred to him, and he turned to Darien. "I am most humbly grateful, Your Highness, that such behavior offends you. It dispels the notion you are unseemly in action and thought and fortifies my belief in your underlying goodness."

"Of course, such behavior offends me!" Darien declared, a little out of joint at the statement. Still, he understood why Glendon mentioned it. Darien spent so long cultivating and reveling in a bawdy reputation, the club was the sort of place the Bishop would presume Darien preferred. "I speak naughty and sometimes act naughty, but never in my wildest imaginings would I ever lower myself to such base behavior. I prefer the chase to the capture and even then, the capture should be worthy. That sort of business offers no chase at all; there is no enticement, no challenge. Ugh!" He shuddered. "It makes me want to scrub myself clean and avoid all Earthian women just as a precaution."

When they got back to the Sheldon ranch, they were at a loss of how to describe their evening. They had to explain something; all three obviously were involved in some sort of altercation. Carrol busily cleaned their cuts and bruises.

"Well, what happened?" Stuart demanded.

"I would rather not speak of it in front of the princess," Glendon said politely.

"Why not?" Carrol asked, surprised. "You were all to go relax, not get into a quasch. What happened? What kind of club is this strip club?"

"Naked women danced for the salacious observation of strangers," Gareth snapped after the other two did not speak up. He was mortified to explain anything to anyone about the events. "It was the most disgusting thing we ever saw in our lives. I for one never want to witness such again and would prefer not to mention it again either."

Carrol stood before him with an antiseptic cloth in hand, her mouth open and her eyes wide. She was shocked at his words. Brent, home for a quiet restful weekend from his adventures on the Isador, had much the same look on his face.

"Did you manage to free them?" he asked.

"They did not wish to be freed," Gareth muttered. "It is their method of employment."

Brent and Stuart uttered snorts of dismay.

Glendon said, "I suppose even a beautiful world like this one has a nasty underside, but I wish I had not been a witness. Surely, they cannot believe it is their only option for garnering wages."

"You see, this is just the sort of thing over which the Bishop will scream," Brent told them. "To say nothing of what Aura will do! We must not mention this in any of our general reports. It took us some time to discover it ourselves. Perhaps if we stick to the plan to keep to ourselves after the Armada arrives, the rest of Thuringa need never be exposed to this kind of unpleasantness. God knows I never want my good boy Triton or my dear Isador to be saddled with this sort of mental imagery, nor do I wish it for myself."

"It is not the sort of entertainment shown on their broadcasts here on Earth," Stuart mused. "Every society has its seamy underside, as Glendon said. In our society we have the sweet poems of the Vita Kanerra in our public libraries, but we also have the Tarinade that our adventurous youth and our ardent and daring lovers claim. If that is the worst that Thuringi society has to offer, then we are far and away ahead of the Earth."

"The Tarinade has some extremely scandalous passages, itself," Carrol pointed out before she realized what she said. The men studied her apprehensively. "You seem to believe only men read, and you also quoted it endlessly on our journey here. Isador read the Tarinade, too; it did not make her any less worthy of respect."

"No, but the Tarinade is chiefly meant for private inspection between consenting adults," Darien said. "It was never meant to be on display in a public forum."

"I will not mention this in my reports," Stuart decided. "I did not bear actual witness to it. But now we are aware of the matter and can avoid it in the future."

"True," Brent agreed. "But how is it this Earthian pastime disgusts us, yet we take such perverse delight in singing along with their 'One Fine Day'? Is this not at cross purposes?"

"I let my imagination take me where it may go, when I sing that song," Darien told him. "It is not something that is placed before me to rob me of private interpretation. It is the difference between being naughty by suggestion and being disgraceful by action."

"Well, Earthians do not realize when they agree by saying 'yes' they have no idea that to us, it sounds like 'yjass'," Gareth said. "But Darien is right: suggestion is a far cry from what we witnessed tonight." He took the antiseptic from Carrol's hands. "We were fortunate the police did not capture us after the fight. Then it would have had to go into the reports, and your father would have found me unworthy for even unintentionally witnessing such a display."

"You had no way of knowing," she told him. "How did you

escape?"

"The women showed us an exit through their dressing room."

"You were among them, among those exposed women?"

"Well, yes," he said, and she hastily gathered her medical supplies. "It was the only way out."

"I can just imagine," she said, obviously not believing him from the tone of her voice.

"Honestly, Your Nibs," Gareth protested. "The only other way would have put us in the path of the Earthian Naradi. It was not unpleasant."

"Oh, of course not," she said, and retreated to her medical office in the parlor.

"Well, what do you want!" he exclaimed, following her. "I did not look upon anything but their eyes. If you think I looked anywhere else, then I am even more offended than you by the accusation!"

"Lover's quarrel," Darien judged. "She is in the wrong, you know. Gareth was every bit as shocked as we were; he was simply more practical about our situation. Someone had to keep his eyes open for a way out. I confess I hid my eyes."

"I stared at the ceiling," Glendon confessed, abashed. "Gareth was strong enough to handle the situation."

Stuart shook his head and laughed. "So, both the Naughty Boy and his noble Guardian were too rattled for practical application! It was up to our Everyman to get you out of harm's way! Well, let the two of them work it out. Let us clear our minds with a treat we walked to the store and purchased today. We have a cold confection called chocolate ice cream." He led them into the kitchen.

In the parlor, Carrol told Gareth, "I do not doubt your word. I simply cannot fathom your even wanting to be near such creatures; such Chassiren." She shook as she put away her supplies.

"Oh no, Your Nibs! Chassiren are not anything like these women! Chassiren are gracious and low-key companions. And I beg your pardon, but I did not want to be near these women. I wanted to get out of there without running afoul of the local constabulary. It would jeopardize our whole mission to run afoul of the law, as well as jeopardize any hope I have for your father to allow me to court you." He reached out and took her hands in his. "How can you think I could willingly look at such brazen people, how could you imagine that I would ever wish to consider anyone but you? You wound me, Your Nibs."

"I simply do not like the idea of some strange woman eyeing you," she said crossly. "A woman so brazen might believe that any handsome man might be hers for the taking, and I do not care to have them assume such of you."

He peered at her. "Nibs? Are you jealous?"

She frowned and looked at him. As she did, her frown altered into a rueful smile. "Well, I suppose I am. You have the ability to turn a woman's head, you know."

"I did not know," he whispered. "I have not made it a habit to notice other women since the night I held you dancing at Festival." She seemed to melt against him, and they kissed passionately.

"Have you settled your differences yet, or have you killed each other?" Darien called from the kitchen. "The silence is deafening."

"We have settled," Carrol called back, and stole another kiss from her beloved engineer.

"Well, if you do not both get in here soon, there will be no chocolate ice cream for either of you," Stuart told them. Gareth and Carrol grinned at each other and tried to see who would make it into the kitchen first.

Only one conversation concerning the club started Monday morning at the oil field site. Darien was asked how he liked the girls last Friday. He gave his inquisitor such an intense glare that the man nearly wet himself from trepidation. "(I cannot believe you treat your women so carelessly)," he responded. "(Is there no regard for human dignity here)?"

"Hey, nobody forces women to dance," the man replied.

"(No, and no one can force me to encourage such activity. I enjoy the pursuit of a woman as much as the capture itself. If she is so wanton as to advertise herself among many, there is no challenge. You people believe in seeking the easiest path. It makes you soft and weak)."

The grand roll of his royal voice reminded the men that he was foreign-born and perhaps very old-fashioned; everything about him emanated royal blood in exile. Perhaps their family fled Europe after the war. The men knew little about European monarchs except that at one time many countries were ruled by them, and now most were republics. This man obviously never lived the life of the common man, yet he returned to the oil field day after day because some sense of duty was stronger than his disdain. Recalling the ease with which he saw Darien throw men across the room at the bar, the man at the bar that night let the matter drop and advised the others to do the same. Darien was given a wider berth from then on.

Dickie Forbes called Darien over to his truck one evening before they packed up to go home. Darien was cold and stiff and annoyed as usual at Pete and George and already in a foul mood. He hoped that whatever Dickie Forbes had to say would be brief and be done with it. He was.

"Darien, you're a darn good worker but right now production isn't really needed around here. Our rigs are going out in the western part of the state to drill at some new sites but we're cutting back on some of these reworks. What I'm saying is, I'm going to need to lay you off, you being the new guy and all."

"You will lay me off." Darien did not understand the term and his stare of concentration looked as if he was contemplating murder.

"But I'll need you later, don't get me wrong!" Dickie hastened to add. "I never saw a man with as much gumption and drive as you! To be honest, I…well, since you don't have any work papers or a passport yet, I have to pay you under the table in cash. Out on the new rigs the big bosses want us to provide Social Security numbers for all the work hands, so I'll have to keep you here."

"Under the table? Social secure…? Sir, my hands have never been completely secure at this social manner of work the entire time," Darien admitted.

To his astonishment, Dickie Forbes laughed at him. "You have the strangest ways of talking, I swear!"

"I would say the same of you."

"I'll explain it to him, Mr. Forbes," Lloyd offered.

"Good! I reckon we'll need him back this summer, but right now they want the rigs out at the new spots. Are you coming with us, Lloyd?" Believing this bewildering conversation was over, Darien strolled off for Lloyd's pickup.

"Yeah. I'll explain to Darien on the ride home."

"Okay. I sure appreciate it." Dickie lowered his voice for Lloyd's hearing only. "Darien kind of scares me when he gets that mean look on his face, almost as much as that brother of his. Brr, I still get the shivers over him!"

"Stuart's a good man, Mr. Forbes; you just caught him on a bad day and the boys picking on his brother, that's all."

"Yeah, well, these people sure stick together!"

Lloyd explained to Darien on the ride back as carefully as he could. He did not want to face the large man's wrath, either.

"See Darien; we're just reworking the old fields to get as much oil out of the ground as we can. They're drilling in new fields out west, but you don't have any identification. Dickie's been hoping you could get new passports or green cards or something from your embassy, but I guess he just can't wait any more. He'd like to bring you out there to work because you're a good strong worker, but you've got to have some I.D."

"I do not know why I cannot get new passports," Darien repeated what he was told to say by Michael. "But what is the meaning of paying under tables?"

"He means he's been paying you off the record in cash because he can't write a check to a guy who doesn't have any legal standing, see. It's called paying under the table, sort of out of sight."

"Oh."

"When they come back, it won't be to any of these fields we've been working. It'll likely be to some east of here, sometime this summer. So, I'm sorry but you're being laid off."

"What does that mean?"

"You won't have any work; you won't be working with us for a while."

"I woe not?" Darien's whole face lit up with relief. "Excellent!"

"You don't mind?"

"Not at all! It is cold and I am unused to this strange weather, and the black product from the ground makes me ill. It will be a relief to get away from it for a time."

"Well, thank God! I was afraid you'd be mad!"

"No woe, not at all! We shall have a grand time of it without the Dickie Forbes' people annoying us!"

"Well, that's another thing. I'm going to be going with them during the week, and then on the weekends I'll drive home to see Katie and Monica. I have to earn a living, and Katie will have to go it alone for a while. So, I was wondering if you'd mind kind of, looking after them for me while I'm gone. You know, in case of an emergency or something."

"I would be honored," Darien assured him gravely. "My family will take care of them as if they were our own numbered kinsmen."

"Uh…okay, that sounds good!"

Darien was in a jovial mood when he came into the house. "I am laid away!" he announced. "I will not toil in the black fields until they return in the summer!"

"When is that? When it gets hot again?"

"I believe so. Ah! Let me wash away this nastiness for the last time!" He strode off to the bathroom cheerfully.

"I am so relieved!" Carrol heaved a big sigh. "Every time he goes out in that field, he comes home ill." When Darien came down to dinner, he was delighted to see heaping plates of vegetables ready to be eaten. "These are the vegetables we stored last summer," Carrol explained. "It was our harvest, as meager as it was. Perhaps this year we will be better prepared and can all help Glendon prepare the ground."

"These are as good as the fresh kind from the market," Stuart noted. "We shall plant the entire yard full of edibles."

"Leave some room for Kellis," Gareth protested. "One side yard, at least!"

"That is not unreasonable," Stuart agreed.

Glendon discovered the usefulness of bicycles and acquired one. It was primarily for Carrol, Stuart, or Gareth to use to ride into town on weekdays, and Glendon rode it for pleasure on Sunday, his day off. Sundays off appealed to all of them, but to Glendon it was especially sweet. Regular businesses were closed, and he was free to bicycle all over the surrounding roads without crossing much traffic. He especially liked to stop outside the churches at mid morning to hear the hymns. He did not understand much about the Christian religion, but he respected the enthusiasm for their beliefs.

The black churches fascinated him. Their music was lively and vibrant with energy, and he was drawn to them. He peered around the door into a service one Sunday, curious how these boisterous sounding services were conducted. A friendly black gentleman at the door waved him inside, so Glendon eased around the door. He only wished to observe unobtrusively in the back, but at six feet ten inches, a yellow-haired, green-eyed Thuringi could not be unobtrusive in an African Methodist church under any circumstances. He was the object of curious glances and stares.

"Come on in!" invited the preacher. "Everybody is welcome in God's house." Glendon took a seat on the back row, and realized how much he did not blend in. But their enthusiasm for their religion was infectious, and in time he clapped along with the rest of the congregation and enjoyed the delightful harmonics of the music.

"Man, that is one big ol' white boy," one man whispered to another. After services, they approached Glendon and chatted as they walked outside. The men were in their early thirties in age, and the one who spoke to him was named Franklin Morris. "I remember you now. You work over at the feed store for Mr. Gentry, don't you?"

"Yes, I do."

"Shoot man, I saw you carry around big hundred-pound sacks of feed like they were nothing. What do you eat to get you there, anyway?"

"I like peaches," Glendon ventured, not understanding the question, "and chocolate."

"Peaches and chocolate?" The men looked at each other and laughed uproariously. "I don't think I'll tell my children that; they'd be eating nothing but peaches and chocolate from now on, thinking they'll grow to be mountains."

Glendon went on his way after a time and reflected on how pleasant strangers were. It did not surprise him that Earthians encouraged religious beliefs. These followers made a much kinder citizenry.

At the gas station later that week Glendon noticed a little black girl barely into her adolescence as she hurried down the road, schoolbooks clutched tightly to her chest. She glanced back over her shoulder continuously, and Glendon saw why. An automobile with four teenage Caucasian boys followed her and as the car passed her, they yelled vile epithets at her. Glendon concluded his gas purchase and followed the girl in order to call out to her.

"Would you like a ride?" he asked. She shook her head, and he drove on. In the rear-view mirror, he saw the car with the boy circling around and approached her again. Glendon stopped his truck and got out. The car pulled in front of the girl, and Glendon saw the way she bit her bottom lip in agitation and fear. The boys emerged from the car, making crude suggestions and more vile taunts than before. One pulled at her pigtails, and she jerked away from him only to run into another boy, who plucked at her blouse.

"Leave her alone," Glendon ordered. They turned around to see who spoke, and two boys backed off immediately. The other two, a surly looking pair, sneered at him.

"Well, the Englishman is a n----r lover," one remarked.

"This child is not up to the task of warding you away, but I am," Glendon told them. He came around the front of the car. "Leave her alone and stop calling her such vile names."

"Ooh! Such vile names!" one of them mimicked and the others chuckled. "Can't you freakin' count, Jeeves? There's four of us and only one of you."

"Yes, it is so terribly unfair. Earlier, there were four of you and only one small girl. Now the odds are even: only four of you, against me." He motioned to the girl. "Get behind me, child. These vermin will not harm you; I promise you that." She pushed past her assailants and hurried to do as he instructed.

"Man, I'll kick your ass," the ringleader of the group vowed as he stepped forward. Glendon backed up a couple of steps to the front of the car. "Look, the retreat of the Light Brigade," the ringleader pointed out to his friends.

Glendon reached down and got a firm hold on the bumper of their car. With a hearty jerk he ripped it off the vehicle in front of the stunned boys. He tossed it aside carelessly and said, "Come kick my ass, boy," with a particularly unnerving anticipation in his voice.

"You took off my bumper!" the driver howled with indignation.

"Come forward, and see what I remove from you," Glendon told him. A police car approached and stopped behind the group of boys. As the officer got out, the boys rushed to him and proclaimed their innocence. They pointed to the bumper, then to Glendon. The girl stood next to the Thuringi and gave the tall stranger a sad look.

"I'm sorry, mister," she told him. "I'm all kinds of trouble to you."

"No, you are not," Glendon said.

"What's this about you tearing up their car?" the officer asked.

"They accosted this innocent girl and then threatened me when I intervened on her behalf," Glendon replied. "I thought it best to warn them as to the possible outcome."

The officer looked at the car and noted with a startled jerk, how jagged the bumper brackets were, literally torn off rather than figuratively. He glanced at the girl and recognized her. "This ain't the first time these boys have shown their tails, is it Becca?"

"No, sir."

"We didn't do nothing to her," the leader of the gang claimed.

"That's a damn lie," called out a woman from her yard nearby. "These hounds called her names and had her so shook up she was downright ashy. Then this giant came along and took up for her, and they were all for going after him, too."

"What about the bumper?" asked the officer.

The woman leaned against her fence and raked the blonde and gray wisps of hair back from her face. She looked the officer straight in the eye and said evenly, "I couldn't say for sure. It must have fallen off." The boys objected loudly to her statement, but the officer stopped them short.

"You pack of wolves; don't think I don't know about you. If you're not stealing cigarettes from the machine at the laundromat or sneaking beers, then you're harassing someone weaker than you. If you're looking for something to do, I have a cell back at the station you can fill for a while. Now I've told you before to leave this little girl alone. She ain't bothering you. Get out of here."

"What about my bumper?" the driver demanded. The officer looked over Glendon and turned back to the boy.

"I'd say you got off easy. Go on now, git." The four boys opened the trunk and stuck the bumper in as best they could. "And don't think about making trouble, either. I know your daddies and they ain't gonna like you pickin' fights." The boys got into the car and left. "Them four are going to win an all-expense trip to McAlester Prison one of these days," he told Glendon. "You're the English guy that's working over at the Gentry's, aren't you?"

"Yes, I am."

"I heard there were a bunch of English guys that caused a big fight over at a club in Muskogee the other night. You wouldn't know anything about that, would you?"

"No," Glendon replied. It was no true lie. There were no people from England concerned with the events at the club as far as he knew.

"Uh huh." The officer wagged a warning finger at the girl named Becca. "You find yourself another way home, girl; don't make it easy for those jaspers to get at you." He went back to his car and drove away.

"I am willing to take you to your destination," Glendon offered, and she took him up on his offer this time.

The next day Franklin Morris from the African Methodist Church came to the feed store to see Glendon. "I appreciate you taking up for my little niece. Those boys have bothered her ever since her brother won a football award one of them thought he should have." He shook Glendon's hand. "You're welcome at the African Methodist Church any time you'd like to come." Glendon thanked him.

Chapter 7: The Amen Corner

The Thuringi scouts grew accustomed to their new outpost planet by painfully slow increments. They were used to the Stellar Council worlds, where the populations were much smaller, the races more definable and the languages easily translated through the Sengan-designed Universal Translator. Earth's population was greater than all the worlds of the Stellar Council combined, plus the estimated numbers of the Shargassi Empire. Instead of one religion per world (except for the Borelliat who boasted three variations, and the Sturbin who had none) Earth had multiple religions, multiple political systems, multiple countries, multiple races, and multiple civilizations. It was hard enough for the Thuringi to keep abreast of American differences, much less try to incorporate the rest of the hemisphere or the other continents of the world.

They liked the variety, however. There was nothing like the animals of Earth to be found anywhere else. They had never seen a cat before, nor elephants or monkeys. Gakkis were found on every world of the Stellar Council. Physically they all boasted a singular horn in the center of the forehead, but the coloring and genetic differences could identify the home world. Each world bred gakkis to meet its own specific requirements but did interbreed its racing gakkis a little since racing gakkis was a source of planetary pride and interplanetary coin for the known worlds.

Instead of cattle, the Stellar Council worlds had cabrett, which had stouter legs than Earthian breeds, and each world had its own variation but only one. One could tell by looking at the difference between a D'tai cabrett and a Thelan cabrett. Chesser were originally from Senga but had been exported to other worlds. This was good for Borelliat's agricultural society but nearly disastrous for Thelan. Their lake-filled world provided an easy-to-evade landscape for loose chesser, and the piglike creatures multiplied so rapidly in the wild that they were considered a nuisance and dangerous. Annual hunting seasons were necessary to keep the population of the wild chesser in check.

Chickens were not native to Thuringa, but Borelliat had birds called nobi that were equivalent to chickens, and the Hunda and D'tai had domesticated fowl. Most of the other worlds did not bother to domesticate birds. They took eggs as they came across nests, provided the protective parent birds allowed it. Birds had variety among the Stellar Council worlds, and some types of birds were best to avoid entirely at certain times. The Thelan farba, for instance, had a wingspan of twenty feet and was used for transportation by early Thelans centuries ago. The farba were not domesticated but tolerated humans on their backs until mating season, when no one rode a farba for any reason and expected to live.

Earthian chickens were small, relatively harmless, and versatile for all sorts of domestic purposes. They were also very appealing, and Carrol liked to pet chickens whenever she got the chance. She adored the soft "awwk, awk awk awk" sound brooding hens made, as if commenting to their feathered sisters.

Despite the number of new things to learn and remember about Earth or perhaps because of it, it was a much more enjoyable place than any other outpost the Thuringi ever knew. Earthians, at least the Americans they met, were curious and exasperating and talented and suspicious all at once. Brent's journeys took him all over the world, but he did not approach people much if at all. His gills and webbed fingers were hard to explain without preparation, and he had far too much area to explore undersea to bother with non-aquatic life. He left that up to his Airmen kindred.

The Sheldon ranch included the surrounding pastures with the beef cattle and stock pond in back. When Michael came to visit one spring day, he noted the wistful way his friends regarded the local horses on the farm next door. "You know, it probably wouldn't hurt to get a horse for you to ride to and from town. It would keep you from illegally driving more than you have to except for grocery trips. But then, you will need to buy some sweet feed and hay."

"Why can we not grow it ourselves?" Glendon suggested. "There is a perfectly large block of land adjacent to the yard."

"Do you know about ranching?"

"Gareth comes from a long line of farmers."

Gareth looked up from his work at the dining room table, where he was rebuilding a small engine. "Yes, but I know little about Earthian farming."

"It is not so different from our way. Michael, your gakkis and cabrett eat hay, is this correct?"

"Yes, it is. I will tell you what: if you can find a way to plow up that whole forty acres over there, then you can plant it with hay, cut and bale it, and then plant winter wheat, you might get two crops in."

"Wheat? That is like our bran?"

"That's right, Stuart. Wheat and bran are I guess the same, essentially. But you'll have to string up the fencing to keep the cattle out of it. They will eat anything but especially whatever you worked hardest to cultivate, it seems."

Michael thoroughly enjoyed the enthusiasm and willingness to experiment that his Thuringi friends seemed to live by. He only had to demonstrate how to string up barbed wire and the next thing he knew, Stuart and Carrol were out digging post holes in order to extend the side fence all the way back to the end of the pasture so they could close off forty acres for a hayfield. Michael reported back to his father that his friends were good stewards of the land.

"The old house never looked better, Dad, and they are planning to grow hay in the forty acres to the west. I really wish you would meet them."

"Look Michael, if you say they are doing a good turn of it out there, that's fine by me but frankly, I really don't care what you do with the old place. It's yours now and I don't have time to go back out there right now. Maybe one of these days. Aren't these friends of yours ever going to find jobs?"

"They do have jobs. One works for Dickie Forbes and another for the Gentrys. Two are doing scientific research for their country and another is an inventor. And the leader is the one who is heading up the farming."

"Oh. Well, all right then, go ahead since they're improving the place. Funny how you never gave two hoots in hell about the ranch before now."

"I never needed it, but they do. I guess I am seeing it through their eyes, and I see its worth now."

Carrol liked to wear the blue denim pants. They fit snugly like uniform breeches and were amazingly durable. She liked the swishing sound the legs made as she walked through the tall grasses in the pasture. Fencing was difficult, tedious work but someone had to do it and there was no point for her to make the men do all the hard tasks. Stuart handled the post hole digger expertly after a few initial mistakes that would have left the fence line staggeringly out of line. Carrol took her turn at it and thanked the God of All that her Arda-powered healing ability made quick work of blisters. All along the fence line they dug holes, planted posts, and then strung the barbed wire strands tight across the posts. They had to take down some of the fencing in order to drive all the cattle out of their planned hayfield, but the oversight was understandable.

Michael brought out a bay mare which Carrol promptly named Bishop. "I always thought Bishop Trapis would benefit from a bit in his mouth and someone to rein him in," she said dryly as she gave Bishop the horse a good rubdown.

Glendon bought a plow rig from Franklin Morris's family and hitched Bishop to it. He tilled the west side of the yard from the roadside all the way to the back-yard fence near the corner of the barn, a considerable garden space. In their enthusiasm, the Thuringi planted a great deal of vegetables and set out many starter plants from the Gentry's store: Corn, bush and pole green beans, snap peas, tomatoes, bell peppers, three kinds of squash, loose lettuce greens, cantaloupe, and watermelons. They were enthusiastic about potato plants because potatoes closely resembled friaks, so they planted twenty hills of those as well.

Stuart realized it would take days to till the acreage with one horse and a single-disc plow. He studied the problem with his usual zeal until he came upon a multiple cultivator. Michael leased it and brought it to the ranch, and instead of the horse they hitched up the Good Lad to it with a slight modification by Gareth. Thus, the Good Lad was the first and so far, only Thuringi fighter ship to be used in Earthian farm work. Stuart and Darien plowed the frontage acres at night so people would not see the ship in action. The back acres hidden by the rolling Oklahoma hills were plowed during daylight hours. Then the brothers took turns spreading the grains and tilling them into the soil.

Gareth took no part in the effort, which mystified them all at first. He watched from the side yard fence one day, his arms crossed over the top strand of barbed wire as he took on a jaunty hipshot stance. Carrol and Glendon approached him from either side, and Glendon slapped him on the back and exclaimed, "Reminds you of the good old days, does it?"

"Well," Gareth replied with a barely noticeable tremble in his voice, "It is indeed similar to how my father used to do it."

Carrol and Glendon exchanged regretful glances. It had not occurred to any of them how this farming venture might affect Gareth, so enthusiastic were they. "Oh, Gareth...I am so sorry," Carrol stammered.

"No, no. It is very admirable for the sons and daughters of kings and nobles to till the soil like a farmer from Carzon. Very commendable indeed." He brushed it off with seamless bravado and picked up a hoe to weed the garden.

That night, Carrol told Stuart and Darien about it as they quietly talked on the porch after sundown. "There we all were, playing at farming while not giving a single thought to Gareth's reaction. That is why he did not have any enthusiasm for it. He had to do it every day of his life plus his other tasks and never got to attend Academy the way he should have done. We see it as a novelty, an amusement. I am so ashamed of myself."

"I never thought of it that way," Stuart anguished. "Poor Gareth! We must look as foolish wastrel noblemen to him."

"No," Darien said after a moment's thought. "He holds no harm against us in his heart. Perhaps he only recalls his father and how much joy he might have felt to know his son traveled all this way to watch a pair of princes revel in his task."

"In fact," Gareth said from the doorway, "That is exactly how I feel." Carrol rushed to him and hugged him tightly with a sob. He patted her on the back. "There now, Your Nibs; do not carry on so! Your brother has an amazing gift of the heart, for that is what I thought this afternoon. Imagine what Father would have said, had he lived to see this day! Prince Stuart and Prince Darien and Princess Carrol and Lord Glendon, finally enjoying what he had the privilege to enjoy all his life! My only regret is that he did not live to see it. I think he would have laughed and slapped his knee at the sight."

I like him, Darien thought. The entire class system has been turned on its ear by a single gentle man from Carzon.

Franklin Morris invited Glendon to Easter services at the African

Methodist Church. Stuart decided he might like to go along and soon all six curious Thuringi headed down the road on a bright warm Sunday morning for the church in Iron Post. "They told me to come early so as to not have to walk so far," Glendon explained to the others. "I am uncertain why it would be a problem, but we should do as they suggest." It was obvious why once they got to town. Every available space on either side of the street held a car as well as several side streets down from each church. The Thuringi had to park blocks away and walked along the aging concrete sidewalk toward the house of worship.

It was a walk that was well worth the time and effort. Spring had come to Oklahoma, and lush green grass covered the lawns of the neat little homes they passed. Riotous spring flowers were on full display in their proudly tended gardens. Glendon stopped now and then to sniff a blossom and invited the others to enjoy the aromas. The morning was pleasant, warm enough to walk without a coat yet cool enough to bring a tingle to the air. The smell of freshly mowed lawn grass locked its fragrance into their memories, and the new green leaves of the trees splashed with sunlight added to their senses for pleasant recall.

They came across a variety of Earthian dallahs along the way. On Earth, the closest dallah they saw that even came close to resembling its Thuringi counterpart was a yellow short-haired pointer. This Sunday, they marveled at the sights of a black and tan hound, a beagle, a dachshund, a poodle, a shepherd, a Pekinese, and a pair of Chihuahuas. Or, as Stuart listed in his journal, "a burned-looking dallah, a small solidly built multi-colored animal, an unnaturally long creature, a partially naked pouf-haired animal, a long-haired dallah, an unfortunate creature with a disfigured face, and two noisy partial rats." Most of the dogs barked at the Thuringi, although the shepherd wagged its tail and allowed Gareth to pat its head. The dachshund trotted back and forth across its porch and Darien could not get over its length.

"Surely these animals are from different species. They cannot possibly all be dallahs," he tried to reason to himself. The sight of the poodle sent them all into gales of laughter. None of them was as ill mannered as to point at the clipped poodle, but they could not hold in their audible reactions. The chihuahuas unnerved Carrol when they raced from under their porch to yap at her heels. She let out a shriek and jumped into Stuart's arms. He held her out of harm's way as Gareth and Darien shooed the little dogs away.

"Their eyes are protruding, they might be mad," Carrol declared as she clung to her brother for dear life. She was anxious about the fact that she wore her Chanel suit and pumps; she would have been much more at ease in her uniform and boots.

"Don't worry, miss," called a friendly voice from one of the house's windows. "They're annoying little beggars, but they won't hurt you. Chico! Groucho! Get back over here before I make you into sausage!" The chihuahuas headed back to the house, but not before issuing a few more barks.

"Interspecies genetics," Darien muttered, and the others agreed.

There were many people outside a little church, but Glendon shook his head. "This is not the right church," he told his companions. "This is full of light-skinned persons. The one we seek is two blocks down."

"First Baptist Church of Iron Post," Brent read the sign out front. "How impressive. Their places of worship are numbered." They were invited to join the Baptists by a nearby man who overheard him. Glendon explained that they were invited elsewhere.

"What is the difference in Baptist and Methodist?" Gareth wondered aloud. "Does the God of All differentiate between the races? Are not the Martins, Methodists?"

"We have all sorts of people in all the churches," said the man who extended the invitation. "We have some colored families here in our church, but most of them like their own church, you know. The Methodist church with mostly white folks is about four blocks that way, but the one you're looking for is right down that street there."

"I propose we split up and attend both this one and the one we seek. We can compare notes later," Darien suggested. Brent, Stuart, and Glendon went on along toward Franklin's church. Darien, Gareth, and Carrol stayed with the Baptists. Carrol admired the lovely frocks on the ladies and little girls of the church. The freshly ironed, lacy pastel-colored dresses reminded her of the high celebration days in the Cathedral of Arne.

The doors opened and the crowd surged inside the church to sit. The Thuringi did not have the luxury of relative anonymity on the back row; the three found themselves in the center of the crowd on one side of the aisle. A large portrait of the long-haired chap was front and center, suspended on wires in front of a wide curtain. The portrait showed the chap kneeling before a large stone and a brilliant light shone down on him from a point in a cloud to his upturned face. All around the altar area were vases of waxy white flowers and greenery.

The entire church smelled of wood polish and old books. Earthian people of all shapes and sizes were in attendance and many of them looked over the Thuringi curiously but politely. Gareth wore his color contact lens. Darien wore dark glasses; Carrol could wear a pair of color contact lens for about four hours before her Arda power dissolved the lens in her eyes, as if the lens were foreign bacteria to be destroyed. They were three large handsome blonde people with English accents who smiled and nodded at the surrounding Earthians. The Earthians in turn accepted them with remarkable ease.

"Where is your home church?" a woman in the row of seats ahead of them asked as she turned around in her pew.

"I last attended the Cathedral of Arne," Darien replied in American with a straight face. "The vicar rang the bells for the occasion."

"Cathedral? Oh, you must be Catholic, or Episcopal," the woman said, trying to figure it out. "Well, I'm proud that you came here to visit us on Easter."

"We are pleased to be here, madam," Darien replied graciously.

"If you need to be saved, this is the perfect time to do it. My granddaughter's going to be baptized today," the woman went on proudly.

"This is the way of all Baptists, hence the name," Gareth attempted to clarify. The church organ sounded before she could reply, and the woman turned to face forward again.

The congregation rose to their feet to sing from their books and the Thuringi rose with them but did not sing. After the song, the leader of the church rose to speak to the re-seated crowd. He spoke of the meaning of Easter, of the sacrifice of Christ and the resurrection. He was eloquent if often loud, and Darien at last understood the connection between the child of Christmas and the long-haired chap Jesus of Easter. Darien lost his cynical smirk and listened carefully to the story, impressed beyond measure with the tale. A warrior with no sword, facing certain doom and agony from those who would turn against him, and even forgave them for their error! It sounded so very altruistic, so very Thuringi. Perhaps this Jesus chap would be of interest to Father and the clergy.

Gareth felt chill fingers run up and down his spine. Resurrection was a subject that gave him the shivers. He took Carrol's hand in his. She squeezed his hand and inched closer to him. She was unaware of his state of mind and thought only that he found the subject as fascinating as she. Gareth kept his eyes on the chap in the portrait and wondered how such a powerful prince – a son of God, no less! – could allow such cruelties to be inflicted without fighting back. He noticed how much the Jesus chap resembled a Thuringi warrior of old with his long hair and flowing garments.

But this chap was a prince of peace, not a traditional soldier in the manner of a Maranta Shanaugh or a Hartin Medina. Ideally, a Thuringi would seek peace but the instinct to fight to the end would not have seen him end up attached to a wooden cross. Such a sacrifice was awesome and required the surety of a divine purpose. Gareth wondered if perhaps the Earthians might very well have hosted a Godly son. Another hymn was announced, and he gladly stood with the crowd, relieved for the distraction it gave him. His thoughts were Thuringi blasphemy.

Carrol thought the tale was moving, but then many Thuringi warrior tales were of sacrifice and admirable bearing. She considered the notion of a holy birth to be figurative, much like the parables told by the Jesus chap. She was too used to a Universal God embraced in various ways by the Stellar Council worlds to take the Earth's self-contained beliefs seriously. But the sincerity of the Earthians was impressive and she did not doubt the strength of their faith.

They were seated again, and the minister then announced that children were going to be 'cleansed in the waters of baptism and the blood of the lamb'. Darien sat up straight. He never liked children to be involved in adult affairs, and this blood business sounded serious. He wondered about the phrase 'saved', and how did they know these particular children who now approached the altar from the congregation were in danger? He could detect nothing unusual about them.

The children went obediently into a small space that had been concealed behind now-opened curtains behind the altar. The minister also went into this space, and the Thuringi heard the unmistakable noise of splashing water as the minister clambered into an unseen tub. The first child in line joined him as he sermonized loudly now of dying and living again and washing away sins and being lambs of God. The hairs on the back of Darien's neck stood on end. Then the minister placed a clean cloth over the child's face and dipped her backwards into the pool.

Darien leaped to his feet as he grabbed for the sword and pistol that of course were not at his side. "You bastard! You seek to drown that child to prove your point?" he shouted, so rattled it came out in Thuringi. Fortunately, he did not have his universal translator. All the Thuringi were fluent enough in English now to not wear them. Gareth grabbed Darien by the arms to prevent him from climbing over the pews to throttle the Earthian preacher's throat.

"My, he's filled with the Spirit!" observed one of the church members in admiration. "He's speaking in tongues!"

The child was brought back up, and Darien saw she was wet but smiling, as if a main goal were accomplished. The Thuringi prince stared blankly at her and then looked at Gareth.

"You do not honestly think this crowd would allow him to slay all those children in front of them, do you?" Gareth whispered to him in Thuringi. "It is all right. Sit down, Naughty Nibs."

Darien did so quickly, because his knees suddenly buckled and he could no longer stand on them. Some of the congregation whispered to each other, and the man next to Darien leaned over to him.

"You never saw a baptism before?" the man asked.

"We do not believe in the practice of endangering air breathing children by holding them under water," Darien snapped at him in American, thoroughly unnerved at what he witnessed. Other children were dipped backwards into the water and Carrol reached across Gareth to take Darien's hand.

"It is their belief, peculiar to their John Baptist tale," she whispered. "They are imitating their spiritual leaders."

"I do not like this in the least," Darien whispered back fiercely. "The sooner we are away from here, the better." At the beginning of the next rousing hymn, Darien bolted for the door as soon as the congregation stood to sing. He paced outside on the sidewalk to wait for Gareth and Carrol and tried to shake the fear in the pit of his stomach.

He understood the story of Christ. He understood the concept of baptism, of atoning for sins, the entire spectrum of Christian belief, but he could not bear the thought of a child being put under water if it was not a waterman. The thought of any child in danger made him nauseous.

As a young officer, Darien went out on a patrol that received a distress signal from an outpost. It was from the D'tai, and Maranta groaned when he heard it. "The D'tai never take precautions as they should," he explained to Darien.

When they arrived at the outpost, it was already too late; it had been too late from the start. The D'tai manned an outpost among already established inhabitants and brought along families to settle the post. But the natives became embroiled in a civil war with the D'tai caught in the crossfire. The survivors were alive only because they barricaded themselves in a cellar and emerged when they heard Thuringi speak in their lyrical language through the cellar air vents. A truce was secured long enough to recover the D'tai.

It was at the entrance to the cellar that Darien saw her, a little child not much older than seven or eight, Monica Martin's age. She arrived with her mother too late to get into the cellar before it was barricaded, and the mother died at the top of the stairs trying to protect her child. The child lay face down, a large knife in her small back. One little arm was against the door in a last attempt to turn the doorknob. Darien never forgot the sight of that helpless child with the weapon piercing her still form in all its wicked triumph.

People emerged from the church and offered to help him pray; some asked if he would like to know the location of the church where they spoke in tongues. Others asked him if he needed saving. He glared at them.

"No," he said shortly. "I wish to leave and attend my own services in our own cathedral. I am not a Baptizer. I am a Thuringi." Carrol and Gareth joined him, and they walked on up the street in search of the African Methodist Church.

"We are all in need of saving, apparently," Carrol remarked dryly. "They believe we are Catholic because of our Cathedral, and in fact they nearly insisted on it."

"I said I was Thuringi. Are their ears clogged with water?" Darien growled. "If they are devout enough to believe that the God of All sent a son here, why must they make divisions among believers of the same source? Baptist, Methodist, Catholic – no wonder they are so confused."

They heard the AMC congregation long before they got to the building. They peeked inside the doors and got a glimpse of a group of singers all arrayed in matching robes, singing in multiple harmonies. Every time the song died down, the preacher launched into a part of a sermon, then the choir started up again in a different song, then he continued, and they sang out again, almost seamlessly. The congregation had a grand time dancing and clapping and singing with the choir.

In the middle of the back row, flanked on both sides by Franklin Morris and his family, were three tall Thuringi, singing and clapping along with their hosts. Brent roared out "Amen!" every now and then, and Glendon swayed in tandem with a couple of teenagers. Stuart could not wear any contact lens at all, so he wore tinted glasses to hide his yellow eyes. He belted out the hymns with Franklin Morris. He saw the three Thuringi at the door and waved them over.

"They do not push children into pools of water here, do they?" Darien asked.

"Not today," Franklin's mother told him in a lovely slow patient drawl. "This is Easter, baby."

Darien climbed over the back of the pew to join his brother. Gareth and Carrol were invited to join another group of people in another row. They were not aware of the passing of time, but by the time the service was over, the sun was far past midway in the sky, and it was hot outside. Franklin's wife Janette took Glendon by the arm.

"You're all invited to stay for the Easter egg hunt," she told him. "It's fun and the grown-ups like it as much as the children do."

"Easter egg hunt?" Glendon repeated. "What is it?"

"It's a little thing we do," Janette said. "We dye boiled eggs different colors, and the adults and the Easter Bunny hides them for the children to find." Franklin had warned her that Glendon and his 'family' were not familiar with a lot of holiday customs, and she tried hard not to laugh at the look on Glendon's face now.

"The Easter bunny hides colorful eggs," he repeated gamely.

"What are those children doing?" Darien asked about the growing line of excited children holding baskets at the edge of a large, mowed field dotted with colored objects. Franklin's father chuckled beside the big Thuringi.

"They're going hunting," he explained. "If any of the children find the prize egg, he or she gets a big ol' chocolate bunny."

"What do the others get?"

"A bunch of boiled eggs," the elder Mr. Morris said.

Someone blew a whistle, and the crowd of children ran into the field, squealing and laughing as they plucked the scattered colored eggs in their path. Darien decided this was much better than sticking children under water and mentioned the baptism ritual to the man.

"Oh, we do the same sort of thing. We just don't happen to do it on Easter Sunday. It's nothing to be worried about, boy. The children are happy to join the family of God through baptism. It's not just white folks. Shoot, they're probably out hunting eggs right about now, too."

"Does everyone search for these eggs?" Stuart asked.

"Just the children," Mr. Morris said. "'Cause man, if I thought I could win me a big ol' chocolate bunny I'd be out there too, yes sir." The three men laughed.

The Thuringi declined the invitation to the church picnic, opting to walk back to the truck for home. Carrol hopped up into the cab of the truck and immediately removed her pumps and wiggled her toes in relief. Glendon blushed and concentrated on driving.

Word, Carrol was beginning to be as unconcerned about certain proprieties as Gareth! A woman should not bare her feet and move her toes about in the company of a man not her husband! – especially when her feet were as small and pretty as Carrol Shanaugh de Phillipi's.

"Yeep! Your Highness," Glendon said at last, "if you please, would you replace your footwear?"

"But my feet hurt. We walked a long way," Carrol protested. "I am sorry, Glendon, but these dreadful shoes have caused a blister on each foot." She tucked her legs around in order to hide her feet under the seat a little. "I must never wear those awful things for anything more enduring than a brief excursion again. You must make certain Janis never tries them."

Glendon nodded as he wiped the sweat from his brow with a

quick swipe of his shirtsleeve. Oh God, the thought of Janis's feet was also going to be on his mind now! He hoped Brent's water tank out by the barn was still clean; he might have to jump into its cold water to calm down.

"What did you think of their Christ tale?" Gareth asked nonchalantly to the others in the back of the truck. He was a little worried that he was the only one who found the story admirable.

"I think these people should be loaded with guilt," Brent said immediately with his answer. "Imagine, such devastation throughout history being brought to bear in the name of one innocent man!"

"I found it interesting. I wonder how best to describe it for our clergy," Stuart said. "Just the premise of God finding favor with one group of people on one planet in the entire universe will put the Bishop's nose permanently out of joint."

"Oh, perhaps not," Darien said as he leaned his head back just enough to let the wind blow his hair away from his face. "These people have had absolutely no contact with any other world before. If we were raised in the same room in the same house with no windows or doors, we would rightly believe that it is the entirety of existence. Surely even a myopic bishop will recognize that."

The general consensus was that Earthians tended to interweave their most serious religious doctrines with fanciful tales of the unbelievable. Just why was unclear. They also celebrated with elaborate dinners involving specific foods and most of the time sweets and chocolate were involved, often brought by imaginary creatures in return for the good behavior of children. These things amused them and contritely enough, made the most sense.

The Thuringi stopped at the Gentry's house on the way home according to the request Glendon received from Margie. She came out to the truck with six little baskets, each holding two colorful hard-boiled eggs nestled in green tissue paper, and each basket also contained a little chocolate bunny. "Happy Easter," she said. "Are you sure you won't come in for Easter dinner? All my family's stopping over."

"Thank you so very much," Stuart replied, "but feeding six hungry Thuringi is far too burdensome a task for such a kind heart such as yours, already laden with guests. Happy Easter to you, Dame Gentry." She laughed and waved as they left.

"They must be from royal folks, the way they give titles to everyday people," she mused. "It's as if they don't know any other way but a highborn way."

Once they got back to the ranch, the Thuringi scouts sat on the porch to nibble their bunnies. "I wonder what the Earthians would think of us if they were the wanderers, and they had come to Thuringa," Stuart mused. "They might have wondered about our sole breed of dallah and our one type of gakki and our modest land mass."

"They would have liked Festival," Glendon said. "And I imagine they would have admired our Dorea trees."

"They would probably have hunted our illini to extinction," Darien said dourly.

"We are fairly boring people," Gareth put in, "and yet in comparison, we are not a bad sort. Their diversity makes for a fractured people. Can you imagine if the Shargassi found them first, instead of us? It makes me sad that they are so naïve about the universe around them."

"They irritate and entertain me at the same time," Carrol laughed. "They are so Thelan!" They all laughed and agreed.

"The Thelan would probably enjoy the odd pursuit of colorful eggs," Gareth said, and suddenly jumped to his feet. "Give me all the eggs, and go into the house," he instructed. "I will hide them, and you five will search for them."

"That is a child's game," Darien told him. "How hard can it be to pick an egg up from the ground?"

"I am not going to hide them for a small mite to retrieve, I am going to hide them for you nibby lot," Gareth told him saucily. "The five of you will have to search hard for them." They went inside and put their chocolate bunnies in the refrigerator. By code of honor, they did not peek out the windows. Five minutes later, Gareth knocked on the door. "Get your baskets and search!"

They went out on the porch and looked around. "Where are they?" Glendon asked.

"That is for me to know and you to discover," Gareth said. He sat in the porch swing and watched as the five poked around. "Twelve eggs," he called out.

"You have them all in your pocket, you did not hide them," Stuart guessed.

"No, I did."

Carrol squealed and pointed up into the rafters of the porch roof. There on a cross brace sat a blue egg. She plucked it down, put it in her basket and beamed at Gareth.

"Ah-Ha!" Glendon found a red egg nestled in a tuft of flower greenery by the porch.

A mad scramble was on. In the end, Darien found four, Carrol three, and Stuart and Glendon found two each. Brent found his one the hard way: he stepped on a warped board on the porch and felt the crunch of the egg where it had been hidden under the plank. He laughed and declared it the prize egg. They hid the eleven uncrushed eggs again for Gareth to find and teased him during his search. Then the boiled eggs were eaten picnic style on the porch, followed later by the chocolate bunnies.

"It will be time for the Cartwrights soon. Brent, you must stay for tomorrow," Glendon said. "You must view more of the Gunsmoke."

"Why?" Brent asked.

"It is so very Thuringi," Glendon explained with enthusiasm. "A Naradi of the Old West of Earth defends an outpost against thieves and rogues and other bad sort. There is a wise Elder medical, and he is aided by a Naradi lieutenant called a Chester. There is also a woman bartender of the outpost cantina."

"Closer to my kind of story," Brent grunted. "They are quite keen on entertaining. Why, even their religious ceremonies are a songfest. Perhaps these strange religious ways are more to your liking, eh, Gareth? I know I like the singing, and the Amening."

"It is rather appealing," Gareth agreed.

"It is so sad," Carrol sighed. "I do not understand how they can enjoy their Christmas, knowing of the child's fate. But I suppose if he lives again, it has a happy ending of sorts."

"Barbaric, ungrateful people," Darien muttered. "They are not Thelan; they are Gharadee or Borelliat. With the exceptions of the Gentrys and the Martins and Michael Sheldon, you can have the whole damn lot."

The spring rains came, and it seemed to the noblemen that after each rain, the garden and hayfield issued forth something new to behold every time. Soon every waking hour was taken up in weeding and thinning and checking for insects in the garden. Gareth came out of the house and after one look in the hayfield, he laughed so hard he fell down helplessly on the ground. He finally picked himself up and stumbled out to the field where Stuart doggedly chopped at the ground.

"No, Crown Nibs," he chuckled, "one does not need to weed the bran field so diligently." He steered him toward the vegetable garden.

Darien stopped by the Gentry's store one afternoon to find Glendon off on an errand for Margie Gentry. As he waited for Glendon's return, he saw Ed Gentry preparing to change a tire on his car. Darien approached him. "May I aid you in your task?" Darien asked. "I would enjoy the chance to return the many kindnesses you have given our family."

"Well, all right," Ed said, relieved. He was about to go in to call the local garage, since the lug nuts were too tight for Ed's arthritic hands to loosen with his tools. He stepped aside.

Darien rapidly unscrewed the nuts with his bare fingers. Ed stared in disbelief as Darien plucked the tire off the hub and plopped the spare in place easily, as if everything were made of cardboard. He screwed the lug nuts on and tightened them by hand. Ed stood by with the unnecessary tire tool in hand, astonished. Darien straightened and dusted off his hands.

"Is there anything else you need?" he asked, and Ed shook his head wordlessly. Glendon returned from his errand at that moment. After he took some paper sacks inside to Margie, he re-emerged with dangling truck keys in his hand.

"Have you been behaving?" he asked Darien.

"Lord Gentry is far too kind a man for me to misbehave in his presence," Darien said, and bowed to Ed. He and Glendon got in their truck and went home. It was at the end of the workday, and they were happy to go. Ed Gentry walked inside the store and stood by the gumball machine, lost in thought.

"Ed? What's on your mind?" Margie asked when she saw her usually restless husband deep in pensive thought.

"Those folks of Glen's. They are the strangest folks, but I like 'em, Margie. I do."

"Lots of folks around here do," she agreed.

Glendon and Stuart took the truck into the larger town of

Muskogee one Saturday to gather scrap metal for improvements to Gareth's ships. Gareth stayed up most of the night to work on a design and was still asleep at mid-morning. Carrol studied a strange animal they caught, a fat gray creature that had rings on its furry tail and a pointed face with black around its eyes. It was not a domestic creature but did not appear to be a particularly dangerous creature. It was adorable to her, however. She enjoyed giving it little knobby berries through the mesh in the wire cage Gareth made.

"Look at your little hands!" she exclaimed in delight. "Oh, why did we not have such clever creatures on Thuringa?"

Darien decided to walk to the Gentry's store for a fizzy drink that afternoon. He admired the strong material called denim and was especially pleased the fabric did not allow the little barbed weeds to scratch his legs. He watched some gakkis as they ran in a field for a while and whistled at a herd of cattle in another. He rounded a curve in the road and saw a minor auto problem ahead. He recognized the car.

Evidently Ed Gentry lost control going around a curve in the road. The car slid off the pavement and was now at an angle that would not allow it to get out of the ditch. Darien continued to stroll until he reached the vehicle.

"Automobiles are not kind to you, are they?" he asked, and Ed laughed.

"Well, that's so. I'm figuring to get somebody to get me a wrecker and just pull it out."

"And it will be all right to drive then?"

"Yeah, I hit a slick spot on the road back there and just slid off as pretty as you please. But look at that tire back there. It can't get no traction, you see, and with it straddling the ditch there's no way – "

Ed Gentry's voice trailed off as Darien went around the back of the car, seized the car firmly by its trailer hitch, and moved it over until the back wheels were on the same side of the ditch. He walked around to the front and gestured to Ed. Ed started the engine and put it in reverse, and Darien helped the car back out of the ditch. Ed motioned to Darien to get in the car, and together they drove to the store. Ed cleared his throat several times but could not say anything at first. Finally, he managed to speak. "I have never seen anybody as strong as you and Glen before in my life. You folks are just real unusual."

"That is true," Darien agreed.

"Just how do you spell where you're from?"

"We are from Thuringa," Darien replied. "I am not certain how you might spell it."

Ed nodded. "Well, I sure appreciate your helping me out, I couldn't have done it by myself."

Darien cheerfully bought an icy cold fizzy drink before he headed back home to the ranch, explaining he enjoyed the stroll. Ed watched Darien walk away, shoulders back and head erect with the easy grace and power of a jungle cat. The gait reminded the Earthian man of his son in the military and wondered if Darien served in the army on Thuringa. He was stronger than he appeared, and maybe he was older than he looked.

Darien went in through the front door and wondered at the silence in the house. He heard the back door click shut and walked that way to look out the back window. Gareth evidently just awakened, for his hair still bore the signs of bed rest. The mechanic scout approached Carrol from behind while she hand-washed linens in a pan of soapy water. She stood in profile to the window, but neither noticed Darien observed them.

Gareth gently placed his hands on her waist and stepped up close behind her. Her hair was in its usual braid, and Gareth nuzzled her neck, coaxing the hair aside in order to have access. Her shoulders sank in a relaxed response to his affection, and she leaned her head back to rest against his shoulder. Gareth's hands did not wander; his mouth did not seek hers for hungry kisses. They simply stood still. Carrol's eyes were closed in dreamy delight, breathing deeply in enjoyment of the moment. Gareth's eyes were also closed, his lips touching her ear.

Whether the good major was whispering to her or not, Darien could not tell but the emotion of the moment brought tears to the Warrior Prince's eyes. So much passion and such longing were embodied in those two still, quiet forms that he was quite overcome. There were no naughty movements as Brent and Isador might have made; no suggestive gestures as Darien himself might offer up to a woman. There was only the quiet strength of love, a love that needed no crude action in order to flourish. This, then, was how a Duncan courted, and how a Phillipi in love should react.

In the distance Darien heard the return of Glendon and Stuart in the truck. Gareth kissed Carrol's neck and stepped over to add a teakettle of hot water to her washtub. The truck pulled into the back yard, and the two riders emerged from the vehicle. Gareth went to see what kind of scrap metal they found, and Carrol continued to wash out her laundry.

Subtlety was a quality high on the list of desirable traits of the well-born, and from that day forward Darien considered Gareth Duncan de Gordon to hold all the requirements necessary as a suitor for Darien's sister the princess.

That evening, Ed got out his atlas and inspected every country with a magnifying glass.

"Ed, aren't you coming to bed?" Margie finally asked. "It's late. You've been looking at those maps all evening long. What's going on?"

"There is no Thuringa," Ed said thoughtfully, and put aside his magnifying glass and the atlas. "Every country that speaks English is listed here, and it isn't here. There's a region in Germany with that name, but those boys don't have German accents, not even a hint of it. Margie, he lifted my car out of the ditch as easily as Glen moves around cast-iron stoves. Things the rest of us couldn't possibly do. Darien twisted the lugs off the car with his bare fingers."

"Well, he's always been a very nice boy to me," Margie said with a shrug. "I don't know what you're so worked up about. They're just strong boys."

Ed rose to his feet and saw a superhero comic book on the coffee table left by some friends' child during their last visit. "Maybe they're not boys at all," Ed said to himself before he went to bed.

Chapter 8: Memorial Day

The next time the Gentrys saw any of the Phillipis, it was Carrol astride Bishop, the bay mare Michael brought out to them. No longer needed for the plow, the horse was petted and pampered by the Thuringi princess. She fashioned a saddle from thick blankets and some flat braided smooth rope that doubled as a cinch from other strips of cloth. Another flat rope was attached to the saddle/cinch combination and its two ends were looped to form stirrups.

Margie Gentry noticed how regally Carrol rode, straight and proud. She was not a common sight in town and curious people stopped what they were doing to watch "the war bride" go by. Of course, they thought she was too young to be an actual bride of the world war, but the original notion about her remained. She purchased a few items at the grocery store and then rode back to the ranch, her long hair streaming out behind her like a flag of glory. A couple of young men accompanied her on horses of their own and provided amusing companionship along the way.

Once there, she thanked them for their stories and rode on up to the house. Like any proper gakkisman she cared for her animal first before she entered the house with her purchases, but the time spent in task did not diminish her excitement.

"Oh, there will be exciting things tomorrow! It will be a Day of Memorials, an American Bauni, in which the Americans will recall great battles and deeds of their warriors! Could we go, Stuart? There will be a parade in the larger town just past Iron Post, and there will be bands and waving flags!"

Carrol knew just what kinds of buttons to push to elicit a yes from Stuart: tales of great battles and warriors accompanied by music and cultural pride never failed to stir him up.

Brent was home from the sea with a gash on his right leg that needed Carrol's healing, and Stuart was not as willing for him to wander the often-violent Earth by himself any longer.

"It was not the violent Earth this time," Brent assured his brother-in-law. "It was an Earthian parmenter and I should have known better." He did not recognize a barracuda before the encounter, but he was not going to forget one in the future. He was able to convince the mission leader to let him return to the sea after a rest period.

The only Aquatic Thuringi among them wore a neck brace to cover his gills and loose-fitting clothing over his websuit for visits among Earthians. His shaggy locks of sun-bleached hair gave him the unusual exotic air of a California surfer, and quite by chance he discovered Beach Boys music in his travels up the Pacific coast. "It is a most excellent choice of music," he confided in his Airmen fellows. "Even you lungers would like it."

"We 'lungers' already do," Glendon told him. "You would do well to catch up."

The next morning, they dressed in their best American clothing and went to the host town for the parade. It was a modest-sized town, large enough that its school hosted separate buildings for the younger and older children. The main street was eight blocks long from the start of the parade to the finish and red, white, and blue bunting decorated nearly every storefront in some fashion or other. Cars were not permitted to park along Main Street before or during the parade so the townspeople could line up along the street.

Shopkeepers were busy ringing up sales and in front of several stores, veterans sold Buddy Poppy flowers. None of the Thuringi understood what Buddy Poppies were, so Brent in his friendly breezy fashion politely asked. He and his companions were regaled with the story of Flanders' Field of World War One, which naturally fascinated the alien warriors.

None of them looked much over twenty-one years of age, and the Americans were pleased to see how interested the "foreigners" were in war stories. Other veterans wandered over and the Thuringi were treated to very warm, personal narratives although it was impossible for the Thuringi to separate the tales of Wars One from Two.

"Such courage!" Darien declared upon hearing a story about Iwo Jima. "Word, that is the stuff of legends!"

"And these Germans, they sound like a quarrelsome group," Gareth added. "Or were they the chaps who fought in the woods?"

"They were in the woods, the Japanese were in the islands," Brent corrected. "I am unsure as to where the 'Limey' chaps fit in."

"Well, that's just what some folks call you Brits," one veteran said kindly. "I imagine your fathers didn't care to tell you that was what your folks were called, it's not the nicest thing I guess."

"I do not mind," Brent replied cheerfully. "We in particular call

all of you short." The veterans and Thuringi all laughed together at his saucy comment.

A siren rented the air and made the six scouts jump in strong reaction at the unexpected sound. It was only the police car signaling the beginning of the parade, but the onlooking Americans naturally assumed it reminded the youths of air raid sirens.

One man took Carrol's hand and patted it. "Now don't you worry one little bit. You're in America now; you have nothing to fear."

Carrol smiled at his thoughtfulness but felt sorry for him at the same time. He had no idea that beings like the Shargassi were out there, or he would have been frightened out of his innocent Earthian mind.

The parade was so much like an Armed Command review day that the six Thuringi were caught up in the familiar excitement, but it was awash in so much American patriotism it was easy to stay focused on their surroundings. They liked the marching bands and the pretty girls waving from convertibles, and the floats were curiosities that made the Thuringi laugh with giddy glee. The politicians were insignificant, and the scout troops looked like some sort of cadet review, but their favorite part of the parade came last, the horseback associations called the Round-Up Clubs.

There were six of these groups and the Thuringi were astonished and thrilled at the varieties of gakkis before them. Carrol and Darien played a longstanding game from her childhood, choosing which gakki they would wish to have in their own stable. Gareth held out his hand, and a gakki turned to him and sniffed curiously at the alien scent.

When the parade was over, they returned home in the white truck. "I wonder how we Thuringi would have handled hand-to hand combat on our own soil against our own people," Darien mused. "I cannot imagine the hardship of raising a hand against another Thuringi over an ideal or belief that is contrary to mine. Oh, a brawl or an argument certainly; but a war?"

"Did you see the cemetery we passed just now? Many graves were marked with little flags," Glendon said. "It is nice that they set aside a day just to recall their warriors' efforts, just as we do."

"There are many ships under water that attest to those battles," Brent told them. "I was curious about them, but most are in very deep waters, and I did not bother to explore any."

Michael was offered a position running a private school in Texas that fall and could not stay in Oklahoma all summer as he hoped. He came out to the ranch to celebrate their first anniversary on Earth and was pleased to see their progress. The ranch was a hive of activity. The garden produced food at an astonishing rate. The ripened vegetables were welcomed with enthusiasm, and the Thuringi toasted their unified gardening effort. This soon gave way to an embarrassing bounty of foodstuffs, far more than anything they expected. There was simply no end to the number of tomatoes and beans and squash. The more they harvested, the more there was to harvest. Soon all of the modest jars from the year before were reused and additional jars were brought in to fill. The day came early when there was no more room in the cellar or in the kitchen or the parlor or back porch.

"I will make a new cellar behind the barn where there is adequate room for expansion," Darien offered.

"You are working for the Dickie Forbes again," Stuart protested with a groan. He was unwilling to think of the name Dickie in terms of a nickname and always used it as a title. "You will overwork yourself if you are not careful."

"But Stuart, working in the soil is a relief for me. Yes, the oil work is nasty but if I can get my hands on sweet Earthian loam, it is refreshing in a way and makes the oil task easier to bear."

Stuart helped his brother plot out a twenty-by-twenty-foot area immediately behind the left side of the barn. Once he saw that contact with the soil really did ease Darien's nausea, he turned the entire project over to him.

Darien dug out the area, larger than the tiny root cellar next to the house. He made it twelve feet deep so they would not have to stoop when inside. He used his powerful fists to slam into the dirt and pack it firmly. It helped take out his frustrations from work this way, plus it made the storage cellar strong. He roofed it with large timbers and covered that back over with the original topsoil. He installed shelving and fitted a door so cleverly concealed that it took Michael Sheldon over an hour searching for it before he gave up and had to be shown its location.

He finished it just in time. Michael never saw so much canned food in a home cellar in his life as he did that summer. There was always something in the pressure cooker to be canned, and when a fruit grower came to the Gentry's store with baskets of peaches for sale, Glendon brought home four bushels. He was dismayed that the peach trees he planted the year before showed no signs of bearing fruit but since peaches were readily bought, it made no difference.

The small flock of chickens Carrol acquired from a nearby farm demanded grain and gave eggs for Thuringi use. There were so many ways to prepare eggs, mealtimes were never dull. Michael cautioned them as to what foods could be preserved and what should not. They decided pickled eggs were not one of those items after all; not a single Thuringi could stand the taste.

The back porch was completely screened now to make their canning operation less accessible to flies and other insects. They made a bed for Michael on the porch. It proved a wonderfully comfortable place to be lulled to sleep in the summertime by the drone of cicadas and the far-off call of the whip-poor-will.

"We used to listen to the rheamor sing for the same reason," Gareth told Michael. "They preferred the country because they are shy creatures, but there were many gathers of them in the woods just outside Arne."

"I loved the rheamor's song," Carrol sighed.

"Oh, it's a song? Or is it a long bird call?"

"Rheamors aren't exactly birds, although they do fly," Glendon explained to the American. "They are beautiful creatures of multihued plumage, but they have the capability to create beautifully complex harmonic songs. They are very honored by our kindred, but they are also very nervous. So many died of stress during the fall of Thuringa that only a small percentage survives."

"Well, that beats our whip-poor-wills all to hell," Michael acknowledged. He noted the ripe hay in the field. "So how are you planning to cut and bale the hay?"

He got blank looks from all six Thuringi. "Well, we did not think that far ahead," Gareth admitted. "Just to see it grow was an accomplishment."

Michael arranged to get a hay baler and tractor, and he and the Phillipi brothers cut and baled the forty-acre pasture. They were prepared to take after it with their swords if necessary, so the baler was a welcome labor-saving device. It was nothing to the Thuringi to stack bale after bale of hay into a wagon and then from the wagon to the barn. They hardly broke a sweat over it. "We sure could have used some of that muscle when I was a kid," Michael complained good-naturedly.

"How will we use that for our bread with it crushed together that way?" Carrol asked.

"Oh, you misunderstand! Hay is what we grow for our livestock; wheat is what we use to make flour, which makes bread and other cooking."

"I see. We are used to only using bran or seeda for everything."

"Say, your corn is looking great! You will be able to cook that and remove it from the cob and can quite a bit of that."

Gareth laughed. "We wondered if we would need to use a jar for every stick of corn. Or ear, that is."

The next morning the heat came early and brought a sticky humidity with it. The wind was dead calm and by noon it was unbearable. Glendon rode Bishop the horse home from town and brought with him an ominous report. "The Gentrys said this is excellent storm weather."

"Yeah, this is Tornado Alley, and thunderstorms love to crop up this time of year. How was the spring?"

"We had many storms, Michael! It rained for three entire days at one point," Carrol told him. "Even Brent missed the sun, but I do not think he ever complained, exactly."

They heard a distant rumble at which Michael glanced to the southwest. "Yeah, see those clouds over in there? They will be coming up from there; it's just a part of life and you can't avoid it if you live here in Oklahoma." The wind began to stir at last, and the coolness was a blessed relief. The clouds continued to build into towers of white puffy clouds which grew bluer and darker as time passed. Then at four o'clock, Darien returned from helping a local farmer clear a field of stumps.

"We stopped early; there is damage to the west of our area, and he did not wish to have us in its path. We 'knocked off early'!" He was pleased to use a slang phrase that he actually understood without needing explanation first.

Michael turned on the television for the weather report. "Y'all, we had better get down to the cellar. Come on, let's go. You can't fight a tornado and that is what they're saying to expect."

They struck out across the backyard and explained to him about the necessary new cellar, but even they were taken aback by what they found behind the barn. The room was downright cavernous. Having run out of shelf room in the original area, Darien took it upon himself to expand it twice as large and placed a long low stone bench along a wall. He had in mind to use it to hold trays when they came to retrieve jars for meals in the winter, but the bench served well as a place to wait out the coming storm.

Gareth brought down a com and tuned it to pick up whatever it could.

"It is raining now," Brent announced. Because Darien had packed the walls and floor so tightly, they held up admirably, but the rain dripped down through the topsoil and between the timber. They hastily threw a tarp up and nailed it in place over the boards.

"A ceiling, a ceiling," Darien muttered as a personal reminder.

"What about the chickens and Bishop?" Carrol asked.

"They should be all right," Michael told her. "Wait, where is Stuart?"

"He is outside. Do not fear for him. Stuart has an affinity with the air currents."

"He might on Thuringa, but this is Earth. Maybe he isn't ready for tornadoes and things." Since the door to the cellar was inside the barn, they were able to open it without getting wet. Michael and Darien went up to the large wide back opening.

Stuart stood in the middle of the doorway, his arms stretched outwards from his sides, head back and with a blissful smile on his face. His hair and clothing were rain-soaked, and the wind blew it all back, but Stuart Phillipi de Saulin was having the time of his life. "Mmmm!" they heard him say in delight, "Freedom!" He turned his head and looked their way. "Stay right there," he advised. "Do not come this way for any reason."

"Be careful of the lightning!" Michael shouted.

"Yes," Stuart said cheerfully. "I know."

"Move to one side, Michael," Darien said as he walked toward Stuart. Michael did as he was told, for he noticed Darien's hands held small blue bolts flickering between his fingers. He joined Stuart and grasped one of Stuart's hands. At that moment, a sudden electrical blue bolt struck the outstretched fingertips of their free hands and danced back and forth between both hands, and the instantaneous strike of thunder roared inside the barn. The sound made Michael leap backward in alarm, but the Phillipi brothers remained where they were. Michael heard them sing a strange song in an unusual minor key, in harmony.

Brent wisely grabbed Michael and pulled him back downstairs with the others. "Better stay down here with us for the now, brother."

"What is happening?" Michael gasped.

Carrol explained, not only for Michael's benefit but for the others as well. "As Phillipi, we have the power to control Arda liquid, a form of energy from our home world. Every Phillipi is born with a certain extra gift that is heightened by Arda liquid, and only those of Phillipi blood can tolerate and control the power from it."

"But… but that is lightning; it could kill them!" Michael gasped.

"It could if we were not Phillipi and energy not a part of our makeup. Our father can manipulate ore and process it into metal and manipulate the metal into form. Stuart has mastery over air currents and over the years he has developed a liking for the rush of electrical energy as well. Darien has a different kind of talent, a talent for chemicals and sensitivity for the chemical balance in living things. And my talent lies in my ability to heal, which also utilizes sensitivity toward living things."

"Then why aren't you upstairs with them?"

"I am not strong enough to enjoy it, and even Darien is not strong without Stuart tempering the power. Besides, I do not like the lightning," she replied. "Too flashy; it is annoying."

"Annoying, she says," Glendon grumbled as he dodged a new leak in the tarp. "I do not see why they even need Naradi Famede."

"Because Stuart cannot create lightning, he can only direct or absorb it. And because Darien is his twin, the jolt will not harm him, but he cannot do what Stuart can. His abilities are different. Anyway, our Arda abilities have nothing to do with our need for security. Darien especially needs a Naradi Famede because he does not mind his manners and is the last word in annoyance to others."

The other three Thuringi agreed wholeheartedly with her, and Michael laughed aloud in spite of his earlier alarm.

Once the storm passed, Darien set to work with his laser pistol to make a crystalline ceiling and walls for the cellar and made the floor slightly rougher with the use of sand on the surface in order to be less slippery. Michael could see no sign of electrical burn anywhere around the barn door.

Glendon soothed the jittery nerves of Bishop the horse as Gareth peppered Stuart with questions. "Why does not every citizen of Thuringa know of your abilities? Word, that would silence the malcontents!"

"They might claim we are too powerful or spread a false tale of harm against others," Stuart explained. "We do not like to boast on our gifts, since it is not our doing that we are this way. It is solely the gift of the God of All. We are merely stewards of the gifts."

"What determines what sort of things you can do?"

"There is no way to tell. It is similar to one's gifted task, there is no way to know at birth what talents someone has. On old Thuringa we Phillipi kept our Arda gifts quiet; only a relative few know what we have, and Father told me even we do not know our full potential."

"What does that mean?" Michael asked. "Since Carrol heals people, does that mean she could bring someone back to life?"

"Oh no!" she exclaimed. "I can heal but I do not have that sort of power! I must absorb the pain and injury myself first, and if I absorb a deadly injury, I must be extremely careful to regenerate in time to save myself or my patient. When death occurs, there is no turning back. The last healer Phillipi who tried to save a fading life, lost both."

"Are there other kinds of gifts?"

"My grandfather King Auguste had extraordinary hearing, which served him well on Thuringa but did him no favor in space. His ship floundered on his way to the Stellar Council, and we lost him, Grandmother and forty-seven crewmen," Carrol said wistfully. "I never knew them."

"My great-uncle mourned for days; they were very good friends," Glendon said. "We have had many healers among our royalty, a number of metallurgists and a few air commanders. There has not been a chemist such as Darien in an exceedingly long time."

"I thought you didn't know much about it," Michael said, puzzled.

"My great-uncle Argo told me after I became a Naradi Famede. I wondered about certain peculiarities of the Royal Family for which there was no ordinary explanation. I was not aware of the depth of the talent, however."

The Phillipi brothers returned downstairs, hearty and restless after the intense charge they experienced. "I could plow a field for corn right now," Darien boasted.

"Scoundrel, you lie!" Stuart taunted.

"I will prove it! Gareth, hitch me to the Bishop's plow and I will take on that entire bran field we just mowed!"

"We do not need that much corn," Gareth objected. "Give us just a little corner." The idea of the prince in plow traces amused him, so they went out to do just as Darien intended. The other four went out to the back of the barn and into the pasture. The wind still blew briskly, and Stuart lifted his hands and took off running into the face of the wind. He whooped with delight.

"Had I only known about these two's abilities back in our Academy days, we would have had quite the roar of a time," Brent commented. "There was a cantina in Dane that I would have enjoyed seeing Darien pull off its foundation. Throw me out for excessive revelry, would they!"

They all suddenly gasped at once. Before their eyes, Stuart made a leap and found himself body surfing on the wind current still stiffly blowing from the south. He rose nearly forty feet in the air diagonally and floated for a brief time before suddenly sinking twenty, and then he caught himself temporarily. Then he plunged the rest of the way to the ground. He leaped to his feet and turned toward his friends and family. "Did you see that? Did you see? Oh, what a thrill!" He tried it again but could not go aloft again.

"Show off!" they heard Darien bellow from the side field.

"Envious!" Stuart yelled back.

"Stuart does not normally speak so brashly," Carrol confided to Michael. "I imagine he is still feeling sparky."

Darien plowed an acre of land before darkness fell. Despite Michael's warning that the corn might not ripen before first frost, Darien and Glendon planted the acre in corn the next day.

They awoke one Wednesday to the sound of distant explosions. Glendon did not go into work. "The Gentrys said I was not to work today, but they did say we should come to town and be their guests for the holiday."

"What sort of holiday?"

"I...I do not know. They simply kept saying it was the Fourth of July. Perhaps it is another observance with sweets and fanciful tales. They will host a meal, and that always means some sort of religious day."

"Another? Word! Perhaps we could enjoy oh, say – August thirtieth," Brent scoffed.

"What happens on August thirtieth?"

"Does it matter? It is the same as July fourth!"

Katie Martin called to invite them to come to the local fireworks show at Iron Post. "It's Independence Day when our country was born. There won't be a parade in Iron Post, but there are some in other towns. But Iron Post is going to have a celebration and Monica's been anxious to invite you to go with us! We're not sure Lloyd will be back from out of town. His truck's been pretty unreliable lately."

"Then we shall accompany you," Stuart said cheerfully. "Perhaps you can enlighten us about some notions. We are going to the Gentry's."

"Oh good! They invited us over, too!"

They picked the Martins up in the white truck and headed for the Gentry's store. Behind the store was a sizable back lot between the store and the Gentry's two-story home. Margie Gentry waved at them from the front porch and ushered the group through the house to the back yard. A picnic table was set up covered in a brightly colored tablecloth. Ed was busy at his charcoal grill, slathering cuts of meat with tasty homemade barbeque sauce. "Hello, there! I hope you're hungry!"

So much meat! While it smelled delicious, the largely vegetarian Thuringi groaned to themselves. This would mean a disaster for their digestive tracts if they ate more than a few bites of the meat Ed offered. Fortunately, Margie had an array of vegetables side dishes, and Katie and the Thuringi brought food with them.

They heard small explosions all over town, and the sound made the warriors jump at every pop and bang. Ed chuckled.

"That's just firecrackers, boys; they won't hurt you none." He had several fountains and sets of sparklers to amuse them, and the Thuringi whooped at the sight with enthusiasm.

"In our homeland, we light rockets to celebrate a birth," Glendon explained to their hosts. "But in your country, you light rockets to celebrate the anniversary of your country's birth. See how more alike we are!"

They were well into eating dinner when Lloyd's pickup rounded the corner of the store. The engine sounded terrible. "Sorry I'm late," he said as he joined the group. "My truck's just about a goner."

"Perhaps I can help," Gareth offered. "I will look it over after the meal."

"I'd sure appreciate it."

True to his word, Gareth poked around in the engine compartment after the meal was consumed. Darien helped clear the table, unwilling to get around the greasy dirty engine compartment of an automobile. The other men watched Gareth and chatted. Ed warmed to the other Thuringi as easily as he had warmed to Glendon. He saw them all at the store at one time or the other, but now that they were in a purely social setting, they were as friendly and enjoyable as one could wish.

"What do you think?" Lloyd asked Gareth about the truck after a while.

"I could repair it, but I am uncertain I can manufacture the proper parts."

"Oh, we can get the parts after Hill's Garage opens tomorrow morning," Ed said. "Lloyd, you don't have to go back to the rig, do you?"

"Yeah, I do. I thought I could just come home and then zip back over to the rig tomorrow and be at work Friday, but it started acting up on me about thirty miles from here. I didn't think I'd make it back before it broke down. I don't know what I'm going to do."

"Why, you can use our vehicle," Stuart said impulsively. "You have done us so many good turns, we would be remiss to refuse you aid in your time of need. Then when your vehicle is ready, we will swap them."

Lloyd gratefully thanked him for the offer and gladly took him up on it.

"If you can crank it up and move it over to that spot right there, you can work on it right here," Ed offered. "You won't have to go far to the parts store that way."

Katie Martin watched the men from where she and Carrol cleaned off the picnic table. "Your brothers sure are some handsome men, Carrol."

"Oh, please do not tell them that; it will only inflate their egos."

"That's hard to believe; you are all so modest! Um…would you mind if I asked you something?"

"No, of course not."

Katie made sure that Monica was with Darien cranking the ice cream maker, and out of hearing range. "Were you married to Gareth's brother?"

"Why, no."

"Are all of those boys your brothers? I mean, are Darien and Glendon brothers? They don't look very much alike."

"No, Darien and Stuart are my brothers."

"I thought Glendon was your brother?'

Too late Carrol remembered their ruse, and she thought fast. "Darien and Stuart are my brothers-in-law."

"Oh! That's right, your names are Phillipi."

I hope I can remember all this later, Carrol thought. No wonder Sunny does not like to lie.

They enjoyed homemade ice cream and enjoyed admiring the colorful sparklers. Gareth threw a block and tackle over a sturdy branch in the tree over the truck. As they all listened to a country band play music in a nearby park, he pulled out the engine. Darien and Stuart helped but were sickened by the greasy residue under the hood and encrusted on the engine block. They loaned the Martins their pickup and rode home in the back of it to the ranch.

The next day Gareth and Glendon rode into town on Bishop. Glendon bought the necessary parts from the garage and brought them to Gareth. One of the garage mechanics followed him back over to see an amateur at work. He came away impressed by the quickness and strength of the Big Blonde Boys, as the Thuringi were called in town.

Gareth was not pleased to simply fix the engine, since he found problems with the brakes as well. More parts were bought and put on, and Gareth toiled away all day under the elm tree in back of Gentry's store. He and Glendon talked and laughed in their lyrical native tongue, and Margie liked to listen in. She had no idea what they were saying since they did not wear their universal translators anymore, but the language was so pretty, just the tune was enough for her.

The other mechanics dropped by and wondered what Gareth thought he was doing. He made modifications to the engine that they would not have thought to do but were perfectly sound once they thought about it. They even loaned him some tools just to see what he would do with them. "Where'd that ol' boy learn how to work on trucks, he's pretty damn good," one of them asked Ed in the store.

"I don't know; I guess he just picked it up somewhere." It was true enough and Ed did not want to invite further speculation with a careless extra word.

By the time Lloyd returned to town that Saturday, his pickup was ready and in far better shape than he dreamed. It still looked like his truck, but the improvements under the hood made the engine purr like a pleased kitten.

"Why don't you get work in a garage?" one of the mechanics had asked Gareth at one point. "I bet our boss would hire you in a New York minute."

"I have far too much to do at home," Gareth replied easily.

The hot summer months were made bearable by visits to the river. They happened across a large blackberry patch while taking a different route back to the ranch, and they returned with buckets until all the ripe berries were harvested. Most of the berries were preserved and put in the large cellar, but they could not resist treating themselves to a jar once a week.

Michael spent several days at a time with them. He showed them how early Americans made butter with a dash and churn and how cheese was made. They in turn taught him the Thuringi alphabet and helped him learn to read from the Thuringi Book of Prayer. Michael liked to be able to write in a private journal and to never worry about any of his family snooping in it. They could not fathom why he persisted in making odd scratchy markings and calling it a language. "Oh, Michael's just playing around with language," his father told the rest of the family. "You know how much he liked learning Morse code as a kid."

Michael took his Thuringi friends to a baseball game involving local minor league teams and explained the game to them. Brent thought popcorn was foolish and preferred watching it pop to eating it, but he liked the idea of potato chips – "friak crisps". Darien was pleased at the sound of the crack of a bat hitting a home run, and Glendon liked to watch the players run to catch a ball. There was nothing from Thuringa to compare with baseball and it was an amusing diversion. Gareth liked the seventh inning stretch and explained to Michael that Kellis players would laugh at the thought of so many rules and regulations.

In Kellis, there was only one rule: "Bury the Dead!" As long as the ball was carried into the point zone of the opposing team, it did not matter what one must do to get it there. One could grab, twist, steal, throw, drag or run with the ball and as long as no one could stop you, a point could be scored. Wrestling one's opponent was fair game, and it was always interesting to see an entire team locked in a tight quasch until someone with the ball broke free and charged forward if possible. Honor prevented unfair jabbing of fingers into eyes or biting, but in the heat of contest even these things were up for debate as a defensive ploy.

"Baseball is a game with so many rules - how do you have time to enjoy any of it?" Gareth wondered to no one in particular.

Glendon often stopped by the Martin house to check on Katie and Monica during the week. He was always polite and unflappably calm. Just seeing him on the porch made Katie feel safer. She hardly needed anything since she was a very capable young woman, and his visits were usually only brief check-ins. The one time she needed help was when her water heater went out. Glendon arrived with Gareth, and the two men worked on the tank.

For Gareth it was child's play, so Glendon only had to pass tools to him. They chatted to each other in their native Thuringi, and it sounded like a musical duet to the Americans listening in. Once the heater was repaired, the two men worked on other odd jobs around the house - a patch in the wall here, a table leg tightening there. They turned away her offer to pay by reminding her that they were friends and had promised Lloyd to look after his family during his absence.

As the Thuringi left, Glendon turned and bowed to her on the porch. "Do call at any time, Lady Martin," he told her, and he fondly chucked Monica under the chin with a playful fingertip. "It is a privilege to give back in friendship."

He did not think anything of the gesture, and neither did the Martins. It was just like the Thuringi to make such lovely gestures and say such nice things, and neither Katie nor Monica thought it odd. Their curious neighbors, however, saw the handsome foreigner with Lloyd's wife and daughter, smiling and bowing and God knows what, and speculation about two attractive people began to blossom.

The rasp of cicada wings in the night pleased Darien Phillipi. Darien's voice was often raspy, and he was one of the very few Thuringi ever known to not have the ability to sing. This did not mean he did not try; only that perhaps he should not and call it a day. His speaking voice possessed the natural singing style of Thuringi speech, but when he tried to lift his voice in song the tune often wandered far from the original key, flattened and awful despite its enthusiastic delivery.

This did not matter to Darien Phillipi de Saulin. Ever aware of the potential to annoy friends and acquaintances, Darien sang for the joy of the action, and it did not matter at all if the tune was lacking. He could not tell anyway. The difficulty of giving birth to two large royal Phillipi babies was hard on his mother, and Queen Oriel used methods she learned from the mystical Hunda to save the threatened life of her younger son. Darien could not sing, nor did he have the kind of outwardly powerful Arda abilities like his brother. His gifts were of an internal nature, more subtle and something he did not discover until he was grown.

He did not like the buzz of mosquitoes, and all the scouts grew to dread the telltale whine of the insects. Evenings in the yard were often spoiled by a mosquito infestation until bats flew in to feast on them. Unlike Earthians, the Thuringi liked the bats and thought they were no worse looking than many short-nosed dogs they saw.

Wasps and hornets were creatures upon which Darien waged a fierce war. He was stung several times by wasps in the barn, so he got out his laser pistol and made quick work of ridding the barn of the things. He was especially anxious to destroy the nests since he knew Glendon would always throw himself between the royal siblings and whatever they came up against. He did not want the loyal Naradi to continue to suffer simply because Darien preferred to take an impatient swat at flying stinging creatures.

The cat in the barn gave birth to four kittens and the Thuringi were delighted with the adorable babies. Even Brent liked them since they did not try to bite at him the way the mother cat did. The playful kittens provided endless observational fun for the scouts, although one was almost permanently welded inside a new scout ship by mistake before Gareth fished it out. They were natural mousers and often presented Carrol with gifts of field mice on the back steps of the house. Carrol was alarmed at their profuse generosity and wished she could explain to them that she did not require such offerings. Glendon was able to give all the kittens away in the due course of time since very few customers at the Gentry's store could resist his friendly salesmanship.

One of the recipients was Margie Gentry herself. Glendon had a feeling that if his daughter Echo were there on Earth with them, all the kittens would remain on the ranch. She was consue age and Thuringi adolescents were fond of small cuddly creatures just as much as Earthian teens were.

That fall the Thuringi discovered the County Fair, and Margie urged them to enter some of their canned goods in it. Carrol selected some jars that looked prettiest, and she also entered some of their favorite chickens and Bishop the bay mare in the livestock competition.

The six Thuringi discovered a whole new world of delight and surprise. Their green beans won third place, and although it was the only jar of theirs that won anything, it was nevertheless a proud moment and one that Stuart was pleased to note in his journal. They met Katie and Monica Martin on the grounds, so Darien rode some of the midway rides with Monica "since it pleased a sweet child to do so." Gareth and Carrol rode the Ferris wheel repeatedly for the pleasure of looking out over the peaceful countryside without worry about detection of their ships.

Stuart accidentally broke the "test your strength" bell when he struck the sledgehammer on the target at the bottom and the measuring striker knocked the bell off the top. The carny worker was not happy, but he did not find it prudent to argue the matter with five large men at hand, especially when Brent scoffed, "Well, if that is all your toy can do then it deserves to be broken."

Darien knocked down enough bottles to win Monica a plush toy, so Gareth set to work and won Carrol a toy too. The other three Thuringi looked at each other, then at Katie Martin and promptly set out to see who could win her the largest prize at separate booths, because "Lloyd would surely wish for his lady to have the best, and we shall win them in his stead." Katie blushed at the knowledge that three handsome men playfully vied for her approval.

Stuart chose a shooting gallery and won a pink and white dog half as tall as Monica. Brent played a ring toss and would not stop until he secured a large black cat with a bright yellow ribbon around its neck.

Glendon threw three-balls-a-chance at a target. In his typical Garin perfectionist way, he took careful aim and threw the balls so hard the first two times that the balls not only knocked down the target, but they also nearly punched a hole in the booth's canvas backing. The third ball crashed through the target with an odd crunch, and the proprietor hurriedly offered Glendon a choice of any prize he wanted. The decision was turned over to Katie, who chose the largest plush toy of all. The proprietor was unable to close down before Gareth decided to play and Darien was not pleased at the small item he won for Monica, so he insisted on playing too.

Brent wondered why the carny worker at the ring toss looked so pleased about the action at the ball toss booth. The carny confided to the Aquatic, "I've been wondering if he's playing a rigged game or not but as hard as your friends are throwing, it sounds like they've broken through whatever he's got holding the targets up."

"Indeed! Well, a bad intent always returns to its keeper with equal malice."

Glendon overheard the conversation and called out to the players: "See here, you two! Make certain to knock those targets down! You must leave no doubt in my mind." He winked at the ring toss carny, who grinned conspiratorially.

Laden down with the spoils of victory, they moved on. The Thuringi all tried but could not eat cotton candy for fear the sugar rush might put them into a coma, but what little taste they got was absolutely delightful.

Once they learned that Monica had entries in the 4-H section, they all went with her in a show of solidarity. Darien was irritated she was awarded only a green fourth place ribbon for her depiction of The Life Cycle of Corn. It was his loud and defiant opinion that her work was by far the more superior display on hand, and that the judges were woefully blind and senseless.

"Do not be dismayed by this travesty, small bones," he intoned grandly to the little girl, "The great ones are often the most modest to the eye."

After walking through the contest barn and the information booth barn, they came to the livestock barn and roamed for an hour. They admired the cows and the pigs and horses and sheep and chickens but were particularly drawn to the goats. Goats were unknown on Thuringa but according to Brent Ardenne, goats had "the most marvelous little faces of virtue ever placed on a creature."

Bishop the bay mare won no official acclaim, but her masters were pleased just the same as if she had. Carrol spent several minutes telling the mare what a noble animal she was, as if the horse could understand. Bishop sniffed Carrol's hand but gave no other reaction.

The amusement rides on the rest of the fairgrounds held no particular charms for alien warriors who once regularly toured the wormhole traces, but the rodeo in the nearby arena captured their imagination like nothing else. Glendon was especially delighted and even managed to talk his way into entering a contest. After observing a bulldogger in action and admiring the way the cowboy wrestled the cabrett to the ground with a twist of the head, Glendon decided that was a challenge he could not resist. Stuart encouraged him to try, since Glendon never asked for much for himself, and it was for the good cause of discovery.

Outside the arena, Glendon practiced sliding on and off Bishop, not an easy task considering the looped stirrups of the makeshift Thuringi Ground Command Cavalry saddle that Carrol had made. He had no partner to ride on the other side of the steer to keep it running in a straight line, but he finally found someone willing to do that for him. He only wanted to try the event, not compete, but the rules were the rules, so he paid the coin necessary to enter. As he rode Bishop into the arena, whoops and howls erupted at the sight of his very abbreviated saddle.

"And now we have Mr. Glendon Garin from Iron Post: this is Glen's first time ever at bulldogging, so let's give him a big hand!" the announcer proclaimed, and the spectators gave Glendon a rousing cheer of encouragement. All around the small knot of Thuringi, people made comments about Glendon's strange saddle rig.

"I don't see how he's gonna be able to get in and out of that thing."

"It looks homemade!"

"Lord, that boy's gonna git killed out there."

Carrol nervously seized Darien's arm on the right and Gareth's arm on the left. "Oh my, they are right. He does not have the proper tack. What are we going to do?"

"We?" Darien exclaimed. "I am not certain what Glendon is going to do, but we shall sit and observe."

Glendon and Bishop lined up in the proper position next to the gate holding the steer as he observed the rodeo cowboys do, and when the gate sprang open and the steer leaped forward, Glendon urged Bishop to follow. With the helpful cowboy keeping the steer in line, Glendon leaned over as the crowd held its collective breath.

Thuringa did not have rodeos, but as with the Ground Command, the Naradi regularly practiced different ways to dismount in case of emergency. The bulldogger's way was similar to a technique used by the Naradi for some forms of riot control. Glendon slipped his feet out of the stirrups and kept his long legs gripped around Bishop just long enough to slide over and grasp the horns. He quickly threw his right leg over Bishop's withers, dug his heels into the ground and plowed into the dirt. It was then a simple matter to flip the steer over the way the cowboys did, and he held him down until the whistle blew. Glendon leaped to his feet and pumped both fists in the air, whooping in triumph.

"Audecer fallen botay!" he shouted to his fellow scouts as the audience cheered his unexpected success.

All five Thuringi bolted for the arena floor, laughing with delight, and talking all at once in their musical Thuringi language. Carrol hugged Glendon around the neck as Gareth and Brent pounded their fists on his back in congratulations and led him off to the side of the arena, yelping and cheering all the while. Stuart ran out to collect Bishop from the other cowboy, but Darien trotted briskly to stand before the release gate, where in his excitement he forgot to speak in American.

"(I must do this game as well, this looks like great fun! Where may I go, who am I to see about throwing around cabrett)?" The cowboys on the gate stared at him dumbfounded with no idea what this tall foreigner was saying to them. "(Well, come now! You have no claim on all the fun, do you)?" After exchanging uncomprehending stares, Darien turned around to Glendon and bellowed, "(I say! With whom must you toy to have fun here)?"

"In American, Darien," Stuart shouted as he rode Bishop up in a generous gallop. He leaned over and held out one hand. Darien reached up and in one fluid motion he pivoted around to land on the bay mare behind his brother.

"I said, I wish to play this sport as well! How does one go about throwing around cabrett?" Darien asked the cowboys.

"The two of you are more than Bishop should bear," Carrol called out, but it was too late. Bishop did not think she should bear both brothers either, and she gave a grunt and began to buck. Darien did a backward somersault off the mare's rump and landed on his feet but was just off-balance enough to stumble back a few more steps before sitting down hard in the dirt. Stuart clamped his legs around the horse and pulled back on the reins. The crowd got a bonus bareback bronc riding exhibition as the ill-tempered horse continued to buck and twist in an effort to throw the Thuringi from her back. Darien jumped to his feet and let out a wild happy yell along with the rest of the crowd. Stuart held on in a sincere desire not to be thrown off in front of all the onlooking Americans and wished Darien would stop making so much noise.

The steer headed toward a nearby open gate in preparation for the next contestant, and Darien was impatient to try this "throwing about business". He quickly ran to match the steer's stride, grabbed the animal by the horns and threw it down again.

"I say, that is great fun!" he chuckled as he released the steer and swatted it on the rump. The crowd was astonished that he was able to grab and throw a steer so easily but as the accomplishment sank in, they cheered again, and for the still-mounted Stuart. The steer ran for the gate, eager to get away from all the manhandling. Darien crawled up the fencing to sit beside the cowboys, who stared at him even as they clapped their hands. "You chaps will need to meet my kinsman Sandan Medina; he will enjoy throwing animals to the ground! Why did we never think of this before!"

Stuart managed to stay on and get the excited horse under control again. He turned her around and rode for another gate, which was opened for him by a group of hat-waving cowboys.

"Well, I reckon we have us some natural cowboys from... er...wherever these fellas are from," the announcer told the crowd. "Let's give 'em all another round of applause!"

For the rest of the evening, the Thuringi enjoyed the rodeo from behind the gates and inquired about the techniques used in each event. They were fascinated by the rigging and the timing and the sheer bravado of it all, and they could not resist entering themselves in bareback and saddle bronc riding contests. Carrol met with opposition when she tried to sign up for one.

"I'm sorry, ma'am, but this is too dangerous for ladies," the registrar said kindly.

"But my brothers get to play," she objected in bewilderment.

"Well, that's just what I mean, this isn't play. Them's thousand-pound horses up against a little ol' gal like you; it's too dangerous."

"But I... Stuart!" she pleaded, pulling his attention away from a conversation. "This man will not let me even try. He says it is too dangerous. I am a Thuringi; of course, it is dangerous. It would not be fun otherwise."

Stuart laughed at her protest and turned to the registrar. "Good sir, I assure you my sister is not afraid of this contest. We come from a different culture and our women may look delicate, but they are wonderfully admirable warriors. Please do let her ride or she will become morose and dejected."

"Yes, by all means, let our little sis ride!" Brent told the man. "I would wager heavy coin that she can stay on longer than your simple eight seconds."

"She'll tumble in seven!" Darien taunted and earned a swat on the head from her for his effort. He cackled in amusement.

"Well, all right but don't say you wasn't warned," the registrar grumbled. "You make sure you sign that waiver so you can't sue us if you get hurt."

"Call upon your legal representatives? I should say I would not!" Carrol snorted with mildly wounded pride. "It is my choice and further, my fault if I do not stay on."

Gareth sighed and whispered to Glendon, "Oh my; I shall have to soak in a cold tub over the sight of Her Nibs with her legs wrapped around a sweaty animal!"

Glendon suddenly inhaled and accidentally swallowed a gnat. He coughed and tried not to laugh or curse at his friend. Gareth's was a comment that a man could tell his long-time friend but not Her Nibs' relatives. It was also a notion that resulted in exceedingly unseemly thoughts for the proper Garin.

"Yeep! Why did you have to put that in my mind," he croaked.

"So, we will both be miserable!" Gareth chuckled.

"You are shame!"

Carrol borrowed a glove for the rigging from one of the cowboys, who were all very eager to help the pretty girl with the long blonde hair and sparkling white smile. Her Thuringi kinsmen gathered to tease and goad her.

"Do not cry to me if you land on your rudder," Stuart admonished.

"Are you sure you do not want a pillow?" Darien asked.

"I have you on for eight seconds at least," Brent instructed with a wag of his carefully positioned finger so as not to show the webbing. "Do not shame me with anything less!"

"Then are you riding?" Carrol shot back playfully.

"I am not some silly lunger looking for needless punishment," he replied smugly.

"Be careful, Nibs," Gareth said as he winked at her.

"This will be Thuringa's greatest triumph!" Glendon cheered, and all five men started up an old Kellis cheer. At the sound of some of the Thuringi words, several cowboys grinned and elbowed each other in amusement but no one stopped the song. They had no idea where 'Thuringa' was, but such bold people were bound to be bolder yet to sing words like that in public.

The gate swung open, and Carrol dug her heels into the horse's shoulders as she was instructed to do. Because the Thuringi did not wear spurs and only had Thuringi boots for footwear, the cowboys hoped these likable greenhorns would not elicit much response from the animals. But the other Thuringi made such a noise every time one of them rode, the horses were already jumpy and by habit and training, they bucked as soon as the gate opened. Carrol's bronc had a good whiff of Brent's Aquatic skin, and it did not recognize this mysterious creature, so it ran spooked for a few yards before it bucked and spun around. Carrol held on for six bone-jarring seconds before the bronc slipped out from under her, and she went down under the stamping hooves. Before the Thuringi could launch themselves off the rail to her rescue, the clowns were already on the job and distracted the animal away from her.

Carrol uncurled from the little ball she formed of herself and hastened to the fence. She was disappointed not to make the eight second limit, but the experience was exhilarating, and her smile and excited laughter told the crowd she was safe from harm. They cheered, and she waved at them. Once behind the gate, however, she put her hand to her side and stood still for a moment.

"Are you okay, miss? That was quite a fall you took there," a barrel-racing contestant from earlier in the evening, asked with concern.

After another second or two, Carrol straightened and smiled at the girl. "I am prone to take too many risks, in hindsight. But I am well, thank you!"

"I swear, that was the bravest thing I ever saw! I wish my daddy would let me ride the broncs! Maybe now he will."

"Well... perhaps if you are used to this sort of sport, you can do far better than I. I do understand the registration man's concern, though."

"Bull riding is next, but I don't think y'all ought to try that; it's just 'way too dangerous even as strong as you are," a cowboy told Stuart. The Phillipi brothers eyed the Brahma bulls.

"We shall accede to your hard-won wisdom," Stuart said.

"But –!" Darien began, but Stuart stopped him with a warning look.

"Darien. If you ride, then Carrol will want to ride and that is not going to happen. The hornless gakkis are one thing but these oversized cabretts are out of the question."

After they watched a few bullriders in action, Darien agreed that perhaps they had enough experimentation for one evening. Somehow along the way, Glendon was given a straw cowboy hat by one of his fellow contestants, and he was more pleased by it than any trophy he might have been offered.

They went home thoroughly exhausted but exhilarated by their adventure, with Bishop and the chicken cage in a borrowed horse trailer hitched to the pickup.

"We must be certain to tell Father about this," Stuart said. "Imagine, deliberately encouraging a gakki to misbehave for the sake of sport! That was such fun!"

"Well, I do not know that I would want a gakki's horn up my lane for the sake of sport," Gareth corrected, and they hooted in amusement.

Glendon looked at Carrol. "I suppose you understand now why it is such a fearsome deed, this bron-criding?"

"Yes, I do." She grimaced as she inspected her shirt. "Bother! My garment is torn; I shall need to mend it."

"Anything else that was torn?"

"Yes, faithful Naradi Famede ever at the ready," Carrol chuckled as she tapped his slender nose with a finger. "I broke a rib but that was easily repaired."

"A rib!"

"Shh! Yes, but I was not about to allow that registering man to be smug."

"If we enjoy any more such sport, it will have to be at home," Darien said thoughtfully. "I was asked many questions about Thuringa that I was unsure how to answer: where is Thuringa, how long were we to stay here, things of that nature. Michael warned us not to – what was it? Stick out? We must be certain to tell the same tale."

"But you must admit, it was great fun," Gareth pointed out, and they all readily agreed.

They checked on the Martins every day by phone or in person. Speculation grew concerning Katie Martin and Glendon, chiefly because Glendon was the best known of the Thuringi in town and he was an obvious choice for romantic daydreams. Katie was quizzed every time she arrived at work in the beauty shop about her activities while Lloyd was away in the oil field. At first, she did not know where it was leading. Once she found out, she was quick to tell the gossipers Lloyd had asked the Thuringi to help her and Monica out in his absence, and they did that and nothing more.

Carrol rode in on Bishop one day with a basket full of eggs for the Martins. Katie invited her to stay for a little while and chat. It was a treat for Carrol to talk to another woman for a change, so she stayed and let Katie paint her nails.

"Are all those guys out there where you live, your brothers?" a client asked as she popped her head out from under the dryer hood.

"No. T- three of them are," Carrol replied, correcting herself to include Glendon as her "brother".

"They sure are good-looking."

"Thank you."

"I hear tell that one that works at Gentry's is married; is that right?" one of Katie's co-workers asked. Her hair was piled on her head in a very becoming fashion, similar to the way the noblewomen of Thuringa styled their hair.

"Yes, he is."

"Why, he's too young to be married!"

Oh, if only you knew! "But he is, and he is madly in love with his wife." Carrol hoped that would be the end of the conversation, but it only gave the two other hair stylists and three customers something to chew on.

"Well, where is she?" asked a customer.

"She is back in our homeland."

"If you don't mind me asking, what are you all doing here?" Katie's boss asked.

Carrol was ready for this formerly troubling question now. "We are here studying American farm practices. I must say, we were extremely impressed by the county fair! Why, there were so many crops and animals and goods on display!"

"I heard that your brother is kind of sweet on Katie here," a stylist said archly.

"We are all fond of her; she and Lloyd have been very kind to us, and of course little Monica is simply charming!"

"Well, I keep saying, she and that big green-eyed movie star Glendon make a mighty pretty couple!" the stylist teased, and Carrol noted the flush in her friend's cheek as well as the annoyed glance she gave the co-worker. Katie did not welcome the comment and did not support it. The Thuringi princess understood the problem at hand and assumed the same patient stance that Queen Oriel Phillipi de Saulin might have taken.

"Of course, they are each attractive people, but it is a poor tale you tell. We were just saying to one another recently how much we admire Katie and Lloyd's love for each other. And of course, my brother's reputation is impeachable and his regard for marriage is sacred. One might think you were spreading something as dreadful as gossip, but I am certain you did not intend for it to sound that way."

The gossip circle did not quite know how to take that. On the one hand, the mysterious girl with the intense green eyes spoke so prettily and lordly; yet on the other hand it sounded as if she had just told the woman to shut her lying mouth. With her back to the group, Katie glanced up at Carrol and smiled.

The salon owner was not quite through. "Did I understand that you were married, too?"

"Yes, I was."

"You're…well, you're a little young, aren't you?"

"I am blessed with a youthful appearance, but yes, I married young." A little falsehood for the sake of safety was something she had learned from The Proper Garin.

"What does he do?"

"He was a soldier, and he was killed in the line of duty." She let that sink in before adding, "It is not a subject I like to discuss. I miss him very much still."

The other stylist started to say, "But what –" and the proprietor snapped, "That's enough, Judy!"

"Who's that other fellow out there with you, that short one? I hardly ever see him, or that other one with the foxy attitude," a customer said.

"They are friends of ours, specialists in their fields. We have all known each other for a long time."

"Are they married; do they date?"

Carrol smiled. "They are both spoken for. Such robust, handsome men are not likely to sit idly without attracting a love interest."

"No, I suppose not. I swear, all the good men are taken!" This started off a round of idle chatter, and the crisis was averted.

As soon as Carrol paid for her manicure and went on her way, the proprietor turned to the gossipy stylist. "Don't you get it?"

"Get what?"

"Are you that dense? Her husband was a soldier killed in the line of duty. Her brother works for the Gentrys, who took him right into their bosom as soon as they got here. See? I bet she was married to

Gary Gentry! They must have married overseas or something, and that's why they came here to this podunk little town! That Glendon does remind me of Gary in a lot of ways, so sure, the Gentrys are bound to favor him."

"But that doesn't make any sense," the stylist objected. "Ed and Margie would have said something by now about Gary getting married."

"Not if his wife was a teenager, I bet they wouldn't," a customer pointed out.

"They sure are some pretty people out there."

"Well, y'all just cut out the trash talk about them folks. You know I don't tolerate anybody talking trash about a soldier." The proprietor patted a framed picture of a Marine that sat on the table at her station to underscore her point. "And if you don't want Ed and Margie Gentry to come after you with a rake or one of those big Phillips brothers to wrestle you to the ground like a steer, you'd best leave the subject of Glendon and Katie be, too."

"There is no 'Glendon and Katie'," Katie reminded them firmly. "Good grief; they are all friends of my husband's! Haven't any of you ever heard of 'family friends'?"

"Nobody that good-looking, no," said a customer. "I wouldn't mind getting a mite friendlier with one of them."

Work in the oil field started back up for Darien, but his was an erratic schedule that did not require his presence every day. A few farmers hired him out to stack hay bales in their barns, and this he did gladly. He did not ask for coin and even protested when it was offered to him, but they paid him anyway. They were grateful they did not have to do all that heavy work and that he enjoyed doing it.

Stuart wanted to document their projects for his report, so one day Glendon accompanied Darien out to the oil field with a camera. What he saw alarmed him greatly.

Darien was in the middle of the drilling operation, handling the heavy equipment and working among the brackish, filthy "mud" pipe lubricant right along with the rest of the crew. His skin was a ghastly pallor, and he was sick to his stomach the entire time, but they were short of a crew member that day and he had to stick it out.

Glendon was likewise eyed suspiciously by the crew. "Anyone

that pretty is probably a fairy," Pete confided to George at midday during a break. George looked beyond him, and his eyes widened so much they nearly bugged out of his head.

"Maybe, but I don't think I'd want to test that boy's patience if I was you." Pete turned around and nearly choked on his coffee.

Darien was covered in the muddy liquid, and Glendon had stripped off his tee-shirt for Darien to use to remove what liquid he could from his skin. Glendon's musculature was impressive, which was only to be expected of a Naradi Famade who spent the last year hefting heavy sacks of feed and fertilizer around all day. When Darien removed his shirt in order to use it for a mop as well, Pete and George did not say anything out of line for the rest of the day. They remembered Stuart's warning about Darien's having killed many men in war, and now they believed it. He looked like he could take on anyone and come out whistling despite the Thuringi claim he looked undernourished.

Brent spent much of the first part of October in the Pacific until the Columbus Day Storm in the northwestern part of the United States. It brought him to the Willamette Valley in Oregon to aid in rescue work at ranches. His heart grieved over the loss of the lives and the destruction of property, and he was extremely impressed by the storm system that caused it all. Storms like that were rare on Thuringa. The Earth's wind and turbulent seas were like nothing he had ever experienced before but it thrilled him greatly. No one questioned his background or noticed his appearance during the rescue work, they were simply glad to have a willing pair of hands in a time of need.

Two days later on the fourteenth he was called back to the Sheldon ranch to help evacuate in case the Cuban Missile Crisis took deadly measures. The Thuringi observed the political events with mixed reactions. Stuart was appalled at the standoff; he had hoped to approach the president but was rebuffed in the attempt given the tense atmosphere in Washington. Carrol was impatient at the foolishness and Glendon privately hoped Stuart would decide to destroy the missiles as a measure of introduction.

In the end they remained at the ranch and waited like the rest of the world and breathed a sigh of relief that their outpost would not be destroyed before the Armada arrived.

"Stuart, Earthians are going to blow themselves up and take us with them, and there will be nothing for our people here but a big smoking rock. What is it about that tiny little island that is so important?" Brent scoffed at the dinner table one evening. "Even its name is unremarkable. Coo-ba. I looked at it. It is nice but for pity's sake, America has an entire country from one great water to the other."

Darien picked at his food at the dinner table and finally spoke his mind. "I do not understand how this miserable planet ever reached this stage in its history. We can hope for peace between them, or we can be instrumental in seeing that peace is achieved. And frankly, hope is just the breeze going by for all its effectiveness."

"How do you propose that we see peace achieved?" Stuart asked.

"Ramming it down their throats seems to be the only thing some of them understand," Darien said. "But the six of us cannot do that by ourselves."

"Not even the entire Armada could do that and still call ourselves Thuringi."

"Well, we need to do something! As Brent said, they will destroy themselves and our hopes with them. It would have to be a concerted effort. With strategic placements of our battle cruisers and battle ships –"

"Are we back to that again!" Stuart groaned. "Which word in 'we cannot' is troubling you on the matter? Forcing someone to do your will serves cross purposes; it will only breed resentment."

"Then what do you propose? Asking them nicely to play with us?" Darien asked acidly. "They like to swagger and brag about their might; let them get a taste of what might really is."

"You work with them. I should think you of all people would understand their peculiar sense of resolve," Stuart said with an effort to keep the irritation out of his voice. "We hated the Shargassi for fighting with us –"

"What part of 'we are not the Shargassi', can you not understand?" Darien shot back. "I am not out to destroy Earthians and do not wish to rule them in perpetuity. We need the space of a number of years of guaranteed peace; that is all. Then we can leave."

"Guaranteed peace? This world has millions of people, with millions of issues with which to deal. Just how can you guarantee anything that they themselves, who understand the issues better, cannot?" Stuart snapped. "I want to approach President Kennedy, but we must make certain that we are not perceived as another threat!"

"Would you pass me the corn?" Gareth asked Glendon. "If they start pounding on the table again, I would like to at least be able to sit back and eat while I watch the show."

"What show?" Stuart asked, distracted.

"The Stuart and Darien Nightly Argument Show," Gareth replied cheerfully. "You both say the same things over and over."

"But Darien never says just whom he would threaten and how, and you never manage to outline a peaceful solution," Glendon added.

"What you two need to do is gather the facts and present them to Father," Carrol said as she passed the corn to Gareth. "He will be the one to decide the course of action, if any."

"Well, when the world blows itself up, he certainly will have only one choice of action, then," Darien declared. "Scrape up what is left of us."

"I look forward to seeing Hartin Medina's reaction to Marilyn Monroe," Gareth remarked, as he buttered his corn on the cob. "He will not know whether to be offended or cover Lady Melina's eyes and stare at the woman."

"He will be too busy gazing at Ann-Margret, I wager," Glendon remarked, with a peculiar gaze into space. He snapped out of it quickly and grinned sheepishly, and Carrol pounced.

"What is it about red haired women, with you," she laughed.

"It is a fascinating color," Glendon said with a shrug. "Perhaps I shall bring back some hair color when we return to the Armada, and Janis will become the first Thuringi redhead."

Stuart and Darien looked at each other with wry grins. They knew exactly what the others were saying to them: Shut up.

"And just what will you say to explain this sudden change that will not make her jealous of your time here?" Darien asked.

"I shall dye mine red, too," Glendon chuckled, and they laughed at the mental image.

"I will color mine brown," Gareth said. "It is usually streaked with grease, anyway." Carrol poked his leg under the table with her toe.

"It is not," she said.

"I will dye mine black," Darien decided. "To match my black

heart."

"I will dye mine white," Stuart said. "Too much more of our arguments about Earth, and it might turn that way, regardless." They looked at Carrol, who was nibbling her corn. She blinked at them.

"What, I am not about to color my hair any differently," she declared. "All this length? It would take days to color and dry. I like good old Thuringi yellow, thank you."

They lifted their glasses of luket and toasted the color yellow.

"The color of caution," Darien observed.

"There is nothing wrong with a little prudence," Stuart began, and the other three moaned.

"Let us color our hair blue, the color of the sky," Gareth suggested.

"That would earn me a rousing degree of sarcasm at an oil field," Darien told him.

"Anyone who has the nerve to color his hair blue should hardly be challenged by people who do not," Glendon told him.

On Thanksgiving Day, Michael Sheldon came out to the ranch and brought a turkey to roast. He helped them prepare and eat a traditional American Thanksgiving meal, and in the late afternoon they introduced him to the traditional Thuringi game of Kellis. It was a bone-jarring collision of muscle and struggle that quickly made Michael sit the game out. The other five continued to play, so Michael took pictures of the happy, laughing group all weekend.

He was astonished and impressed by the ranch's improvements: the barn was once again a solid structure, and the livestock were healthy and well-tended. The house was remodeled with all manner of improvements, and he liked the heated tub on the back porch for Brent's use. The fences were all kept up and the people of Iron Post had nothing but good things to say about his large house guests. No one cared any more about where they were from or what they wanted. The Thuringi were friendly and bright and did not cause trouble for anyone unjustly. They kept to the ranch much of the time but when they did appear in public, things just seemed better for it.

All the scouts attended Monica's Christmas Pageant. To Darien's disappointment, she was not a sheep but in the context of things she had an improved role: this year she was an angel. It was the same play from the year before and the roles were recast, so Darien knew what to expect in terms of songs and setting. His companions were delighted by the play and cheered enthusiastically. Gareth went out in search of the perfect Christmas tree with Lloyd and delivered it to the Martin household.

"Now we need to get your folks one," Lloyd said, but Gareth shook his head.

"It is not our belief, Lloyd Martin. It is an admirable religion, and we respect your decision to follow it, but it is not ours. To claim the trappings of this Christmas would be false to our own ways."

Monica pleaded with him to stay and decorate the tree with them. Darien drove up with a truckload of firewood and proceeded to offload half of it, and the other half would go out to the ranch with Gareth and him. He agreed to help Monica decorate so Gareth agreed as well.

"You know, I noticed that y'all don't seem to have any holidays of your own. Is that true?" Lloyd asked Darien after they unloaded the wood and came in to set up the tree. Gareth already had it in the stand and was testing the lights.

"We have our own holidays, but no one here knows anything about them," Darien explained. "They are not large and grand affairs like yours; they are but simple observations with no meals or sweet candies or gifts. Word, your calendar is sprinkled with merriment, while ours boasts a steadier, somber sort of appreciation year-round."

"You don't believe in Jesus?" Monica asked round-eyed.

"No, but we honor his ideals," Gareth replied. "That should suffice. We do not expect anyone here to believe in everything we say and do." He finished stringing the lights on the tree.

"I guess so. Are you and Miss Carrol going to get married?"

The question left Gareth open-mouthed and blushing, to which Darien snickered and answered, "He had better. I think Carrol has her heart set on it."

"Oh, I do not know that she does; there are many other more worthy men than me," Gareth stammered.

"Name one!" Darien dared brashly. "I have observed you, Sword-and-Fist, and I can think of no other man who measures up to you. And I am a notoriously hard man to please when it comes to deciding whether some noddy is good enough for my sister."

"What about her late husband, er, your brother? What was he

like?" Katie asked.

Darien had to think for a moment before he understood what 'brother' she meant. "He was an admirable man in every way, but I must say that I had my doubts. He was a career soldier and there is no certainty he would have treated her with the same gentle regard as our everyman Gareth. Oh, Maranta was grand, but I much prefer Gareth for her, and that is no mean reflection on either man."

Gareth pondered that statement in silence. He joined Maranta Shanaugh's squadron in the Air Command before Carrol was born and had been with him until the day the general died. Darien was right, Maranta was a career soldier. When Gareth learned of the general's affair with the princess, he wondered what she saw in Maranta beyond his good looks and sterling reputation. Maranta was an ideal warrior, a man who did not flinch from duty or regret; but would he have made a good, loving husband? He had a big heart and a generous spirit, but he also had a stoic outlook and a hard work ethic. Perhaps Carrol changed that part of him; perhaps she would have softened the flinty edge and encouraged him to relax and enjoy life. But if she had, it would have been late in his life and changes did not always last. Maranta always derisively referred to himself as a "killing machine", a title he did not like but acknowledged as accurate. It was a title that Maribel Duncan scolded the general for accepting as true.

"And why aren't you married?" Katie teased Darien.

"I? Good woman, I am a scoundrel of the first order and have no business spoiling the dream of some hapless well-intentioned skirt! It is best to leave me to the wastelands of domestic existence."

"Aww," Lloyd scoffed softly. "I bet you'll be settled down with some doe-eyed gal before long. Just when you figure you'll never find her, the woman you waited for all your life will be right there in front of you."

"Then she had best get out of my way, or I will trample her with my unrepentant ways!" Darien snickered. He went out to the truck and returned minutes later with a large boot box wrapped in a brown paper bag, flattened out so it could be taped smoothly over the box. A single white ribbon was tied around the package. "And so Small One, it appears you have a gift to place under your symbol of the season." Monica squealed and shook the package excitedly. "Here, now! Is it the custom to rough up the gift?"

"Yes," Monica giggled. She heard a soft swishing sound from within. "What is it?"

"What, indeed." He knelt and turned his face so he could receive a kiss on the cheek. "Give us a farewell buss and we will be gone. Merry Birthday to the Jesus child."

They all exchanged good wishes and goodbyes, and Darien and Gareth headed home.

"I am grateful you favor the idea of courtship for me and your sister," Gareth said eventually during the ride.

"I see no reason not to favor it. Ah! Here is an idea! Let us gather more toes of mistle and drape them all over the roof. Then we can watch Stuart and Glendon squirm with the implication of impropriety between you and Carrinkle and tease them for their salacious suspicions!"

"Us? No! You can gather the toes of mistle; I am going to tune up this truck, it sounds terrible." Darien could not tell the difference, but he knew Gareth could.

On Christmas morning Monica Martin opened gifts from many people, including doting grandparents who inundated her with goodies. Lloyd and Katie lavished their only child with toys and clothes and books. But her favorite gift was a fifteen-inch-long homemade porcelain doll with skin the color of sand, yellow eyes, and delicate features, and had real human hair of a sunny color embedded somehow in the china head at the proper place. The doll was a collaborative effort that could only move its arms up and down and wore an exotic but simple outfit, handmade with delicate stitches. Because the doll was taller than her fashion model dolls, she called her Carrol. She did not put other clothes on the Thuringi doll or move her around; she preferred to keep it nearby to add elegance to the play area. She never let her friends play with it either, but she did let them admire it. Long after the other dolls fell out of favor and put away in lieu of other interests, the Carrol doll remained a beloved decoration.

The snow that had been so lovely and interesting at first proved to be quite something else the more they experienced it. Darien's work in the oil fields during the winter was uncomfortable, but his pride in overcoming obstacles would not allow him to quit. The snow turned to slush underfoot and under the weight of the vehicles in the drilling area. The Americans knew how to dress for the weather, and Darien figured it out by trial and error and observation. Once again, he was the target of mild ridicule and found the phrase "dumb Limey" exceptionally irritating. He wore his long black traveling coat because it was made for space travel and kept him warm, but to his fellow oilfield workers it resembled a formal swallow-tailed morning coat.

"Hey, Little Lord Darien, you wanna bring that wrench over here before you head for the embassy ball?" Pete taunted, and Darien had to grit his teeth and concentrate on not throwing the wrench at his head.

"You boys better leave him alone," Dickie warned.

"Aw, we're just funnin'."

It was hard work; the hardest Darien ever did in his life. His was not a sheltered life, not in the least; he endured consue and training in the Air Command, Kellis and battle with the Shargassi. But never before had Darien ever gone out in the cold surrounded by unfamiliar work to draw forth liquid from the ground that made him physically ill and tolerate the teasing of working-class men. So many challenges at once! He was beyond resentment and anger; it was now a point of self-control, to prove to himself he could maintain his cool and do a good job.

One mid-afternoon, dark gray clouds moved in and obscured the sun. The winter chill deepened, and Dickie decided the weather was too harsh to lay any more pipe without someone losing flesh on the cold metal surfaces. The workers packed up and headed for their vehicles, bound for home and warmth.

George and Pete were to ride back to the café with Dickie Forbes, whose truck was parked next to a sharp incline below the site. Dickie had the truck started and intended to drive away from the incline to give them more room to open the cab door. As he did two things happened: the truck's front wheels struck a slushy spot, and George and Pete lost their footing and slipped down the incline. Pete slid under the midway point of the pickup and was pulled under the back wheels of the helplessly bogged down truck. George's legs were wedged beneath the slushy mud below and the hot exhaust pipe on the undercarriage of the vehicle.

Their screams of alarm and pain brought men from all over the work area. Dickie stopped gunning his motor as instructed by the bystanders, but the weight of the heavy truck with equipment and supplies and heavy toolboxes was still on top of the two men. The front wheels were bogged down to the axle, and shouts of confusion and helplessness filled the air.

"Get it off of them!"

"He can't, it's stuck!"

"Somebody call a tow truck!"

"That'll take too long! We need to get them out of there now!"

"I'll tie my truck to the bumper –"

The babbling voices died down as the back end of the truck lifted up, and George stopped screaming for help. Darien Phillipi stood at the trailer hitch, his legs braced against the earth and his hands firmly in place on the underside of the back end of the truck. The cold eddies of wind swirled his hair and strange foreign coattails around him and gave him the appearance of a magic sprite, come forth from the depths of the earth. He calmly said, "Pull them out from under the vehicle, fools."

George was swiftly pulled out, but Pete was still wedged under the tire. Darien re-adjusted his hold and stepped forward. The truck rose higher. As Pete was moved, he uttered a high-pitched shriek. "No, no, I'm dying! Oh God, my hips are broken!"

"We can't move him yet, we need something to slide under him, so we don't do any worse to him," Lloyd called out.

"Then find something," Darien instructed. His voice was the only one present that was not pitched with trepidation or pain, and his breathing was easy. He glanced about almost casually, as if he were not holding up a half ton of metal with his bare hands. "That walkway board over at the drilling site will do. Go get it and try to slide it under him."

As two men hurried to do as he suggested, Dickie Forbes shouted, "Darien, we'll get a jack for you, just hold on."

"It would be simpler if you concentrated on Peter and not waste time with your little tools," Darien replied. "I am in no distress."

The walkway board was one of several plywood sheets placed over the soft ground around the concrete rig apron. It was ideal as a temporary stretcher, and the men slid Pete onto it and away from the truck as fast as they could. When the all-clear was given, Darien lowered the back of the pickup to the ground and wiped his hands on a red rag. He went to George and pushed people out of the way to reach the burned black man.

He pulled a kila from his pocket, a small dagger used on Thuringa like a pocketknife. He swiftly cut away the burned fabric on George's pants legs. He then scooped up handfuls of fresh clean snow nearby and covered the burns with it. "You need medication and unfortunately I have none of the now," he told George. "The cold snow should stop further damage to your flesh. You fellows, place your coats on his body, he needs to stay warm." His instructions were followed, and Darien turned his attention to Pete.

Pete was in a bad way, and the first aid kit for the job site was of poor benefit to the injuries. Like George, he was covered in blankets and coats, but little could be done for a broken pelvis. Darien ran his fingertips over the man's pelvic region and muttered his thoughts aloud. "It is broken, snapped like a twig. The arteries were spared severing, but his vessels were crushed. He must be taken to a medical station immediately." This was not his usual Arda gift, but the need of the moment superseded his assumed limitations. Darien placed his palm over Pete's forehead and uttered a chant in a language that sounded vaguely Grecian. The injured man still groaned, but he closed his eyes and took easier breaths.

"Larry's got his pickup over by the graveled part of the road out of this section," Dickie told him. "If we can get them into the back of it, we can drive them to the Cushing hospital."

Darien got a firm grip on one side of the board and reached over the injured man to the other side. He stood up easily. "Show me which vehicle," he told Dickie. Dickie led the way, and two other men used a fireman's carry to bring George to the pickup. Darien stepped into the back of the truck, board and all, and placed it securely in its bed. He then put George beside Pete and jumped down from the truck. "Take them quickly; time is their enemy." Workers piled into the back to steady the two injured men, and Larry drove away.

Without another word, Darien returned to Dickie Forbes's pickup and moved the back end and then the front end onto solid ground. He climbed into Lloyd Martin's truck, where astonished crewmen came to him.

"That was amazing, the most incredible thing I've ever seen. I never knew you were so strong!" one man said when no one else would speak.

"None of you know anything about me," Darien snapped at them, his unEarthly yellow eyes flashing with indignation. "You have done nothing but taunt me from the first, amusing yourselves at my expense, and you only show kind interest when it is to your advantage. There is much more to me that you do not know, and I now choose not to disclose it. The way you treat those who are different from you is appalling and I want nothing further to do with you. Lloyd Martin, let us be away."

Lloyd got in and drove the Thuringi home. He saw glimpses of Darien's strength at earlier occasions, but he never dreamed his friend held such power. He did not dare speak since Darien had been so surly, but after a few miles Darien spoke.

"You and your family and the Gentry family are among the few people outside my home who have treated me kindly and not as a freak. Stuart has great confidence in others of your kind, but I do not." He felt a tickle in his nose and suddenly a sneeze erupted from him. "Waugh! What a terrible sound!"

"God bless you," Lloyd said automatically.

"He had best do a better job of it," Darien agreed grumpily. He did not feel good; his throat felt tight, his sinuses made his face feel stuffy, and the top of his head was strangely heavy. He sneezed again. "Chuala detra copus (This shit is getting old)!" he exhorted in Thelan.

"Er...what?"

"This is a terrible business. What can it be?"

"Sounds like you're coming down with a cold. I'm a little worried about the way you strained yourself back there. I heard of times when people get super strong in times of stress, but I never thought I'd see it for myself."

"That? That was nothing," Darien told him. "I picked up that vehicle simply because it was the decent thing to do. I cannot begin to count the number of times I have withheld from doing damage to some of those men. Uff! They are lucky they were alive this morning, not accounting for this evening's events."

"They are pretty rough on people, I know. I would say 'they don't mean anything by it' but that's not really true. It's more like hazing, you know; a way to break in fellas and see how far they can take it."

"In my homeland, such activity would bring the wrath of several entities upon their heads. In some cultures, they would be slain outright for their impertinence! Bah! Yours is a naïve society. What you consider important I deem foolish, and what you call modern technology is but archaic testaments to timid research and blatant ignorance. But for you and yours, Lloyd Martin, I would deem your entire civilization as slackards."

"Well, that's pretty harsh," Lloyd drawled. "Of course, if I say anything against you, I know you could twist me into a pretzel. But tell me this: what is it about your people, aside from your eye color and your strength, that sets you on higher ground?"

Darien considered the question long and hard and slowly realized his words were harsh and aimed at the wrong man for the wrong reasons. He did not mind Earthians that much, but his body ached in ways he never knew before, and he had lashed out without thinking. He finally replied, "I suppose you could say it is our arrogance, bested only by our astonishing propensity for inappropriate rudeness."

Lloyd smiled. "Apology accepted."

He dropped Darien off at the gate and waited until the big Thuringi made it into the house and closed the door before he drove home. Later that evening, he phoned Darien, who sneezed into the phone. "Waugh! This malady has not dissipated," Darien groaned. "What is it you seek?"

"Didn't know if maybe you'd like to know about the fellows."

"Yes, I would. Are they alive or dead?"

"Uh – ha! Well, I guess I should have expected that! George's got third degree burns but it will heal over in time. He'll have some hellacious scars, but he says he would rather that than what could have happened. Pete – well, it's obvious Pete's never going to work in the oilfields again. His pelvis is broken, and he'll be in traction for a long time, but they said he was very calm on the way to the hospital. He told the boys over and over that you saved his life, and he didn't feel as much pain as he did before you talked to him. His family is sure grateful to you; George's too."

"Hmm. Well, a bitten dallah holds more compassion than one who has never felt teeth."

"Darien, you say the strangest things. Oh, Monica said to say you are a hero."

"Monica says the strangest things as well."

An unfamiliar car came down the driveway and stopped in front of the house the next morning. From it emerged a black woman and three small children. She introduced herself as George Foster's wife and asked to speak to Darien.

Darien wrapped himself in blankets and sat facing her on the couch. The children's eyes widened in fascination at the sight of the yellow-eyed white man, and they stayed tucked behind their mother. Occasionally they peered out at him. "Good day, Dame Foster. How may I be of assistance to you?" Darien intoned. His voice was even deeper than usual, and he gladly accepted one of the cups of hot tea Carrol offered to their guests and him.

"I...I wanted to thank you for what you did for George and Pete. Mr. Forbes said you picked his truck up and saved their lives." One child looked at Darien from over her shoulder, and the sight made Darien smile.

"Well, it is called a pickup truck," he replied. This made his guest relax and smile.

"My husband is the breadwinner in our family; I'm a housewife and with our children being so small, I don't know what I'd do if he had to stay out of work for a long time or if he was killed. He always admired you, but he said he scared your sister one day by accident and that you didn't like him."

"The incident has been forgiven, but I cannot say much for the friends with whom he chooses to associate. They are rude fellows, and he would do well to distance himself from them, but then there is no accounting for odd friendships. I have never met people of your color before; we come from a faraway land and the Negroid race is unknown to us."

"Really?"

"Yes. The brown skin is quite attractive when I see it close to, as now. Will he return to the oil field, then?" Darien's leap from one subject to another caught her off guard for only a moment.

"Once his legs heal, yes."

"We are glad to hear his recovery will be complete."

Glendon was seated at the dining room table with a book in hand. Naradi Famede did not allow their charges to meet with outlander visitors while ill unless the guard was in place. Despite Darien and Stuart's insistence that Glendon had been following all orders correctly, the Naradi felt guilty he was not on hand to assist his Warrior Prince and somehow prevented his illness from striking. He resolved to at least guard him at home. Glendon wore no weaponry, but he needed none on this occasion, and his pistol was out of sight but accessible. The children had this second strange man to study, too.

"Is there anything I can do for you, Dame Foster?" Darien asked. "If your man is yet ill, how will you garner coin to pay your expenses?"

"Oh no, my family and his family are helping us out, we'll be all right. Really, Mr. Phillips, you have done all I could ask for by saving George. He's a good man, he really is."

"I am certain of it. Only a man with righteous footsteps earns the hand of a noble lady such as yourself."

The easy delivery of this unpracticed gallantry flustered Mrs. Foster a little, and she blushed. "Well, I had best be going. I just wanted to tell you how grateful I am – we all are."

"Thank you," her little boy added. Darien smiled, and with that smile came an ease of heart for the family.

At the table, Glendon broke into a smile of his own. This was the Darien Phillipi the Naradi had long hoped to witness. He wished Maranta Shanaugh could have lived to see this day.

Carrol decided to look further into Earthian medical care and took Darien with her after she cleared his sinuses. It gave him enough relief to feel fit enough to go. They visited Pete's room at the hospital, and George happened to be on hand as well. Pete was not the brash, insolent man who once tormented the Thuringi with unchecked glee. He was pensive and when he spied the man in question in the doorway, he motioned him in.

Darien entered, his large frame dwarfing the door and almost overshadowing the sister beside him. Carrol slipped in and glanced over the equipment and monitors attached to the injured man.

"You do not look as alarming as before," Darien remarked as they approached the bed.

"Everybody here tells me I'm lucky to be alive, and I agree with 'em. If it hadn't been for you…oh, hello ma'am. Your brother is a real hero," he said to Carrol in the strained voice of a man in pain. She smiled, and the monitor recorded the increase in his heart rate. She reached in pretense to smooth down the man's hair, but she actually wanted to read his physical condition with her healing Arda gift.

"Darien has many heroic qualities, but has had very few opportunities to display them," Carrol informed him as she leaned against the bed rail to work. "Of course, he has always been a hero to me. Did you not know how strong he is?"

"N… no ma'am, I didn't." Pete was mesmerized by the touch of her hand.

"Your injuries are grievous," she murmured. She looked at George, who lay in the second bed of the shared hospital room. "And are you better, Lord Foster?"

"Oh yes ma'am, yes I am, much better," he stammered in the presence of the statuesque beauty with the brilliant green eyes. "We'd both be goners if it wasn't for your brother."

"Pray do not address so much gratitude to me," Darien said low, nearly in a growl. "It was simply common courtesy, from one man of toil to another."

"I know I've been pretty hard on you. Everybody there said you didn't hesitate for a minute, you were like 'Big Bad John' or something, that Jimmy Dean song," Pete said, obviously impressed with the large man before him. "They said you picked up that truck like it was paper."

"Mmm," Darien acknowledged without enthusiasm.

"I hate to think what would have happened to us if you hadn't been there," George put in again, and it was at that point that Darien's patience broke.

"And if I had never done a thing, if you had never fallen or the snowfall did not soften the ground and conspired with the elements of chance to harm you, you would still belittle me," he said bluntly. "I would much rather you address remorse for your unkindness rather than gratitude for my actions. Honor stirred my hand, sir, only honor. It is not our way to let the ignorant suffer and die, however distasteful their habits may be."

"Darien," Carrol objected mildly, "It is also not our way to boast on our suffering."

"No, I had that coming," Pete told her. "I guess I ought to take it like a man if I'm gonna dish it out."

"Indeed," Darien said, "at last you speak with a contrite heart."

"Yours are still terrible injuries," Carrol told Pete. "Are you in much pain?"

"As long as they keep me doped up, I'm all right," He wondered at the way he felt no pain at the moment and attributed it to the distraction her looks offered. She, on the other hand, appeared distressed. "It's kinda wearing off. Uh, Darien never talks about you much."

"The honorable require no advertisement," Darien said shortly.

Carrol shook her head at her brother before she replied to Pete. "I am a widow, and my brothers are quite protective of me. There is really nothing more to tell. He knows little of you, as well. We only wished to check on your progress. Darien will not return to the oil fields for a while." Darien noticed the increased strain in her face.

"He won't? Why not?" George asked, as surprised as Pete. "We need strong men out there."

"He has suffered terribly, and our finances do not require him to put his health at risk on an unfamiliar venture. Tell me: does the black oil you extract make you ill?"

"No. It stinks and it's a bear to wash off, but it don't hurt any," George told her.

"It does not suit Darien at all. There is no reason for him to stay continually nauseous. I asked him not to return, and he promised to do as I ask until we find a solution."

"She is persuasive to the point of nagging," Darien remarked. "Quite pushy, really."

"You dance upon your own truths," Carrol reprimanded before she turned back to Pete and stroked his face gently. "Well, we shall go now and let you get more rest. Do recover well, gentlemen."

Darien nodded to them and put his arm around Carrol. She walked as if nothing was amiss, but Darien had to support her part way down the hall until she was strong enough to walk under her own power. "I am sorry it took so long. It is harder when I cannot simply place my hand on the injury, but that would have been most unseemly, as Father would say."

"Father would be right in this case," Darien said with a grin.

"Did you ever see such a beauty in your life?" Pete asked. "Man, I swear when she had her hand on me, I didn't feel any pain at all."

"Well, I don't think you're going to get anywhere with her if Darien has any say in it, and I wouldn't cross him if I were you," George cautioned.

"Oh, hell no! Georgie, he lifted a half-ton truck and just stood there with it! He lifted it off us like it was nothing!" The temporary relief from pain he experienced in Carrol's presence was gone, and he clawed for the nurse call cord. "I wouldn't cross him ever again. Boy, sometimes you just don't know when you dodge a bullet. Damn it all, that hurts!" His right leg twitched with sudden tingling.

George said slowly, "Pete, I thought you couldn't move your legs at all."

Pete stared down at his legs. "I can't. Or rather..." A big toe twitched. "I did that. It wasn't easy, but I did it. My legs feel like they've been asleep and are just now waking up."

X-rays later revealed to astonished doctors that the bone and muscles in Pete's legs were somehow inexplicably repaired, and the crushed blood vessels were inflated again and carried blood to and from his extremities. The medical records were combed over carefully but they found no explanation for the 'miracle' that happened. George's family believed it was divine intervention, and Pete's family thought it was some sort of medical cure.

Pete was unsure. In time he could walk with crutches and graduated to a wheelchair, and from there he walked again. He wished he had gotten to know the strange foreigner better before he teased the man and been introduced to his lovely sister. He had found such unusual comfort in her touch. It did not occur to him to put two and two together. Pete was not the sharpest of men.

Carrol got a hot bath ready for Darien as soon as they got home to warm him up. Despite her best efforts, she could not rid him of this particular ailment. He sneezed with great exhortations of expelled air that alarmed them, especially Gareth. Despite the constant warmth of the continually tended wood stoves and heaters, Darien felt chilled. When Darien mentioned that he felt strangely warm all of a sudden, Gareth felt Darien's forehead with his hand and became agitated.

"You must not go back into the field, Naughty Nibs," he said sternly. "This is nothing with which to play."

"Oh, it is not that bad."

"No!" Gareth barked out, and they regarded him curiously. They rarely heard anything so harsh coming from their happy-go-lucky major. "That is how I lost my father and my brother Clive, to weariness and sneezing and the cough. You must stay home, Your Naughtiness. Nibs, this is a dangerous thing."

Carrol saw how very alarmed Gareth was. "You have an Earthian cold," she told Darien. "We have no idea how their diseases might affect us. Stay home and let me treat you." She patted Gareth's back affectionately. "Have no fear, Royal We. Earthians are known to overcome this sickness. We will utilize some of their methods as much as we can."

"Can we overcome this?" Gareth asked.

"Yes. There is much about fighting the cold in their journals and productions," she soothed. "There will not be a reprisal of Clive's fate."

"Who is Clive?" Darien asked after another sneeze.

"My late brother," Gareth told him, and Darien bit his lip in thought.

"Yes, Clive Duncan. I knew of him. I will stay home for the sake of Major Sword-and-Fist's concern," he agreed.

Carrol made vegetable soup and fed it to her brother as he lay in bed, covered in blankets. He was miserable and felt rather silly at the same time. He was a Thuringi warrior, the Warrior Prince, accustomed to holding his own against any with a sword, and yet he lay bested by a germ. He felt weak and hot, and his head ached.

Stuart was also not well, and Carrol declared that they were all quarantined until further notice. Brent brought back a great deal of fresh fruit from his travels, and it made their symptoms bearable. Glendon called the Gentrys and explained about their illness and his subsequent quarantine. Margie promptly brought over a casserole and a pot full of chicken soup with noodles. She also gave them a recipe for a whiskey toddy. Brent kissed her cheek and declared that she was a woman after his own heart. She giggled and went home with a smile.

"We really must do something kind for them in repayment," Darien said, feverish and near delirious. He waved a hand cloth around like a surrender flag. Stuart brought home boxes of paper tissues expressly to clear their nasal passages and bring relief to their sinuses. They all had need of tissues by the end of the third day. Brent mixed up the whiskey toddy in the enamel pot they used for canning, and they all had a good strong dose of it.

Gareth moved around like an old man as he shuffled his feet wearily. Stuart ordered him to bed. Stuart and Glendon had the sniffles and slight coughs as did Brent, but they were not as hard hit as Gareth and Darien.

"It is because they work so hard all the time," Glendon speculated, "out in the weather and what not. It is why it is called a cold." Carrol rushed back and forth from room to room, worried.

Brent pulled her aside. "Your great love will not die. There is no sense in making yourself sickly as well. Gareth is a strong man, and he will weather this illness. Little Sis if you do not slow down, you shall come down with it, too. Then I will have to throw you in bed with him, and you can be ill together." He laughed as he considered his words. "That may be a welcome thing for the two of you."

They moved Gareth into the princes' room, and Brent in with Glendon. Stuart slept in the front room in order to keep the stove going. Carrol nursed the two ill Thuringi back to health by plying them with chicken soup, juices, and experimental medicines like the whiskey toddy. Darien awoke one afternoon to see his sister at Gareth's side. She held his hand and whispered endearments. Gareth still coughed but he looked better than the last time Darien saw him. Stuart entered with hot drinks in cups for them.

"I am told that plenty of bed rest is effective for dealing with this illness," he told them. "Therefore, as long as this terrible weather lasts, I do not think it wise for Darien to return to working outdoors. No," he said when he saw Darien stir to protest. "We need our Warrior Prince at the peak of health. Our situation is not dire and does not require you to work in the unaccustomed cold. Gareth must rest more as well. He has completed the Isador and a small reconnaissance version of the Good Lad and almost the renovation of the Naughty Boy with hardly a moment's rest. After he rises from his sickbed, we must make sure Major Sword-and-Fist is better rested even if it means waiting until the weather returns to warm. Spring, it is called."

"Very well," Darien moaned. His nose was tender and sore from blowing it so often. The thought of returning to the freezing oil fields was dreadful and he was privately relieved not to go. He took the drink from Stuart's hands. "What is this?"

"It is called hot cocoa. Katie Martin told me how to make it," Stuart explained.

"Mmm, you did well," Darien's throat rumbled in delight at the taste.

"We have a pot full downstairs. Drink all you please." Stuart handed the other cup to Gareth. The mechanic/engineer sniffed at the brew and cracked a smile.

"Is it a cure of some kind?" Gareth asked.

"No, but as I drink it, I no longer mind being sick," Darien observed.

Gareth's fever broke that evening. While he took a warm bath in the tub, Carrol changed the sweat-soaked sheets on his bed. Darien watched her as she hummed contentedly while she worked.

"You are very fond of our good major, are you, Carrol?" Darien asked.

"Why, you know that I am," she said with a smile.

"You were worried you would lose him, yes?"

She paused in her task for a moment to consider his question and then continued to make the bed. "I will always be afraid of losing him," she admitted. "I do not think I could bear it. And he was afraid for you, as well. He did not want to lose a man so much like his own brother and in a similar manner in which he lost him."

Darien was comforted by the thought as he closed his eyes and snuggled into his bedding. Gareth returned in the loose clothing of slumber, his hair toweled dry and sticking out at all angles.

"I feel much better," he assured Carrol, his voice gravelly with the cold's effect on his throat. She turned back the covers, and he got in and let her tuck him in. "Are you certain you cannot join me?" he whispered.

"Why, major, what a question," she whispered back. "You know I cannot."

"We rested together blamelessly in Darien's apartment before we came here to Earth," Gareth reminded her. "I do not think he would object." She leaned over to tuck the covers around his shoulders and took the opportunity to kiss him lightly.

"He might if we picked up where we left off," she told him. "You need to get some rest now, dear one."

"Stay a little while?" Gareth insisted, and explained, "I miss your touch, Your Nibs." She laid her head against his broad chest and curved her arms around his shoulders as she curled up to him. "I do not believe I have ever been so ill before," Gareth confessed to her. "It is so alarming, this coughing."

"I understand. It must bring back terrible memories," she whispered.

"Darien reminds me so much of Clive, it alarms me to hear him cough. Clive was a rascal, a ladies' man, such a live wire, just like your brother. He was naughty, but nice."

"I would have liked to have known him," Carrol said.

Gareth coughed again. "Oh, he would have toyed with your heart, but at the very core of him he was a very decent fellow. He tried to warn me not to take an interest in Lia Neo. Clive collected women even though he never wanted to settle down, but she was one of the few he did not care to add to his collection. When she discovered he had Bran Fitt she lost interest in him and took up with me. Clive said it was a relief. I felt badly, as if she had traded up for a healthier model, but Clive simply moved on to another love interest." He coughed. "I am so glad neither of us ended up with her. Mother would have boxed our ears. She did not like Lia one little bit. She would have liked you, Nibs. You have quite the nicest bedside manner."

The warmth of her body against his own, coupled with the comfort of the bed, made him drop off to sleep and she did the same at the same general time. Darien opened his eyes and grinned at them. Stuart came to the door, looked in, and smiled.

"She is a dedicated medical," Darien told Stuart. "Let her stay, Stuart; it is a comfort to them both." Stuart put a blanket over his sister and her admirer.

Chapter 9: 1963

The ground was green with grass and flowers were coming out all around the edges of the house. Stuart went to Washington before dawn, to a meeting Michael arranged with a congressman. Glendon and Darien were at their respective jobs. Carrol opened her window and experienced a rush of spring fever. The balmy breeze blew in through the screen. She went downstairs and out to the barn, where Gareth put the finishing touches on a two-seater.

"It is just about done," he told her.

"Good," she said, "I want to help test it."

"Get in, then, and we will fly." She jumped in the back seat, and he sat in front at the controls. They flew out the doors of the barn easily; if they turned sideways, they could have only used one door. They flew low to the ground, only a few feet from the ground. Taking the craft further back into the secluded pastureland behind the ranch, they tested the controls, the roll, the pitch, the yaw. Gareth put the ship down next to a low dip in the middle of a clearing and got out to inspect the undercarriage.

"We will take it out for speed at night," he told her as she got out to join him. "It seems to be holding together."

"It is wonderful how you can craft this together so cleverly," she marveled.

"But it is Earthian steel," he said with regret. "I wish I had some Pleonian steel or could successfully cut down a scout ship for it without taking all year."

"You are too hard on yourself," Carrol told him. "You have done well." She peered up at the bright blue sky, and the puffy white clouds overhead. "How grand to fly on a day like this, free to journey as we pleased!"

"It would be," he agreed. Satisfied with the reassurance that the ship was in good shape, Gareth turned his attention to her. Her hair was loose, the way he always liked it, and she wore Earthian clothes of slacks and a light top. The sun warmed the day well and the breeze was invigorating but not at all chilly. The fact that they were alone together was not lost on either.

"Oh, I wish we were back at the ranch house," she said as she put her arms around his neck. "I have some literature there." He laughed and hugged her tightly.

"'My glorious thrill, my unending joy, is found in the fulfillment of my wishes and wants, lost in the embrace of you.'" he quoted, from the Vita Kanerra.

" 'What passion in your eyes'," she countered, from the Tarinade, " 'That undress me with a thought'."

For a moment, they were quiet. Then Gareth said plaintively, "I want you, Carrol." It was the first time he called her by her given name directly, and the sound of his voice caressing her name touched her heart more deeply than she ever dreamed.

"I want you, Gareth," she replied.

They slowly and deliberately undressed each other in the small dip in the field. He laid his shirt out on the ground, and she placed her top next to his. She ran her hands over his bare chest, and he shook in anticipation. "For the life of me, I cannot recall another single word from either book," he whispered as he gathered her in his arms.

"Then we need to write a new verse," she suggested.

They lay together on their discarded clothing and explored each other in mutually satisfying foreplay. Gareth and Carrol made love under the sunny skies of Earth, free from the bounds and dictates of bishops and Elders and royal edicts. Carrol discovered how absolutely right the rumors in the Standard had been about Gareth being the right man for such duty. As for Gareth, he offered this wonderful woman all his passion and received in kind the sort of joy and pleasure he craved.

It was late afternoon when they returned to the ranch, after they carefully tucked their shirttails into their trousers and made sure everything was properly fastened. They could not remove the smiles from their faces or the happy satisfied glow from their expressions. They sat on the front porch swing with a close hold on each other.

"Your Nibs," he said at length, "I can avert my gaze, and I can hold my speech, and I can take cold baths to ease the heat of my longing, but I doubt I will ever be able to keep in what I feel for you. It has already been an unspoken fact among us all."

"I cannot bear to hide another secret," she told him. "It is a waste of time to deny what we feel. I am happy to be in your arms, Gareth, and there is nowhere else I would rather be." She nestled against him.

"You feel good," he murmured to her. A familiar white truck came down the road and turned in at the driveway. Neither lover moved from their comfortable and loving embrace. Glendon parked the truck and leaped out of the cab with a bag of groceries. As he approached the porch, he slowed with each step until he saw that they were not changing their positions.

"What are you two doing?" he sighed. "You know the rule."

"The rule be damned," Carrol told him evenly. "There is no shame in an embrace; no wrong in honesty."

Glendon blinked in surprise. He of course had no idea what transpired, although he was beginning to get a fairly good idea. "You place me in an uncomfortable position. Your father's wishes are clear."

"My father told me to be happy, and I am," Carrol stated.

"He told me to be worthy of her," Gareth said.

"And he is," Carrol added. Glendon shook his head helplessly. "Glendon, you have been exemplary in your duties as a Naradi but for the love of God, can you now simply understand?" Carrol pleaded.

Glendon looked at her face, then at Gareth's. The strain was gone from his longtime friend's face, and from the way his royal charge gazed at Gareth, Glendon knew that no Naradi could hope to stand between them now.

"There is no wrong in honesty, I suppose," Glendon finally sighed, and came up the steps. "Any word from Stuart?"

"No," Gareth told him. "Perhaps it is a good sign." Lloyd Martin's pickup dropped Darien off at the end of the driveway, and the prince walked up the drive, whistling an unfamiliar tune. It was unfamiliar chiefly because Darien was not musical enough to always keep it in the proper key. He saw the couple on the porch swing and whistled notes of surprise and daring.

"And what say you, on this lovely day?" Darien's voice boomed out. "Do I have a fighter ship?"

"After a fashion," Gareth said. "There is still a little work that needs to be done."

"Um hm. And do I have a fighter sister?" he teased.

"Oh, I can fight," Carrol replied. "I just choose not to, not anymore."

"No?" Darien asked and leaned against a porch post. "Then what do you choose to do, instead?" he challenged saucily.

"To love my heart's choice," she answered calmly.

Darien's eyebrows shot up high at her bald confession. Glendon grinned and shook his head. Now that he surrendered his own guardian position, it amused him to see not even Darien believed that Carrol could out-Darien, Darien. Gareth, too, turned to stare at her. He could not believe her bold words either, but he hoped he had heard them. She kissed him in front of her brother and Glendon.

"And what say you, Gareth?" Darien asked, hardly able to ask.

"I would never think of disappointing Her Nibs," Gareth said, and boldly returned the kiss.

Glendon groaned. "All we need is for Stuart to come home and listen to the explosion."

"There woe not be an explosion from Stuart!" Darien laughed, stubbornly mangling the will not contraction. "He may even wonder how he might best convince that chill woman he married to gain inspiration from these two."

When Stuart returned, it was evening time and the night's meal was served. They greeted him enthusiastically, but their enthusiasm waned at the look on his face. There was no anger or anxiety, just an impassive expression that did not change. He shook his head when they asked about Washington and told them they would discuss it all later. During the ensuing meal he ate without comment, answering only with a brief "let me eat first."

When dinner was over Stuart volunteered to clean up, even though it was Carrol's turn. He gently shooed her out of the kitchen and did his task with a great deal of silent contemplation.

At last, he emerged from the kitchen and sat in the living room with the other four. Darien cut to the chase. "What happened today, Stuart? What has brought this blue mood to our happy brother and leader?"

Stuart sat still for a moment, his elbows on the arms of the chair. His hands met at the fingertips, and he studied the tips as if with great interest. Then he spoke.

"This blue mood will pass. But first, how was the day here? Anything interesting happen?" he asked. One glance at their faces told him a great deal. Darien's mouth twisted into a saucy smile, and Glendon preferred to look anywhere except at Stuart. Gareth straightened slightly and took a deep breath, and Carrol tried hard to look Stuart steadily in the eye.

"The events of our day can wait," she told Stuart. "It would seem your day is the more pressing."

"Whatever may have transpired here today must not be much more than of personal anecdote," Stuart suggested. Gareth nodded, along with the others. "Is it a good thing?" Stuart asked directly to Gareth.

"Yes," Gareth replied without hesitation. "We believe that it is."

"Then it can wait. I can use happy tidings once my tale is told. Now I will tell you a tale of the day's events, but I ask that you listen and not ask questions until I am through," he said quietly.

They all solemnly agreed, even Darien. This was not like the sunny Crown Prince Stuart, and they were all concerned. He cleared his throat and began his story.

Stuart tried for months to arrange a meeting with President Kennedy. He could not get past the layers of advisors and aides without revealing his true nature, and he did not want to expose his people to so many so soon. In Stuart's mind, the United States president held the same power as a king, and King Lycasis of Thuringa was much more receptive to unusual matters than his often-unsympathetic advisors. He searched for another way.

Michael heard of a young congressman, Anthony Price, who was interested in space exploration and was on the committee which funded the National Aeronautics and Space Administration. He was reputed to have an open mind and a friendly disposition, so Michael arranged an introduction for Stuart. NASA would be the most logical way to present the Thuringi to the government and the world.

The congressman was held over in another meeting and asked to talk to them over lunch. They met him in a Georgetown restaurant. Congressman Anthony Price was an intelligent, curious man in his mid thirties who listened intently as Michael and then Stuart carefully laid out the details of their visit.

"I met young Stuart here by accident when the ship he flew unexpectedly came out of the clouds and into the path of my car. I swerved off the road and he saved my life. Then as I got to know him and his companions, I came to realize how fortunate I really was. The technology Stuart and his friends possess is beyond anything we have here in America, or anything on Earth. You see... Prince Stuart is from another world."

"Uh huh." The congressman was as skeptical as Michael warned Stuart he might be.

"We are not concerned whether you believe us or not; eventually you will when the rest of our ships arrive," the Thuringa prince explained. "But please know that we have no intention of bringing harm or hardship to any of your people. We only need a place to rest and recover our health after our long flight, and then we will be on our way again. This is not our ultimate destination."

"And just what is?" Anthony Price asked as he absently stirred his drink.

"A world far into the unknown area beyond this one. Your world is past the edge of the territory of our Known Worlds, and no one has explored this far with any serious intent."

"And just why are you going there?"

"Our world was destroyed by a race who has harbored a long and needless resentment toward us. We know the target world is uninhabited and we explored it briefly once, but we cannot travel the quickest route there because our ships are too fragile for the journey. That is why we need to rest on your world. We need the sponsorship of your president and his council and hope perhaps you will guide us to that end."

Stuart saw the bored lift of an eyebrow and the raised bottom lip of a man prepared to brush off an imaginative but time-wasting story. In desperation he pulled off his dark glasses and looked the congressman in the eye. "Please, Lord Price. We came here to establish proper diplomatic relations, but I realize that your world does not take space travel seriously. You believe it the stuff of fantasy and...and poorly made films. Yet your own country is in a race to go into space. Is it beyond your belief that other worlds might not also exist, and also have such dreams in mind? That such dreams have come true and have been in place for centuries? Is it easier to believe that Earthian humans descended from related mammals, or that life can only be found on this one planet because its inhabitants declared it so?"

"Well..." Anthony Price sat up. Come to think of it, the boy made sense and besides, Anthony never saw eyes like that before. "And you only need a place to rest, eh? Just how big a place, what did you have in mind?"

"We have three large general population ships, one oceanic ship, one for our botanicals, one for our surviving creatures, a medical ship, several battleships and cruisers, a few hundred fighters, and nearly forty thousand people. We have lived in our ships for the last ten years; any amount of space that could be spared would be welcome. We only need a chance to repair and improve our ships for the rest of the journey and perhaps improve the health of the populace with some fresh air and sunshine and some hearty meals of fresh vegetables and fruit. We have the kind of technology your people seek. Perhaps there could be an exchange."

The more he heard, the more excited the congressman became. It was not an impossible claim, as it might have been if Stuart had named some fantastic number of survivors and boasted of thousands of ships at his command. It was the story of a beleaguered nation under fire with the sort of needs one might expect of nomads fleeing for their lives.

When Stuart produced a small rectangle the size of a deck of cards, Anthony did not know what to expect. He saw a clear crisp picture of a beautiful sunny blonde woman and a boy on the small deck-sized screen. The small screen alone was a revelation of technology unknown to him. With the press of a button, the screen displayed a triangular-shaped aircraft the like of which Anthony Price never saw before, not even of the experimental variety. More and more pictures were shown on that small screen, each one with more exotic, unearthly scenes than the next. There was something about the casual way the people in the background stood and the gorgeously appointed details in the pictures that told him that this was not the product of Hollywood or some advertising agency.

In close quarters, little details about the Thuringi were more noticeable than at first: Stuart Phillipi had no hair other than on his head, his eyebrows, and eyelashes. There was not even hair on the back of his hands or on his arms. He looked like a teenager but even at that, his face did not even bear any 'peach fuzz'. He had smooth skin with small pores and no indication of follicles. His eyes were undoubtedly naturally yellow and not the product of colored lens; his irises expanded and contracted with the changing of nearby light. When he spoke, it was not always in sync with the way his mouth moved. Most of the words were but there were a few more complex words or phrases where the two did not match. He noticed the small cord extending from behind Stuart's left ear.

After lunch Anthony and Michael followed Stuart to his ship. Here was something Anthony could touch, something tangible: irrefutable fact. Stuart let him look over the ship thoroughly and then took him for a quick trip around the world. As they reached the upper atmosphere of Earth and orbited, the congressman had to pinch himself to make certain this was more than an elaborate dream. It was real.

Congressman Price not only believed in Stuart; he was enthusiastic about enlisting support for the Thuringi cause. Michael cautioned him to use discretion when approaching these scientists. Anthony assured him he would begin with theoretical scenarios at first in order not to be viewed as a "nut case" himself.

He told Stuart and Michael that as soon as he could arrange a meeting, he would let them know. The best way to garner the president's attention and prove who he was would be to impress the scientists and engineers behind the president's pet project. Many factions of the government would be interested in opening diplomatic channels with the Thuringi, especially the Air Force.

Michael was suddenly uncomfortable at the mention of the Air Force and asked they be left out of the loop.

"Well, I don't know why not," the congressman said. "After all, the Air Force and his Air Command could share helpful information with one another, a sort of arms trade deal. Let me see what I can do. I'll start with the scientists but one of them might contact the Air Force anyway. These guys know funding and how to get it, and I can't very well control that without sounding suspicious, myself."

Stuart could not dictate terms at that point and did not argue. He took Michael back to Boston. On the way, he asked the Earthian man what troubled him so.

"I wish I could say, Stuart, I really do," Michael told him, "I do not have a problem with Anthony Price but frankly, I do not trust the Army or Air Force or Navy any further than I could throw them where it concerns you Thuringi, and I have no concrete reason." Michael drew a breath, and blurted out, "Contri faldo."

"He said what?" the other scouts exclaimed at home that night when Stuart told them.

"He said, 'contri faldo'. I heard it as plainly as I am saying it to you," Stuart said. "Although how Michael Sheldon could have possibly overheard that phrase, or figured it out from talking to us, I do not know. But he said, contri faldo - 'deception with a smiling face'. I asked him if he knew what that meant. He said it sounds like Italian, but he did not know why he said it, he does not understand Italian."

"What does it mean in Italian?" Carrol asked.

"It means nothing, as far as I know," Stuart said, "but I know what it means in Sturbin."

There were several instances of cross-reference between the Known Worlds and Earthian dialects: some odd, some amusing. This, however, was not the kind of coincidence that could be tossed away. Michael once told them he did not know many foreign Earthian terms except what he found on menus, and this was certainly not the case. If he had used a Thuringi term for 'deception with a smiling face', it would not have been as startling as a phrase from a world whose language he did not know at all. "I will alert Brent to double his efforts in locating an island upon which to settle New Thuringa," Stuart told them. "We may need to go swiftly if there is deception in the air."

"Deception from Michael?" Glendon asked in dismay. "Or from this congressman?"

"Not from Michael," Stuart said, "and the congressman seems ready and eager to help us, but one can never truly know the hearts of acquaintances. Now then," he said, brightening at last, "there was a mention of good tidings earlier. What is it?"

Gareth resolutely kept his mouth shut. With his abysmal way of speaking, he would only make a mess of it. Glendon and Darien looked at each other, also uncertain of what to say and how to go about it.

But Carrol knew what to do. Catching Stuart's eye, she took Gareth's hand in hers and smiled at her older brother.

"We are all aware of your fondness for each other," Stuart pointed out, unimpressed.

"Then accepting the fact openly should be no large matter," Carrol said cheerfully.

"Now, wait," Stuart cautioned, and was suddenly aware of Darien's nefarious grin. "What are you smirking about?" he demanded suspiciously.

"I do not think it is open for debate, Your Crown Nibs," Darien said, borrowing from Gareth's favorite phrase. "Our sister has made her choice, and he has made his."

Stuart looked at Gareth, who was still silent. "You have never woven a tale of partial truths, Gareth; you have always been quite up front about everything. Tell me what this is all about," Stuart said.

Darien and Glendon waited in curious expectation of something amazingly blunt, and they were not entirely disappointed.

"You said yourself that you were well aware of our fondness for each other," Gareth told him plainly. "We are quite certain of that fondness ourselves and intend to continue to share it with each other. Discreetly, of course." The last three words were the clincher.

"Dis... ah... of course," Stuart managed. "Where were you?" he suddenly demanded of Glendon.

"At the Gentry store. Darien was at the oil field," Glendon said.

"We cannot be in two places at once," Darien argued.

Stuart looked at Gareth for a long minute. If Stuart were father to a daughter, he hoped she would find someone like the man before him now, the man holding Carrol's hand so reverently in his own. "Nor can I," Stuart said in reflection. "I do not believe Father has any objections in Major Sword-and-Fist as your suitor, Carrol. In fact, I suspect he sent you both here together to get you away from the Elders in the hope of it. His chief concern was public opinion of the Armada. Despite what we personally feel, our subjects expect our conduct to be exemplary. Here, we are not on the Armada, and I do not plan to lose any sleep over your deportment. But have a care! That which is acceptable here on Earth will be under different scrutiny among our people of the Armada. When we return, do not be too comfortable with each other."

"Who knew that I am more at ease among Earthian ways than our own," Gareth mused. "I promised discretion, and I will give it. And I will begin by turning this conversation to other things, thank you," he told them, and Stuart smiled in agreement. "Darien's two-seater is ready for a speed-trial run. Everything else checks out."

Darien leaped to his feet with a triumphant cry. "It will be dark within the hour. I will be more than happy to test the speed of the Naughty Boy, myself."

"We can go find Brent Ardenne and tell him of today's events in Washington," Stuart suggested.

The brothers went out to test the Naughty Boy alongside the Good Lad. Glendon went upstairs with some boxes. Gareth and Carrol watched curiously as the Naradi gathered all his possessions and packed them. Finally, Carrol had to ask the obvious.

"Glendon, what are you doing?"

"I have trusted my instinct about Michael Sheldon, and I still trust it. If he is uneasy about involvement with the Earthian Air Force, then I intend to gather us together on the chance that we may need to leave in a moment's notice."

"Do you really think it is that grave a situation?" Gareth asked.

"An Outlander who uses an obscure Sturbin phrase to explain an inexplicable feeling impresses me enough to feel that it is." Carrol saw the point and went downstairs to pack away her research equipment, so Gareth packed up some of his tools and personal items. "You are bitten by good fortune, Gareth," Glendon told him as they worked. "Losing Lia Neo was the best thing that could have happened to you on many levels."

"In retrospect of the chain of events, you are right," Gareth said, "but winning Carrol Shanaugh is the very best."

"Oh, winning yet! Are you that certain of her heart to claim a win?"

"Yes." Gareth's succinct response told Glendon enough to ask nothing more.

Brent Ardenne stood atop the Isador with his feet apart and his hands on his hips, grinning broadly at the incoming ships. The gently rocking waves of the South Pacific made the oceangoing ship bob about in the water, but Brent's clinging bare feet held him in place firmly. He had a gloriously glowing bronze skin tone, and the sun also bleached his yellow hair almost white. He kept his hair cropped fairly short for a Thuringi, just brushing the top of his shoulders. The length was twisted up and held in place by a clamshell he fashioned into a hair clasp. He cut off his slacks until they were scant shorts, and shirts were things that were left inside the Isador as long as the sun shone.

Brent was once again a lord of the seas. On Thuringa he rode the waves of Lycasis's oceans, seeing to the well-being of fish and watermen that lived there. His intense passion for life was in concert with the restless wind and waves, and it suffered with him in the cold airless reaches of space. Now he was back in his element, and Brent Ardenne would never again willingly agree to fly the black vacuum for a long journey without it.

The ships that approached were undeniably Gareth Duncan designs, curious triangular crafts of gray metal rounded off at all edges. The wings dipped slightly down at the tips, and the nose of the ships also dipped down. They hovered just above the waves. Stuart and Darien opened their cockpits to hail him.

"Are you the Little Mermaid?" Darien called out. "Monica Martin admires your story."

"Are you an ill-tempered reprobate who is the constant source of irritation for his long-suffering parents?" Brent called back to him. "And who is that with you, the unfortunate captive of my repressed sister?"

"I am until we return to the Armada, and I give her dancing lessons," Stuart answered. This brought out whoops and catcalls from the other two. "How is the search for New Thuringa going, Brent?"

"I have just about narrowed it down to a select three possibilities," Brent said. "Fresh water, out of traffic lanes and trade wind routes, and useful land mass. Why have the sons of Thuringa decided to play with their new toys and fly here to ask me what I would tell them in two days?"

Stuart came out to sit on the nose of his ship, and Darien did the same on his. This brought them within ten feet of each other. "There has been a new development which may be either a boon to us, or trouble," Stuart told him, and repeated the story he related to the others.

When he was finished, Brent shook his head. "Amen. Michael Sheldon is a very trustworthy lad, so I share your concern about his uncertainty in the American air command. Come with me to the islands I have chosen and see what you think. There is one in particular of which I am fond, but you may find advantages in the others I do not. The sooner we get away from the mainland, the better."

"Spoken like a true waterman," Darien snorted.

They gave each island a brief flyover in the late afternoon of the South Pacific. One was almost entirely an atoll, much too small for the entire Armada's compliment, but it did have a wonderful lagoon and was in a very obscure location. The second one was a bit larger, but almost entirely just above sea level. Any storm could easily cause flooding.

They flew to the third island located along the 25th parallel south, and Darien and Stuart saw at once the potential it held. It was roughly a mile and a half wide and five miles long. A long sandy beach stretched along the western side and around the north end and down the eastern side until it narrowed at a natural arch. From there, the southern coast was rocky and jagged. The interior of the island was crowded with vegetation. At the wider southern end of the island was an extinct volcano. There were natural springs and surprisingly, little wild goats.

"We have a winning contender," Stuart said. "What do you think, Darien?"

"I agree. Is this the one you had in mind, Brent?"

"Yes, for the fleet; but personally, I am fond of the first one of course."

"We should claim this now as New Thuringa in the name of the king," Stuart suggested. He and Darien landed on the beach, and Brent eased the Isador up onto the surf's edge.

"We claim this land," Darien shouted toward the center of the island, "in the name of King Lycasis Phillipi de Trennon, twenty-fifth king of Thuringa!"

"The Isle of New Thuringa," Stuart shouted beside his brother. "Prepare to be settled!"

"You goats be warned," Brent shouted beside the princes. "Lonely men approach the island!" The Phillipi brothers gave Brent twin looks of consternation.

"No wonder Aura is repressed," Stuart told him. "You are of a peculiar bend of humor."

"Aura is a prig with no sense of humor at all! If mine is bent, it is because it must do double duty on behalf of our generational contribution," Brent said as he walked toward some coconut trees.

"Amen!"

Early the next morning the other three Thuringi came out to the island, using the scout ship Her Nibs as their vehicle. The daytime brought out the lush beauty of the island, and Brent was able to show them all the places he thought were especially helpful. The natural arch at the southern tip of the island was a part of the rocky range to the highest point of the island. The deep waters just off that part of the island would be a good berth for the Oceanic ship Freen. A sharp ridge ran along the eastern side of the island, which rose from the flatter northern end up to the apex that commanded the southern tip near the arch. Flat space near the center of the island would serve well as a landing area for the Armada. The Quantid and the General Population Quarters ships could nestle at the base of the cliffs, which were pocked with caves. Much of the land along the northern part and on either side of the ridge was thick with jungle growth, including several pools of water.

Skeletons of five past inhabitants were found on the northern tip of the island. Each Thuringi studied the camp to piece together why there were no living descendants to be found. Perhaps they were sailors whose ship foundered, since there was little evidence of useful tools settlers would bring to build a new life. One skeleton's leg was shattered, perhaps from a fall from the high craggy cliffs or a tree, and infection surely set in beneath the ineffectual attempt to fashion a crude splint with two tree branches and some rags. Two bodies lay near each other outside a crumbling hut, and the metal weapons near their hands suggested a deadly quarrel with no winner. Inside the hut the last two bodies lay on pallets of banana leaves with jugs near each.

Carrol speculated that they were ill with fever or suffered soft tissue injury, to have died in bed. Brent agreed and told his friends about the hazards of jellyfish and sea snakes. Carroll noted the skeletons were all adult males which further supported the shipwreck theory rather than settlers with families. The Thuringi gave the luckless victims proper burials and carefully burned the hut to guard against possible lingering disease. No other human remains were detected on the island. Only birds and reptiles lived there, and Glendon suggested that the goats might have been a part of the sailor's cargo. Somehow, they made it to shore and thrived on the lush vegetation and lack of large carnivores.

The scouts each made a rough map of separate sections of the island and flew back to the Sheldon ranch for further discussion. Stuart did not want to leave the ranch unwatched for a long period of time. They put together their chartings and came up with a resultant detailed topographical map, to scale and set up in the center of the now nearly empty research parlor. Gareth found items close in scale to the Armada ships: cylindrical oat cereal boxes representing the GPQs and a small cut-down cereal box with film canisters glued to it represented the Daven Bau. These were placed in different locations on the island map, each Thuringi debating the merits and drawbacks of each placement.

King Lycasis would have the ultimate say on the placement, but he would take their suggestions into serious consideration since they were familiar with the Earthian conditions. In the meantime, this preliminary plotting would help them decide where to set up an outpost and living space. No one wanted a reprise of the five sailors' fate.

One of the main reasons Brent chose this particular area of the Pacific to search for an island was that it was out of commercial shipping traffic. It was a shame there was no snow, he told the others, but the large island at the southern axis of the world held an incredible amount of the cold white stuff.

The Thuringi always enjoyed the radio and got a better grasp of English from it. They listened to the music curiously. Thuringi music was comparable to Earthian folk music, largely acoustic and told stories through its lyrics. The first time Carrol heard 'Sh-Boom', she could not figure out what it meant. "La-da-da-da-da-da, Da-da-da-da-da' meant nothing to them, to say nothing of the mystery of what or who Sh-Boom was. The instrumentals were well liked; 'A Summer Place' reminded Glendon of a winding drive in his speeder back on Thuringa, and the smooth sound of the violins were as pleasing as the sholti players that entertained during Festival at Arne. None of the scouts understood 'The Twist', but at least they could guess with help of the lyrics.

Darien was out with Lloyd Martin for the evening. Gareth happened upon the opening chords of a song on a different station on the radio in the living room, and he paused to hear it. It was then that the five Thuringi got the most unexpected shock Earth gave them yet.

'Louie Louie' was something of a minor scandal among Earthians, for the slurred delivery of the words on the recording tickled the lurid imaginations of many. But for the Thuringi, it was as if the Tarinade was put to music and broadcast over public airwaves. The slurred 'I said' sounded like the Thuringi asaya, or 'let us go'. Wegodgoe was a slang term for the sex act, which closest Earthian equivalent began with the letter 'F'. Therefore, when the Earthian singer sang the Thuringi-sounding invitation, the listeners in the front room of the Sheldon ranch house froze in place.

In English the words were slurred and almost indistinguishable but in Thuringi, most of the words sounded like a lurid account of casual sex for a lecherous man and a wanton woman. They were so startled by this brazen account that no one thought to simply turn off the radio. They sat listening to the song until it ended, and a commercial came on.

"Word," Brent said as a smile spread from ear to ear. "If not for the fact that he cannot sing a note, I could swear Darien somehow did that."

"I cannot believe I just heard that!" Stuart bellowed. "Name of All!" But he too smiled because despite being mortified, he was inwardly amused at the unseemliness of it all.

"Yeep!" was all Glendon could manage.

"And we were concerned about Darien misbehaving in a cantina." Gareth blew out a long breath as if decompressing. "These people are even more unwittingly offensive than I."

"What a shame that the tune was so infectious," Carrol commented. She sat in the floor and covered her face with her hands. "It is hard to get out of my head now." Gareth tried to find another station, but 'Louie Louie' was going up on the charts and they came across it everywhere.

"There are some things, Stuart, that you are simply going to have to leave out of your report to your father," Brent told him. "The song about the lustful flower is one of them."

When Darien came in the door, they all tried at once to tell him about the song 'Louie Louie', but he could not follow what they meant. Carrol turned on the radio and searched until she happened upon it. The song lit up Darien's eyes. He in turn corrupted his brother and best friend into singing the chorus with him.

Darien was the ringleader back in their Academy days, and Stuart and Brent were usually right with him in the thick of it all. They became quite adept at wreaking havoc in the Standard in Arne. Stuart might back off from their hijinks out of duty to the crown, but Brent reveled in the bad behavior and was likely to try to top it.

'Louie Louie' did not put off Gareth at all. He enjoyed the notion that this was one time when an odious deed could not be blamed on a simple country boy from Carzon. He joined them in the chorus and winked at Carrol as he did so. Glendon was a proper Thuringi, but he was also a man who enjoyed a good joke. This was completely out of his hands; he could not regulate the amusement of Earthians even if he wanted to. This was simply too ripe not to pluck.

For her part, Carrol stuffed her fingers in her ears and made faces at them all.

They laughed uproariously at the conclusion of the song. Darien told them about his evening in the Earthian cantina with Lloyd Martin and that it did not offer this much amusement.

"Can you imagine," Glendon chuckled, "the looks on our wives' faces if ever they hear this tune? Isador would probably laugh. Janis would blush but she would find it privately amusing, Of that, I am sure."

"Oh, and Aura!" Stuart began, and he and Brent looked at each other for a second before both men roared with mirth. Darien and Gareth and Glendon joined in, and even Carrol laughed at the prospect of Her Haughtiness hearing 'Louie Louie' in all its unholy glory.

"We must remember to do a rendition of it for her when we return," Darien snickered. "To say nothing of the songs, 'One Fine Day' and 'He is So Fine'."

"Darien!" they all roared, outraged. Darien reminded them about the use of the word 'fine', and Brent could not hold back a wicked laugh.

"Aura will simply need to become deafened between now and the time she arrives on Earth," he chuckled.

"How much did you have to drink tonight, Darien?" Stuart asked as casually as possible.

"I only had two of their rancid beerz in all. Word, that weak sauce can put hair on the tongue with no effort. Ugh."

The oil field Dickie Forbes's company worked in was fully developed, and the Forbes drilling company moved on to another field further away. Darien declined to go with them, citing his reluctance to travel far from home. He was told he was welcome to join them again, and he politely agreed to consider it. Lloyd shook his hand as Darien left the truck on his last day. "Monica's still going to want to see the Magic Man," he told Darien. "I'm not sure how long I'm going to stick with roustabout work, myself. Don't forget us, now."

"I woe not," Darien promised.

He had plenty to occupy himself. Most of his time was spent on New Thuringa, where he developed the caves into living quarters. Blasting at the rock took a careful touch; excavating too little made for small claustrophobic rooms; too much, and the structure was in danger of collapsing altogether. He took advantage of the freedom of the island, and soon his hair was sun-bleached almost to the lighter shade of Stuart's and his skin bronzed nicely. He enjoyed the strength of the earth and the balmy caress of the breezes. Darien was able to relax and laugh on the island, in a very different frame of mind than what he had when they first came to Earth. Indeed, he had not felt this good since before the first attack on Thuringa by the Shargassi.

Through Congressman Price, Stuart was introduced to a rocket engineer with the Mercury program. At first Stuart was regarded as just another starry-eyed fan of the space program, albeit a large one. But after the engineer saw a few of the basic formulas and equations from elementary Thuringi physics, he desperately wanted to know more about where Stuart got his amazing information. Stuart was reluctant to give information without obtaining some diplomatic pluses for Thuringa. He did not divulge his whereabouts to the scientist or the congressman, remembering Michael Sheldon's strange reaction to the Air Force personnel. Anthony tried to convince the engineer to keep the knowledge quiet so as not to alarm the Thuringi, but he was not sure how long he could keep the curious scientist satisfied with mere promises of more information. What he got from Stuart was enough to keep him puzzling over for a while, but he would want more soon.

Glendon secured several old Army generators from a surplus dealer, and Gareth put those to use as power generators for the island. He finished the new ship for Glendon, and the Golden Boy was somewhere between the size of the scout ships and the smaller two-seater fighters. They decided to keep the Her Nibs and the Sword and Fist as scout-sized ships so they could eventually return to the Armada with a minimum of needed large ships and a maximum of occupancy in each. Glendon found appliances Gareth could repair, improve, and send to the island. Carrol stayed in Oklahoma with Glendon and Gareth to run the household and work in the garden. Glendon moved into the Phillipi brothers' bedroom, and it was a cozy companionable summer for them.

On pleasant nights, the three went to the local drive-in theater. Glendon sometimes sat in the courtesy seats at the concession stand until the young women gathered to visit with the handsome man with the odd British accent and emerald green eyes. Then he returned to the truck and continued to watch the film from there. In his presence Gareth and Carrol were well behaved, but Glendon could tell by the unkempt hair and clothing and the fogged-over windows that tomfoolery had been exercised in his absence. He even found himself apologizing for his early return.

Some Proper Garin I turned out to be, he thought wryly.

Gareth constantly worked on something at the ranch. There were projects all throughout the barn and in the house, and just outside the back door. Once in a while he decided to take a break, and if that break happened to be in the loving company of Carrol Shanaugh's soft bed and arms along with their copy of the Tarinade, no one was there to object to it. When Michael Sheldon came out to visit, he was always welcomed with enthusiasm. Michael still could not keep his eyes off Carrol, but he picked up on her and Gareth's new relationship change quickly.

Glendon made friends with the local lawmen and occasionally rode along with them on patrol out of curiosity for American law enforcement. The 'local Naradi' as he called them liked Glendon since the day he stopped the tough boys from harassing little Becca Morris. Glendon learned aspects of police procedure that Thuringi did not often experience – theft, rape, homicide. The police discovered how handy it was to have Glendon's muscular presence there to hold down a struggling suspect, and drunks were easily subdued. The policemen hoped Glendon would join them, but he explained he and his friends were having a difficult time replacing their passports and he could not apply.

One night Glendon awoke to a strange sensation. He looked around but could no longer feel it. It must have been in a dream, he thought, but he was now wide awake. A strong urge to get up tugged at him. He pulled on his boots and a robe and felt around for his pistol. He settled for his sword and went out into the darkened hallway.

He glanced into Carrol's bedroom and saw her peacefully asleep in her neat orderly bed, awash in the moonlight through the window. He checked on Gareth across the hall, and saw him sprawled across his bed, his limbs tangled in his sheets, in a deep sleep. Glendon went down the hall, down the stairs and opened the back door. He felt compelled to move his legs forward, out to the Golden Boy and without understanding why, climbed into the ship and flew off into the darkness.

He went toward town and saw the Gentry's store and the rambling two story house behind it. An odd pressure seized his head, not quite a headache but not a normal press. He lowered the ship down silently to land behind the tangle of honeysuckle vines along the fence. Glendon stood in the side yard feeling more than a little foolish until a flashlight beam from an upstairs window caught his eye. He heard muffled voices of alarm. He sprinted toward the house and recognized Ed Gentry's voice.

"I'll give you whatever you want, just don't hurt my wife, please."

"Shut up, old man, and get your safe open."

"I told you, I don't have a safe in my house. I don't know where you heard I do." Glendon heard a sickening thud and heard Margie cry.

"Please, if we had one, we'd open it for you, but we just don't," she cried. "You don't have to hurt my Ed."

Glendon stepped back from the house and looked up. There was a second porch, a widow's deck as Margie called it, located over the main front porch. Crouching down, the Naradi leaped upward and caught two balcony banisters with his hands. He pulled himself up and onto the porch soundlessly. Drawing his sword, Glendon stepped over to the door and peeked in through the little glass window.

The bedroom lamp was on, and by its light he saw Margie on the edge of the bed with her arms tied at the wrists behind her. A man in dark clothing and sporting a rough beard held a large knife in one hand and held Margie by the hair with the other. Ed Gentry picked himself up off the floor dully. A callow-looking younger man in mismatched clothing stood ready with a wooden club. Glendon saw that Ed had been hit more than once by the club, and a large bruise developed over one eye.

"Come on, old man. I heard you never go to the bank 'cause you got a safe here in the house," the youth was saying. "Shut her up; I can't stand to hear no blubbering."

Margie tried to keep from sobbing, but she was afraid and could not contain her fear. The man who held her slung her forward to the floor, and Margie landed hard on her knees. The man looked at her impassively and started for her.

Ed Gentry thought the door to the widow's walk exploded. Out of his good eye he saw a large, robed figure burst into the room with a sword, singing in an unfamiliar language. The sword flashed, and the man with the knife cried out in pain as a long gash appeared on his arm. He dropped the knife to grab his wounded limb. The robed figure advanced forward and lashed out with his foot. It caught the man in the side of the head and knocked him off his feet and back onto the bed. The club-holder swung at the figure with his weapon, and the sword flashed again. The club holder then held a six-inch stub of wood in his double-fisted grip, and the rest of the club fell to the floor with a thud. The fist of the swordsman caught him in the jaw, and the club holder stumbled backward, dropping his stub of wood. The figure picked him up by his loose shirt and shook him like a rag.

"You dare bring harm to these people, you wretch!" Joe and Margie both recognized Glendon's voice, in his clear English accent. "These kind good people? Do you have a death wish, boy?" Glendon heaved the younger man across the room at the other man, who had regained his senses enough to try to scramble from the bed. Both of the assailants tumbled hard against the headboard of the bed.

Ed pulled Margie out of harm's way. They stood to one side of the room, astonished to see their gentle Glendon in an unprecedented rage.

"Come to me if trouble is what you seek! Come to me if it is a fight you want! Foul istays, you shall know the taste of Garin steel!"

"Who the hell is that?" one of the men squawked. "Freakin' Richard Burton?"

"That's my boy Glendon, you son of a bitch!" Ed shouted triumphantly as he untied Margie's binds. "Margie, go call the sheriff from the kitchen."

"But your eye, Ed!" Margie fretted.

"I'm okay, go get Fred to come over here!" Margie hurried downstairs to make the call. One of the men made a run for the broken door to the widow's walk, and Glendon deftly stopped him with the threat of cold steel. The would-be thief rejoined his partner in crime.

"Are you in distress, Lord Gentry?"

Ed patted the tall Thuringi's shoulder affectionately. "Not anymore, I'm not! You came right in the nick of time. God, am I glad to see you!" He shook a fist at the trapped men. "I told you sons of bitches; I don't have a safe in my house! It just don't seem like I go to the bank, because I like to be discreet about handling my store's money. I ought to have young Glen here give you a taste of your own medicine! The idea, trussing my Margie up like a holiday turkey and scaring her like that!"

"Shut up, you old man," the younger thief snapped.

"Nacona delees fatuttan," Glendon rasped, and for the first time the two men under guard noticed that the Gentry's tall champion had yellow eyes. Eyes as yellow as the sun, as a sunflower, and he spoke in a language that was lilting and musical as a song, yet the mysterious words were clear in tone as to their content. The younger man shut his mouth abruptly. Glendon's boots were gray from wear, and his white robe came together in the front only barely held in place by his hastily tied belt. There was no other body hair on the tall figure before the robbers, and his white undergarments seemed to be just another part of the whole costume.

"Sweet Jesus," the bearded man whispered, "they got a damn guardian angel."

"And I am filled with righteous fury," Glendon added as he recalled part of a sermon he heard at Franklin Morris's church.

The sheriff's car and a second patrol car pulled up in the driveway, and they heard sounds of slamming doors and running feet. Margie led them up the stairs. The two would-be robbers were put in handcuffs right away, and the local doctor came in to look over Ed's bruises.

"That big angel cut my arm open," the bearded man complained.

"Too damn bad," a deputy told him. "If you hadn't been robbing a house, it wouldn't have happened."

"What did happen, Mr. Gentry?" the sheriff asked.

"These two broke in and tied up Margie and beat around on me. They thought I had a safe hidden here in my house, which I don't. Then, just when that bearded guy pushed Margie down in the floor, the door just blew open and Glendon came in and saved the day, like… like a big blonde Superman!"

"Oh sure, I recognize him now. What happened to your eyes?" the sheriff asked Glendon.

"Nothing. It is genetic," Glendon told him. "It is a burden that some in my family share."

"Well," the sheriff said, deciding to pass over this little mystery for the case at hand, "What made you come out here in the dead of night? Did you see what happened?"

"No, I cannot explain it exactly. I awoke with a terrible feeling, and I felt compelled to wander about. I came upon the Gentry's house and saw the lights and heard distress. I got on the second floor and entered through the door as swiftly as I could."

"I'll say he did," the deputy said, looking over the damage. "How'd you do this?"

"With a kick."

"He's a strong boy; picks up wood stoves like they were nothing," Ed Gentry said proudly, as if to brag on his own son.

"It's a miracle," Margie said as she hugged the Thuringi around the waist. "I prayed and prayed for a miracle, and God send our Glendon out here to help us. He moves in mysterious ways, His wonders to perform."

"The God of All knows the way of all things. Who can say how God aligns the stars?" Glendon quoted automatically.

"Don't believe I'm familiar with that verse," the doctor said as he bandaged the bearded man's arm.

"He's an avenging angel," the bearded man croaked. "He said he was filled with righteous anger."

"So am I," the doctor snapped. "Ed and Margie are good friends of mine, you sorry bastard."

"I always thought he was an angel," Ed told Margie in satisfaction.

The sheriff seemed satisfied after a few more questions, and remarked it was a fortunate coincidence Glendon was restless that night and chanced upon the scene of the crime in time to prevent further harm to the Gentrys. The sheriff heard of other such premonitions from time to time and did not doubt it was the case in this situation. Thanks in part to Glendon's occasional ride-alongs with the sheriff and his deputies, they knew his character and his motives were beyond reproach.

Glendon called Carrol to come get him in the truck. "And bring Gareth," he said in Thuringi on the phone in the Gentry's living room. "He will need to be let out early so he can fly the Golden Boy back home without being seen. It is hidden behind the honeysuckle fence."

"What?" Carrol asked sleepily.

"Just do it," Glendon urged. Gareth and Carrol dressed hastily and did as instructed. Gareth found the Golden Boy in its hiding spot and carefully flew it home low to the ground, slowly to not attract attention. Carrol collected her 'brother' and got a glowing account from the Gentrys, the doctor, the sheriff, and the deputy about his brave and timely actions.

"I remember him helping out the little Morris girl," the deputy reminded the sheriff. "He's a pretty handy fellow to have around. He said he comes from a long line of policemen back where he comes from."

It was not until after the Thuringi left that the police wondered how Glendon managed to walk five miles in the moonlight at night with a big sword. "Well, he kicked their widow's walk door clean off its hinges. I guess your avenging angel type of guys can do that sort of stuff," the deputy yawned.

The Gentrys told everyone who came into the store of their harrowing time and of Glendon's heroics. Glendon would have preferred that they not mention it at all, but by the end of the next workday it was all over the county that Glen Garin rescued his patrons from a deadly pair of robbers. By the day after that, it was all over the local papers that Glen Gary Gentry rescued his parents from a group of killers. And in the Sunday edition of the Tulsa World there was a brief mention that Iron Post native Glen Gentry saved his parents from escaped convicts in the family store.

Darryl Sheldon asked Michael if he knew anything about it, and Michael said he did not, but it would not have surprised him a bit if it was all true. Michael came out to visit and to ask Glendon about the story in order to ease Darryl's mind.

Glendon sprawled out on the front porch swing, cooling off from a morning of hoeing the vegetable garden. He groaned and pulled his straw cowboy hat down lower over his eyes. "I cannot explain what possessed me to go to their house, but I did, and I am very glad of it. The Earthian Naradi cannot explain how or why I managed to safely travel five miles in the dark on foot, but they accept it. Darien always felt we should try to do something for the Gentrys, and I hope that in some way this may repay them for a portion of their constant kindness."

Stuart at last heard from Congressman Price, who told him scientists were curious to meet him. He was able to make some inroads through his connections with the White House via NASA and petitioned President Kennedy to give him some time. Kennedy was having trouble of his own in his personal life, as his wife had recently lost the baby she was carrying. Stuart could not interrupt a family in mourning and chose to wait. In the meantime, he worked on contact with Anthony Price's people.

It had not been easy to bring up the subject of Thuringi to the average man. No one had heard of the Isle of Thuringa, let alone that it had a king. Like Michael, Anthony Price was reluctant to tell the whole truth about the Thuringi. He did not want to come off sounding like a nut who watched too many movies. He wanted their presentation to the world to be taken as seriously as it warranted.

The scientists were intrigued with what they considered Stuart's radical but theoretically intriguing space flight theories – information that was painfully elementary to Gareth and something Stuart learned at Academy in regular coursework. After several more weeks of arguing and vacillating, a representative for the scientists called the congressman to arrange matters and insisted it be at a Langley, Virgina address. Anthony contacted Stuart, who flew in to meet him at home when arrangements were finalized for a Thursday meeting.

Stuart spotted Anthony's car and flew through the low-hanging clouds as inconspicuously as possible. On the way, he noticed a dark sedan following the Congressman's car. At a lonely stretch of road outside Langley, the sedan pulled in front of Anthony's car and a second sedan came up from behind. In a concerted effort, the two sedans slowed the congressman and brought the car to a stop. Men jumped out of the car and pulled Anthony from his vehicle and into one of theirs. They searched Price's car and seemed quite perturbed at failing to find what – or whom – they wanted. The sedan with the congressman in it sped away. Stuart followed, uncertain whether this had been arranged by Anthony Price or if something was amiss.

They did not go to the location marked on Anthony's map. Instead, they took the congressman to an auto garage and pulled him inside. Stuart landed quietly on the roof of the building and drew his projectile pistol. He reconsidered using a deadly weapon and retrieved a handful of small sharp throwing discs the size of his palm. He eased down the fire escape and gained access to the building's interior. Cautiously he stayed in the shadows and peered out in the direction of the men's voices.

The congressman sat in a chair surrounded by men in dark suits as well as Air Force uniforms. Anthony Price appeared more angry than anxious. Stuart crept closer to hear the conversation and figure out his best plan of action.

"Mr. Price, ordinarily your story would be marked down as the rankest of puerile fiction but there are some points we drew from your conversation with our physicists that has us very interested. Tell us more about this so-called space man and the kind of technology he's offering."

"So, that's why you snatch me out of my car like some kind of thief? You can't just chat openly on the street like normal folks? Who are you people really? Do you have any idea what you're doing?"

"Suppose you tell us what we are doing, congressman."

"I'm not telling you anything! I'm a United States Congressman, damn it, and I'm not going to stand for this kind of treatment."

"You inferred that an alien from space would be with you. Where is this alien?"

"Look, I didn't say anything about space. I just said this man is an emissary, a scientist from another country, don't you get that?" Congressman Price snapped. "How's it going to look, you kidnapping a government representative? Puts an awfully nasty light on the United States military, don't you think?"

"An emissary from where? I don't think the nasty light on the military will matter in the face of national security issues. Where is he now?"

For a moment the congressman was quiet, and then he spoke deliberately. "He must have decided at the last second not to come. I don't know, maybe he didn't like the idea of riding in a car today."

"Where did he go?"

"How the hell should I know, what, do you think I've got a complete itinerary of a man I practically just met? Maybe he was just pulling my leg. Hell, he probably doesn't even own a model airplane for all I know."

"You related some very specific information on the phone to Dr. Forrester dealing with quantum physics; theories that frankly Mr. Price, you just don't have the education to pose off the top of your head."

"Pose this off the top of your head," Anthony Price snorted, boldly displaying the middle finger from his fist to the man. "I don't know about quantum physics, but I do know an asshole when I see one and buddy, you're brown."

His interrogator started toward him, but one of his companions stopped him.

"You are the one who contacted us, Mr. Price. You said specifically that this friend of yours has fantastic knowledge of space flight and those specifics you mentioned interested us very much. There was another man mentioned. Who was that; that was a contact, wasn't it? What's his name, congressman?"

"I don't remember now," Congressman Price spat out. "It was a name that started with the syllable, Quantum. You guys don't exactly make a guy feel at home, you know."

"You're a single man in a busy city in an office of considerable power, Mr. Price," the head interrogator pointed out. "Any number of things could happen to you. You could be mugged by someone who wouldn't even realize you were a representative of the great state of New York."

"Are you threatening me, officer? Do you not think for a minute that my family will investigate my disappearance; that they will find out who I called and spoke to?"

"Do you not think for a minute, Mr. Price, that telephone records can just disappear? That there will be nothing to trace? There is a man in your acquaintance," he shouted at Anthony Price to vent his rising anger. "He is apparently privy to important information and access to a great deal of rocketry power. Your cooperation could mean the difference between the safety of the United States or the triumph of Khrushchev's Russia. How do you know he isn't at this moment at Red Square striking a deal with the Russians?"

"How do you know he isn't exactly what he says he is: an emissary, looking for a place for his refugee nation to apply to for sanctuary?"

"If he has this sort of power, why would he need sanctuary? We've never heard of Thuringa."

"Neither have I. I can only tell you what I've been told. He says they are refugees, and he flies a ship. I don't know about rocketry; I'm a freakin' congressman, not Jules Verne!"

One of the other men spoke up in a cold voice. "Forget it; he's a waste of time. What we want is the space man."

"What about him?" asked someone meaning Anthony Price.

"Deal with him." He turned to go.

Anthony Price spat out a filthy but appropriate epithet, and all but two men left the garage. Stuart waited until he heard the doors shut to step out of the shadows. One of the suits pulled a gun from his jacket without taking his line of sight from the congressman.

"You are not going to do this," Anthony said in disbelief.

Stuart got out one of his discs and threw it at the gunman. The disc struck the gunman's arm, and the gun fell to the floor. The other man turned with his weapon, so Stuart threw at him as well. His aim was hasty, and it struck the man in the head instead of the hand. He fell as if he were shot. As the gun clattered to the floor Stuart rushed to strike the first gunman with his fist. All the gunman saw was a large figure with a billowing cape rush at him and two bright points of light flash blindingly in his eyes before the blow rendered him unconscious.

"Quickly, follow me," Stuart told Anthony Price as he swiftly retrieved his discs. They went out the back door and up the fire ladder to the roof. Stuart threw the stunned congressman into the ship, and they flew away, out over the Atlantic and from the continent. "Who were those men?"

"I don't know; some thugs from the seamy underbelly of some governmental alphabet department, I guess. I honestly did not contact anyone from the Air Force after Michael asked me not to, Your Highness. From what I gather, one of the physicists I spoke to had some of the mathematical formulas you gave us, and word got out that no one of this world could have come up with it, not even close. That doesn't say much for our science community."

"No," Stuart tried to reassure him, "Your people have not reached that point quite yet."

They flew to Boston where Stuart hid the ship, and they carefully made their way to Michael's rental house. They waited and presently Michael came home untroubled and unaware. Stuart stepped into view as Michael came up to the porch, and the educator stopped short in surprise.

"What is going on?" Michael asked cheerfully. "Have you contacted someone already?"

"Come with me," Stuart said. "You may be in danger."

He took Michael and Anthony away from Boston and hovered the ship a few feet above the waves in the middle of the North Atlantic. Anthony was agog at the power and ability of the aircraft and equally astonished that Michael took it as a matter of course.

Stuart brought Michael up to date of the events in the auto garage. "I have done you a grave disservice. I have endangered others in my quest to contact your people. I should have immediately contacted your president when we landed here rather than wait and then bring this upon you."

"I am the one who advised you to wait," Michael told him. "I was afraid harm would come to you; I did not even consider someone might threaten a congressman."

"What'll we do now?" Anthony Price asked.

"I must seek out the president," Stuart said. "You said you know him."

"You bet I do," Anthony said. "Just get me back to Washington."

But back in Washington, they could not arrange a meeting; they spotted military personnel stationed outside Price's congressional office. Anthony did not trust anyone at NASA now, so that avenue was closed as well. The final blow came when they arrived at his apartment and discovered it thoroughly ransacked. The only reason they could avoid the stakeout team was that the team did not anticipate their quarry having a ship that could land and take off from the roof. The threesome retreated to an obscure motel to discuss their options.

"There's one person left that I know who could possibly be of help to us. It's a long shot, but I've met him and he's a great guy." Anthony dialed and presently someone answered on the other end of the line. "Hello Bobby," Anthony greeted. "This is Congressman Anthony Price of New York. Yeah, that's right, the space gink. I wonder if you and your big brother could help a space gink out of a serious jam." He laughed, glanced at Michael and Stuart, and winked.

Michael realized who was on the other end of the line at once, but Stuart was in the dark. Anthony's friend was the president's brother and Attorney General of the United States. Anthony briefly explained that Stuart was a scientist with a radical approach to space travel, and that somehow the Air Force was under the mistaken idea that he was a space man from Pluto or something! He and his old pal Michael Sheldon, Harvard class of '53 - yes, a fellow alum, Bobby! – were being hounded by a bunch of thugs from Jetsonville, all on a big mistake. However, his friend did have some exciting theories and formulas regarding space flight that would help the space race immensely.

When he finally concluded the call, Anthony turned to them. "Bobby says to relax, he's going to make a few calls to get this straightened out and get back in touch."

"And you trust this Bobby?" Stuart asked.

"I trust Bobby Kennedy with my life," Anthony told him.

"You are going to have to," Michael said.

"You did not trust him enough to tell him the truth," Stuart pointed out.

"There's telling the truth, and then there's judiciously editing what you say," Anthony pointed out. "We told a few people about you and ended up almost eating a bullet. What little technology and information you shared was enough for shady elements in our government to go after you and, by extension, go after me. We'd better rethink your approach. Unless you have got military muscle on hand to make the Air Force back down, you and your people need to lay low.

"So far, nobody else knows about you and you'd better keep it that way for a while. You're a research scientist if you have to be anything at all. Mike, there's going to be a real curiosity circus going on about you once they start asking around where he came from, and who sent him to me. No doubt there's a squad of air force goons checking out your activities, and sooner or later they'll find the ranch. Fortunately, my staff doesn't even know what our meeting was about this morning, so they won't be able to say much. I'm sorry, pal; I honest to God believe you are who and what you say you are, but if anyone asks me again, I'm going to stick to my goofy scientist story."

"I understand," Stuart said.

"How long is this going to last?" Michael asked.

"It depends on the Kennedys, really. Bobby's an enormously powerful man, the brother of the president, and if anybody can help us, it's him. He and I will meet with Jack Kennedy when he gets back. He's going to go on a re-election stump for the governor of Texas in Dallas tomorrow."

This information was met with solemn reflection at the ranch. Stuart said, "The Congressman is claiming ignorance of matters, saying only that he was passing along information he gathered but has not true grasp or knowledge of from whence it came. Brent has found a suitable place for a better outpost, and I think we should move operations there. Michael is in Tulsa at his father's estate and believes he may be able to avoid being questioned through influential friends of his father's, in the government. The time may have come, my friends, for us to flee our home again."

They all digested this news as the telephone rang. Stuart answered it. "Yes Michael, it is I," he said. "Are you? That is good news." He was silent, listening to Michael speak. Finally, he said, "I understand. I will be watchful." He hung up.

"You will be watchful about what? What did Michael say?" Darien asked.

"He and Anthony Price met with Bobby Kennedy. Apparently,

their Harvard academy is a very close-knit brotherhood. Kennedy has arranged for the Justice Department to treat Anthony Price and Michael Sheldon as special protection cases. There will be no more bullets to be eaten."

"That is good to hear," Glendon said.

"For Michael and his friend, yes," Stuart agreed, "but we are not under quite the same roof. As long as President Kennedy is in power, we will be under the protective auspices of the White House. Should he lose the next election, we will no longer enjoy having influence to help shield us. If we are able to meet personally with him after tomorrow, we will press the truth to him and forge a treaty."

The next day, Glendon came home to the ranch early, pale and shaken. "Gareth, where is Stuart?"

"He and Darien are looking at an actual gakki, I mean horse, that Michael's father sent out here. Why, what is wrong?"

"Lord Gentry heard it on the news," Glendon said, hurrying to the television to turn it on. He and Gareth stared in anguished disbelief as they heard the news announcement that President Kennedy died of the gunshot wounds he received that day at the hands of an assassin's gun. The six hastily assembled Thuringi sat dejectedly in the front room of the Sheldon ranch house.

Stuart was shocked. The Naradi Famede of Thuringa spent their tasks in protection of their monarch, and it was Stuart's understanding that the Secret Service was the American equivalent of Naradi Famede. He could not separate the idea of king and president from his mind. Why, this was tantamount to slaying King Lycasis, and Stuart shuddered at the thought.

How could this have happened? Were madmen allowed to run free in a nation already so lax in its behavior? And what was to become of their plans now? If it had been difficult to approach the president with the radical idea of alien visitors before, then doing so now might prove impossible at this point.

Darien swore and paced back from the stairs to the front door and back. "What good does planning do when this violent world slays the very people who are in power to help us? Even if we had been successful in contacting the president and gained his support, all is for naught. Now the people who were set to harm Congressman Price will be here after us and Michael Sheldon."

"Then we must leave Sheldon ranch immediately," Stuart said. "We must leave no trace of our being here to spare Michael any trouble in the future. Glendon, if you must bid farewell to the Gentrys, do so casually. Tell them you are going to visit friends back home. Gareth, let us load all your mechanical marvels in the Sword and Fist that we can and ferry them out to the isle as soon as dusk settles."

"What about all our effects here? The heaters, the furniture?" asked Carrol.

"Take them, too. We must leave this place clean but also sterilized of all things Thuringi."

They moved quickly and quietly. Gareth disconnected all his inventions and repair work, and by the time dark finally enveloped the ranch grounds the barn was empty and the house bare. Everything was flown out in the Sword and Fist and Her Nibs. All that was left was to wait for Stuart to return with the Sword and Fist to get Gareth and Carrol, and Glendon and the marshmallow white truck he drove into town to say goodbye to the Gentrys.

Gareth and Carrol rocked on the porch swing and enjoyed their final, if stressful, evening on the ranch. "It was nice while it lasted," Gareth commented.

"Gareth, do you ever envision a time when we will not be fleeing to a new home?" Carrol asked wistfully.

"I think New Thuringa will be safe enough for us. It is easier to defend something that is completely in your care rather than worry about say, Darryl Sheldon's cabrett getting caught in crossfire." She nodded.

Stuart landed the Sword and Fist in the front yard, and Darien did the same with the Naughty Boy.

"Where is Glendon?" Stuart asked the pair on the porch. "I thought he would be finished by now."

"So did I," Gareth said. "It surely does not take even the garrulous Glendon Garin this long to say goodbye."

"I will go see what might be holding him," Darien said. "They know me there more than any of you." Stuart agreed, and Darien flew the Naughty Boy to the feed store.

"We are returning to our homeland at last, and I wanted to say goodbye to you. This tragedy today in Texas has frightened Carrol very much. It makes her think of war and of losing her husband." Stuart could never have brought himself around to telling out and out lies, but Glendon had no such compunctions. If it would provide a safe environment or escape for his royal charges, Glendon Garin could tell classic whoppers.

The Gentrys were sorry to hear about Glendon's "plans". They were very fond of the friendly young man with the lilting accent and bright eyes. He spoke to them longer than he intended. He was about to leave when he felt an odd chill run the length of his spine.

"Would you mind if I went out through the back door?" he impulsively asked Margie. She said no, of course not, and gave him an affectionate hug. He shook Ed's hand and left. As the door softly closed, the front door to the store opened and in walked two men in dark business suits.

"Are you the owners of this store?" one of the men asked.

"Yes, but we're fixing to close for the night. What can I do for you?" Ed asked.

"We're here to ask you for some information. Have you recently been in contact with some foreign nationals?"

"Well now," Ed drawled, stalling for time but not really understanding why, "let's see, now. Foreign, you say. What kind of foreigners are you talking about? We do get a lot of visitors in here."

"Suppose you tell us, Mr. Gentry," the man said, not unpleasant in his tone. "How many foreign visitors do you get out here?"

"We had some folks from Italy visiting the Everetts not long ago, but that was for old Miss Isabella's funeral." He could see past the two men. Through the front screen door of the feed store he saw Glendon's white truck silently pushed out of its parking place toward the street. He heard the engine turn over a split second before the blast of an approaching freight train on the nearby tracks blared, and the truck took off down the road.

"We're interested in someone possibly from England settling in around here," said one of the dark-suited men.

"Oh, yeah, there's a couple of folks around here. There's a boy that comes in to do odd jobs for me, you know, just for spending money. Real pleasant fellow, real polite."

"Know where he lives?"

Flight of the Armada

"No, no, can't say that I do for sure." Ed Gentry was his usual friendly smiling self, his homey manner easily answering the questions even as he felt the sweat trickling down his backside under his plaid shirt.

"But he works for you; you don't know where he lives?"

"Oh! I thought you meant where he's from! He lives down to the old Sheldon ranch."

"And how much did you pay him for his work?"

"I paid him a couple of dollars an hour, but it was just a token. Boy, could he work!"

"Two dollars an hour? Can you tell me how he was able to afford new appliances and furnishings his family reportedly bought from the local stores?"

"Well, I don't know but they all seemed like real regal folks. I imagine they got money from back wherever it is they come from. He just came in because he's a young man and he was bored, I think. Really proper boy, he didn't care for all the frippy little girls who hung around him at all."

"He had a wife back home," Margie added. "He sure missed her a lot. They planned on going back home."

Glendon drove the white pickup down the road at as fast a clip as he could safely manage, passing under Darien's Naughty Boy in the deepening twilight. Darien looked ahead and saw the men walking out to their car from the feed store. He waited until their car headed in the opposite direction of the ranch before he landed the Naughty Boy outside the Gentry's store's back door. Margie was getting ready to lock up and peered out the back screen.

"Oh! You startled me!" She gasped and laughed, then gasped again. Darien's yellow eyes glowed in the dusk.

"Thank you for all your help, Lady Gentry," Darien told her quietly. "We are a peace-loving people seeking rest and succor on our journey. Your kindness will surely be returned to you tenfold."

"We don't want any trouble," said a voice beside him. It was Ed Gentry, and he held a shotgun to Darien's head. He had quietly come out the side door and crept up on the Thuringi.

"Neither do we," Darien replied, keeping his hands so Ed could see that he held no weapons.

"What did those men want with you folks?" Ed asked nervously.

"They seek to do no good," Darien said. "They fear that which they do not understand."

"Are you folks spies or something?"

"No. We are simply homeless people persecuted for our particular knowledge and abilities. We were seeking aid from your President Kennedy and when he was slain, we fear we will be persecuted once again by certain factions of his government. He was our protector, you see, and they will be after us."

"Where are you from, really?"

"From a world ravaged by war and overrun by parasites," Darien told him. "Lord Gentry, have Glendon or I ever caused you concern?"

Ed lowered his gun a little. "No, you haven't."

"Do you trust what others tell you, or what your heart tells you?"

"I trust my heart. Why were those men looking for Glendon?" Margie asked.

"I could not say as to their motives," Darien replied, "but Glendon is not a man for you to fear." He bowed to her and Ed. "Trust me, good people. We come in peace." He turned to his ship and quickly got in. In their excitement at his unexpected appearance, they had not even noticed the ship in the back lot. To the astonishment of the onlooking Earthians, the Naughty Boy vertically rose before them and darted away into the night sky.

"Damn it, I knew it!" Ed declared, slapping his leg with his hat. "I knew the minute I saw their yellow eyes!"

"Don't you say a word," Margie told him, her eyes on the disappearing lights of the Naughty Boy overhead. "They wouldn't harm a fly."

By the time the government men were finally able to find someone willing to talk about the Thuringi and locate the Sheldon ranch, there was no trace of the mysterious strangers with yellow eyes. The barn doors were wide open, but its inside was devoid of anything. The house showed signs of inhabitation but other than a television aerial still atop the roof and indication that furniture had been in place in the rooms, there was little physical evidence. The oddest thing they noticed were the piles of sand all along the floorboards all over the house.

The information they got from the people of Iron Post wildly varied. They were homeless bums or deposed royalty, happy-go-lucky or tragic figures. They had passports or lost them or were new citizens or tools of the Devil himself. But not one citizen in Iron Post ever saw anything flying out at the Sheldon ranch. The harvest was over, and the garden had been turned over to rest for the winter, and peace settled over the pastureland like a comforting blanket, giving no hint of alien visitors or mysterious ships.

Darien and Glendon left in the Naughty Boy with the pickup suspended under the ship as they winged their way to New Thuringa. The pickup was loaded down with the last items from the ranch, and they were thankful for the cover of darkness.

"Will they bring harm to Michael?" Glendon wondered aloud.

"He ought to be able to claim he was tricked by a sad story from a band of liars," Darien said although doubt tickled his thoughts. "I would."

They reached the Isle of New Thuringa without incident and ate a brief dinner of grilled fish and opened coconuts to nibble on the white meat for a post-dinner treat. For a time, the six scouts sat in dejected silence in the bed of the pickup and listened to the waves rushing against the sandy shore. "We are once again forced to flee our home," Gareth sighed at length. "How long will it take to reach Farcourt, and will we be permanent there?"

"It may take some time, but the effort will be worth it," Stuart said. "We must stay positive."

A glint came to Brent's eyes and developed into a full-blown twinkle. He trotted off to a small tidepool where he removed an unopened wine bottle from the cooling water. He returned to his five companions. "We have been thrown from more than a few cantinas too, have we not? That never stopped our thirsts!" He poured the wine into halved coconuts as the others' spirits brightened. "Now then my lads and lady, let us drink to the future and what we will make of it!"

End of Book One

305

Other Books in the series

Glossary

Arne - the former capital city of Thuringa
Atest (uh-TEST) - Thuringi church service
Audecer fallen botay (AW-day-sare FA-len bo-TAY) - literally, "Just try to top that!"
Bauni (BAH-nee) – Thuringi Remembrance Day
Beran – large furry animal, fierce
Bran Fitt (brawn feet)– respiration disease
Brent – literally, "powerful stroke"
Brenton – a noxious Thelan weed, similar to ragweed
Burillier (Boo-RIL-ier)– portable Thuringi medical diagnostic tool
Cabrett (ka-BRET) – cow of Thelan origin
Chesser – Thelan pig
Chumpet – flat Hunda wizzar drink
Cootoon – Thuringi flute
Crita von (KREE-tah vahn)- Shargassi term; literally, "where do you dwell?"
Dakarte istay (da-KAR-tay IS-tay)– literally, "you filthy fucker!"
Dallah (DOLL-a) - Thuringi dog, similar to a short-haired retriever
Dolo – Thuringi pearl
Dorea – large, strong, tough Thuringi trees
Ersanta Vorassi – "time of enlightenment" (Thuringi honeymoon)
Fiday – Thuringi xylophone
Friak – Thuringi potato, staple food
Forid – a tiny Thuringi frog
Fortrude – Thuringi fish, similar to tuna
Gaff – a thick sturdy Thuringi tree, widely used in landscaping. Diamond-shaped leaves
Gakki (GAK-ee) – horse with a horn in its forehead, found on many worlds
Gallina (gal-EE-nah) - a grand seaport city on old Thuringa
Ginta (ginn-TAH) - a nine-day week
Illick charranay - literally, "he is a fool who would hesitate at such bounty" or generally, "I am an opportunist"
Istay – an unwelcome individual with suspicious motives
Kila - a small dagger
Luket (loo-KET) - a nourishing milk-like substance from the pushkas plant
Melator - Thuringi piano
Naradi (na-RAH-dee) - Thuringi law enforcement; police

Naradi Famede (na-RAH-dee fa-ME-day) – royal palace guard
Nobi – Borelliat domesticated birds, or chickens
Parmenta (PAR-Tah) – Thuringi barracuda/piranha
Pienna (pee-IN-uh) – "sour face" a Thuringi fish
Poddack (POD-dack) - Thuringi daily school system for ages 5 to 18
Pushkas – plant that produces luket
Quasch (kwaw-shh) - a wrestling match
Shargassi (SHAR-gah-Say) - enemies of Thuringa
Skit – a decorative shrub
Stack – gakki foal
Tarinade - (TARE-en-Aid) - banned Thuringi sex manual with poetry and illustrations
Tiff – Pleonian flax plant used for making flexible armor
Vaguno (va-GOO-no) - sandy soil of Thuringa favored for grain crops
Ver hirum caute (ver HE-room CO-tay) - literally, "is this real?"
Wegodgoe (WEE-god-go) - Thuringi for an enthusiastic sexual encounter
Wizzar - sweet fizzy non-alcoholic drink
Yeep - a proper person's usual response to a startling or embarrassing situation
Yjass (yass) – passion

www.ingramcontent.com/pod-product-compliance
Lightning Source LLC
Chambersburg PA
CBHW051140030726
47504CB00004B/962